PROMISES FULFILLED

Traci Wooden-Carlisle

D1521888

COPYRIGHT

PROMISES FULFILLED
(Promises to Zion Series)

Table of Contents

DEDICATION

Thank you, God, for placing this seed inside me before I knew the gift of what was being planted. The fruit you are bearing through these books is food to my soul and I praise you for it.

Thank you, Daddy, for your continued love and support. No matter how heavy the subject your cheers of delight lighten my heart every time I call you to celebrate.

I dedicate this book to each one of my friends who were by my side at the beginning of this journey but have since transitioned and get to witness the culmination of this dream from heaven. I miss you and I will see you again.

ACKNOWLEDGMENTS

Thank you to the Fabulous Five who help make my world go around.

Thank you for your love, inspiration, strength, and encouragement, women of God. You know who the ten of you are.

Thank you

Dana for lending your talent to my book covers.
A.I.R.R.E. Firm for smoothing out the edges in my timeline.
Paula thank you for editing this book.

Thou shalt not bow down thyself to them, nor serve them: for I the LORD thy God am a jealous God, visiting the iniquity of the fathers upon the children unto the third and fourth generation of them that hate me; but showing love to a thousand generations of those who love me and keep my commandments.

Exodus 20:5-6

PART ONE

Chapter 1

Thirty-nine years ago

"Thank you, Charlie," Brenda said, smiling at the doorman as she walked through the opened door of the upscale apartment building.

She glanced around surreptitiously, still having a hard time believing this place with its gold ornate framed mirrors, red-accented Persian rugs, and tan, leather club chairs were part of her home. She'd lived in Apartment 5A for eight months now, and walking into the lobby still made her a little breathless.

She'd done it. She'd used her intellect and education to secure one of the most coveted positions in Chicago. More than that, she wouldn't have to crawl back home and marry the first man her mother and father paid to take her. Every night that she walked into this building after work was another day she had won.

Brenda took measured steps across the lobby to her mailbox, ignoring the eyes on her. She belonged here. She had dreamed bigger than what she should. So her mother told her. She was stubborn, proud, and too smart for her good. Her mother had tried to convince her that coy glances, shy smiles, and an overabundance of flattery, and of all things, losing any game on purpose to a young suitor was the way to a man's heart. It made absolutely no sense to her that allowing a man to beat her would make him want her more. She thought it would be the opposite. What would a man want with a dense woman? Why wouldn't he want someone that challenged him intellectually? Someone who would move him to be even better? Her mother had it wrong.

Still, Brenda may have even begun to consider her mother's error in opinion if she hadn't met Luca Sable. Luca Sable was, in her opinion, a true man. His name was said in whispers among other business owners in Chicago. He was a formidable businessman and highly intelligent as he'd proven to the accounting firm he'd taken her from.

She was realistic and not at all in the habit of lying to herself. She knew what she looked like. She also knew it was a bit of a challenge for men her age, and sometimes older, to get beyond her beauty to seek out the woman behind the golden eyes. Luca was the first man to see her for her.

He noticed her ability first, her talent with numbers, her gift with equations. She believed he noticed her dry humor, lust for life, and ambition next. Maybe even in that order. She found his ability to see beyond people's looks alluring. The fact that he saw through hers, only made him more attractive to her.

His swarthy good looks, tall, lanky build, jet-black hair, and matching eyes didn't hurt either. He was older. Some would say too old, but what little conversation they shared, outside of projects she was working on, was easy and showed her that they had quite a few things in common. She could have contented herself to adore him from afar, to admire and hold a quiet, yet intense, crush on him if he didn't look at her with a similar longing at times.

She should have taken some of her colleagues up on their offers to dinner or a show. She might have been able to talk herself out of her infatuation, but she had never been known for doing things the easy way. She worked the hours it took to get each project done whether it was eight or twelve. She came in on weekends if needed and made sure she was accessible even after she left the building. If anyone asked why she worked so hard, she would tell them that she loved her job, and working at Sable Financial was her life's dream. They didn't have to know that Luca was the one she loved, that he was her life's dream.

No one would ever know about those two beautiful weeks they shared when he'd given in to the desire she'd seen in his eyes on occasion. He'd treated her like a queen. He'd doted on her when they were away from the office. He sent her flowers and wrote her small notes. She'd sensed that he had a romantic streak. He was Italian after all, but his attentions even surpassed her biggest dreams and fantasies. He was attentive and very much the gentlemen when he took her out. He even looked a little boyish when he asked her if he could make her dinner at her home for the first time. It was a memory she would treasure always.

"Good evening, Ms. Gorman," greeted Philip. He'd worked as the night shift security guard since she'd moved in.

"Good evening, Philip. How's Marion?" Brenda asked as she rang the call button for the elevator.

"She's doing much better. She tried the lemon and honey recipe you gave me with the cayenne, and it made her sweat like you said it would. She went back to work today, so we'll see how she's doing in the morning.

"I'm looking forward to a favorable report," Brenda said as the elevator doors slid open. She stepped inside and gave him a warm smile.

"Me too, Ms. Gorman. Me too." He gave her a mock salute before the doors closed and obstructed her view.

Ms. Gorman. The name had taken some getting used to. There were still moments when people addressed her, and she had the urge to look around for her Grandma G. It was understandable. Brenda had only been going by the last name for four years. She'd left undergrad as Brenda Lattimore and was supposed to go back home and find a suitable husband who could continue to keep her in the fashion she was used to. The only problem was, she didn't want to be kept. She didn't want to find a suitable man. She didn't want to go back home. After a fight to end all fights with her father, who threatened to disown her if she didn't come back, she changed her last name to Gorman to honor her grandmother who had put such notions of becoming an accountant in her head—and anger her father. She took what allowance she'd saved—which was most of it—and enrolled in her school's graduate program.

Brenda glanced down at her watch as the elevator climbed to the fifth floor. Her gaze caught on the platinum and diamond tennis bracelet peeking out from the edge of her cuff. Luca had given it to her on their first night together. He'd placed it on her wrist after dinner and later, even after he'd undressed her, he'd left the bracelet on. She'd worn it every day since, only taking it off to shower and sleep.

She'd lived a fairy tale for two weeks, and on the fifteenth day his wife and children came home from visiting relatives in Italy.

Brenda hadn't asked to see him again after their time together. She'd kept her end of the agreement in hopes that he might one day consider continuing their affair…if the perfect situation presented itself. She'd cried when it was over but not in front of him. She'd even sulked a little in the privacy of her home, but it wasn't as if she didn't know what she was getting into. She just didn't expect to fall so hard and so completely in love with him.

At first, the memories of Luca sitting at her kitchen table, on her couch, and in her shower were a comfort, but as time went on without him visiting or calling for any reason outside of work, the memories began to haunt her until she finally had to move. She refused to put her life's work and freedom in jeopardy by not adhering to their agreement just because she fell in love with the wrong man.

She'd put her heart and soul into her work, not wanting to give Luca any reason to think their time together had a negative effect on her professional life. She'd done a pretty good job of distancing herself and might have considered herself almost over him until she was sent out of town to Las Vegas on business last week. Since she no longer had a reason to go home for her birthday, she welcomed the assignment. It would be a change of scenery, and she could treat herself to a spa day if the work wasn't too strenuous.

There was no work. A few hours after she'd arrived, there was a knock on her door. Thinking it was room service, Brenda opened it

4

wide only to find Luca standing in her doorway with a bouquet of red roses. It was one of the most amazing weeks of her life, and when it was over, she boarded a plane back to Chicago with the understanding that their affair was over. She didn't cry that time.

Brenda stepped off the elevator and walked down the carpeted hallway to her door. She let herself in and dropped her keys in the glass bowl on the entry table. She shut and locked the door behind her as she leafed through her mail. One piece caught her attention. It had no return address, and her address had been printed. She set her purse down on her kitchen table along with the women's dress catalog, mailers, bills, and the off-white envelope.

She was curious, but whatever it was it would have to wait until after dinner. She was starved. She would have loved to come home to Luca's spinach ravioli. She'd never tasted anything like it. Sometimes she'd stop by an authentic Italian restaurant on her way home from work and order the meat lasagna. It wasn't the same, but it was close enough to give her goosebumps when she took that first bite.

Brenda walked into the bedroom and changed into a pair of oversized sweatpants and a T-shirt. She would have given anything to walk around in one of Luca's shirts, but he never left anything behind. Nothing except the bracelet. She ran her fingers along the smooth, icy surface of the diamonds as she thought over her choices for dinner. She had frozen potpie, frozen meatloaf, and garlic mashed potatoes with green beans, frozen barbeque chicken with corn and peas, and freshly sliced pastrami that she'd picked up from the corner deli earlier that week.

Cooking had never been something she could master. She had one or two recipes that she made better than her mother, but even she could get tired of spaghetti and beef stroganoff. She knew her mother was disappointed in her homemaking skills, but Brenda wasn't built that way. She didn't have any natural inclination to have or take care of children and a husband. Well, she could have been convinced to do so by one man, but he already had a family.

Brenda walked into the kitchen and randomly pulled a frozen dinner from the freezer. She didn't care what she ate. It was only meant to sustain her. She turned the oven on and sat at the kitchen table as she did most nights to go through her mail while it preheated.

She opened the odd envelope and pulled out the contents, her hand freezing as her mind worked to make sense of what she was seeing. Her hands began to tremble, so she placed the note and pictures on the table. Snapshots of her and Luca walking into a theater. She took a calming breath. What was she afraid of? They had always handled themselves with professional decorum when they were out in public. Just about any of their outings could be explained away.

Her heart rate was slowly returning to normal when she caught sight of another piece of a photo. This time with what looked like bared skin. She slowly pushed the top photo forward revealing more skin, her skin, and in a much less innocent photo with Luca holding her towel-clad form as he kissed her. The diamond bracelet catching the light of a streetlamp as it entered her hotel room curtains.

She'd opened the curtains earlier just enough to watch the way her bracelet sparkled against her wrist in the moonlight. Luca was dressed to leave, but the photo caught her in the middle of changing his mind.

She reached for the note, dreading what she was going to find.

And here I thought you were hired for your gift with numbers. What a pleasant surprise to find that you are alive under all of that ice.

I'm sure you don't want anyone to find out about these pictures, especially Luca's wife. If you don't share, neither will I.

Let's make a deal. If you melt for me, you can keep your sparkling reputation. If you don't meet me on the corner of Fern and Silo at midnight, all of your efforts will be washed away.

A.M.

Brenda yanked her fingers from the paper as if it burned her. She was being blackmailed? Her mind spun. How did this happen? Why would this happen? She kept to herself mostly. She followed the "rules" and didn't ruffle any feathers. Her thoughts became erratic, jumping from one thought to another. She wasn't a saint, but she worked hard to blend into the background and do her work.

The note alluded to her wearing or being made of ice, at least on the first layer. Maybe it was the shock, but she couldn't think of a single soul she'd met and rejected to the degree that would justify this action.

Brenda had kept her head down. She didn't go against her immediate boss, Michael Fordor, Sable's Chief Financial Officer, on much of anything. If there was something that needed his attention, she wouldn't go over his head if he didn't listen to her when she first presented issues to him. After their first and last heated conversation, when he was reprimanded by Luca for not taking action on a situation she'd brought to him that cost the company money, Mr. Fordor told her that if she failed to get his attention with her first attempt then to keep trying until she was successful. Since he didn't treat her like the scourge of the earth or as if she should be shining his shoes, instead of polishing business accounts, Brenda took him at his word, and with extra patience submitted her concerns to him until she got a response.

It had taken a year to gain his trust and another six months for him to gain hers. They had a similar goal in keeping Sable Financial the smoothest and most soluble company in Chicago. It allowed them to share a level of respect for one another that kept their lines of communication clear.

Even still, Brenda knew what they called her around the office. It was mostly talk from men who didn't like the thought of a woman, or even more to the point, a black woman in her position. She had been asked out a couple of times from men on her floor—executives—but thought it best to decline their offer. She had been asked to join groups for drinks after work and had accepted a couple of times, but they made the next day a living nightmare, so she had started declining. She wasn't in Chicago to play.

She'd never made friends easily. Her mother watched the people she interacted with very closely, which made getting close to anyone she liked, impossible. Brenda was used to being envied, scorned, and misunderstood. It was what happened when you were put up on a pedestal.

She believed people thought she had it all, but in actuality, she was only fighting to keep her freedom. Her Iceness—that's what men called her—but she couldn't recall anyone with the initials A.M. who worked for Luca Sable's company that she interacted with on a daily or weekly basis.

She thought back to the men she'd served at one of Mr. Sable's late evening meetings. She'd recognized a few of them. Their names and pictures had been in the *Wall Street Journal* several times. It had been rumored that some of them ran legit businesses by day and less than reputable establishments once the sun went down.

Brenda had taken Michael's place while he was on vacation, attending the meetings and preparing the financial documents being discussed. She suffered the leers of some of the men as they arrived, but no one approached her or spoke to her beyond courteous gratitude.

Once she'd distributed the paperwork and poured the rich-smelling coffee to those who requested it, she'd be dismissed, rather tersely, she thought, by Mr. Sable. Brenda looked around the room for a second to make sure she hadn't done anything wrong, but after catching some of the men's gazes, she understood his reason for wanting her to leave. Brenda was both thankful for his protection and disgusted that she would need it.

It had been nearly a year ago. She closed her eyes recalling the picture she'd taken with her mind of the men sitting around the table. She slowly replayed it, scanning face after face, but was still unable to point out any unseemly attention in any one man's eyes. She tried to recall the names but without knowing them all to begin with, that exercise didn't prove fruitful either.

Brenda sat the table going over her options again and again until she could only see one way. She turned off the stove and checked all her windows and blinds. She went back into her bedroom to change, picked up the pictures and note, and as quietly as possible, left her apartment with all her lights on. She walked to the elevator, looking over her shoulder every so often. She checked her watch. There was a chance Luca was still in the office.

When the elevator opened at the lobby, Brenda waited for a few heartbeats before exiting. She didn't know why her heart rate sped up at that instance or why a fine mist started on her upper lip, but it made her wary of what she was about to do. She glanced around her as she made

8

her way to Phil standing at the security desk. She caught his attention when she was still a few steps away. She opened her mouth to ask to use his phone but saw a man she didn't recognize sitting in one of the leather chairs just beyond the pillar.

"C-c-could." She stuttered to a halt for a second, looking blankly at Phil before regaining some composure.

"Could you call me a cab? I've decided to dine out tonight."

"Very well, Ms. Gorman."

He stared at her for a moment. "Are you all right, Ms. Gorman?"

"Sure. Just hungry. I think my sugar dipped as I got off of the elevator," she rushed to explain.

"Okay, where do you want to go?" Phil asked with the receiver to his ear.

"Um..." She ran through a list of restaurants in her head that had a dimmer light setting. "Michaelino's on Thirty-Eighth and Fleet."

Phil nodded and made the call for her. She stood next to his desk until he finished.

She made sure her body blocked, from most of the lobby, what she was about to hand him.

"I need you to hold something for me. I've written the name of the person who will pick it up, on the package. If they don't pick it up, then I will get it from you when I come back from dinner." She slipped the envelope around the back of the desk to make sure no one saw her hand him anything. She hoped from anyone else's point of view it would look like she was chatting with him until her cab pulled up.

Bless Phil's heart. The man didn't blink or give anything away.

He nodded gravely, and she felt a modicum of fear and anxiety lift from her shoulders.

A few minutes later when her cab pulled up, she had completely regained her composure. She sat in the cab as it maneuvered around the evening Chicago traffic, glad that she didn't have to concentrate on driving in the state she was in.

She stepped inside of Michaelino's and paused a moment to let her eyes adjust to the dimness of the romantic Italian restaurant. She had been there a few times, but it was a little pricey with its cloth napkins,

9

marble floor, and hand-painted ceiling. She liked the sound of her heels on the floor the first time she walked through the dining room. Tonight she hoped the rubber sole of her wedges would smother her footfalls and she could be ushered to her seat drawing as little attention as possible.

She was greeted by the maître d' and ushered to a seat toward the back of the restaurant as she requested. She summoned the sommelier, ordered a drink, then asked him not to deliver it until she got back to her seat.

Brenda unfolded her napkin then got up and placed it on her seat to show that she would be back. She walked in the direction of the restrooms and was happy to find that her memory served her well when she saw the pair of payphones in the narrow hall.

She glanced around to make sure she wasn't followed then dialed Luca's office number. She didn't breathe through the three rings it took for him to answer.

"Hello?" His strong voice rang through the line causing her so much relief she had to hold back a sob. She blew out the overflow of emotion.

"Lu—Mr. Sable," Brenda said, summoning her professional voice at the last second. "It's Ms. Gorman."

"Yes, Ms. Gorman." The pause before his response let her know he was on alert and taking her lead.

"I'm sorry to bother you, but I received a package that I know you will want to see," she said just loud enough to be heard.

"What type of package?" Luca asked, his voice going cold.

"The type that blackmailers use," she responded.

The ensuing silence was deafening. She waited, knowing there was nothing more she needed to say to get his attention.

"From whom?" he asked, over-enunciating, letting her know that he was angry.

"It was initialed A.M., but I don't recognize those initials," she stated.

"What do they want?" Luca asked, and she was very happy the coldness in his voice wasn't directed toward her. The colder Luca's voice got, the angrier he was. When he turned quiet, it usually meant heads were about to roll.

"Me," Brenda said, feeling mollified by the intake of breath she heard on the other end of the line. He cared. She knew it, but it was something else for it to be proven.

"Where are you?" he asked after another long pause.

"Michaelino's. I was told not to contact anyone, so I came here for dinner so I could call you."

"Good thinking. Do you want me to meet you? Do you have the package with you?" he asked, and she could hear papers being shuffled in the background.

"No. That was my first thought, but there was someone lounging in the lobby I didn't recognize. I gave the envelope to Phil with instructions to only give it to you or back to me if you didn't come by to pick it up. I made sure no one saw me hand it to him." Luca had told her Phil was trustworthy. Luca would know since he owned the building.

"I figured if they were there to see if I'd contact or run to you, they would follow me," she said before going quiet.

"Very clever."

They were only two words, but the softness in which they were said and the hint of a smile she heard behind them warmed her.

"I'm sorry, Luca," Brenda said, feeling obligated to apologize. If it weren't for their affair, there would be no need for this conversation.

"Why are you apologizing?" His speech became guarded, and she rushed to tell him what she'd been thinking.

"I knew there might be consequences for my actions—our actions, Bren."

"Do you regret..." She closed her eyes when her throat closed up. She told herself she would never ask him questions that may hurt both of them to answer. The silence killed her a little more with each second.

"No."

The word was quiet but clear. A tear escaped, and she brushed it away impatiently. She cleared her throat and forced back the emotion.

11

"I'll eat here and give you a chance to pick up the package," she said, her voice void of emotion.

"When?" he asked.

She was miffed that she'd lost track of the conversation.

"Excuse me?"

"When do they want you?" he asked again.

"Midnight," Brenda replied. She could imagine him checking his watch. It was silver and open-faced with a heavy black leather band. It was impressive and a little intimidating, but there was little Luca did without considering how it affected others. Well, except for her.

"It's just after seven. We have some time to come up with a plan. You go eat, and I'll pick up the package and make some calls," he said, taking charge. She felt safer already.

"Okay. Thank you," she said, ready to hang up.

"You're not alone in this," Luca said, and she tried to believe him, but if things went sideways, he may have a mark against his name, and the company might temporarily suffer a dip in stocks. Her career would be over.

"Yes," was all she could say before hanging up.

She visited the women's restroom and freshened up. She went back to her seat, took a big sip from the wine placed in front of her, and ordered an entrée she knew her stomach was too active for her to eat.

She pushed her food around for fifteen minutes, taking a few bites. She felt herself getting more nervous with each passing minute until she couldn't take it anymore. She glanced at her watch for the tenth time in forty-five minutes. Luca should have picked up the package by now. She wondered what he thought of them and what plan he'd devised regarding her blackmailer.

Brenda signaled for the check, asked the server for a to-go bag and asked if he could have the maître d' call her a cab. She took her time signing while she finished the last of her drink in hopes that it would calm her some. It didn't.

Brenda stepped outside of the restaurant and pulled her coat closer around her. It wasn't the season for cold nights, but there was a chill in the air. She glanced to her left and right. The sidewalk was crowded

12

with the summer tourists despite the dip in temperature. Brenda waited for a few moments then walked toward the waiting cab, feeling an urgency to get back home.

The hairs on her arms stood up, and the urgency upgraded to panic. Maybe coming out wasn't such a good idea. She talked herself out of running the last few steps and placed her hand on the door when someone grabbed her arm.

Chapter 2

Startled, Brenda looked up into the cold, dark eyes of the same man who had been sitting in her lobby when she'd left. Her heart, which had been beating double time only a few seconds before, stuttered then continued its frantic beating. The man was massive with shoulders that blocked out the light from the restaurant now behind him.

"Mr. M. is feeling a bit impatient. He would like to see you now," he said in a rough voice that sounded like he smoked a few packs of cloves a day. His height and breadth made her feel small even though she was of average height.

She knew his size was supposed to evoke fear and intimidation in people and though it was working, she wouldn't let him know it.

She yanked her arm out of his grasp. "Tell Mr. M. that patience is a virtue."

She placed her hand on the door of the cab and again her arm was taken, but this time the grip was much tighter.

"He insists," he said with clenched teeth, right before he pounded on the top of the cab in a signal for it to move on.

She watched with growing dread as the taxi pulled away only to be replaced by a black sedan with dark tinted windows. He opened the back door with one hand and kept hold of her arm with the other.

She dared not get into the car.

Brenda began to struggle, hoping to catch someone's attention if she couldn't release herself from the man's grasp. She tried to pry his

14

fingers from her arm, but it was like trying to remove a steel band. She stomped on his instep in hopes of getting him to loosen his hold, but he only shook her.

She opened her mouth to scream, but he covered her nose and mouth with his oversized palm. She went into panic mode as her airways were cut off and would have missed his words if he hadn't whispered in her ear.

"There is nothing you can do to keep me from getting you in this car. What happens once you're in there is up to you." He shook her again as if to punctuate his words.

"Nod if you understand me."

Brenda nodded in a jerky motion, just wanting to get in a good breath now that heat started in her lungs. It took another couple of seconds for him to remove his hand, and she knew he'd done it on purpose when she saw the cruel lift of his lips. She realized that he liked hurting people, and the dread she'd felt before bloomed into fear.

The man didn't release her arm but did gesture for her to climb into the back seat of the sedan. Brenda looked around to see if they'd caught anyone's attention. She met the eyes of a man across the street, but when the man holding her followed her gaze, he growled, and her opportunity to be rescued turned and walked away.

"I won't say it again. Get in the car." He pulled her toward the door.

"Wait. Wait!" she said, trying to stall. She didn't want to die, and she knew there was a good chance that she would disappear if she got in the car.

"Would you want this to happen to your daughter? Wouldn't you want her to fight?"

"If I had a daughter, the first thing I would tell her was not to sleep with married men," he said with a gleam in his eyes.

Brenda stopped struggling for a second, stunned by his words. He knew. How many others knew? Was her career over? She would have palmed her forehead if her free hand wasn't braced against the hood of the car. Dead people didn't have careers unless it was to push up grass and daisies.

15

"Please. Mr. M. said midnight. I have until midnight," she said, working hard not to beg.

"You have until Mr. M. says until you have," he said, getting in her face, spittle hitting her cheek and chin, and she had to tamp down the urge to brush it off.

Obviously tired of her attempts to delay them, he placed a hand on her head and pushed her into the car. She tried to get back on her feet, but he shoved as he followed her. In one last attempt, she scrambled to the other side, fumbling with the handle. She didn't care if she opened the door to traffic. Anything was better than waiting to see what fate lay at the end of this ride.

A clicking sound caught her attention. She turned slowly to see the man pointing a gun at her. He said nothing. He just waved it toward the back of the seat. She righted herself, facing forward. The car pulled away from the curb, and she watched as they moved farther from the restaurant she'd just exited. Did someone in the restaurant realize what was happening? Had they called the police? Should she have tried to hold out a little longer?

Luca. She wished she'd thought to drop something he would recognize. Then he would know she was taken. She wondered how long he would wait before looking for her. She was grateful she hadn't talked herself out of calling him, otherwise it might be days instead of hours before he or his men began combing the streets for her.

Did he know who A.M. was? Would he know where to look for her? Her mind jumped from one thought to the next in desperate need of keeping her occupied. She knew if she had more than a few seconds to dwell on all the things that could be done to her, she would throw her dignity out of the window and start crying in hopes of reaching whatever souls these men had.

She started thinking of different ways she could distract them so she could escape. One look out the window told her that they were moving too quickly for that. Maybe at a light…

Idea after idea entered her mind but was quickly dismissed. After she'd considered more than a dozen, she tried something she hadn't let herself do in years. She prayed.

God, if you can hear me. I would consider it a really big favor if you could see me out of this? I'm not ready to die. There are so many things I've never done. Please don't let them kill me.

She hadn't lived in any way that would put her higher on God's list than anyone else she knew, but she hoped it was a slow-task day for God.

Brenda thought about putting her seat belt on, but on the off chance they stopped at a light next to a police car, fire truck, or garbage truck, for that matter, she could make an easier escape without it fastened.

After a few minutes, which seemed more like hours, the streetlights appeared less and less until they turned on what felt like a dirt road. It wasn't, but it was rough. Then it occurred to her that they hadn't placed a blindfold over her eyes. Oh. This didn't bode well for her. It didn't take much to guess that her escorts were part of the Italian mob: the abduction from a busy street without anyone attempting to stop it was a huge clue.

The next pothole shook all of them. Was the driver aiming at them? The man sitting next to her continued to point his gun at her side.

"Maybe you should put that away." She gestured to the gun. "The driver seems to be targeting every hole in the ground. You wouldn't want to accidentally shoot me. I don't believe Mr. M. would be happy with you."

The man's expression never changed, but she saw his eyes frost over. Brenda tensed just before the breath was knocked from her body with a blow to her ribs with his gun. She doubled over, trying to delay the pain and force her diaphragm to cooperate.

"You think this is a joke?" he said next to her head. "You won't when Mr. M. is through with you. Now, shut up."

She stayed in the position, working her throat to pull in air until her body heaved and oxygen filled her lungs. Along with the expansion of her lungs came an excruciating pain in her side, so she made sure her next breath was more shallow.

The car stopped outside of what looked to be an abandoned warehouse. She glanced through the rear window. They were in an

17

industrial area after business hours. As much as she didn't want to get in the car, she really didn't want to get out there.

The man sitting next to her opened the door and slipped from the car. He grabbed her wrist at the last moment, giving her no choice but to follow. Her instinct was to resist, but he yanked hard, almost pulling her shoulder from the socket which did nothing to help the pain in her side.

She stumbled after him on the small pathway leading to the huge bay doors. *What must they house in here to need such big doors?* She knew the thoughts were irrational and irrelevant, but her mind was having a hard time concentrating on any one point.

Brenda glanced down at her watch as she held her side. Luca might have noticed her tardiness, but he wouldn't start growing alarmed for another half hour to an hour. Who knew what could happen by then? She needed to come up with a plan to save herself. It seemed she was farther down on God's list than she hoped.

She was shoved through the doors and stumbled to a halt at the change of scenery. The huge hangar-looking room was sectioned off into different areas using rugs, furniture, and dividers. She would have considered it plush and almost cozy if it weren't for the cars parked around the space.

Brenda could make out a dining room with a table that sat at least sixteen, in one corner. A living room with a white shag carpet and oversized couches were to her right, and what looked like a bedroom was behind a frosted glass partition. A small shudder went through her body, and she looked away quickly.

"Ms. Gorman, thank you for gracing me with your presence." She turned, recognizing the voice even before the man came into view. Brenda looked beyond him at the darkened end of the warehouse and was relieved to see that he was alone.

"Mr. Mauro," she returned the greeting with little emotion. She wasn't surprised. She wouldn't have been astonished had it been any of the men she served the night she sat in for Michael at Luca's evening meeting. This just confirmed her guess from earlier that evening.

"Call me Angelo," the barrel-chested man said, walking up to her and capturing her hand. He leaned down and pressed his lips to her knuckles making her stomach turn.

Angelo Mauro was uncharacteristically handsome. He was on the shorter side at five foot ten, but what he lacked in height he made up for in presence and what she guessed was charm. Too bad it was lost on her. His green eyes reminded her of the pieces of glass she found on the shore at North Avenue Beach. She could tell he used his long-lashed dark eyes and full mouth to his advantage. She wondered at his heritage with the Grecian nose, its straight bridge, and a slightly pointy end.

She stared back at him.

"Ms. Gorman. Your first name is Brenda, right? May I call you Brenda?" he said, giving her a smile that reminded her of a feline's who cornered a mouse.

"I would rather you call me a cab," she said dryly.

His lips tipped up at one corner making him look more ominous than amused.

"Sorry, my dear. I can't do that," he said, stepping back and sweeping his arm out toward the living room section. She followed his silent command. From what she'd surmised during the meeting, Angelo Mauro was not a man given to vain gestures, flowery words, or compliments nor did he seem to feel the need to prove his authority. The movement was bigger than what she remembered him making during the meeting, but his eyes held warning.

What little relief Brenda was beginning to feel dissipated as he guided her to the couch with the oversized pillows and sat down with his knee touching hers. She tried to shift away and create more room between them, but the hold he had on her hand tightened painfully.

"Then it is definitely Ms. Gorman to you," she said, not looking away. She was in this warehouse in the middle of nowhere with a man she was sure wanted something she didn't want to give. If all she could do was stare him down, she would do it with everything in her.

She looked down at the hand holding hers prisoner then back up at him. He chuckled and let go.

"I see what he sees in you," Angelo said as if he were assessing her. "You have a fire in you that lights up your eyes even more, but you also have steel in you that temps me to distraction. I wonder what it would feel like to break you."

She used every skill she had to keep him from seeing her reaction to his words. He was dangerous and something she'd never come in contact with before: a man who enjoyed causing people pain.

He blinked slowly, but she remained stoic and steadfast in her resolution. When he fixed his gaze back on her again, his eyes were warm and playful.

"I trust you received the package I sent you?" he asked, leaning back against the cushions.

"I have a feeling you already know," she said, realizing at that moment that the words were true.

His look intensified, and she realized she was giving him what he wanted. She shuttered her expression and saw his lips bow in response before he sighed.

He got up and went over to the cabinet sitting kitty-corner from the door. She wondered if she could run fast enough to reach the door before he did. She threw that idea out of the window. Even if she made it to the door she would probably run into his henchmen. Plus it was probably what Mr. Mauro wanted. She would not give him any more reason to cause her pain.

"Would you like a drink?" he asked.

"No," she said sharply then added, "thank you," for good measure.

He didn't turn from what he was doing. "What about water? Yes, I think water would be good," he said, going on to answer for her.

Brenda huffed and continued to look around for a window or door she'd missed at first glance.

A half glass of water appeared in front of her, but instead of reaching for it she looked up at him.

"No. Thank you," she repeated slowly.

The congenial look he was wearing disappeared. "I insist."

She reached out for the glass, grasping it tightly.

He sat back down next to her. "What were we talking about? Oh yes, you told me you got the package. What did you think? Pretty nice pictures, right?"

He looked at her for confirmation.

She gave him no inclination that she'd heard him, but he went on.

"I have a man who does great work. He treats it like art. I believed he liked having you as a subject," Mr. Mauro said, watching her. If she were thinking about answering—which she wasn't—he probably would have spoken over her. He wasn't having a conversation with her so much as telling her what he knew.

"I can understand you feeling angry or betrayed about the pictures taken of you. It can feel like a violation. Someone coming into a place you consider sacred. Where you can feel secure in what you have built and earned with many hours of work."

As he went on, Brenda got the distinct feeling that he wasn't just talking about the pictures taken of her and Luca. The words held a double meaning, and if she were correct, he was sending her a message.

Did Helena Sable know about her affair with her husband? Was that why she was here? If it was, life as she knew it, was over. She tried to hide her distress, but Angelo picked up on it like a bloodhound.

"Smart enough to be afraid and fiery enough to not cower behind it." He looked at her with something akin to admiration.

"Drink the water," he said, his gaze going steely.

She opened her mouth to tell him she didn't want any water.

She looked down at the glass of water, and her hand began to shake. She stilled it with her other hand. She looked back at Angelo, not caring what he saw in her eyes.

"Don't worry. It isn't poison. Just something to relax you."

"I am relaxed," she deadpanned before taking a sip. The water definitely had something in it. It tasted bitter.

He inclined his head gesturing for her to take another sip. She hesitated.

"You've been favoring your right side. Do you think something's broken?"

She glanced at him, surprised by his change of subject.

21

"I don't know," she said honestly.

"Did Tim do that?" he asked.

"Tim?" she repeated before realization dawned. The idea of the hulking man who abducted her from outside of the restaurant being named Tim was so absurd she would have smiled if she wasn't so afraid for her life.

"Yes," she responded.

"Does it hurt a lot?" he asked, reaching out to touch her. But she shied away.

"Enough," she replied.

He pulled his hand back, nodding his acknowledgment of her answer.

"If Tim, whose only job was to escort you here, was permitted to do that if you didn't follow orders." He pointed at Brenda's side. "What do you think I've been given permission to do?"

Mr. Mauro looked up into her eyes, and Brenda saw the threat lingering there before he spoke again.

"Drink the rest of the water," he said, not looking away this time.

She slowly finished the contents of the glass. Whatever was going to happen now was out of her hands.

He took her glass and got up to place it on the cabinet.

"You read my note in the package I sent you?" he asked as he came back to the couch. He leaned back and crossed his legs.

She nodded, her tongue beginning to itch.

"I think it was well written. It didn't give too much away, but it conveyed what I meant," he said, going back to his bizarre monologue.

"Do you remember what it said?" He glanced at her.

She shook her head slowly, lying, and cleared her throat.

He clicked his tongue. "That's too bad. I worked hard on that note. I was sure you would appreciate my cleverness."

She blinked a few times to clear her vision, which was starting to swim.

"You must be a purist. I didn't expect it to affect you so quickly. Oh well, I'll get to it," he said, sitting forward again.

"I told you what would happen if you shared my note with anyone. You shared it with Luca without my permission, therefore I will share..." He leaned in close enough for her to feel his breath on her face. "You."

She moved away in what seemed to be slow motion, but he followed her. She moved back as far as she could but came up against the pillows, and still, he came closer. She thought he would kiss her, so she turned her head to avoid his lips.

Her mind moved as slowly as everything else, so it took a moment for her to understand what Angelo said. The shot of adrenaline the fear brought cleared her mind a little, and she struggled to get up from the couch, but Angelo stayed her, one hand on her shoulder.

"Ssssh, it's okay. This won't kill you, though you may wish otherwise before the end of the night.

His face swam in and out of focus, and she drew on her last bit of energy to push him back.

"Who are you?" she slurred.

"I'm what nightmares are made of," he crooned softly. "It's really too bad that you're such a lightweight. I wanted you a little more sober when all of the festivities begin."

She turned her head when she heard footsteps coming from the back of the warehouse. She tried hard to focus on the man who walked into the room followed by three more, but their faces blurred to the point where keeping her eyes open made her nauseous.

"Wonderful," Angelo exclaimed like an excited host. "The gang's all here. Now the party can begin."

Brenda tried to push herself up, but her limbs wouldn't cooperate. She heard a snap and searched with her eyes for the cause of the sound. She could barely make out one of the men pulling on a pair of latex gloves, and the sight made her stomach bottom out.

I'm sorry, God, for what I've done. I changed my mind. If you aren't going to rescue me now, I don't want to live through this.

She waited for any type of response. She listened intently, but all she heard was the slowing of her heartbeat just before hands reached for the top button of her blouse.

23

Chapter 3

The devil had come for his due right away, Luca thought as he looked down at the swollen and battered face of the woman he'd betrayed by not keeping his emotions and actions in check. Two broken ribs, a dislocated shoulder, and bruises covering her back and thighs and more. He'd sat there listening to his doctor go over the list of injuries, wanting to go after those who had done this to her, and it didn't take but a moment for him to realize that he was the main culprit.

After reading the message Angelo had left for Brenda, Luca didn't want to leave Brenda unattended. He had been right to send Patrick, his driver, to follow her back to the apartment: just too late. Patrick reported following the sedan Brenda was forced into as he pulled up to the restaurant.

He informed Luca that once he arrived at the warehouse, he watched the men take Brenda inside. Patrick was known for holding his own in a fight, but the two men, clearly built for talking with their fists, were more than he thought he could handle. Not to mention whoever else was in the warehouse. He went back to the closest pay phone and called in some reinforcements. By the time they arrived, Brenda had been in the warehouse for nearly half an hour.

Patrick had advised his colleagues to cover their faces just in case things went sideways. They'd been able to sneak up on Angelo and his associates. While the others held guns to the men's heads, Patrick pulled Angelo off Brenda, wrapped her in a coat, and left the way they'd come.

Luca had been both devastated and relieved by Patrick's account until he was told the address of the warehouse. The relief turned into rage then self-loathing. He'd done this. The moment he'd kissed Brenda, he'd set her on this path of destruction. He knew better. He didn't live in a black-and-white world. There were too many layers of deceit for every move to be accounted for. He was sure Brenda had an idea of some of his business double-dealings. She'd handled some of his business accounts as well as more personal accounts. She wasn't an innocent, but Brenda had not been brought up in his world and though he should've known better, he'd been too weak to stay away.

Still, he never thought their interactions would bring this down upon her, and that wasn't his only error in judgment.

Angelo Mauro didn't seem like the type of man to obsess about a woman, kidnap her, drug her, brutally rape her, and invite others to watch or whatever they were there to do. Angelo, the next in succession to inherit and run the Mauro family business of illegal gambling and legit pharmaceutical testing, always struck him as aloof and somewhat disinterested in people as a whole. Luca wouldn't have pegged him as the creator of the sadistic scene Patrick described, but it was obvious that Luca was going to have to reassess his judgment of Mauro and have his investigator go deeper into the man's background.

It was crucial to him and his family's survival that Luca know everything there was to know about the men he chose to do business with, legal or illegal. Angelo Mauro seemed like a good man to do business with because he didn't like owing people. Luca had discovered this during a conversation they'd had many years ago during a dinner party Luca and his wife hosted. He found the trait both commendable and a good asset. Little to no debt meant very little risk of Angelo being blackmailed or extorted into compromising the dealings of his company or others in their circle.

It was easier to consider that Angelo Mauro owed someone a favor and they'd called it in. Normally, Luca would consider the payment of debts honorable, but this act seemed personal and intentionally cruel, like the type of punishment a lioness protecting her cubs would dole out if she felt threatened. He felt safe in that assumption after finding out the address of the warehouse.

The rustling of the sheets brought Luca back to the present, and he looked down at the frown marring Brenda's face. It seemed that even under heavy sedation she couldn't find peace in her sleep.

The rage that had abated under guilt rose back to the surface with renewed energy. He wanted to order a Sunday massacre, and bring everyone who had hurt her to their knees. It was a bitter pill to swallow knowing he couldn't seek retribution without cutting his own throat in the process.

As ruthless and fierce as he could be in business, it seemed his wife wasn't above cruelty when it came to protecting their home.

He'd sat in this townhome bedroom turned hospital room for hours watching Brenda breathe in and out to reassure himself that his carelessness hadn't cost her her life. He considered her future and how he could help preserve her career. She'd admitted on more than one occasion that it had been her dream to work in a high-powered environment. He didn't want to take that away from her, but he knew it was less than wise to keep her in his employ.

He reached out, lightly running his fingertips along her hands, marveling in the softness of her skin so unlike his own. As dark as he was, her cocoa-colored complexion made his digits look light. It was alluring. Most of the women and men from his homeland were milky or creamy in complexion. The difference was startling and appealing.

He remembered the first time he saw Brenda. He, as he was sure many other men before him, thought she was one of the most beautiful women he'd ever seen. Her hair had been pulled back in a severe bun at the crown of her head. It enhanced her high cheekbones and the slant of her extraordinary eyes. She was young, maybe twenty-three to his thirty-six years, but she held herself with a self-assurance and poise that belied her age.

She'd spent the first few seconds going over the numbers in one of his company's accounts she'd been called in to explain. When she'd finally looked up at him, it was like a punch to the gut. Her features alone were stunning, but with her golden eyes, she was phenomenal. For the first time in his life he wished he was someone other than the head of an Italian crime family steeped with obligations: anything that would make being with her permissible.

She had been very professional, not giving any hint that the inner turmoil he was experiencing was mutual. His choice to take her from the smaller firm had been due to her exceptional mathematical skills and the fact that he wanted to have her close, even if he could never have her.

It was reckless, and he justified his decision by telling himself that he had been everything everyone wanted him to be: a loving husband, loyal son, devoted father, and a formidable successor to both of the family's names. He deserved to have something of his own even if he could do nothing but look upon her a couple of times a week.

He'd overestimated his strength and underestimated her allure. She did nothing overt. If she had, it would have been easy to deny her. She held herself away... above even himself which made getting close to her a challenge and staying away from her an impossibility.

Still, he'd done it for two and a half years. He'd rationed his glimpses and time spent in her presence. Sometimes he would make sure she was included in projects that needed his approval so he would have a reason to talk to her. Her intelligence extended beyond numbers. He'd known from her background check that she came from a family with considerable wealth and that she had gone against their wishes by enrolling in graduate school. When they made it clear that they wouldn't continue to support her if she stayed in school, she took her grandmother's last name and stepped out on her own. He was impressed, but the thought of *his* children doing something so rebellious gave him a couple of sleepless nights.

As time went on he feared and hoped Brenda would start seeing someone that he couldn't intimidate, get married, and move away. The temptation would be over, and he could go back to a life without her.

Fiscal year-end projects caused most of the people in Brenda's department to stay late for close to a week. Dinner would be brought in, and he would get a chance to catch up with his employees. Everyone seemed eager to share except Brenda. Her answers were halting and monosyllable at first. She was standoffish, and he wondered if it was because she was only one of two African Americans employed at the executive level, but she seemed disinterested in being more than acquaintances with anyone.

It turned out that Brenda wasn't good with social cues and would rather stay by herself than embarrass herself. She'd admitted as much after he pressed her about it one evening when they'd ended up working alone. He couldn't understand why she constantly rejected invitations to parties and outings he heard the employees going on together. When he found out about her turning down invitations to Christmas parties, he made attending the Christmas office party mandatory.

At first, Luca regretted his decision to force her to associate. He'd watched her sit in one of the corners most of the evening until Michael pulled her up from the chair. Luca had to tamp down on the jealousy that swiftly rose in him and reminded himself that he wanted her to interact with others. On the way to the dance floor, Michael pulled two more women to their feet and led them all to the dance floor.

Luca watched her grow more and more comfortable with the music until her movements became fluid, and a smile appeared on her face causing her eyes to glow. He realized he'd never witnessed her smile and made a promise to himself he had no business making. He would bring that smile back.

Occasionally, Luca would come down to her office when he knew she was working late and bring a snack with him. He would cajole her into sharing it with him while they talked then he would send her home by his driver. The shared snack would sometimes be a full dinner he'd ordered, but they would do some work while they talked. He loved those evenings, and by sending her home in his car he could guarantee her safe arrival. This went on for months, and the more she revealed about herself the more he wanted to know.

On the evening she told him about her hard time with social cues, Brenda had been running through some numbers for him on a company he wanted to take over. She told him the numbers didn't add up, and he chuckled thinking she was using a play on words, but when he glanced at her, thinking they would share a look of comradery, he caught her staring at him with a puzzled look on her face.

He stared back at her trying to judge the moment. "I thought you were joking," he said.

"About this not being a good venture?" she asked, confusion clouding her features.

"About the numbers not adding up. It could be a play on words. I thought it was," he said sheepishly.

"Mmmm," was the only noise she made before going back to her paperwork.

"I rarely see you laugh or smile. Why is that?" he asked, watching her expressions for any sign that he had been mistaken. Maybe she didn't enjoy their moments like these. Maybe this was truly one-sided. Sure, she looked at him like he hung the moon, but that could be purely work-related hero worship. He received it from new male hires all the time.

"Am I bothering you when I come here and share a snack or dinner with you? You can tell me. I won't fire you or reprimand you," he said before clumsily letting the sentence fall.

He watched her set the paperwork down on the desk, but it was a while before she looked up at him. She looked nervous, and he regretted making her feel uncomfortable.

"I smile. I laugh. When I feel joy I react like everyone else." Her hands disappeared in her lap, and her eyes strayed over to his right. He was tempted to see if there was someone behind him, but since he was facing the door, he knew no one had come in.

29

"I miss things. I don't get most jokes, innuendos, sarcasm, and most plays on words. It has always been that way. They just don't make sense to me." Brenda finally brought her gaze back to his eyes, and he understood the depth of what she was sharing.

She again averted her gaze, but this time she stared down at her paperwork. "I'm glad you made the Christmas party mandatory, now. I was angry with you at first because I was so nervous and afraid someone would say or do something funny or ironic, and I would miss a punchline or cue, and everyone would know I was different."

He didn't point out that she was different. That her gift with numbers and ability to memorize equations, different calculations, and eight-digit numbers, like others remembered their phone number, was extraordinary. She was excellent at what she did. Her focus with numbers and problem-solving couldn't be rivaled. She was a brilliant and beautiful woman who kept to herself because she hadn't learned how to mask her cynicism with humor. She thought she was missing something, and he thought she couldn't be more perfect.

"What do you want, Brenda?" he asked, wanting to know what would bring that smile back to her lips.

"What?" She looked back up at him, startled.

"What do you want in life? Where would you like to go after your work here?"

She was quiet for a moment, and he gave her some time.

"I thought this was my end goal. I didn't expect to get here so soon, so I've had to recalibrate my finish line. Maybe my own finance company," she said, but it lacked conviction.

"Let me know when you're ready to make that move," he said and meant it. He would hate to see her go, whether it was in two years or twenty years, but she was destined for greatness.

"Really? You would help?" she asked, and the awe in her voice moved him. She didn't know that he would move the Chrysler building if she needed more space to grow.

"Really," he said and was gifted with a smile that lit her from the inside. He could feel the warmth of it to the very depth of his being and he wanted to be consumed by it. He leaned in slightly not even aware of what he was doing.

The smile slowly faded from her features, and her eyes grew round, and he felt shame at that moment like he'd never felt before. He'd been wrong. She thought she couldn't read cues. What was he doing?

He began to lean back, but Brenda moved in quickly and clumsily pressed her lips to his. When she pulled back, he didn't know who was more shocked by her action. Her coloring didn't make it easy to detect blushes, but he saw the color rise in her cheeks and was enchanted. He couldn't let her think he didn't want what she offered, so he placed a palm behind her head and brought her lips back to his.

Later that evening he justified his action, telling himself that he might be a good man, but he was a man. Any man would be hard-pressed not to fall a little in love with a woman who looked at him with such admiration. It was heady. He often felt as though he could do anything when she was around. He'd missed that feeling with the obligation and constant duties of life. He loved his wife, but there was something about the way Brenda looked up to him. It made him feel eight feet tall. And she never asked for anything. She expected only what she could work for, which made him want to give her the world.

***

A shifting of the bed once again brought Luca out of his reverie. He lifted his head from his hands and sighed wearily upon seeing Brenda's brows scrunched together. If he'd been asked even five years ago if it were possible to love more than one woman, he would have answered with an unequivocal no. His time with Brenda had him rethinking what he knew about love.

More than once he'd asked himself if what he felt for her was just an intense lust and infatuation and had to admit in the beginning what he felt for her was just that. Maybe if he hadn't gotten to know her or spent time with her, he may have been able to pretend that she was just a beautiful woman to look at.

31

He had so many chances to walk away, place distance between them, keep her far away from the underbelly of his world, but he had tested temptation too many times and he'd gotten caught in his own trap.

He checked his watch one more time, hoping she would sleep longer, but anxious to see if Mauro told her who was behind her kidnapping. If she knew, would she hate him? Would she demand that he stay away from her? He would do it. He would have to. It was the least he could do.

He stood up and leaned forward to place a kiss on her forehead.

"I'm sorry, Bren. You didn't deserve this," he said then forced back the emotion that threatened to overwhelm him because he couldn't promise her retribution or restitution. He couldn't promise her these things because it would mean confronting the owner of the warehouse where Patrick found her. It would mean choosing her over his wife and that he could not do.

Chapter 4

When Brenda found her way to the surface for the first time, scenes fast-forwarded and slowed without her bidding. It made her dizzy. Too many faces, too many hands. Too much pain. She sought the dark and wrapped it around her like a cloak hoping the next time she had the strength to seek consciousness, it would be easier. It wasn't.

Pain. It was what her world had shrunk to. That one word consumed everything. She took a breath and felt pain. She tried to think of where she was, but that took feeling, which brought pain. Lastly, she tried to pry her eyes open, but what little light snuck in caused more pain. A moan inadvertently slipped passed her throat, bringing with it… more pain.

A picture presented itself in front of her closed lids, and she swatted it away like a pesky fly. She couldn't deal with memories right now. Just the present. Just the here.

"Brenda? Are you awake?" The uncertainty in his voice made her inwardly cringe.

She feigned sleep. Just a little longer. She needed a few more… what… minutes, hours, days? She couldn't answer that. She just needed time to get back some of what was taken from her.

***

Dawn broke slowly and softly. It was so serene it pushed at the chaotic thoughts that had been bombarding her for the last twenty-four hours. Brenda watched the colors blend and fold in on themselves, and she took its instruction and did the same with her emotions. She didn't move anything except her eyes, afraid of waking the sleeping form in the corner of the room.

Her gaze went back and forth between the sunrise and Luca, hoping he stayed asleep long enough for her to commit this moment to memory. It didn't take a rocket scientist to realize that she had just barely survived the end of an affair. Brenda breathed in slowly but shallowly so as not to make a sound. She'd learned with her first deep breath that it had to be the last for a while, or she would cry out from the pain and probably knock herself out in the process.

Brenda thought if she could make it, she would limp out of there without disturbing Luca. She didn't want to see the pain and regret in his eyes. It would hurt her more than that monster did. She didn't want what they had shared to be overshadowed by one night of violence. It was over, and she would go back to work in a week or two and keep her head down while Luca served his form of retribution against the men who hurt her. She wouldn't even ask him about it, but she was sure there would be something in the news about parts of their bodies being found at the bottom of Lake Michigan or whole bodies burned beyond recognition.

In a couple of years, she would start her own firm and build new dreams. She hoped Luca would keep his word about helping her, but if he didn't she would do what she needed to do.

Brenda looked around the room noting, not for the first time, her relief at not waking up in a hospital surrounded by strangers with pitying smiles on their faces. She wouldn't have given any answers because she wasn't stupid, but the last thing she needed was an overzealous caseworker or cop trying to seek justice on her behalf. They couldn't do it half as well as she was sure Luca would.

She took a deep breath trying to summon the strength to sit up, forgetting about her bruised ribs which now felt broken. Her breath hitched, and she gave up on the thought. She squeezed her arms against her torso, feeling the binding wrapped below her chest.

"Bren?" A strong hand with long fingers wrapped around hers gently, and it was all she could do to keep the tears, that came with the pain a few seconds before, from falling.

"Oh, Bren, my sweet, sweet Bren. I'm so…"

"Stop," she said on an exhale, interrupting him. "Please don't. It wasn't your fault." She opened her eyes as she spoke the last words, and his face looked like a beautiful watery mass.

He raised her hand a couple of inches to his lips, kissing then rubbing his roughened cheek against it. She stood it for as long as she could then pulled her hand away. He didn't look up immediately at her movement, but when he did he was composed.

She steeled herself at seeing the moisture in his eyes. "How did you find me?"

He leaned back in his chair assessing her. "I'd sent Patrick to see you back to your apartment. He followed you to the warehouse and went back to get reinforcements. It took longer than I'd wished."

"Yes, but since I still have all of my fingers and toes, not to mention my life, I won't complain too much." It was all she planned to say. There was no reason to torture both of them again.

Luca stared at her for a full minute. She could tell he wanted to ask her questions, but she gave him a warning look, and he finally relented.

"Did you have your doctor attend to me?"

"Yes," he said with a solemn nod.

"Then you know everything."

"Everything except what Angelo said to you, but we can talk about that later," he said with a dismissive wave.

"No, let's do it now, so we can get it out of the way," she said, taking a few shallow breaths.

"Are you sure? Things may still be a little hazy. The doctor administered some medication for the pain he was sure you'd have, but nothing more because of what Patrick thought you'd been given by Angelo." He leaned in.

"Help me sit up, and I'll relay what Angelo said. Just what he said. Nothing more." She didn't lose eye contact with him, and he finally nodded.

35

He stood up and helped her sit up. Brenda had been right about not being able to limp out of there earlier. She could barely sit up without breaking a sweat. She knew it would mean she would stay in this room for a couple more days, and she hated the thought.

Once she was relatively comfortable and had gotten down half a glass of water, she relayed everything said by Tim, Angelo's henchman, and Angelo himself, verbatim. Her gift for remembering things didn't stop at numbers, though for once she wished it did.

She watched Luca closely as she replayed what Angelo said about his photographer and was rewarded with the reaction she was looking for. The stark paleness of Luca's face confirmed his wife's involvement. It caused her to wonder though, and she reconsidered not asking him to avenge her.

She finished the retelling and went quiet as she watched the emotions play across his features. He could be stingy with his expressions during business meetings and when he was thinking about a deal, but he had never tried to hide anything from her when they were alone, and this time was no different. The regret was clear and it ate at her.

"We promised each other that there would be no regrets, Luca," she said after she caught her breath again.

He sucked his teeth at her as if she were being ridiculous.

"I had an idea of what could happen. I didn't walk into this blind," she said and watched as he looked at her with something akin to wonder.

"We had an agreement, and I will keep my end of that agreement if you keep yours," Brenda said.

She saw as realization dawned on his face.

"You want to keep working for me?" he asked, sounding incredulous.

"Yes. A dream is a dream, and I'm not giving up mine because of last night. I guess the question is, do you think last night will appease her?" she asked, trying to keep the hope out of her voice.

He stared at her for a moment, his eyes burning with anger. "Since the outcome wasn't to be death," he said, and she watched his jaw clench. "She should be appeased."

"Fine," she said as pragmatically as she could. "I think I'll need a week before going back to work."

"Two," he said without hesitation. She wasn't inclined to argue.

"Two," she responded.

He watched her for a moment then reached for her hand again, and she let him take it.

He started shaking his head. "I never would have—" She cut him off because she knew where he was going.

"I might have," she said, startling him into silence.

She watched as he scanned her face, taking in all she was saying. She still loved him, as stupid as it was, and she let him see it all... one last time.

He kissed her hand without taking his eyes from hers then closed them for a moment as if looking at her was too painful.

"If I could—" he began in a choked voice, but she cut him off again.

"Avenge me."

His eyes popped open, and the pain in them stole her breath.

He swallowed loudly before giving his head a brief shake. "You don't know what you're asking."

She'd known without question that he loved his wife, but there had been that fleeting hope. She now knew unequivocally that the two of them would never be anything more, and it stung.

"Not your wife, Luca," Brenda said, trying to hide some of her hurt.

"Angelo. I want you to hurt Angelo then Tim and the other men who came to watch," she said as firmly as she could with the pain in her body and heart.

She watched him as he stared at her. His face went from sad to grim, then he nodded once.

Brenda squeezed his hand as if to finalize their pact. "I need to sleep now. Can you help lower me a little?"

He got up and assisted her just as gently as he had before and kissed her on the forehead when he was done. She closed her eyes with a small smile on her face and fell asleep still holding his hand.

Chapter 5

He'd hurt his wife.

Luca knew there would be a reckoning for what he'd done, especially after what happened to Brenda. Helena was neither meek nor subservient. He hadn't wanted a woman he could walk over, and he hadn't developed a taste for disciplining a woman like one would a child. When he met Helena he fell in love with her strength and love for life. Once she made up her mind she was all in. She loved him and their children the same way. If they disagreed, she didn't have a problem speaking her mind, but she always respected his place in their family. She could get passionate about her opinion, but she wasn't crude or cruel. It was because of these characteristics that he was baffled when it came to his wife's recent behavior.

She hadn't come to him when she'd found out about his affair with Brenda. She had just dealt with what she must have considered a threat or opposition. She hadn't ordered Brenda killed, but Helena's message was more than clear.

He wondered if she'd known about the two weeks he'd spent with Brenda while she was in Italy or if it had been the spontaneous trip for Brenda's birthday. He knew he was playing with fire. He should have kept to the promise he'd made to himself and ended it after those two weeks.

He was fortunate in the fact that Brenda had not broken their agreement or demanded more. It turned out, she was the least of his worries.

It could have been the same person who took the pictures of him and Brenda in her apartment. He had Patrick doing some quiet research in that area.

He walked out of the master bathroom into the sitting room of the palatial home he'd bought for his wife when she was pregnant with their third child. He picked up the report on his grandson and the foster family he'd arranged to take him to. They had fallen in love with the boy and wanted to adopt him. Antonio had put up some resistance but agreed that an open adoption was best for everyone. Luca had taught his son to value family and put them first. It would seem Antonio listened better than he had.

Helena was sitting up in bed reading a book. She glanced at him when he crossed the threshold into their bedroom but returned her attention to the book without saying a word. This had gone on since she'd come back three days ago from the month-long trip she'd taken with some friends to the South of France. When he asked her how her trip had gone she'd given him monosyllabic answers, and he had given her more time and space. He knew he had no right, but he missed his wife. He missed the woman with the intense eyes that made him feel fortunate to have gotten her first.

Luca took a deep breath then sat down on the edge of her side of the bed. Helena shifted her legs away but didn't look up from her book.

"Helena," he said, seeking her undivided attention.

She released a heavy sigh and placed a bookmark at the page she was reading then set the book aside and looked up at him.

He wanted to touch her, to connect so she understood the depth of his sorrow for hurting her, but he kept his hands still.

"You, Helena, have been more than I imagined a wife could be." He watched her eyes go from impassive to blazing hot. He fought the urge to back up.

"I have seriously wronged you, and I shamed myself when I broke my vows," he began again but stopped when she held up a hand.

"Are you still sleeping with her?" she asked, her voice giving away little of what he saw in her eyes.

"No," he said, relieved to be able to give her that truth.

"How long, Luca? How long were you with her?" She didn't look away which made him want to squirm. He'd seen her do it to their children, but he would take it. He still wasn't sure if she knew about the first or the second time so he told her the truth, knowing it would hurt.

"Two weeks earlier in the year and then I was with her for a week about a month and a half ago. At that time I told her we could not continue, and she accepted my decision. I have only been alone with her once since that time, and it was to see she received the medical attention she needed. I didn't think it would be smart to have her go to a hospital. Too many questions."

Helena chuckled but it was devoid of humor. "Smart, huh."

"The smart end to a dumb decision," he said, hoping the self-deprecating statement would either bring her temper forward or calm her. This aloofness, no matter what her eyes said, was daunting. It meant she didn't feel she could trust him with her feelings, and he wanted to at least have a chance to earn it back.

"You put your family and business legacy on the line. It was reckless and irresponsible, and for what? So you could have your ego stroked?" she said.

He didn't respond, knowing she was letting off some steam as he'd hoped.

"I thought you were more. I pitied my friends whose husbands cheated on them and considered myself fortunate to have found one of a few men who took their vows seriously and put his family above everything, including himself. Shame on me for feeling secure in your love and friendship. Shame on me for taking your loyalty and concern for my well being for granted." Her words cut as was their intent, but the pain that extinguished some of the fire in her eyes would have brought him to his knees if he were standing. He had taken something sacred and beautiful and all but demolished it.

"I'm so sorry," he said, meaning it to his core. He'd hurt his wife, and if it weren't for her deeply rooted Catholic faith, she would probably be thinking of divorcing him.

He began to reach for her hand but pulled back. He saw her eyes follow the movement before she closed them briefly.

41

"I hear she still works for the firm," she said, her voice as hard as cement and just as colorful. She finally met his eyes again, and they were frosty.

"Yes, but I have no direct contact with her. Any project she's on that needs my signature is conducted with two levels between us," he said.

"So you keep tabs on her even if it is only to make sure you are not in the same room at the same time," she stated, and he hoped she wasn't going where he thought she was.

"What do you want?" he asked before he could keep the words from forming.

"I want you not to have cheated on me. I want my friend not to have betrayed me. But since I can't have that, I want all temptation of it happening again gone," she nearly spat, and though he could see what that little bit of control cost, he couldn't give in to her.

Early in their marriage, he and Helena agreed that she would not interfere in any of his businesses, and he wouldn't interfere with hers. If he solicited her advice or opinion on a special project, that was one thing, but requests, orders, or commands were not welcomed. It was an agreement neither of them had broken until that very minute.

"No," he said without room for misinterpretation.

She blinked. "No? No, I'll think about it? No explanation as to why you wish to keep the woman who helped you break your sacred vows?"

"No," he repeated. "She is the best accountant in Chicago, and I messed up by seducing her. Not the other way around. I have wronged you and lost your trust, but I want to earn it back, and I will do anything but allow you to tell me how to run my business," he said with conviction.

He thought she was going to spit on him. He may have welcomed the loss of control. It might have put him on more even ground with her. He watched her hazel-green eyes glow with an almost unnatural light as she stared back at him.

"I got a call from Angelo yesterday," she said, her chin going up defiantly.

"Not in here, Helena. Do not bring that man into our bedroom." He worked to keep his voice low.

She went on as if he hadn't said a word. "He said he's heard talk that you are lining up others to take his place at the table."

"He had no right to share that with you. You are not a part of that business. You cannot know about any part of that business. He is putting you in danger, and I will not have it."

"No, Luca, you did. You put me in danger. The moment you married me, you put me and each child we would have in danger. And the moment you climbed into bed with that woman, you put each one of our lives in her hands." Her voice had gone from loud and urgent to resigned.

He looked past her shoulder because he knew where she was going, and though she had a strong argument, he did not want to do what she was going to ask. He'd made a promise.

"Stop, Luca." Helena's voice had defrosted some.

"No," he said without shifting his gaze.

Her small fingers touched his cheek, and the feeling startled him into looking into her eyes.

"Stop, Luca." Her voice went from cool to cajoling. "I hired him to do a job. He did it. It has nothing to do with your business."

The burning that had started in the pit of his stomach at the sound of Angelo's name grew, and he didn't know how long he could keep it from erupting. She didn't see Brenda when Patrick carried her into his townhome. She hadn't witnessed the brokenness. No matter what side she fell on, Brenda was someone's child.

"He's a bulldog."

"A trained bulldog," Helena responded, and he pulled his face out of her reach.

"How did you know?" he asked, not really wanting to know how she'd obtained information he hadn't.

"Marjorie gave me his name. She used him to discourage Niccol's mistress," she said.

"You told Marjorie our business?" he asked, feeling his anger rising. Marjorie, Helena's sister, couldn't hold news in a cistern.

43

"No, I gave her someone else's name. You know you would have gotten a call from my brother Solomon by now if he didn't just come to your business. I couldn't have that," Helena said, sounding distracted.

His mind took in everything she was saying. "How long did you know before you set your bulldog on her." He just stopped short of saying her name.

She leaned away and pulled a package out of the bottom of her nightstand and threw it on his lap. He knew what it was. He didn't need to see the pictures again.

"When?" he asked.

"While you were in Vegas." Her voice had returned to steel.

He swallowed back the bile that rose with the anger.

"If we have any chance of finding our way back to what we had before, you will stop preparing to replace Angelo," she said, putting the package of photographs back in the nightstand. He noted their placement so he could take them out later and burn them.

"He's a monster, Helena," Luca said, forcing images of Brenda out of his mind. He wouldn't even give credence to her thinly veiled ultimatum.

"One more reason why you want him working for you instead of coming after you," she said, but he noticed she wasn't beseeching or cajoling anymore. He took in her expression and realized she was testing him.

"He's a dime a dozen. Why is this important to you?" he asked, continuing to stare at her.

"Because I need to know that the promises you make to me are more important than the ones you make to her." Helena didn't blink. She didn't fidget. She didn't move. His wife was very intelligent. It was obviously one of the things he found attractive. Some men liked legs. He was attracted to extremely intelligent women. Brenda's intelligence grew despite the people around her, and Helena's intelligence grew due to her ability to observe and read people, so he didn't have to ask his next question but he did so anyway.

"How did you know it was her request?" he asked, beginning to feel sick.

"Because I would have asked for the same thing."

He glanced away briefly. His shame complete. He was about to break his word yet again.

What he didn't know was how much it would cost him.

***

"I'm pregnant." The words hit their target as if they were launched from a gun.

Luca had to admit that finding Patrick leaning against his car in the parking structure was odd, but it didn't prepare him for Patrick alerting him to Brenda's presence before he opened the back door for him.

He slid in and came face-to-face with Brenda. He had been avoiding her at every turn for two months, but now and then he caught a glimpse of her profile or back, and he knew she wasn't out of his system. Now that he was in such close proximity to her he couldn't help but permit himself to drink in her beauty. It could be that he'd starved himself, but she looked more exquisite than he remembered. Her skin had an almost unearthly glow, and some of the rounder features of youth in her face had become slightly angular. It was hard to concentrate on what she was saying, let alone keep himself from touching her. He balled his hands into fists as a last resort. Then she spoke those two words, and it all faded into the background.

"Did you hear me?" she said with an anxiousness he'd mistaken for excitement just moments before.

"Yes," he said, nodding. He didn't know how to react. There were so many questions, but they all seemed inappropriate, so he had her take the lead.

"Tell me what I need to know," he said.

He caught the look of surprise in her eyes and knew she'd expected him to try and separate himself from her, and she would have been right to think so after he'd gone back on his word to avenge her.

She licked her lips before she began and smoothed her bun with a shaking hand. He hated seeing her agitation and took her other hand long enough to squeeze it gently before letting go.

She gave him a brief smile of gratitude before she began. "I'm ten maybe eleven weeks pregnant. She ran a shaky hand across her forehead. "Uh... I thought I had a bug a few weeks ago that wouldn't go away, so I went to the doctor yesterday. I didn't know. I promise I didn't know." She shook her head.

He shushed her because he needed to get as many facts as possible. Her pregnancy could cost her her life, and he needed to find a way to protect her. Brenda took a couple of deep breaths before she began again, and he was relieved that he didn't have a frantic woman on his hands.

"I know we took precautions except for the time in the shower during my birthday week. It could also be from a week later," she said, before glancing away for a second then seeking out his gaze again.

"What do you want?" he asked.

"I don't know. I'm just terrified someone is going to find out," she said.

He knew she was beyond panic because her last statement made no sense. Unless she was asking what he thought she was asking.

"Do you want to see it to term?" he almost whispered. It was not something he ever thought he would ask a woman. It seemed blasphemous even to think it.

"I think I must," she said.

He thought her answer was odd since she neither sounded affronted nor afraid.

"Why?" he asked.

"If I were to try to wait for the paternity test, it would be too late to do anything," Brenda said, looking at him solemnly.

He took a deep breath before asking because his heart was pounding in anticipation and dread. "Why should it matter?"

"I would keep yours no matter what," she said as if he should already know the answer.

"Why? It still wouldn't be possible for us to be together, for me to be in your or our child's life," he said apologetically and watched the words chip away another piece of her. It never failed. When they were together she lost.

46

Brenda stared down at her hands for a moment then looked back up at him, and he saw the answer plain as day.

"Because I love you," she said with eyes that turned sad then resigned.

She covered his hand for a moment, and he wanted to cry at what he'd done to this beautiful woman. He should have found another job for her in another state after her convalescence, but he wanted her close. He saw that now. He wanted to be the one who helped her dreams come true. It seemed his ego hadn't had enough.

"I know what you are thinking, and I'm an adult. I make my own choices. I could have left at any time, but I wanted to stay. I told myself I would just wait to see what you did to Angelo, but he is still working with you." She watched him closely for a moment. He couldn't have spoken if his life depended on it.

"But if I'm to be honest. I just wanted to be close to you," she finished quietly.

Luca took in the dark brown hair, cocoa-colored complexion, slanted golden eyes, high cheekbones, full lips, and strong chin, and took a snapshot in his mind.

Enough.

He had been selfish and thought himself just big enough not to have to deal with the ramifications of his actions, but they were reverberating through his life and the life of those he held most dear. It was time to stop.

He moved back toward the opposite side of the back seat and hardened himself against the flash of hurt in her eyes.

"I will do everything I can to keep you and this child alive." He gestured to her stomach. "But if you don't do as I say, I can't help you."

Brenda stared at him for a moment then nodded. "Okay. Thank you."

Her gratitude made him physically ill, so all he could do was nod for a few seconds.

"I will call you with directions before the end of the week," he said.

Luca watched her as her eyes skimmed over him quickly. "You look thinner and a little tired. Please take care of yourself." With that Brenda opened her door and left.

He stared at the spot where she'd sat long after Patrick got in and started up the car. He took a deep breath and reached for his mobile phone. If Brenda was pregnant with his child, he would rather it be brought up by another man than be killed by his wife's bulldog. It left a bitter taste in his mouth, but it was his own doing, so he would have to take it.

As for the vengeance Brenda was obviously still seeking through him for Angelo, he would have to put her off and hope motherhood would distract her. Maybe it would cause her to change her mind, especially if the child were his. He could take a paternity test and give it to her as a wedding present. He shook his head at the wrongness of that thought as he pressed a couple of buttons to a man's phone number who he was sure never wanted to hear from him again.

It was time to call in a favor, of sorts, and sever a tie.

Chapter 6

Brenda sat on her couch, staring out of her living room window at the Chicago skyline. She'd loved this view from the moment she saw it. She noticed it was a clear day, and she could see all the way to Lake Michigan. The blue of the water was so vivid. It seemed wrong somehow on this day when all of the color had been stripped from her world.

Luca was selling her off like a broodmare. Her stomach roiled at the thought. Well, to be fair, her stomach tossed and turned at every despairing thought, strong smell, or fast movement, and on and on.

She'd begun feeling tired and run down a few weeks before. Thinking it was a bug, she took more vitamin C and went to bed almost immediately after getting home from work each day. She would feel somewhat revived in the mornings but would start dragging again in the afternoons. She started taking small naps after scarfing down her lunch, and that helped but when her stomach started rebelling by sending her food back, she began to get worried. It would be her luck to have contracted a terminal disease. She wouldn't go out without a fight though.

She had told Luca the truth. She had no clue she was pregnant until the doctor came back in her examination room with a hesitant smile. He'd probably seen the Ms. on her file and assumed correctly that she wasn't married. Ha. If he only knew the truth. The moment he told her she was pregnant he had unwittingly given her a death sentence.

At the time, the thought of telling Luca she was pregnant made her almost wish for a life-threatening disease. She wasn't looking forward to his reaction or what would come next. She knew if she didn't tell him right away, she wouldn't have the courage to do so. She hadn't shared more than three words with Luca since he'd taken her home once she was well enough to leave his townhome. She thought seeing him at work would be awkward until one week became two then a month went by without her setting eyes on him.

Her gratefulness for his concern turned into annoyance from his avoidance and into paranoia from his complete lack of communication. It was a new emotion. One she didn't know how to deal with so she prepared for the worst: the worst being Luca betraying her.

"Brenda?" The sound of her name from foreign lips pulled her from her thoughts, and she looked over to see the handsome major and Luca's lawyer watching her. It was the lawyer who'd addressed her.

"Have you made up your mind?" he asked with a patience that grated at her. She clenched her teeth to keep from saying the first thing that came to mind. She was being sent away like a petulant child, but that wasn't all. To add insult to injury, she was being married off as well.

She tried to take Luca's plan and instruction as the last-ditch effort he said it was, to save her life. It was hard though. She hadn't known what to expect by his words in his car but it certainly wasn't for Luca to send her away with a total stranger.

She was being exiled. She would sign a letter of resignation that would take effect immediately, marry this man in two days, whose name she'd forgotten again, and move to Panama City, FL. Everything she'd fought so hard to obtain was slipping through her fingers.

She wasn't leaving empty-handed though. No. Luca was a first-class gentleman to the bitter end. For the duration of her marriage to Major Handsome Pants, she would be given a stipend. From the number of zeroes behind the seven, which Luca knew was her favorite number, Brenda could have easily envisioned owning her own business in a year, but her soon-to-be husband was active in the military. If she wanted to remain under the protection of her husband, and Luca

50

indirectly, she would have to give up her dream of owning a brick-and-mortar business.

"Yes, I have," Brenda said, before shifting her gaze to Major Tall Glass of Water. "Any wedding present requests?"

He shrugged his shoulders. "I don't know." He pretended to think for a moment.

"How about fidelity? I would rather not be made a mockery of," he said with feigned ease.

"I think I can arrange that," she responded with the same dry humor. He nodded.

"And you?" he asked.

"Celibacy?" she asked sweetly, not sure if his question referred to the reason behind their forced marriage. She thought some of the looks he'd given her while the lawyer began speaking seemed flirtatious, but she could have been wrong—she had been before. He could have just been watching her.

The small smile that had lifted his lips left as he waited to see if she was kidding. She made sure to keep her features blank.

"Do you have another present in mind? The agreement calls for at least five years," he asked with all seriousness, his attempts at charm seemingly abandoned.

"No, but I will give it some thought," Brenda said with a sickeningly sweet voice.

He watched her for a few more moments then nodded.

Brenda sighed. "Well, it looks like we've come to some understanding."

"Do you need anything before Saturday?" asked Major Finer Than Frog's Hair. She didn't like that she found him attractive or that he obviously found her attractive. She was pregnant for goodness' sake, and he knew it. What kind of man would marry a woman that he just met and was pregnant with another man's baby? Did Luca tell him the child might be his own, or did he share the more shameful possibility of this baby's parentage? She didn't want to know right then.

"No, I think everything has been taken care of."

She looked over at the attorney who was lifting paperwork out of his briefcase. "When will the packers and movers be here?"

"The packers will be here Monday morning, and the movers will put everything on the truck on Wednesday," he recited as if he were going through a grocery list.

She would be shipped off within a week, but before she left, she would get the truth out of Luca. She would get assurances that he would keep his word and avenge her or she would do it herself.

Brenda scooted to the edge of her seat so she could reach the papers the attorney placed on her coffee table. She read through them to make sure everything Luca's attorney discussed with her and Major Babe, was written. Satisfied, she signed and pushed the paperwork over so Major Smooth could sign as well.

She watched him hesitate for a couple of seconds and felt nothing. She didn't know what she was supposed to feel at the moment, but she was sure it wasn't supposed to be this complete numbness. Brenda glanced back through the window while she waited for him to make his decision.

She had come to Chicago to make a name for herself. She fell in love with a mob boss whose wife, if she found out Brenda was pregnant would surely have her killed and was leaving for parts unknown with a stranger who'd owed said mob boss a favor. What type of man married a woman he'd never met as the fulfillment of a favor? If Brenda was sure she could get away and hide with her own means, she would have taken her chances.

She heard the scratching of pen on paper and waited for it to stop before she turned to Major Million-Dollar Smile. "I'm sorry to ask you again, but what's your name?"

"Major Wilson Ellis," he said slowly, setting the pen down.

Brenda nodded. It was extremely odd that she could remember sheets of pages worth of bank account numbers, but she couldn't remember her husband-to-be's name. She even remembered his rank and military branch, but his name was like a whisper that disappeared before reaching her.

"Major Wilson Ellis," she repeated.

52

"Once you both arrive back in Florida you will be required to go to the justice of the peace. We want this to look as legitimate as possible."

"Then you should have started making references in your little book long before our marriage," she said, not even trying to leave the scorn out of her voice.

The lawyer took it in stride. "Funny you should mention that," he said, pulling a sheet from his briefcase and handing it to her.

"As you can see, you and the major have been seeing one another, off and on, for some time. You met six months ago when Major Ellis was in Chicago for business."

Brenda glanced at the man in question. "Were you here six months ago?"

Wilson nodded.

"What kind of business?" she asked, realizing she didn't know how Wilson and Luca were acquainted.

"The kind that I cannot speak about with people who haven't been vetted by Federal Investigative Services," he said without hesitation.

She leaned forward. "How does a person come to owe Luca Sable such a huge favor?"

"Am I doing him a favor? I rather thought he'd done me one," he said, mimicking her movement.

Brenda leaned back, seeing that she wasn't going to get the answers she was looking for easily. She glanced back down at the paper. She read that he'd been in town once again during the two weeks between her birthday and the attack. She was curious to know how they were supposed to have been together during either of those times.

As if reading her thoughts, Wilson leaned in even closer and tapped a finger on the line she'd been reading. "That was the week I came back to tell you that I didn't want to mess around anymore. I wanted us to really work at our relationship because life just wasn't the same without you." He delivered the last with a grin he must have thought made the ladies swoon.

"Does that really work?" she asked with genuine curiosity.

"What?" Major Ellis asked.

She pointed at his mouth. "That thing you do with your mouth. The grin."

He leaned back and shrugged. "I've never had any complaints."

She squinted at him. What kind of man had Luca attached her to? "Do you use it on many women?"

The mirth left his eyes, and it seemed to dawn on him what she was asking. He shook his head.

"No."

She studied him for a moment then shrugged. At least he was quick thinking.

"Would you like to go out to dinner or get a cup of coffee?" he said, looking around briefly. I think it would be good if we could talk and get to know one another better before we get married." She could tell he was being sincere. She didn't think some conversation would hurt. Luca wouldn't have placed them together if he didn't think this man could and would take care of her. The fact that he suggested they go out for dinner instead of dining in her home only reinforced her thoughts.

"Okay. This evening?" she asked.

He seemed surprised by her easy capitulation. "Yes, I'm staying in town, so I can escort you to my home in Florida."

She noticed he said "my" home in Florida. It oddly comforted her. It meant that he hadn't quite embraced the fact that they would be sharing space for at least the next five years.

"I'll be back to pick you up at six, if that's okay," Major Ellis said as he stood up with the lawyer.

"Sure," Brenda said, also rising from the couch.

"A copy of the signed documents will be delivered by messenger tomorrow morning," the lawyer said, facing her.

She nodded her thanks and led the men to the door.

"I'll see you at six?" Major Ellis reiterated.

"I'll meet you in the lobby," she said. It made him pause but with one look at her, he nodded. Either he was being extremely accommodating or all of the television representations of majors in the military were fake.

54

Chapter 7

"So, Major Ellis, are you from Florida?"

"First, please call me Wilson or Will. Second, I was born and raised in Cole, Kansas," he said, before taking a bite of his steak.

"How about you?" he asked.

"Durby, Oklahoma. Have you heard of it?"

"It sounds familiar. Were you born and raised there?"

She shrugged to make light of what she was about to tell him. "We came from a town in Philadelphia when I was eleven." She told him the name, wondering if he would recognize it. When there was no change in his reaction, she relaxed.

"How did you come to work at Sable Financial?"

She looked at him across the table, but he was already forking up another piece of meat. He was only trying to make small talk and get to know her as he'd said.

She breezed through her years of college, her work at the contracted independent firm Luca had taken her from, and her desire to one day have a financial firm of her own.

Once she was done, Wilson looked regretful.

"My job transfers me quite a bit. I don't see how you will be able to do that," he said almost apologetically.

It wasn't anything she wasn't expecting. Though she'd thought the same thing, hearing it from him made her ill. She would have to wait at least another five years, and by then they would have forgotten about her in Chicago. She would have to start all over again in a town where no one knew her.

"Please, excuse me," she said, getting up from the table. She could feel her eyes stinging, and she knew if she saw any more sympathy in his eyes she would burst into tears. She walked to the bathroom as quickly as possible and was relieved to find herself alone. She walked over to the wide mirror above the faucets.

"Suck it up, and stop acting like a baby. You know this is the only way. You're lucky. He seems like a decent man. You will have a home, a husband, and a father for your baby," she said into the mirror, trying hard not to consider the irony of fulfilling her parent's dreams for her. She willed the tears back, angry at the overreaction. She refused to become a crier. She took a few deep breaths and told herself there was no need for the waterworks. She'd made her bed by having an affair with a married man. Now she had to sleep in it. Evidently, with a man she barely knew. She shook her head as she tried to shift gears yet again. She tried her pep talk again, squared her shoulders, and walked out the door of the women's restroom then right back in to use it for what it was meant for.

When she returned to her seat she was as poised as she wanted to be. Since he stood when she approached it was hard to avoid eye contact. She told him in one look that their previous conversation was through.

"Well, since we have established that I will have to place my dreams on hold indefinitely, why don't you tell me why a young, handsome, and I assume successful man as yourself, would agree to marry a woman he's never met who is pregnant with another man's child?" she asked while watching as his normally friendly face closed down.

"I owe him my life," he said. When it occurred to her that he wasn't going to elaborate, she just stared at him.

"Besides, he did me a favor. I work too much to go out or date and coming home to someone I can talk with and share civilian conversations with sounds inviting.

56

"You are so lucky you didn't say 'coming home to a good meal,'" she said, breaking up some of the straightforwardness of the statement with a shadow of a smile.

He looked startled for a second but recovered quickly. "Are you saying you can't cook?" he asked, looking incredulous. But a small twitch at the edge of his eye gave him away.

"I can survive on what I cook in the kitchen. I may or may not have built up an immunity though," she replied.

He watched her for a few seconds and seemed to make up his mind.

"Luca shared some of your... predicament with me." He paused. It was probably because she also paused for a moment. Her hesitation was more obvious since she was holding a fork to her mouth.

"He did," she said, more as a statement than a question and resumed the movement. She was all of a sudden too tired to eat, but she forced herself to chew and swallow the food she'd just placed in her mouth.

He slowly wiped his mouth with his napkin before laying it on the table. He leaned back in his chair and watched her for a moment before speaking.

"Do you know Damian Sable, Luca's younger brother?" he asked.

"Just what I've read on paper," Brenda lied. "Do you serve under him?" she asked, knowing Damian Sable made his enlistment in the air force a lifelong career. He was considered a black sheep in the family because Luca's father thought he had the sharpest mind of all of his siblings and was angry that he would waste it on a military career. It was one of the few things Luca shared with her about his family.

"Colonel Damian pulled some strings, so I could go home to bury my family when my mother, father, and sister died in a car crash."

He said it like he'd said it before, many times and had condensed it all in one sentence. She wondered if he did that to distance himself from it.

"I went home, but after a few days, I ran into some trouble with men who were obviously angry that my family was receiving more attention than they deemed necessary because I honestly can't think of any other reason why they would try to ambush me outside of the mortuary." He paused to take a sip of his water before continuing."

"Damian and Luca, who I'd met only once before came in for the funeral. I was honored that they would come, but that day I was more thankful than anything else. If they hadn't shown up when they did, I probably would have been buried right alongside my family."

"Is that why you say you owe Luca?"

"That is part of it, but they also adopted me. I would say I owe him. He doesn't. In this case, he asked me if I would consider helping him. After hearing him out. I agreed to help him," he said the last with a small lift of his left shoulder.

It was hard to think of Luca asking someone to help him with her like she was a problem that wouldn't go away. She quickly brushed the thought aside.

"How does Damian feel about you sacrificing your bachelorhood?" Brenda asked, drawing a smile from him.

"Damian thinks it's time for me to stop strolling around this world alone," he said, leaning forward over his plate. She guessed the hard part was over or at least he was done with what he considered the hard part.

"Will your family be upset about not being invited to our wedding?" he asked.

"Yes, but the fact that there is a wedding will help to appease them. I think they should be grateful that I am reaching out to them at all since my dad disowned me for putting my career ahead of having a family," she said with maybe too much honesty.

"I know this is very personal, but you seemed in the perfect position to excel in your field. There were ways you could make sure you weren't putting your career or life in jeopardy. Why did you decide to keep the child when there's a chance it isn't Luca's?" he asked, watching her intently.

"Because there is a chance that it is Luca's," she responded without hesitation.

"You love him that much?" he asked, frowning.

"You sound surprised," she said, wondering if she was being tested yet again.

"Not so much surprised as disenchanted. I'm a patient man and until either my charm or distance makes some room in your heart for me, I will be content to be your friend," he said.

"Really?" she asked, not believing him one bit.

"Well, not completely, but I thought it sounded good," he responded, seeming almost reluctant.

"How about this?" she said, pointing her fork at him for a second. "I will always be honest with you about my feelings. I will represent you as best as I possibly can. I won't disrespect or argue with you in public, and I will not get in the way of any parental relationship you wish to have with my child. As far as h or she will know, you are their father."

His look of understanding when she began morphed into something close to admiration. He bowed his head in agreement when she was finished, and they continued their dinner with lighter conversation as they got to know each other's likes and dislikes on a more surface level.

He had been on his own for more than a decade. He had gotten used to being alone, but he wanted a family of his own. He liked a good steak and potato meal, dogs more than cats, though he had neither, and jazz more than any other type of music. His favorite color was navy blue, and he originally joined the air force because he wanted to fly planes but was placed in an analytical position. She was intrigued, but when she asked what he did, he told her it was classified.

By the end of the evening, she'd discovered that they shared quite a few things in common. They would get along, but she knew if they'd met in a bar or the market she wouldn't have given him the time of day once she found out he was in the military. She didn't want to be a homemaker; she didn't want to be forced to travel around the country, and she certainly didn't want a husband who could be deployed for months on end.

Wilson walked her through the lobby to her elevator but no farther. He bowed over her hand, kissing her knuckles when she held it out to him for a handshake. His brown eyes twinkled as he grinned up at her, and she couldn't help the answering smile that came to her lips. He was teasing her, and she'd caught on.

"Goodnight, Brenda," he said before pressing the button to call the car down.

"Goodnight, Wilson," she mimicked.

"Do you maybe want to get some lunch with me tomorrow?" he asked, stepping out of her space.

"I have a lot of work to do, to start to prepare for the packers. Give me a call around eleven, and I'll let you know."

He nodded and left the way he came, his long strides eating up the carpet between her and the door. She thought he had the grace of a cat and wondered if he'd always walked that way or if it was the military's influence. She watched him until the bell rang letting her know the elevator had arrived. It was easy for her to see why he was so confident. He had the looks, height, and swagger.

She stepped in and stared ahead as the doors closed. Maybe one day she might let him charm her with his looks, intelligence, and kindness if he was truly the man he portrayed himself to be, but for the foreseeable future, her heart and mind were full of two things—Luca and revenge. There was no room for anything else. She couldn't give too much thought to her baby at the moment either because if she did, that monster might walk free. She would call Luca again.

***

On Thursday, a week later, Brenda walked into her soon-to-be husband's two-bedroom condo-style home. It was tastefully decorated in tan, beige, and black with the right amount of furniture to make the rooms look bigger than they were. It was quiet, and though on base, set away from most of the other housing. She liked it.

The arrangement of flowers next to a fruit basket caught her eye. She assumed right away it was something Wilson had set up to welcome her.

"That was very thoughtful of you," she said, not noticing how still Wilson had become.

60

He walked around her to the flowers and lifted the card from its holder wedged between the irises and tulips. After glancing at it his shoulders relaxed, and he handed it to her.

"It's for you. It looks like Luca beat me to welcoming you to Florida," he said before walking away.

She watched Wilson pick up the bags she'd left at the door and walk down the hall to what she assumed were the bedrooms. If he was going to get this stiff at just a note, she wondered how he would respond if it turned out that she was carrying Luca's child.

She looked down at the card, a smile coming unbidden to her lips at seeing the familiar scrawl of his name. She turned the card over, and the smile died on her face.

The anger. No rage that engulfed her at reading the words had her clenching the fist not holding the card. She read the words three times. Her anger growing each time until she was shaking. At that moment, the one thing she thought impossible, happened. Luca Sable had failed her.

Hot, angry tears blurred the words, but she had committed the note of betrayal to memory.

Welcome to your new life.
Let go of your old one.
Completely.

Getting on the plane with Wilson was a last-minute decision because, although she signed the paperwork she'd considered going back on her word. Luca hadn't taken or returned her calls last week in Chicago, and the one time she'd shown up at the Sable building, she saw Helena getting out of a black sedan across the street so she didn't go up.

If Luca thought he could put her away and think she wouldn't seek the vengeance she was due, he was mistaken. They all were mistaken.

Brenda would make that monster regret he ever laid eyes on her. She would take away his future just as he'd taken away hers. Any revenge Luca would have gotten on her behalf would look like a slap on the wrist for Angelo Mauro compared to what she was about to do.

61

She shouldn't have trusted Luca Sable with her heart, and Luca shouldn't have trusted her with his less-than-legal financial documents.

She threw the card on the floor and walked on it as she went to see what her new home looked like. She thought it symbolic. Soon, at least, four of the five families doing side businesses with Luca would be under her heel too.

PART TWO

Chapter 8
Present Day

Grace placed the second colored contact in its receptacle before rinsing the moisturizer from her face. She patted her face dry and unintentionally caught her gaze in her reflection. She paused in her actions and frowned at the woman's judgmental gaze in the mirror.

She cut her eyes at the woman in the reflection, refusing to feel guilty for her deception. She was too close to the truth to let one young man's job mess with her conscience. Besides, if she could convince the clerk to hand over documents she didn't have the security credentials to obtain, he didn't deserve to hold the position.

Grace gazed at her still smooth forehead and ran a discerning eye over her elegantly sculpted eyebrows as well as the rest of her face and neck. The older she became, the more time she spent on her nightly and morning regimen. There was some vanity, she admitted to herself, but it was control she was a slave to.

She'd learned to use the same looks, that had cursed her almost forty years ago, to her advantage. Her current husband was still blind to everything but her beauty, which had given her a nice upgrade in her status and the ability to gain otherwise unobtainable information that kept her two steps ahead of her self-proclaimed enemies.

Grace cast a look around the opulent bathroom with its pearl accents at the edges of the marble counter, which was long enough to hold three basins. She didn't know why a private bathroom would need three basins. It seemed like a waste of space, but the custom-made jacuzzi tub, big enough to seat four, and the built-in sauna made that small flaw easy to overlook. The warming towel rack and heated floor tiles only upped the ante.

She meant to take one last glance but stopped to stare at herself. The dwindling light of the day cast a dividing shadow across her face, throwing the left side into darkness while brightening the right. She thought it would be fitting if there was any more light left in her. Grace stepped to her right, dispelling the illusion. She was already surrounded by more than enough deception. She didn't need to entertain light's play at it as well. The movement spotlighted a few lines at the edge of her right eye and she scowled.

The light brown eyes with an abundance of golden flecks stared back at her accusingly. She hated them. They had been the cause of so much pain. Pain by the hands of men who didn't even deserve to look upon them. The anger that constantly burned low, spiked with the memory, and she shut down that thought.

Grace set the towel aside carefully and stepped back from the mirror so she could take in more of her physique. She turned slightly from the left and to the right, comparing what she saw now with the body of the young woman who came to Chicago with wide eyes and huge hopes. It was as close as she had come in a while, trying to reconcile the two. Her gaze traveled up her torso to her chin before she finally turned away.

Grace donned her robe before leaving the master bath. She entered the sitting room of the bedroom she shared with Ross, thankful that his meeting had run late. She measured her movements to keep the anger, that was so close to the surface, at bay. She'd raised two generations of women who carried her mark, her curse, as she called it. If she had her way they would never know just how much of a burden she carried for them and because of them, but it seemed life wasn't finished messing her over, and now it was only a matter of time before her secret was revealed.

Grace ran a slightly trembling hand across her forehead. She refused to go back to the naïve and stupid girl in her mind again. It served no purpose except to haunt her, which it had been doing since Brandon's funeral, and she'd come face-to-face with Richard again. Richard who had known her family and at one time been one of her mother's favorite suitors for her and a majority of the reason for her fight with her father. He had very clearly remembered her, despite the years and subtle changes to her face. She could have had a completely different life, but that was in the past, and the past had not been merciful.

Grace shook her head to dispel the thoughts and sat at her desk. She retrieved the envelope she'd put away the night before along with a copy of the itinerary she'd proffered from the border patrol clerk.

Her last set of men lost Melanie and Marc on the Oregon Trail. No matter what transpired between them, Melanie was still her child. Melanie was not a hiker nor had she ever shown any interest in camping. Grace unfolded the newly acquired list showing that Melanie and Marc had crossed into Canada over a month ago. What was Melanie doing crisscrossing then leaving the country while Paige was grieving? What would take precedence over comforting her daughter and granddaughter?

Grace turned to the clock, sighing at the time that had slipped by her while she was in the bath. If her husband kept with his schedule, which she was sure he would, he would be home in the next fifteen minutes.

The man was a stickler about his schedule. It was one of the reasons Grace liked him. She never had to wonder where he would be, and she made sure she was exactly where he could find her when he looked for her. Ross Dillard was a hard man in the boardroom. She'd witnessed it firsthand. He was one to be reckoned with when he wasn't getting the results he wanted, and he was an unstoppable force when he was. As a contractor with the United States government in its

65

Homeland Security Division, her husband was both ambitious and aggressively competitive. He was a thrill to watch in action and not too boring away from his job.

He was an attentive man. He loved her and took care of her every whim. He liked spoiling her and she let him. They had a comfortable life. There were also interesting conversations to be had. He was a very intelligent man. She learned a lot about new and old laws regarding the protection of their borders and how not to be flagged when leaving the country.

She might have been able to be happy. She could have at least tried to make her first marriage work. Wilson had been a good man. Though he hadn't, Wilson had every right to leave her when she'd turned state's evidence that helped the government indict three of the heads of the four families Luca did business with. They were charged with money laundering, tax evasion, and racketeering.

Grace and her newborn were given new names, immediately placed in witness protection and moved to Kansas. Wilson followed after he'd come back from an assignment. It was a tense month as the military decided whether his intelligence work was worth the risk of him staying in his position or being honorably discharged. Grace was sure he would have left her had he been forced to give up the career he'd worked so long and hard at. It turned out that he was the only one who could do his job at that particular time. He'd told her he'd made friends in very powerful places, and the work couldn't be done without the help of those relationships. It was more information than she'd ever received from him regarding his job. She was just grateful it was true. She would have hated having that on her conscience.

Wilson Ellis, or rather Wayne Morganson, loved her and was willing to wait until her feelings reached the same level as his even though they were thrown together in marriage. She could have tried to make their home happy and peaceful, but she also knew she would have failed, so there was no need in trying something she realized she wasn't going to succeed in. It would only have put more holes in her already battered confidence.

Grace was not a martyr. She did not go after unobtainable things. She wouldn't give up at the first thought though. She would give the challenge plenty of consideration and work out how she could succeed. If there was no plausible way to reach the conclusion she wanted, she would abandon the plan altogether. This was why she chose revenge over peace. Peace was like catching the wind in your hand. Wind could be felt but only seen if it moved something tangible. Peace was also felt, and it could be measured by the effect it had on people's emotions. It wasn't something easily molded and manipulated to suit her. Revenge was a different animal. Given enough anger and hatred and time, revenge could be given enough fuel to destroy lives—even dynasties.

Sure, there would be collateral damage, but no one was really innocent. Revenge fueled by rage didn't always have perfect precision. Those standing too close to the target could get burned. The thought brought Luca Sable to mind.

Luca wasn't her target, but he'd chosen his side when he took her hard-won protection from her by framing her for the assassination attempt on his grandson. She'd underestimated him. Grace knew that now, but at least she'd been able to secure some type of protection for her daughter. She had to hand it to those Sicilian families. They protected their own to the death. Grace would certainly make them prove it. One Sicilian in particular by the name of Angelo Mauro.

The sound of the garage door opening pulled her attention away from her thoughts. Ross was home. She wondered what type of mood he was in. It was late, so she hoped he was tired. Maybe a late dinner, some television, and another bath—with him this time. She needed to sweet-talk him into some vacation time in Canada.

Chapter 9

Paige was tired. So tired. Could one die from being tired? Could a person just sleep until they transitioned or flowed from a corporeal being into the spiritual realm? Paige lay in bed curled in on herself. She ran the palm of her hand along the edge of the mattress, allowing the feeling of the texture of the embroidered edge soothe her. This small relief she could accept. It was just enough to take the edge off. She repeated the motion a few more times before stopping to listen for any noises. Gladys had taken to sitting outside her door and praying quietly at night. Even though Paige could only hear the fabric of Gladys' clothing rub up against the door as she shifted from time to time, Paige knew the child was praying. She'd told Gladys to stop, that she needed her rest for class, but the stubborn girl persisted. She usually went back to her bedroom around midnight, so Paige knew it must be early morning because it was still.

She didn't sleep much at night. It was the sun that seemed to drain the strength from her. Dawn's light would start to creep between the blinds she'd drawn tight, and a lethargy would pull her under for a couple of hours. It was usually about that time that Gladys would knock on her door so Paige would have enough time to wash her face, brush her teeth, and change clothes before driving Gladys to school.

Paige used the drive to catch up with Gladys and then Vivian, who usually called in to talk for a minute or two. Her class schedule allowed her a couple of minutes between homeroom and second period since she was two hours ahead. Paige knew they talked and worried over her.

She wished she could muster up the strength to care more, to feel more, to want more. Most of her fortitude went into acting "normal" enough to keep the girls from worrying more than they did. Paige wouldn't put it past Vivian to talk Mason into coming out to take care of her, and that was the absolute last thing she wanted. So, she pretended to eat full meals, stared at a blank page in her office—when she had the ability to go in—bought prepackaged meals from the grocery store and acted like she did more than heat them, so Gladys would have a meal to talk to her over.

It was as if her emotions and drive had been dampened. At first, she welcomed the respite from the pain and grief. There was an almost unbearable pain that came with the memories that haunted her. Memories of sweet kisses, warm touches... All the things she would never feel, see, or be near again. Then there was the scent of Brandon that would ride in on a breeze when she walked in her front door, bedroom, closet, everywhere.

Suffice it to say, she missed Brandon. Her sorrow was deep even more than a month later, but she could thank God for Victoria, of all people, for pulling her out of the extremely dark place she'd been in when she arrived at the farm over a month ago.

Paige walked on socked feet into the living room and pulled back the vertical blinds to the window next to Brandon's favorite chair. She looked out into the starry night for a few minutes before sitting down and curling up in Brandon's chair. Here she could imagine him waking up to an empty bed and coming in search of her. He would give her one of his looks that said, "What's my chair got that I don't?" Then he'd sit on the ottoman and take her feet in his lap. Paige stared at the piece of furniture for a moment then went back to staring out the window.

Thanksgiving was a little more than a week away, and this silent haven would be temporarily smothered by Brandon's family, Mason, and Vivian. Dominy and Robin were going to spend it with Robin's family since it was Nicky's first big holiday. Victoria and Richard were taking what she considered a third, or was it fourth, honeymoon. Paige had probably worn out her welcome with them, though they would never admit it.

She'd taken Victoria up on her offer to stay at the farm for a month... well, three weeks, while Ava and Elijah stayed at the apartment with Gladys and packed up some of Brandon's things. Some, because she didn't want his presence to be banished while she was away. She thought it was too cruel.

It had been hard to believe that her sister, um, mother hadn't shown up. Melanie had been there for each major event in her life. She could call her and trust that she would be there, but instead of being comforted in the arms of her mother, Paige got a video call. It did nothing to lessen the anger she'd begun to feel in her gut at the unfairness of it all.

Paige got off the plane that first evening still wearing the sunglasses she'd worn throughout the flight from Los Angeles to Oklahoma. They didn't conceal the tears that ran down her cheeks every once in a while, but they did keep away anyone who had a mind to approach her.

She barely got to the baggage claim before being enveloped by Victoria. It was odd, to say the least. Paige wasn't used to Victoria being so affectionate. After some cooing and what she would have called smothering, though she was sure Victoria would have called it comforting, they retrieved her luggage and met Richard at the curb for passenger loading. The only way Paige could describe him was that he was cautiously happy to see her. His hug was warm, brief, and just firm enough to bring more tears to her eyes. *What was it about a man's hug?*

Paige turned down dinner, claiming fatigue, and when she was finally left alone in a guest room, she shed her clothes, slipped between the gloriously cool sheets, and slept for a full day. She knew it was a day because when she woke her mouth was as dry as dust, and the clock on the nightstand stated it was a half-hour earlier than when she went to sleep the previous day. Paige forced her stiff muscles out of the bed and made use of the en suite bathroom then promptly went back to bed.

Paige woke up a few hours later to the smell of grilled cheese. Her stomach rumbled, so she opened one eye to peer between the sheets.

She hoped there wasn't anyone accompanying the food. She wasn't ready to talk. Paige found the room blessedly silent and let out a sigh. She ate half the sandwich then crawled back under the covers and lay there staring at the wall.

It was as good a time as any to search her thoughts, and search she did until she ran smack into the most raw parts of her. The haze that seemed to cover the more intense feelings slipped away, and Paige cringed at the stark pain and anger that assailed her. She immediately wanted to take back her thought. She wasn't ready. She didn't know how to filter these feelings in their raw form. She wanted to scream and rant and rave over the fact that she'd had more than she could have imagined given and taken away within four months.

For the first time in a long time, Paige indulged in her anger, and she understood how easy it could be to give in to it instead of put effort into finding answers that she could accept.

She felt betrayed. There, now that she'd pulled back the industrial-sized, reinforced steel door to her heart as the Holy Spirit had been prompting her to, she gave herself permission to be free with her thoughts.

Paige knew the thoughts weren't healthy. She knew she shouldn't indulge in them. She had even ministered against feeding such thoughts, but she still thought them because she was angry. She was hurt. She felt broken.

He had been her savior. God had introduced her to peace. He'd taught her how to love. He'd taught her how to hold on to that love and believe in something much more than she could see. He'd taught her how to live. He'd taught her how to forgive.

Yes, she felt that betrayal deeply. *And how did that work?* That she would both still believe in Him and desire to berate Him, to wish to hurt Him in some way. She knew on some level, which seemed as far away as heaven right then, that He felt her pain, that He cried when she cried, but He had caused it by not healing Brandon. The two of them could be celebrating the sudden or gradual disappearance of cancer cells in his body. Instead, she lay there alone wishing she could find some way to witness, even in its minutest form, God's pain.

71

O, sweet daughter. You're doing that right now.

She stilled at the sound of God's voice urging her to accept His comfort. Though her physical body remained still, she shifted in her mind, distancing herself from Him. She didn't want Him drying her tears or repairing the gaping hole in her soul. If watching her suffer would cause Him to suffer, she would do it for a little while more. Paige closed her mind to Him even as she closed her eyes, and everything dimmed a little.

There wasn't any doubt that God was still with her. She knew He was still with her, and it gave her little comfort at that moment. She thought it might be better if she felt as though He were no longer with her, that He had forsaken her. Then she might have been able to convince herself that He wasn't watching while Brandon left her. That somehow, He might not have been a witness at that moment when her future ran like sand through her hands.

No, she thought, it would have been better if she had believed God had forsaken her even if it was for only a couple of days. She thought it hurt so much more to think that God was with her and didn't stop Brandon from dying. He hadn't kept her from looking like a fool, at the least, and being devastated at the worst.

She had no sooner finished the thought than an overwhelming heaviness pressed on her soul. Everything went still and dark. It wasn't as if the physical light in the room had gone out, but one close to her soul. It felt like desolation was spreading through her being, swallowing her up. Simultaneously, a resounding hopelessness started to pull her down, and she found herself scrambling for some type of purchase before she was smothered.

Just as quickly as it came over her, it was gone, and the knowing and light were back. It couldn't have lasted more than a few seconds, but it felt like eons.

She'd sobbed like a baby, shaken by the utter bleakness she'd felt.

That was only my essence distancing itself from your spirit. You might think of it as me leaning away from you. Please be aware of what you requested. I cannot, and I will never leave you nor forsake you. I won't go against my promise, so please don't ask me to again.

His voice should have comforted her. It reassured her, yes, but the comfort she'd ultimately been seeking was just out of reach, and it left her conflicted.

He really was a gentleman. He didn't force her attention, but what never left was the restlessness of her soul and spirit, so she smothered it until she felt apathetic to everything outside of her own pain.

When Paige had come downstairs a few days later, showered, and mostly put together, she'd endured another hug then proceeded to answer question after question regarding her immediate plans with Gladys. She glanced at Richard, a little disquieted by his silence. His slight frown was enough to have her quickly averting her eyes back to her lunch.

That was how it went whenever she felt up to coming down and sharing a meal with them or joined Victoria in her garden. She would politely answer questions or participate just enough in whatever conversation they started, to appear present. Then it all came to a merciful stop.

"I thought you would do better than this, Paige," Victoria said three weeks into Paige's stay. "I never thought I'd think this, let alone say it, but I'm actually a bit disappointed in you."

Paige looked at Victoria from the lamplit garden spread out before them. It was finally cool enough in the evenings to sit outside, listen to the crickets, and watch the fireflies dance around the edge of the small pond Victoria had built in the middle.

Paige let out a labored sigh, knowing this talk was long overdue. She couldn't blame Victoria for being concerned. She may have been too if it were her and Lady Menagerie with her mother/mentor indulging in the same thoughts she was. She would wonder if there was a level of maturity one could reach where you wouldn't be crippled by the loss of something or someone you'd wanted more than anything. There was a whisper of conflict at her last thought, but Paige batted it away.

She wasn't irreparably broken, per se, but this was supposed to be a place she could feel comfortable in being vulnerable, while she dealt with Brandon's death. She thought with their daughter Rachel's death, Victoria and Richard would be able to understand some of her struggle. Obviously, she'd been mistaken.

"What do you want from me?" Paige asked with all sincerity.

Victoria's mouth opened, closed, then opened again before words escaped. "I invited you here so you could receive some peace, but it seems you are thwarting every attempt we're making to help you through this."

"I didn't know this trip came with conditions or an expiration date for my grief," Paige said despondently. The fact that she'd mustered the passion to even say the words was something.

"See? That right there is what I'm talking about." Victoria gestured at Paige. "You sound like you've given up."

Paige stared back at Victoria nonplused by her accusation. She hadn't given up. To give up you'd have to start fighting.

"Once again, I didn't know this trip came with a prerequisite. I thought you were giving me a place to step away for a while. Are you rescinding that because I'm not reacting the way you think I should?" Paige asked, already knowing the answer but wanting to make a point or at least end this conversation.

"No, Paige, I'm worried. It's like you are disappearing right in front of our eyes. Even Richard is concerned, and he's a lot more patient about these things than I am."

At the mention of Richard's feelings, Paige's patience with the conversation grew thin, and she spoke with more feeling than she had since she'd met Victoria at the airport.

"Again, Victoria, what do you want from me?"

"I want you to act like the woman of God that you are. I'm not saying you can't grieve because that's a part of life, but I am telling you not to take this trial and turn it into something you will have a much harder time coming back from." Victoria got out of her chair across the table to sit in the seat next to Paige. She reached for Paige's hand, but Paige moved it to her lap.

Paige never thought of herself as *that* person. The one who painted everyone with the same brush and projected her experiences on to them. As she listened to Victoria, who meant nothing but good but was oh so far from right, Paige questioned herself to see if she judged those who grieved.

She never said anything judgmental to those she tried to comfort, but she did wonder what type of relationship they had with God if they could be laid so low by the loss of a loved one, especially if it was obvious that the loved one transitioned to heaven.

It was so easy to say. *Lean on the Lord. Embrace His comfort. Let Him hold and heal you.* If she ever found herself in a situation like that again she would silently pray for them, but otherwise she would keep her mouth shut.

"I want you to get your head out of the sand, and remember all of God's promises to you," Victoria continued. "Not just for you, but for your daughters and the young women who look up to you." Victoria paused for a second, and Paige saw her going in for the kill.

"For me," Victoria finished.

Paige closed her eyes and waited for the blow to take effect. She was sure she would break down and cry from the shame. She waited, sure that she would be keening any second. She counted down, four, three, two... She let out the breath she didn't even know she was holding. Nothing. Absolutely nothing. No remorse, no sympathy, no righteous indignation, and certainly no guilt or shame.

That knowledge was the first thing that had her reconsidering just where she was headed.

***

So, here she was back home almost a week later, feeling pretty much the same. Except there was anger. There was always a kernel waiting to be heated by her thoughts of the unfairness of it all.

Paige blinked several times to bring herself back to the present. She glanced around the living room, which had held a lot more people in the days before Brandon's passing than would be there for Thanksgiving, and still it seemed like too many. She'd gotten a grocery list that afternoon from Ava who planned to arrive the following Tuesday with Marjorie. Paige smiled inwardly. Brandon's big sister treated her much the same as she'd treated him. It didn't matter that both she and Brandon had been fiercely independent. Marjorie was a mother hen who would give her last breath to her family. With anyone else, Paige would make sure there was a wide berth so she wouldn't feel suffocated, but Marjorie wasn't only nurturing, she was observant and pragmatic.

Paige liked Marjorie. She was the only one who hadn't pressed her for her feelings or to talk at all. A couple of days after the funeral Marjorie came and sat in the living room with a photo album filled with pictures of Brandon and their siblings. It was obvious they all adored each other. Paige had a fleeting thought that they could have been hers. She could have been a permanent part of their family. Marjorie pulled her away from her thoughts as she called Paige's attention to the picture of a very young Brandon with his arm around an equally small girl.

"Brandon told you about Peyton, right?" Marjorie asked, pausing before going into what Paige knew would be another funny story.

Paige nodded and leaned over the book to get a better look at the picture of Brandon who looked very much like a miniature version of what he looked like only the month before. He couldn't be more than four, but he was dressed in a suit with his arm around his sister who wore a white, frilly skirt with pink rosebuds. They were an adorable pair and looked like a handful. When Marjorie shared the story behind the picture, she knew the sparkle of mischief in the children's eyes wasn't a part of her imagination.

Marjorie continued on, turning page after page while she shared stories of Brandon as a child that had Paige smiling for the first time since Mason walked down the aisle to receive Christ as his Lord and Savior.

Once Marjorie left, the quietness that initially came with extended family and friends leaving, descended upon her like a suffocating blanket. Paige had to find ways to keep some type of background noise going in the house. She caught the occasional odd look from Vivian and Gladys before Vivian went back to Chicago and Gladys went back to school. Ava seemed to remain in the background, always ready to lend a hand and share a touch of affection. It was the perfect amount of attention and let Paige know that she was still considered family, at the moment. She just wondered how long it would be before everyone in Brandon's family went back to their lives and forgot about her: the woman who was once married to their youngest son.

Paige pushed away from the morose thoughts as a star streaked across the sky. It was so hard to stay focused these days. Her thoughts seemed to carry her away so easily. She hadn't seen her therapist in a few weeks because she just didn't want to, but she knew she would have to go in to refill her prescription, which was getting very low. She'd even lowered the dosage by taking a pill every other day. It obviously wasn't working very well. The compulsion to reorganize the kitchen cabinets at 3 a.m. that morning gnawed at her until she went into the bathroom and reorganized the items under the sink in alphabetical order.

If Brandon were there, he would have taken her in his arms and prayed with her until the urge was gone.

And she was right back where she started.

Paige forced herself to concentrate on the night sky. It was beautiful.

What had she been thinking about? Oh yes. Thanksgiving and a full house, including Mason.

Next week both Mason and Vivian would come in on Wednesday. The one saving grace was that he would stay in a hotel, and Vivian would be somewhat distracted by Gladys.

Mason. She was still getting used to the change in the dynamics of their relationship. Mason called her once a week, every week. He'd called her, even during her stay with Victoria and Richard, leaving messages when she didn't answer. It didn't matter where he was or what he was doing, he called her without fail. Would she answer every time? No, but he was persistent, and if nothing else, it gave her hope that she might get through this fog one day, and he might still be there to be her friend. Was it selfish? Yes, she couldn't even deny it.

Mason had accepted Jesus into his heart. It was the miracle she'd prayed hard for. From the morning she woke up from the drug-induced sleep to that moment when she watched Mason walk down the aisle toward the altar, she had been in somewhat of a stupor. But no one could have sleepwalked through that. Even she felt the profound nature of the situation. The way heaven rejoiced so loud you could hear it in your heartbeat as Mason knelt on the steps to the altar, head and soul bowed. She wouldn't mind experiencing that over and over again. She could almost peek through and see Brandon smiling. She knew he'd been smiling.

She considered that Mason may think she rarely took his calls because she thought the price of his salvation had been too steep. It was a logical point of view, but it wasn't a spiritual one. She still believed everyone deserved eternal life, no matter how it came about.

Paige took a deep breath and caught a whiff of Brandon's cologne. She groaned. She wanted him back so badly. *Was there no balance?*

Sure, she wished Mason could have come to Christ another way and had no doubt that he may have, given time. She rarely took Mason's calls because the excitement in his voice reminded her of how she'd felt when she first accepted Christ. It wasn't Mason's fault. A person could hardly contain their joy during the first honeymoon stage with God, or the second for that matter. She didn't want him to have to contain it. She didn't want him to feel the need to tamp down on his excitement when they talked.

Paige knew Mason had noticed the change in her between the funeral and coming back from Richard and Victoria's, but he didn't push. He was just there. He talked about Vivian, his job, and the new position he was thinking of applying for. He would even mention Brandon on occasion, which she found thoughtful. It was only when he started talking about a new perspective he received in a situation, a part of a sermon that clicked, or a scripture, that Paige began to feel restless and pressed to get off the phone.

It was probably one of the most selfish thoughts she'd had in years. Well, outside of the whole *wanting God to feel her pain* thing. Mason deserved to be able to revel, boast, and shout about his relationship with God. Wasn't that one of the reasons she'd given him for them not being compatible? Boy, how the tables had turned. He was ready to talk about the wonderment and beauty of God and His gifts, and she couldn't bear to listen because she was no longer there. She'd lost too much.

He lost no less than you did.

The thought came out of nowhere. Well, not nowhere. It came from everywhere and deep inside. She clenched her jaw while she turned and stared up at the ceiling. She was jealous. She had trouble taking Mason's calls because she envied the freshness and newness of what he felt for God.

Paige finally felt an emotion other than pain and anger, and it turned out to be jealousy. Her God sure had a way of getting His point across. She would have laughed at the irony if it weren't for the tears that won out.

For I, the LORD your God, am a jealous God.

Paige put her head in her hands, but not feeling comforted by the position, slumped back in the chair. The dawning realization of what she'd been doing for the past weeks made her feel small and very grateful that God had patiently waited for her to come to one simple understanding. She had placed her love and relationship with Brandon above God.

She swallowed hard, closing her eyes. Yeah. She had been very selfish and reckless lately, locked away in her own little world of pity and woe.

"I'm sorry. I'm so sorry, God."

Chapter 10

Melanie couldn't stop staring. She'd dreamed of and hoped against this moment for so many years. If her heart sped up any more she was likely to have a heart attack. Melanie took a deep breath while she took in Brian's features. He looked exactly like a more mature version of the boy she'd last seen crying over her in the delivery room. His dark eyes had intensified, and his full lips had spread in proportion with his face. His jaw had gone from the soft one of a boy to angular, and his chin had squared. He was extremely handsome in a swarthy, brooding type of way, and she prayed for any woman who caught his eye.

She'd wanted to hug Brian on sight, she was so happy to finally come face-to-face with him after so many weeks of traipsing around the country, but she hesitated, and it was just enough time for Marc to post himself at her side. Melanie looked at her husband when she felt his arm come around her waist. She took the possessive gesture for what it was and smiled warmly at him. His grin in response relayed everything that needed communicating.

Hearing Brian say her name pulled at the place she'd set aside for him long ago, but it had decreased in size over the years, and now it was just big enough to hold affection for her daughter and son's father. She didn't know how long they looked at each other on that dock before he suggested that they follow him to his truck. Whether it was milliseconds or full seconds, it was long enough for her to note the wariness and intelligence in his eyes. He glanced around, and she just knew he'd seen a great deal more than she would have. He took in their surroundings as Marc did; like her dad had. Was he in the military or some other government agency?

She found herself at a loss for words on the ride to his place. She wasn't sure if it was his closed features or her hesitation at starting a conversation that they would have to interrupt. She glanced at Brian a few times, which was easy with all three of them sitting in the front of the cab. She made herself blink and look away a few times, but nostalgia kept washing over her and she finally gave up.

She took Marc's hand and squeezed it briefly with the overwhelming happiness she felt. The warmth of his hand kept her grounded and reassured her that she wasn't dreaming.

Brian pulled into the parking lot of an older hotel that looked like it had recently undergone some renovations. Brian turned to Marc. "I need you to go and check in. You won't be staying here, but there needs to be a trail just in case those who are looking for you can track you to this point before you get back home. It isn't likely, but you never know."

Melanie followed Marc in but remained by the door while he paid and signed the log-in book. He took the key from the front-desk representative and walked back to her. He led her back outside and around the corner to where Brian's car was idling. Melanie felt like she was in the middle of some type of espionage film, but it was no less than the zigzagging path they had left for anyone looking for them. Before starting back home, she needed to know just how much this trip would cost them.

The ride was just long enough for her attention to be caught by the beauty of their surroundings. Everything was so green and lush. The road, though it was four lanes, was merely a path carved out of the mountain between majestic red spruces that stood at very intimidating heights. Brown and green followed by an occasional peek of blue of the bay when there was a clearing. It was lovely and alive. She loved it but only to visit. Her small experience along the Pacific Trail weeks before instilled in her the need for concrete, creature-free beds, and espresso shops. Melanie wasn't sure how camping on the east coast differed from the west but she was pretty sure she'd feel the same.

Brian turned off the highway onto a less-used road with thicker foliage and then onto a path with a faded white line dividing the direction of traffic. From there he made one more quick turn that had Melanie's head whipping around and making her dizzy. She had just regained her equilibrium when his home came into view and she gasped. It was a beautiful log-style home with a dock leading to the bay. Judging from the amount of space between what she could see from the side of the house to the dock, there was also a good-sized backyard.

"Have you lived here the whole time?" she asked, staring up at the two-story home.

Brian closed the truck door, and the sound bounced off trees that seemed to stand sentry around the domain. "No, I moved here about eight years ago. I wanted to wait until B.J. was out of school." He said the last over his shoulder as he led them to a side entrance.

Brian was tall like his grandfather, but where Luca was lanky, Brian had more of an athletic build with wide shoulders and trim hips. He wore his strength like others wore T-shirts. He was built like a lumberjack.

He opened the door, and they walked through a mudroom with a washer and dryer, then into a kitchen she would have created if she could have imagined such efficient beauty. It was a chef's kitchen made for a baker. She took in the matching Viking double oven with stove, refrigerator, and dishwasher. Her fingers itched to touch them, but she crossed her arms and followed Brian to a breakfast nook in the corner of the spacious kitchen that had her curious about who did most of the cooking.

"Follow me, Marc. I will show you where to put your bags," Brian said as he passed both of them and walked into the next room. Melanie finished her perusal of the kitchen then glanced around the corner into what she guessed was the great room and caught her breath at the cherrywood-outlined windows and accents. The furniture was comfortable and what she would have considered oversized, but judging from Brian's size, it all fit him just right.

Melanie smiled at the nursery rhyme story that came to mind as she ran her fingers along the edges of the rich-looking credenza where pictures of Brian and B.J. were displayed. Her eyes greedily took in B.J. sitting on his father's shoulders. He couldn't have been more than three. His chubby cheeks tinged with pink despite the knit hat, earmuffs, and scarf he was wearing. She wondered where they were when that picture was taken. She looked at the next photo. It was one of B.J. on his own holding up a nice-sized fish. Her heart could have wept at all the time and memories she'd missed with him. There was no helping it. Despite knowing she'd done the right thing in forcing Brian to take B.J., she was still heartsick. He looked so happy. It appeased her some. She went from picture to picture taking in as much as she could, so she could take the memories with her. One thing she noticed was there were no women in any of the pictures, and her heart went out to both men. She guessed living in secret wasn't conducive to any type of long-term romance. Would Brian have had to hide the way he did if he didn't have B.J.?

The hand on her elbow startled Melanie out of her study of the pictures. She glanced around to see Marc at her side. She straightened and turned back toward the kitchen to see Brian sinking into a chair on the far side of the table.

"Your place is beautiful," she said, walking back and taking a seat next to Marc.

"Thank you. It's come together nicely. You should have seen it when we moved in. I almost had to gut it," he said with a pride that made her pause.

"Did you do the work?" she asked, unable to keep the wonder out of her voice.

His face reddened a little. "It's a hobby. Something to do with my hands when I'm not working."

"A hobby? Really? You're gifted. You don't do it full time?" she asked.

"It's what I do to relax from a day at the office. I'm not interested in mixing the two," Brian said, looking a little uncomfortable under her praise.

"The office? What do you?" she asked without missing a beat.

She watched Brian and Marc exchange glances and closed her mouth for a second before speaking again.

"What?" she asked, looking between them to make sure she didn't miss anything.

"I work for my grandfather. Of course, not as myself. I have an alias, and I work remotely, but I am always quietly in the background of meetings Luca holds," Brian said, looking even more uncomfortable.

She stared at him for a moment then turned to Marc. "Did you know?"

"I suspected, but I didn't know for sure," Marc said, seeming not to be bothered at all.

"Why would you suspect that?" she asked, feeling as though she'd missed something.

She watched Marc's eyes slide to Brian and back to her. "It was just something that struck me in my last conversations with Luca," Marc said with a shrug.

Melanie looked down at her hand resting on the table as she tried to digest that information. If Brian worked with Luca, could she trust him? How much did he know about her life, about Paige's life? True, the more he knew, the easier it would be to explain, but if he already knew about Antonio and Brenda why did he continue to lead her and Marc to his home? There were so many pieces missing.

"What do you know?" she asked, not raising her head.

"Luca was very careful about the information he shared. He wouldn't share any facts with me about you until I was eighteen. I think he knew with me being an adult, I would find ways to obtain it myself, which would probably call attention to all of us." He shrugged before continuing. "I know you received a scholarship to school. I was obviously told about your wedding," he said while gesturing back and forth between her and Marc. "It was a bittersweet day. I truly am happy you found love after… everything."

Her heart squeezed at the apologetic look she caught him sending Marc's way, but after a few blinks it was gone, and he was matter-of-fact with his recitation of what Luca had shared with him and what he'd found out on his own later. He admitted that he could only obtain so much information before raising suspicions, so he left a lot of the fact finding to his grandfather.

"I only recently learned about Vivian being alive, but I think that was more of a discretion on Luca's part." Melanie didn't correct his assumption by letting him know that they'd only learned of Vivian recently as well. There was no reason to cause him unneeded distress.

"Over time, Luca has told me that Antonio has made a lot of guesses and assumptions about my death. Nothing concrete. What *has* caused a few questions lately is the fact that you weren't there to comfort your daughter before or after the death of her husband." Melanie looked up to see if there was accusation in Brian's eyes even though she didn't hear it in his voice. They were pained but otherwise warm. "It was very unfortunate timing and altogether heartbreaking to hear about Paige's husband. How's she doing?" Brian asked softly.

Melanie's heart pinched at the thought of Gladys' latest report. "Not so well. She's trying to pretend for Gladys' and Vivian's sakes that she is doing okay, but she's struggling. Gladys thinks it's more than just that she's mourning Brandon. She thinks Paige is angry."

Brian looked troubled, but she could see that he didn't fully comprehend what she was saying.

She leaned toward Brian. "My daughter." She paused and started again. "Our daughter is an elder in her church. She ministers to people, particularly women about God and His mercy, grace, and forgiveness. She loves and adores Him. He was the one who coaxed her out of her rage years ago after the rape and birth of Gladys and Vivian. She has always sought Him for comfort, for answers, for guidance. There were many times I would have questioned Him for the things she endured, but she never did. Not with doubt anyway." Her voice trembled and she took a deep breath when she felt Marc's hand on hers under the table.

"It's just that if Paige is angry, she may not be in a place to want to be comforted by Him. With me here, I am afraid of her reverting."

"Is her love for God that fragile?" Brian asked, giving her the first glimpse of his spiritual knowledge.

"No," she said after a moment's hesitation.

"Were you the one who led her to Christ?" Brian asked.

85

Melanie couldn't help the frown. What was he saying?

"No," she responded.

"Then trust that those who were with her when she first came to God, will be with her now, and if they aren't, trust that God can reach her," he said with all confidence.

Melanie looked at him for a moment. "Are you a Christian?"

His nod was quick and precise.

Melanie let go of the breath she wasn't aware she was holding. She didn't know what she would find when she sought out Brian, but this was more than a pleasant surprise. Her son's father was a believer. Thank goodness.

"When?" she asked, unable to contain her curiosity.

He gave her an amused look before answering. "Um, summer of my sixteenth year. It wasn't an easy transition."

She was both surprised and saddened by his admission. She had been hoping one of them came away unscathed. Melanie embraced the suffering in hopes that he and B.J. had happy childhoods.

"Who helped lead you to Christ?" she asked, still astounded by the fact that neither one of them grew up in a Christian household but ended up around people who loved God.

"My nonna, Helena. She would take B.J. and me to church with her when she came into town," he said with nonchalance.

The mention of his grandmother caused her to wonder how similar their lives were. "Does B.J. know you're his dad?"

"Yes, I told him when he turned sixteen. I figured he was mature enough to know and understand."

And that's where the similarities ended.

"How much did you tell him?"

"Well, it was pretty obvious that we were very young, but I didn't map out the full situation. I told him you and I were separated by our parents and forbidden to see each other again. We lost touch, and the day you showed up his life would change," Brian said sounding tired.

Once again, Melanie felt like there was a world of knowledge she was missing, but before she could voice it, Brian continued.

"He knows what I know, about you, about Paige, and the girls. It seemed like the easiest way for him to understand the importance of staying under the radar, at least about who we are. He also understands the need for discretion where your visit is concerned." Brian rubbed the palms of his hands together, seeming to get lost for a moment in the movement. "I didn't tell Luca you were coming."

"Not that you need to," Marc said.

She saw the resignation wash over Brian's face before he gave a careless shrug. "True. Very little happens in this family without his knowledge. It was one of the reasons I sent you two through so many loops, and I may have added a few more to ensure he didn't interfere," Brian said, clasping his hands together on the table.

"Okay," Melanie said, gearing up to hear what had to be bad news.

"I need to know why you contacted me, Melanie," Brian asked, throwing her off guard. It made sense that he would ask. She was only supposed to contact him in case of an emergency since no one was to know he was alive, especially her mother.

"Victoria and Richard visited Antonio. Whatever was said during that meeting had them heading to me afterward," she blurted then winced upon seeing Brian's reaction. Melanie took a breath to slow herself down and give herself more time to think. She'd become accustomed to the information that had tilted her world on its axis. The least she could do was to be sensitive to Brian and his world. She looked at Marc, asking him, with a glance, if she could offer up some information. He nodded his agreement, but she kept it as vague as possible.

"Have you heard of Victoria and Richard Branchett?" Melanie asked Brian carefully.

A dark shadow crossed over Brian's expression before he blinked, then it cleared.

"Yes," he said with a great deal less emotion than she thought he would have displayed for his mother. "She's Vivian's adopted grandmother. She owns a farm just outside of Oklahoma City, and her husband, Richard, is a successful investment broker turned philanthropist. In a few choice words, Granddad told me that she and my dad were lovers in college. She got pregnant and tried to use me as leverage to gain a place in the family, but Antonio was already part of a decades-old truce."

Melanie glanced at Marc in confusion, but Marc gave a slight shake of his head. Melanie closed her eyes for a brief moment before speaking. All these secrets were making her sick.

"Why would your biological mother try to use you to gain leverage to get into your family then give you up for adoption?"

Brian's expression went from closed to curious. "Luca said he didn't know her family beyond what he told me but that he stepped in when her parents contacted him to see if he wanted me before she gave me up for adoption."

Melanie glanced at Marc who she could see was grinding his back molars.

"I'm not sure why Luca said those things to you, but from what I've heard from my daughter, Victoria had no intention of putting you up for adoption. Matter of fact, the reason why I brought her up is because she's been looking for you all these years."

Brian's eyes widened only slightly before they narrowed. "What causes you to think you know enough about her... about Luca, to say such a thing?" The hostility rolling off Brian made Melanie cringe, but she didn't blame Brian for his doubt. This whole thing was almost unbelievable. Marc stepped in before she could speak.

"Victoria came to my attention when Paige told us she was contacted to become a living donor for a young girl. I did a cursory check into the family's background to make sure Paige wouldn't be compromised. Sometimes people run scams and try to prey on the donor's compassion to receive more than just the organ donation. Donor companies have some safeguards in place to prevent the donor's information from coming out, but how do you keep the families from meeting if they want to get to know each other? I've seen all types of things in my line of work." Marc took another breath while he rubbed his hands together.

"I ran a check on Victoria and Richard's background. I was intrigued when I found out that Victoria filed for full custody of the child to receive Paige's kidney, so I decided to dig deeper. On paper, they were an ambitious couple that had done very well for themselves but suffered tremendous loss with countless miscarriages and finally the loss of their only daughter two years prior to Vivian's accident."

"Well, see, there you have it," Brian said, relaxing back slightly in his seat, but Melanie wasn't fooled. She could still feel how tense he was. "She's lost all her children, and now she wants me back."

Melanie saw the slight glimmer of hope in his eyes and knew a part of him wanted to deny the fact that Luca lied to him more than he wanted to know the truth.

Marc paused for a moment, shaking his head. "She's been looking for you from the very beginning." When Brian opened his mouth to protest, Marc raised his hand. "Let me finish then we can sort out what's what."

Brian raised his hands, palms up, and spread his arms out as a gesture for Marc to continue. Melanie could see that Brian's defenses hadn't lowered much, but Marc went on.

"It wasn't until recently that they stumbled upon Brenda's medical records, but when Richard and Victoria's investigators started prying, not only into Paige's medical records but Melanie's and Brenda's as well, I decided to get involved.

Paige grew close to all the family members after finding out Vivian was the daughter she thought died at birth. Victoria took to her, and when the Branchetts found out that Paige wasn't Brenda's, but Melanie's daughter, everyone, except for Melanie, started looking for her father. When the Branchetts followed the planted files into your medical records, I thought they were doing it for Paige. Your grandfather never told me about their connection with you," Marc said, holding Brian's gaze for a moment before continuing.

As Melanie looked on, her heart went out to Brian. The conflicting emotions crossing his face made her want to reach out to soothe him.

"Paige mentioned to Melanie, when they were finally speaking again, that Victoria was distraught about what she'd found on a Brian Grossenberg. I started putting the pieces together. Paige said Victoria has been looking for you since her parents and pastor coerced her into giving you up. When Richard found the planted files about your death, Paige said they had to sedate Victoria.

"It could have been overwhelming guilt," Brian said, but Melanie could tell that he didn't really believe what he was saying.

"Man, I get it. It's been forty years. That's a lot of time to dwell on what you believe your mother did. I'm not even going to get into the repercussions, but I wouldn't even mention this if it were just hearsay. There is a thread of paperwork a mile long, dating back to a few years after she signed the documents giving over her rights as your mother." Marc paused to rub his forehead.

"If I didn't know the facts, I would also be inclined to believe Luca. He seems like a man who would do anything for his family. He brought me and Melanie together, helped me keep her safe, and gave me the same choice he gave you: to be in her life or protect her from afar." Marc stared at Brian without judgment but with something akin to gratitude, and her heart swelled with pride for this beautiful man she loved.

"I just couldn't see a future without her." Marc shrugged. "It doesn't make either of us weak, strong, right, or wrong. It does bind us though through Melanie and I would do nothing to jeopardize her safety or happiness. If it means telling you the truth, no matter how it affects your relationship with Luca, so be it, but if nothing else, you deserve the truth."

Melanie searched Brian's face for an expression she could read, but he had become a closed book. Brian nodded once and Melanie spoke up again.

"Occasionally, Marc will get updates on people just to make sure they don't pose a threat to Paige, Gladys, or me. A few of them are Brenda, Victoria, Richard, and Antonio," Melanie said slowly, watching Brian carefully. She would have taken more care if she imagined that Luca had lied about Victoria. She should have known. Keeping the two families apart was the best way to guarantee that no one connected the dots back to Brian.

"Though Antonio has proven to be more challenging since your grandfather's bubble of privacy encompasses him as well as you and your son," Marc inserted into the conversation.

Melanie gave her husband a half-smile before continuing. "Victoria, Richard, and Antonio getting together doesn't bode well for your invisibility."

Brian's expression had turned into one of determination. "If all the misleading files about my 'last days'"—Brian threw up air quotes—"are still in place, why would you think a conversation between Antonio, Richard, and Victoria would constitute an emergency?"

"Because it's not just Richard, Victoria, and Antonio. That meeting between the three was just a fact-finding mission on Antonio's part. The real threat is Brenda. She is using Antonio to gain access to your remains so they can be compared against previous DNA samples," Melanie said, watching Brian's features go hard. "Well, you know, whatever ashes are in your family's plot," Melanie said, waving a hand to dismiss her half-hearted attempt to correct herself. "After all this time, she has him questioning the truth about your 'death.' She mimicked his use of air quotes with the last word. "It was all the hope Victoria needed to start looking for you again. She won't give up. I wouldn't give up if I were in her shoes."

Brian gave her a sad smile. "No, I imagine you wouldn't." He seemed distressed for a moment then shook it off and looked at Marc. "Where would Antonio get the sample to compare against the remains for a DNA match?"

"The sample that was taken from you as a baby for the paternity test. The results bearing the DNA markers are still in the system," Melanie answered before Marc could open his mouth, hoping Brian would tell her that she overreacted and there was nothing to worry about, but he didn't. Instead, Brian's face turned a dark shade of red, which was startling against his already deeply tanned skin.

"How do you know this?" Brian asked, his voice barely above a hard whisper.

Melanie swallowed at the anger in his eyes. She ignored the temptation to squirm in her seat and opened her mouth to speak, but Marc beat her to it.

"I'm pretty much a desk jockey now, and my clearance gives me the ability to monitor certain files. Your grandfather has given me some hard-won permission to get notifications if certain files are part of inquiries, but I took it a little further with Brenda since she's more of a threat.

Some months ago there was an inquiry about the permit used to transport your ashes to your family plot. I traced the search back to one of Brenda's new husband's office computers." He paused and turned slightly toward Melanie before continuing.

"From time to time I have a man observe Brenda. I like to know what she's up to as well as the Branchetts and Antonio. He came back with evidence that Brenda and Antonio were in contact with one another. The degree of separation was way too close for the two of them to be anything but trouble. We left when Antonio started making inquiries at the mortuary where your ashes are being held. I'm surprised Luca hasn't said anything to you," Marc said, sounding as confused as she was.

Brian seemed to be in deep thought. "Yeah, me too."

Marc took his hand from Melanie's and clasped and unclasped his fingers together before shooting her an apologetic look.

"I did some digging into the WITSEC file on Brenda. I did nothing that could be flagged, but I needed to know Brenda's motivation, and I needed to know more than what Luca provided. I respected his request not to go looking for you because one, there was no way to get around some of the triggers he had on certain files, and two, I didn't want to put Melanie's future in jeopardy. I did, however, trace a line back from Brenda to Luca and some of the files she gave over." He took a deep breath and continued to stare at his hands, which made Melanie more than uncomfortable.

Marc shook his head. "She had given over financial records that gave our analysts keys to finding back doors into money laundering, illegal gambling, and sex trafficking. In all of that information, there wasn't one piece to implicate Luca. He was a very clever businessman and had been shifting his business dealings over to the legal side since he'd gained the majority of the shares in his company and votes on his board. Charles Mauro and other leaders, however, lost a great deal after what Brenda revealed. I went back over the information time and again, but couldn't find a motive for her focused vengeance or why she wasn't killed for it. I mean, we are good, but if the Italian mob wanted to assassinate Brenda, there were ways to get to her, especially after she was relieved of the protection."

Most of what Marc was saying wasn't a big surprise to Melanie. Marc had told her what he said he thought was relevant to their safety and asked her to keep it confidential. She'd also looked up Luca, so she knew he once had dealings with organized crime. She hadn't dug any deeper because she didn't want to know. It was enough to have to deal with her mom's lies and secrecy. She wanted to create a serene and loving environment as best she could for Gladys and Paige when she was finally ready to be honest. This information about Mauro was new though. Melanie thought the look Marc gave her before beginning was an apology for what he was going to say about the threat on her mom's life, but upon realizing there was more, she didn't know whether to listen intently or cover her ears.

Melanie looked up from Marc's hands and watched Brian's eyes go flat. He knew. Whatever Marc was leading up to, Brian already knew. Her heartbeat picked up, and her dread ratcheted up to fear.

"From what I was able to find, Angelo Mauro, Charles' son, was being groomed to take over the head of the Mauro business at the time, but between the months that Brenda left Chicago and contacted the FBI, Luca and Angelo had a falling out, an irreconcilable dispute which caused a rift between the two men so large, Luca would only do business with Charles." Marc paused, looking up at Brian. Melanie followed his gaze, catching the staredown between the two men.

"I tried to get further, but I kept getting blocked, and I recognized the pattern. So, now that we are here, there are some questions I need you to answer," Marc said without blinking.

What was going on between these two? Melanie had barely been able to follow the conversation but the tension slowly building between Marc and Brian just hit a crescendo. Brian looked away first, and he took a deep breath.

"This was a bad idea. A really bad idea. I put your life in jeopardy the moment I left you that emergency contact," Brian said, looking at Melanie, and she could see that he knew a lot more than what he led them to believe. In that one look, she saw not only what Brian wanted her to see, but what he didn't. "I should have let you go completely, but you are the mother of my son, and even now I can't imagine denying both of you the possibility of seeing each other even if it will be a very, very short visit.

Melanie, surprised by Brian's last words, opened her mouth to object, but he held up a hand to stop her before looking back at Marc.

"You understand that once I tell you, you can't unhear it. People act differently when they obtain certain information. It's instinctual. There is either fear, confidence, awareness, or a misguided sense of safety that makes them careless. What I tell you will put you in danger, even more so if you act outside of your normal character." He paused to let the words sink in, and Marc looked at her with a growing uneasiness filling his features. "Us coming together like this puts all of our lives at risk. There are only so many places these days that aren't filled with cameras, hidden or otherwise. I hate to say this even before you've had a chance to see B.J., but the longer this reunion is, the more at risk everyone is."

Melanie tried to pretend she wasn't put off by his words. She knew what he said was right, but it put a damper on her excitement in meeting her son for the first time. As if feeling her disappointment, Marc placed his hand back in hers.

"I have every confidence that you lost your tail somewhere in Canada, but I think three days is all we should dare. Once they find out you've reentered the United States, it will only be a matter of days before Brenda's men are led here. Your trail can't stop here for any significant amount of time." He paused to give them a rueful smile.

"You have been out of touch long enough for Luca to suspect that you might be headed here. Well, 'might' is the wrong word after he made a surprise visit a month ago. As we speak, Luca and his family are on a yacht for the week celebrating his birthday. That may make it hard for him to come up with an excuse to leave the Mediterranean and fly back to Portland if he gets wind of anything."

Marc's knee, which had been bobbing excessively through Brian's speech, stopped and he leaned forward. "So, are you going to tell us what Brenda and Charles Mauro have in common?" Marc said, giving Brian his law-enforcement stare. Brian only cracked a smile.

"I'm glad she has you. I knew you had to be someone special for Luca to approve of you marrying Melanie."

Marc shrugged, but she felt him tense at the mention of Luca's authority. "Did he have a choice?"

Brian stared at Marc. "Yes, and he wouldn't have hesitated to interfere if he didn't think you would protect and love her. Luca may be a legit businessman, but he will do anything to protect his family." He turned to Melanie as if to emphasize his words. "Even protect those around his family."

"But I haven't been around you for years. Why would he protect me?" she asked, befuddled by Brian's words. She watched as he shook his head, a sad smile on his face.

"You, Melanie Grace, are family. You are the mother of my son and daughter." His eyes softened around the edges, giving her a glimpse of the boy she used to know, before narrowing. "I was speaking of Brenda. She was the one who was extended protection because of you."

Marc had told her the same thing, but it was still hard to grasp after all these years.

"Oh," was all she could say in response.

She saw a shift in Marc's posture, but Brian held up a hand. "I will tell you what you want to know, but it sounds like B.J. has just arrived, and I would rather not take the tension up any higher otherwise he will notice. He's very astute."

"Does he know?" Marc asked.

Just then Melanie heard gravel spraying out front and the revving of a big engine. She went from slightly agitated to near panic in less than a second. Brian gave them a sheepish glance before standing up.

Brian shook his head to the negative in answer to Marc's question before speaking. "He isn't the slowest driver on earth. It's partly my fault. I indulged him in his love for race. I took him to Indianapolis Motor Speedway after he received his bachelor's degree. I thought it would serve as the culmination of a boyhood dream, but it only drew him in deeper.

As Brian walked across the room and out the side door, Melanie went to the kitchen-sink window facing the driveway. She caught sight of a younger version of Brian who was just as tall but less broad around the shoulders and chest. He had more of a basketball players' physique—all arms and legs. Her heart swelled at the smile and half hug, half shake he gave his dad. They looked like they had a comfortable bond.

She knew the moment Brian told him she was there. His eyes strayed toward the house, and he licked his lips in what she took as a nervous gesture. He rubbed his hands down the sides of his slacks before his dad put an arm around his shoulder and muttered something, causing him to laugh and shake him off before moving from her sight.

She walked back to the table but was unable to sit down as she waited for them to come through the side door. She clasped her hands in front of her then unclasped them, placing one on Marc's shoulder then brought them down at her sides. Marc took the closest one to him and squeezed, giving her a few seconds of comfort while she waited.

The door opened wider, and she watched as Brian reentered followed by B.J., who looked up at her at the last minute. She took in everything all over again from his dark, closely cropped hair to his face and complexion which was a couple of shades lighter than Paige's. He had the same shape and eye color as his father, but her high cheekbones. He was model handsome, but she knew that even if he didn't sport such charming features, she would think him beautiful.

Her feet were guiding her toward him before she knew she was moving, and within four steps she had her arms around him, her heart setting a rhythmic chant through her body. *My son, my son, my son.* The arms that embraced her back brought heat then moisture to her eyes. She inhaled his fragrance, which had a hint of cologne mixed with his natural scent. It felt so good to touch and hold him; she wanted to stay like this for hours and get her fill so she could convince herself he was alive and well, but all too soon he began to pull away, and she let go.

He stepped back but didn't go any further as he seemed to survey her. "I've imagined this moment for many years," he said, his image going blurry at the edges with the tears in her eyes.

"You look"—he stopped speaking and cleared his throat—"you look better in person."

Her son was a charmer.

She pulled him back in her arms. "So do you. So do you," she said, catching Brian's look of contentment before closing her eyes.

***

It took nearly an hour before her eyes stopped straying over to her son. When she caught him stealing glances of his own, she felt both elated and saddened. They had so little time, but she was happy she wouldn't have to spend any of it trying to defend herself or Brian's decision to split him and Paige up at birth. Brian had given her something she didn't deserve. He'd kept her memory fresh in their son's eyes. She was beginning to see how much of a disservice she'd done both to Paige and Brian. Paige would have no idea Brian was her dad if they came face to face, let alone having a brother. She tried to breathe through the guilt she felt and tell herself that she and Paige's family dynamic was different. With their mother, it left little room for honesty where Paige's parentage was concerned.

B.J. pulled her out of her thoughts with his next question. "Do you have any pictures?" She blinked to see him watching her. When she realized what he was asking, she could have palmed her forehead.

"Yes, I do," she said, reaching for her purse and pulling out the small packet of pictures of Paige when she was baby up until she turned

97

thirteen. There were a few of the two of them together from more recent years then a set of Gladys.

B.J. had been passing the pictures to his dad after he perused them. When he got to Gladys' picture, he stopped and stared at it before looking up at Melanie. "Gladys, right?"

"Yes, Marc and I raised her for her first twelve years. We are still raising her, but she's staying with her mom while we're gone. She is a treasure."

"She's just as beautiful as her mother," B.J. said, before going to the next picture, which he stared at for a few seconds before going back to the previous picture.

He held up the second picture. "Vivian?"

Melanie nodded. "Good guess."

He shrugged. "Not really. Even though it is obvious that they are identical, they have two distinct personalities that come out in the way they hold themselves. I would say Vivian is more outspoken than Gladys. She also holds her chin differently.

Melanie smiled as she thought back to the first time she'd met Vivian and the child's inclination to raise her chin just like Paige when she was feeling nervous.

"She and her sister turned thirteen this year," Melanie said, watching their expressions ping-pong between affection and anger. She could see from B.J.'s demeanor that he also knew how Gladys and Vivian were conceived.

The men looked at each other for a moment, and when B.J. looked back at her she was surprised to see moisture in his eyes. "Is she okay?" B.J. asked, setting the picture aside.

"Regarding the drama surrounding Gladys' and Vivian's conception and birth? Yes, I believe Paige has healed. She is resilient and strong."

"Dad told me about Paige's husband. Is she okay?"

Melanie heaved a sigh. "She will be."

B.J. nodded, but the crease didn't lessen from between his eyes as he went back to the pictures.

She continued to watch her son and his father as they passed photos back and forth. Even with what little information the two were able to glean from Luca, they had a great deal more knowledge about her and Paige than she had of them. She felt cheated and guilty that she was still deceiving Paige. She could tell from B.J.'s mannerisms and open affection that Brian was a great father. Paige would be better for knowing him if it didn't put her life in jeopardy as Brian stated.

Melanie was happy Paige had the colonel as a father figure. He had been their rock in so many ways. Unless things changed drastically, Colonel Wayne Morganson would have to be enough.

B.J. leaned forward to hand her back the pictures. She waved him off. "They're yours. It's the least I could do." She watched as he glanced at his dad before bringing them back to his lap.

Brian tapped his thighs and stood up. "How about dinner before we continue with this reunion." His quick movement startled her, but the growl that came from her stomach answered for her. A flush stole over her neck and cheeks.

"I'm sorry I didn't offer sooner," Brian said, moving toward the sink. Melanie jumped up, used to serving instead of being served. B.J. stood up with her but laid a hand on her arm.

"Let's show you what we can do," he said before leading her back to the chair. She let herself be gently pushed back into her seat, returning her son's smile. Her son. A dream she had no business conjuring had come true. She swallowed once then twice to keep the overflow of emotion from seeping from her eyes.

She felt Marc's hand squeeze hers, and she welcomed the comfort it brought. Three days. She had three days.

"So, it's been just the two of you all this time? No special women in your lives?" Melanie asked, able to watch both men since they were working side by side. She noticed Brian's body go rigid before he changed his stance, but his face didn't give anything away. B.J. glanced at him out of the corner of his eye, but other than that, didn't seem to have any personal response to the question.

After a breath or two, Brian looked up at her. "It's hard to have a lasting relationship when you don't exist."

"The heart doesn't care who you are on paper," Melanie replied without hesitation, her own heart squeezing at the look on Brian's face. "What's her name?"

Brian let out an exasperated sigh. "Leslie." He visibly swallowed. Leslie Caine." Melanie saw B.J. go still when Brian said her full name and wondered at the reaction.

"Did you know her?" Melanie asked her son.

B.J. looked at his father, seeming to ask permission. Brian gave it to him when he pushed over some vegetables needing to be cut.

"Yes, she was around for a while. She was really nice. She even took me to school on occasion."

"High school?" Melanie asked, curious about the timeline of this relationship.

"Yeah, I think it was my junior year," B.J. said beginning to cut some peppers. When he went quiet, Melanie looked back at Brian, but he had closed up. She was struck by the fact that Brian had sacrificed a great deal more than she had for their son and daughter, but he had done an amazing job with B.J. She let the subject go for the moment but as almost any woman would, wondered if there was a chance for a happy ending for Brian and this Leslie.

The rest of the day and evening was filled with stories of B.J.'s youth from Brian's perspective and Paige's early childhood and recent years from Melanie's memories. She loved her son's easy smile and open nature. For all that she thought he'd lost or missed by being so sheltered, he seemed very well rounded.

The thought that she might have been played crossed her mind. That she kept quiet all these years for the sole purpose of doing Luca's bidding and keeping the knowledge of an illegitimate birth secret from the public and his family, except from his wife. She shook away the thought, hating the idea and the feelings it brought forth. *There would be time enough to contemplate that,* she thought as she watched Brian and her son work together as though they'd done this hundreds of times before.

Melanie inhaled and took in the sight and sound of the other side of her family wondering if God would answer her prayer and bring everyone together.

Chapter 11

For I know the plans I have for you," declares the LORD, "plans to prosper you and not to harm you, plans to give you hope and a future. Jeremiah 29:11

The first time I read this scripture I was struck by the omniscient presence of the Lord. I was known I wasn't a mistake; I wasn't forgotten or set aside. It sounded to me like a promise already kept. A promise fulfilled because God was not only the one who made the promise. He brought it to fruition at the same time. I've thought a lot about that lately. It gives me comfort. It eases the fear that I've been able to keep at bay on the sidelines of my thoughts.

As with my other notes, I've shared this particular scripture with you not just to tell you how it made me feel, but to cause you to wonder what your future holds. What do you think God has promised you that has already been delivered spiritually, but that you might still be waiting for it to come to fruition? Something solely for you, to you and also because you live. Think about it, my friend.

I'm going to take a nap while you do that. I'll write again soon.

Brandon

Mason reread the page in the notebook Brandon sent to him before he passed. He wasn't sure when Brandon had the time to write all the notes and letters, but Mason was grateful that he didn't have to completely say goodbye to his new and dearest friend. Brandon's personalized notes had been a significant part of Mason's study. He could hear Brandon's voice in his head, inflections and all. If it were possible, he was even closer to Brandon than he'd been the last day they'd spoken on the phone. The man had become instrumental in pulling Mason out of his struggle with himself. It was much like a veil being pulled back from a mirror that he'd looked at for years, which showed him a flawed reflection of himself riddled with failure and guilt.

Mason chuckled to himself as he relaxed back in bed. He sounded like a United Methodist commercial. He glanced over at his clock. At four-thirty on a Saturday he could start dinner or try giving Paige a call. He didn't expect it to last long even if she answered; she'd been quiet at first as he'd expected. He wanted nothing more than to sleep through Rachel's wake and funeral. He wanted to give her every opportunity to show up in his dreams, but he had to wait until Vivian went to sleep each night to do so, otherwise he knew his last reason for living would be ripped from his arms. Victoria had been out for blood and used any and every reason to threaten a fight for custody. He was miserable and caught up in a hell of his own making.

He knew by the reports he'd received from Richard and his daughter that Paige was little more than a zombie going through the motions. He was happy Brandon's family had stuck close, allowing Paige some solitude but always close at hand. He was more than relieved when Paige came back from Oklahoma. It was obvious Victoria and Richard wanted their turn to nurture and comfort Paige, but from what Richard told him, she barely left her room, and when she did she rarely spoke. Richard voiced his concerns with him one evening going so far as to hint that Mason should come and talk to her, but Mason knew that was the last thing he should do. He'd received eternal life during Brandon's funeral. He had no idea what to expect from her outside of a two-minute phone call, where he made it very clear that he was checking in to make sure she was eating, showering, feeding Gladys, and stepping outside now and then to get some sun.

Almost a month and a half later, and that was still the extent of their conversations. It usually went something like this:

"Thank you for answering my call."

"Thank you for calling."

"Have you eaten today?"

The answer to that question varied more if he called in the middle of the day, so he began calling closer to dinnertime, so he could tempt her with ideas just in case she hadn't eaten yet. One thing he did not do was ask her how she was doing. He knew how she was doing. She was hurting from the inside out, and until she allowed the One she blamed for hurting her to comfort her, it would be slow going. Meanwhile, he would be there whether it was on the sidelines or to lend her his ear. Well, until Thanksgiving the next week.

Mason wouldn't deny that he was looking forward to seeing Paige. He also wouldn't deny that he was dreading it. Being close to her again would be agony, especially since the only thing he could give her was more of what he'd already been offering her: prayer, an ear, and continued assurance that he would be there if she needed anything. It was the least he could do with all the times that she did the same for him, whether he wanted to recognize it or not.

Mason glanced at the clock again and blew out a breath. He picked up the tablet on his nightstand and turned it to the recipe he was planning for that night.

It seemed that all of his efforts to tempt Paige into eating motivated him to give cooking a serious try. He'd found a website that walked him through recipes step-by-step, and Mason discovered that with some focus he was more successful at dinner than not. It was a vast improvement by both his and Vivian's standards. He learned if he didn't try to modify or substitute ingredients, there was a greater chance of him producing an edible meal. Go figure.

Tonight he would try his hand at enchiladas. Ambitious? Absolutely.

Mason brought up Paige's name on his phone and pressed the button to dial her number. He moved from the bed as the phone rang and headed into the kitchen. He'd just set the tablet on the counter, resigned to the fact that she wouldn't pick up, and he'd have to wait until Wednesday to talk to her when he heard her voice.

"Mason."

He didn't want to be overly optimistic but the one-word greeting was more than he'd gotten since before Brandon's death. Usually, she just waited for him to speak first. Her voice, almost void of emotion.

"Good evening, Paige. Thank you for taking my call."

"You're welcome. Thank you for calling." The note of irony in her voice had him smiling. She was definitely doing better.

"Have you eaten today?"

"There's more to life than food, Mason."

"Usually not around dinnertime, Paige," he responded in kind.

"Then call at a different time." she retorted, and he couldn't help but break out in a huge grin.

He paused before asking her the question he'd been tiptoeing around for weeks.

"How are you feeling, Paige?"

"I didn't think you'd have the nerve to ask." He could tell her bravado was a mask, but he was grateful she had the energy or desire to try.

"I find I have the courage to do a lot of things lately. This. Provoking your wrath being one of them."

"Bravo." He heard her clapping in the background before the line went quiet. He took his head away from his phone to make sure she hadn't hung up.

"It hurts, Mason. It hurts so much. How do people come back from this? And don't say one day at a time."

Her words cracked something in him. He closed his eyes against the pain she provoked and the answering grief from his own memories surrounding Rachel's death.

"Not one day at a time. No one can hold their breath that long. It is one second, one thought, one moment at a time. Each one you survive, endure, and come out on the other side of, is a victory. It is another movement of the clock that you can look back on and mock because it didn't beat you. How you choose to get through them is up to you."

"How did you do it?" Her voice took on the vacant quality he hated hearing.

"Oh, I don't suggest you use any of my methods. Most of them were selfish and self-destructive."

"You survived," Paige answered quickly.

"I survived for Vivian. And because I wanted to thwart Victoria's plan to gain custody of my daughter," He added for good measure.

"I get up every day. I go through the motions for Gladys' sake, but that's all it is. I know what's expected of me and I do it. Over and over again," Paige said. Mason knew that all too well, but he wasn't able to express that feeling until long after he stopped being angry.

"I don't mean to sound like I'm looking a gift horse in the mouth. I'm actually quite relieved that you're talking, but I'm curious at what brought about this change?"

"Let's just say I got a good dose of what I was giving God, and it pulled me out of myself a little," she said haltingly.

He didn't even pretend to have a clue of what she was talking about, but he was grateful for its effect on her.

"You know, if I could take your pain I would," Mason said, finally giving in to his need to tell her what he'd been thinking for weeks.

He could hear a pin drop on the other side of the line; it was so quiet.

"Why? Don't you think I'm strong enough to get through this?" The edge of defensiveness and anger in her voice took him aback. It was the last response he expected. He was at a loss for words, so he went with humor.

"I guess it's good I didn't take up counseling. It's pretty obvious by the way I was blindsided by your response that I have a lot to learn." He ran his finger along the edge of the countertop, taking in the grooves and flaws in the granite.

"I'm sorry. I don't know why I responded that way. You were offering me… breathing room and I bit your head off."

Mason touched his cheek and forehead as if she could see him. "No, it's all still there."

"What is?" Paige asked.

"My head. It's still there, and I'm no worse for wear."

"Okay." He heard her exhale long and slow, and he felt the disappointment in his bones. She was about to end their call. Even though it was much more than he was expecting when she answered the phone, he loathed ending their conversation.

"So, you and Vivian will be arriving on Wednesday?" He shouldn't have been as happy at the moment's reprieve she'd given him.

"Yes, our flight gets in at one p.m. Since you aren't too far from the airport, we will come by and pick up Gladys before going to the hotel. I reserved adjoining rooms, so they can be together and do what thirteen-year-old girls do."

"That's really thoughtful of you. I know Gladys will enjoy Vivian's company for the week. It should be a welcome reprieve from her zombie-like mom," Paige said making a self-deprecating snort.

"Don't do that," Mason said with all seriousness. "You don't need to add guilt to your mixed batch of emotions."

"You know, it's kind of a relief."

"What is?"

"To feel. For a long time I didn't feel much of anything," Paige said, surprising him.

"Really?"

"Yeah. You'll never guess what my first real emotion after anger was," Paige said. Mason wasn't sure if he was supposed to answer or if her statement was rhetorical, but after a few seconds passed, he gave it a try.

"Self-pity."

"Close. Jealousy," she replied, and Mason found himself surprised once again.

"Jealousy? Why?" he asked, unable to help himself.

"I'll explain it to you one day. Just not today," she said, and he didn't push.

"Okay."

"I'm sorry again for responding the way I did earlier. I think I'm feeling possessive."

Mason was utterly confused, but he was willing to step off the proverbial cliff. "Possessive? Possessive of what?"

"My hurt, my pain, my anger. I want them, so for you to say you would take them if you could, kind of struck me wrong. It's all—" Her voice broke, and he went even more still than he had been a moment ago. "It's all I have right now that tells me that what I had with Brandon was real. That the love we shared was deeper and stronger than almost anything else I've ever felt," she said almost too quietly for him to hear.

"You have the memories," he said before he gave himself a chance to contemplate what he was saying.

"Yes, and there will come a day when I cherish them. Right now they only remind me of what I'm missing, what I can't make more of, and it brings me back to hurt and anger."

What did one say to that? He was more than speechless; he was breathless for a few seconds. Her pain was so palpable.

"I'm so sorry you're going through this, Paige," he said, wanting to give her any kind of comfort he could at the moment.

"Yes, I know you are," she said quietly. "I'm going to get some laundry done before Gladys comes home. She went to the movies with a few friends from school."

An irrational panic filled Mason, and he spoke quickly to keep Paige from hanging up. "Before you go, could I ask you a question?"

"Okay," came her reluctant reply.

"Have you eaten today?" An unladylike snort came through the phone. It was the closest thing to a laugh he'd heard come from her in a long time. He'd take it as a win.

"No, no I haven't. What are you cooking tonight that you want to tempt me with?" Her question made him pause. She'd figured out what he was doing.

"Mason?"

"Uh... yes, I'm going to try my hand at enchiladas."

"Wow... okay, that's, um… courageous."

"I thought it was more ambitious," he said, trying not to be offended.

"Yes, that too. I'm looking forward to hearing how they came out."

"I'll text you about my success, later," he said, trying to sound optimistic.

"Good. Well, thank you for calling, Mason," Paige said, leading them once again into a close of their conversation. This time he would let her go.

"You're welcome, Paige. I'll see you Wednesday," he reminded her. Not that he had to, but it gave him some comfort to say.

"Yes, see you Wednesday." She paused for a breath. "Bye, Mason."

"Later, Paige," he replied before he heard the click signaling the disconnection of their call. It took him a few more seconds to remove the phone from his ear, but when he did he noticed his heart wasn't as heavy as the last time he'd spoken to her.

Oh, Father, please. Please comfort and cover her even more now. Please.

He stood there, hands gripping the edge of the counter, feeling the sharp places biting into his palm. He dropped his head and closed his eyes against the pain in his heart and the burning at the backs of his eyes.

Please.

***

When Mason walked out of the airport loaded with both his and some of Vivian's luggage, he inhaled deeply. It had to be sixty degrees warmer in Los Angeles than it was in Chicago. He glanced back when Vivian disappeared from his side. She'd stopped to take her coat off, which was way too warm for their new climate. He could tell her that he'd warned her, but she'd been a little grumpy earlier that morning and during the flight, so he just patiently waited for her to reorganize herself and catch up.

As they crossed the rental parking lot, he scanned all of the vehicles hoping the crossover he'd rented for the weekend was large enough for all their bags. He was tempted to employ the same rule his mother had when he was young. Which was, only packed what you could carry, but the tension surrounding his daughter as she finally finished packing the night before kept him quiet.

Mason pointed at a smaller burgundy SUV once he compared its slot number against the number on his receipt. He received no notable response from Vivian, so he continued to the vehicle and pressed the key fob to raise the trunk and unlock the doors.

They were halfway to Paige's house before he tried one last time to get Vivian to tell him what was bothering her. "Are you looking forward to seeing Gladys?" he asked as he glanced in his side-view mirror before switching lanes. His daughter didn't turn away from her window, and he thought she meant to ignore him at first, but instead of calling her out on it, he took a deep breath, which was when she turned to him.

"Yes, but Gladys was hoping her mom would be back by now. She loves... we love Mati, but there's so much sadness. It's just hard." She sighed heavily, and he tried to understand where she was coming from, but he was a little disappointed at her lack of compassion. It had barely been four years since the death of her mother. Had she forgotten her pain from that loss?

"I understand. I really do. There are times when I think of a place I went to or conversation I had with Mommy, and the tears just come because I won't get to do that again with her and I miss her, but sometimes when I cry I feel better, so it's a good thing. I want to feel better." She stopped speaking for a moment and played with the hem of her shirt. "I don't think Mati wants to get better," Vivian said the last sentence, glancing up at him with real concern on her face.

Mason reached across the console and took her hand for a moment. The woman he spoke to last evening was still grieving deeply, but it didn't sound as if she'd given up.

"When was the last time you spoke to Mati?" Mason asked, trying to get an understanding.

Vivian shrugged her shoulders, looking deflated. "Maybe a week ago."

He looked over to access if she was telling the truth. She glanced away. "Maybe two."

"Have you talked to her since she came back from Gran's?" he asked, feeling disappointed in his daughter then guilty for putting so much on her. She wasn't a counselor nor had she studied the psychology of people who grieved. Her only expertise came from allowing God to heal her from the pain of losing her own mother.

"Just once," she admitted, her head hanging. There went another year's reward for 'Best Dad'. How did he keep missing these things?

He scanned the road, signaled, and pulled over on a side street from the main vein they were on. He put the car in park and turned to see tears splash on the hands in her lap.

"Hon, look at me," he said, waiting for his daughter to turn back to him. She shook her head to the negative and a heavy lump began to form in his throat. "Why?" She shook her head again and wiped at her tears. He raised up and removed the handkerchief from his back pocket. He held it out to her but didn't let go of it when she tried to pull it from him. She looked at him with red, puffy eyes, and he had to fight the impulse to take her in his lap and rock her until the tears subsided.

"Why?" he repeated.

"She wasn't really there. It felt like she only answered because Gladys was living with her. I'm sorry, Daddy. It was just so hard. It made me so incredibly sad to see her like that. It took most of the morning to pray the feeling away. It was just so hard. I'm sorry, Daddy. I really tried." The last of her sentence came out in low wail, and Mason reached over and wrapped his arms around his daughter. His incredibly sensitive daughter who had no business apologizing because she couldn't carry someone else's grief on her small shoulders, and he told her as much while she cried into his chest.

"It was not your job to make her all better. It was more than enough that you and Gladys let her know that you love her. It will take some time. You see how long it took for me when your mother died, but Paige, no matter how upset she is right now, has something I didn't when your mom passed."

Vivian leaned her head away from his chest, a hopeful expression on her face. "What's that?"

"Not what? Who. She has a relationship with God. A real one where she can be angry with Him when it hurts, but she can also go to Him to receive comfort and have Him wipe her tears. It may have slipped her mind for a moment, but I had a conversation with her yesterday, and although she is still very, very sad, she seems ready to receive that comfort." He used a thumb to wipe the tears from under her left eye. Vivian took a shuddering breath, much like the ones she took when she was a toddler after a fall or a tantrum.

"You think so?" she asked, her voice hopeful.

"Yes, I think so," he said, punctuating his sentence with a kiss on her nose. She scrunched up her nose and tried to pull away, but he held her tight.

"Daddy!" She half squealed and half laughed.

"I love you, Vivian. You are an amazing young lady with a heart bigger than this car." He saw her eyes moving as she glanced around the car.

"Uh, this car isn't that big," she replied, frowning.

He stifled a laugh. "Bigger than our apartment." The frown didn't leave or lessen. "Okay, bigger than all the outdoors," he said, watching the crease between her brows fade and her lips tip up at the corners. "There's my sweet girl." The frown came back, and he did laugh that time before letting her go.

He looked over at her while she dried her eyes. "It will take a moment, Vivian. Brandon was a great man, and Paige loves him very deeply. All I'm saying is not to put her grief on you. Just continue to love her as you have been." Vivian nodded her consent.

He noting that the interior of the car's atmosphere felt lighter, and he thanked God again for prompting him to pause when he would have pushed Vivian into a confession and gained her ire instead of trust. It could have all gone terribly wrong.

"I know another great man," Vivian said in a small voice. He looked over at her to find her watching him and felt a flush crawl up his neck at her praise.

"Well, thank you, hon. I wouldn't go so far as great, but I hope I'm better than I was a few years, even a few months, ago."

Vivian seemed to consider his comment. "Yeah, I'd say you are. Your cooking has definitely gotten better."

He reached over and tickled her behind the ear almost losing his hearing at the sound of her scream as she scrambled to get away. "It's true," she complained.

"Yeah, yeah," he said as he glanced out the sideview mirror and put the car back in gear.

Fifteen minutes later, Ava Tatum opened the door to Mason and Vivian and the aroma that wafted out, caused his mouth to water. "Ah, Mason. Vivian." Ava hugged them, saying their names as if it had been years instead of weeks.

"Mrs. Tatum," he said, returning the greeting. When he pulled back it was to a stern face. "Ava. It's good to see you, Ava." Her stormy expression cleared, and he gave her an impish grin.

"Come in, you two. Gladys has been waiting for forever." She said the last part of the sentence with exaggerated exasperation.

Mason followed his daughter deeper into the living room, watching as Gladys came running from a back room to hug her sister. "I've missed you so much," Gladys said, squeezing Vivian, who looked to be holding on just as tightly. He looked over their heads at Ava and smiled. It would be good for the two of them to get away for the rest of the day.

"My dad said we can get room service," Vivian said once their embrace was over.

Gladys looked up at him and came over for a hug of her own. "Hi, Mr. Jenson. Thank you for the room service." He couldn't help but chuckle.

"You're welcome," he responded, registering that she looked and felt like his Vivian, but her scent was different than his daughter's. He gave the top of her head a quick peck then let her go. When he finally looked up, he spotted Paige standing at the door of the kitchen, watching everyone. She was noticeably thinner, and there were dark circles under her eyes, but the smile she gave him flickered briefly in her eyes and that was more than enough for him.

Gladys slipped out of his arms, taking Vivian back to the room they shared, and Mason let his legs carry him to Paige. "Hey, Paige," he greeted before embracing her.

"Hey, Mason," she replied into his chest. He took an extra second before grabbing her shoulders and pushing her far enough away to see her eyes.

"Did you eat today?"

She shook her head but chuckled, and he felt like Christmas came early.

***

Mason sat at the extended dining table with his daughter to his right and Marjorie on the left. Paige was sandwiched between Marjorie and Ava who kept Paige's plate full. He watched her sigh in exasperation when Ava replaced the stuffing she'd finished with a serving of garlic mashed potatoes. The look she sent him made him bite his tongue to keep from laughing, and it went a long way in easing some of the tension that sat on him since his talk with Ava earlier that day. She'd asked him to give her a ride to the grocery store for some undisclosed ingredient. It wasn't until they reached the store that she blindsided him with her true motive.

"Brandon left some letters for Paige, with me, before he passed," Ava said once he put the vehicle in park. All Mason could think of was how happy he was that Ava had waited until they were still to drop that bomb.

"He said you would know when it was time to give them to her," she continued. *And that bomb as well.*

He looked over to find Ava watching him. He rubbed his hands up and down his face to buy himself some time, but it didn't matter. He could have been given a month, and he still wouldn't have known what to say. He thought back to the most recent conversation he'd had with Paige and didn't like the answer.

"Why didn't he want her to have them right away? Didn't he think they would have helped?" His mind was ping-ponging from the funeral to the note and scripture he'd read last week. *Why would Brandon do this to him?*

"He said he didn't want them to be a crutch but a continuation of their conversation," Ava said, looking unsure. "Do you think she's ready? I'm not sure if she's ready or if I want her to be ready."

Mason thought about Ava's words and tried to push his feelings of betrayal to the back of his mind. This was so unfair. *Okay, think. If Rachel had left you letters to be read postmortem when would you have been clear of mind enough to read them?* Mason shook his head. There were so many dynamics. One huge one being her relationship with God. This could go so wrong.

"I think the only conversation Paige wants to have right now has to do with why he didn't fight harder and when was he going to ask God for a miracle so he could come back," he said while breathing out as he rested his head on the seat. "The fact that she has made some significant strides over the last two weeks makes me shaky with this decision, but there were some things said that makes me think she's not quite ready. Maybe two weeks to a month," Mason said, feeling only a little more secure in his decision after sharing his reason with Ava.

Ava placed her hand on his. "Thank you. I know none of this is easy, but Brandon trusted you and thought of you as a friend." Her words made him chuckle. The irony was so layered.

"What is it?" Ava asked.

Mason looked over at her, his eyes burning all of a sudden. "He's my mentor." He threw her a small smile. "It sounds weird, but he sent me a notebook filled with notes. It's like continuing the conversations we had when he was alive." It struck him almost immediately that he used the same words that Brandon had for Paige, and he wanted to reverse his decision, but when he opened his mouth there was an unease deep in his gut, so he shut it. When he refocused on Ava, she stared at him for a beat then gave him a wobbly smile.

"I trust your judgment. Brandon was right in choosing you to make this decision." She shook her head. "He always had an uncanny ability to choose just the right people to surround himself with."

"I was much different a year ago," Mason said, not wanting her to go away thinking he was some type of saint.

"Oh yes, I know. We talked. That's how I know this is truly God's work." She patted his hand again, and he had to blink back the tears that rushed forward. It was a good thing they were separated by a console because if she'd hugged him, he would have cried like a baby.

***

Mason blinked back to the present and passed a bowl of green bean casserole to his right. The chatter was louder which allowed him to relax. Hopefully, no one had noticed his short trip.

"I see you're back," Marjorie said in his ear.

So much for that.

"Are you all right? You seem distracted." Marjorie continued to whisper.

"I'm good. It's just been a long time since I shared Thanksgiving with so many people," he said, only addressing half of the reason for his unease.

116

"Well, get used to it because we aren't going anywhere," she said, bumping his shoulder with hers.

"I wouldn't have it any other way. Paige is blessed to be able to call you family," he replied, meaning it.

Marjorie blinked twice and looked at him as if she'd never seen him before. "You love her. You love Paige."

Mason froze for a millisecond before forcing himself to relax. What could she have possibly taken from his last statements as a clue that he loved Paige? That was uncanny. He didn't know what her next reaction was going to be once the shock of her own revelation passed. At least she'd kept her voice low.

"Of course. She's the mother of my daughter and has been a very integral part of our lives." He was especially proud of his quick thinking until Marjorie's eyes narrowed.

"Is that all?" she asked, still watching him like a hawk.

"Do you really think this is the time for this conversation?" he replied, trying to dodge more questions.

"Do you want me to corner you later?" Marjorie asked, and he could tell she would. He blinked slowly and nodded his head.

"What are your intentions?" He wanted to laugh at her audacity but bit his cheek to keep from doing so.

"To do what I have been doing all along. Be her friend; continue to love and nurture our daughter, and be there if, or when, she needs me," he responded as quickly as possible before forking some collard greens into his mouth.

"That could be a dangerous place. She could get used to just having you around and fall in love with someone else," Marjorie responded.

Were they really having this conversation with a table full of Brandon's family members?

"If he made her as happy as Brandon did then I would be fine." And he realized he meant it.

Marjorie stared at him for a moment. "Wow. Do you have a brother?" He opened his mouth, confused by her question, but quickly

117

closed it when it dawned on him what she meant. He turned his attention back to his plate to hide his embarrassment.

"Do estranged half-siblings count?" He placed another bite of food in his mouth.

"Probably not, but it makes for interesting conversation," she shot back.

"Wasn't this interesting enough?" he asked, incredulity coloring his words.

"For now," she replied, patting him on the shoulder. "For now."

Mason was almost pained to see if Paige witnessed any of their conversation, but he couldn't fight the temptation. He glanced over to see her watching him with an openly curious expression. He shrugged his shoulders and set his features to "baffled." It bought him a rueful smile that made her eyes twinkle a little. He decided Marjorie wasn't so bad.

Chapter 12

Paige stared down at yet another serving of yams. She ate slowly to keep this from happening but not slow enough. Ava was watching her like a hawk, so slipping food into her napkin or on Marjorie's plate was out of the question. She glanced over to see how empty Marjorie's plate was when she overheard part of her whispered conversation with Mason.

"Do you have a brother?" Marjorie asked. *Why would she want to know if he had a brother?* Was Marjorie wondering why Mason was eating Thanksgiving dinner with Paige and Brandon's family? Paige listened a little more intently while she placed a small amount of mashed potatoes in her mouth. There would be no crunching to obstruct her hearing.

"Do estranged half-siblings count?" Mason responded, his humor seeping through his words. Paige might have smiled if she wasn't supposed to be eavesdropping. The comment was odd, and it struck her that in the year and a half that she'd known Mason they'd only talked about his family once. From what she remembered his childhood wasn't something he wanted to revisit when they first got to know each other. She wondered if anything had changed? She would have to ask him soon.

Paige speared a sliver of turkey and had it halfway to her lips when she heard Marjorie's response. "Probably not, but it makes for interesting conversation." *What? What kind of thing to say was that?* Paige breathed through her nose to cool the indignation that rose up in

119

her. It wasn't like Marjorie to be so callous with people's feelings. Her tone sounded playful, maybe even teasing, so Paige didn't think it was meant to be malicious, but it was Mason. He wasn't as social and outgoing as most people were. It wasn't like talking with Brandon who let most things slide off his back. Paige caught the tense she used but didn't correct her thoughts. They were her thoughts.

"Wasn't this interesting enough?" Mason blurted back, and Paige wanted to high-five him, but again, she wasn't supposed to be listening. She wished she'd sat next to him at the table, but she didn't want to offend Ava or Marjorie who had done everything but bathe and dress her since they arrived on Tuesday. The few times she looked his way he'd done or said something to ease the heaviness in her heart a little. It was ironic she would be drawn to him, but he, more than most, knew what she was going through, and he didn't push her to try to feel better. He just took her as she was. Well, there was that obsession he had with her eating, but no one was perfect.

"Now," she heard Marjorie mutter. She heard what sounded like a pat and looked up. "For now," Marjorie said, and Paige watched as Mason shook his head slightly then took a breath and looked her way. She schooled her features to show innocent curiosity. Mason shrugged his shoulders and looked at her like he wasn't sure what just transpired. She felt a sense of comradery and pity for him and communicated it the only way she could at the moment. She was going to have to get him by himself at some point and find out what that was all about.

Paige looked down at her plate and sighed. She knew Ava wouldn't let her leave the table until her plate was closer to empty. She wanted to please the woman, but no one wanted to witness the second coming of the yams, potatoes, or green bean casserole she'd eaten. She finished her cranberry sauce hoping it was light enough to leave room for the rest of her green beans. She shouldn't have eaten the stuffing first, but it was nice to crave something for a change and Ava's was the best.

"You are doing a great job. Do you want some more of anything?" Ava said beaming. The woman was actually praising her for eating.

"No, I'm not sure I can finish what's on my plate now. Everything is so good," Paige said, stretching and patting her nonexistent belly.

Ava glanced down at her hand, and a look of such profound sadness crossed her features that it took Paige's breath away. In that instant she was transported back to the moment Brandon came home from a doctor's appointment he'd had early on in their marriage. He didn't say anything. He just came in, and after locking the door, put his briefcase down and walked over to the couch where he scooped her up and carried her to the bedroom and closed the door. "Well, hello," she said, giggling, but he didn't respond. Instead, he laid her on the bed, took off her shoes, and crawled in next to her. He wrapped one arm around her and placed his head on her belly.

She ran a hand over his hair and reveled in the fact that he wanted to be near her, but when she felt the wetness from his tears, she became concerned. She wrapped her hands around any part of him she could reach and just held him. It took two days for him to tell her that the doctor had told him they had a 1 percent chance of conceiving due to all of the medications he was taking. She told him, that with God, even 1 percent was more than enough, but he went quiet and refused to talk about it anymore. It was the one big issue in their marriage that he shut the door on in regards to conversation, and it made her angrier than she thought she could ever be with Brandon.

Paige met Ava's moist gaze and reached out a hand to comfort the older woman. Ava blinked rapidly to pull back the tears and gave Paige a pathetic smile while she patted the hand Paige had placed on her arm. Paige wouldn't allow her head or heart to visit that dark place she so often escaped to when memories overtook her. Instead, she leaned over and kissed her former mother-in-law on the cheek because she couldn't think of anything to say. She, a public speaker and writer, couldn't think of a single comforting word, so she kissed her again, squeezed her hand, then went back to her plate and focused on clearing it.

During the rest of the meal, Paige pushed herself to stay present. Ava's slip in composure was a small wake-up call. She wasn't the only one hurting, but she was the only one who had locked herself away and rejected everyone's attempts to comfort her. She had been a lot more selfish than she first realized. She couldn't even promise herself that she wouldn't slip back into her hole once everyone was gone, but for the next week she would try harder not to compare how different things would be if Brandon were still with them.

"How are you doing?" Mason asked, taking the seat recently vacated by Everzie who had been sharing all of the baby pictures Paige had missed of Peyton, named for her aunt. The child was adorable and had this uncanny way of knowing when her picture was being taken. *A diva's born every minute*, she thought to herself.

Paige held out her hand in response to his question. "I am now charging everyone a dollar each time they ask me that question. Mason looked at her as though she were joking. She gestured for him to give her what she asked for by waving her fingers. She watched with no little humor as he leaned forward to pull his wallet from his back pocket.

"I don't know why you're charging me. I rarely ask you how you are doing, if at all," he mumbled as he sorted through the bills in his billfold and pulled out a dollar. She reached for it, but he brought it back to himself.

"How much money have you made so far?" he asked, narrowing his eyes at her.

She reached out and quickly snatched the bill out of his hand. "One dollar."

He sputtered for a moment. "Why me? Why not Marjorie or Phillip or Makayla?"

"Because I knew you would fall for it," she said, placing the bill out of reach. Mason looked like he wanted to reach around her to go after the bill but then thought better of it. He grumbled something unintelligible before slipping his wallet back in his pocket.

"How are you holding up? I know you're not a fan of crowds," Paige asked, bumping his knee with hers.

"Ahhh, this is pretty nice. They are... you are such a close-knit family. It's like being enveloped in warmth, and the twins are having a great time babysitting. Vivian told me they've watched *Frozen, Kipper, Dora the Explorer, Doc McStuffins* and *The Red Balloon.*"

"Today? That's like five things. I didn't know their attention span was that long," Paige said, feeling completely clueless.

122

Mason chuckled. "I would bet they started watching *Frozen*, and a couple of the children got bored then they moved on to an episode of *Kipper* then *Dora*. I think there were snacks and dinner somewhere in there, a few games, and more shows. I'm afraid they have destroyed the twins' room."

Paige felt panic slide over her and had to tamp down on the urge to go back and see for herself. She checked her watch. It was early yet. If most of the relatives with children left in the next couple of hours she could clean up for at least four hours before she wore herself out.

"They are children, Paige. They mess things up, and they will continue to do so until they leave next week," Mason said, glancing at the football game on the widescreen that most of the men in the room were watching. Many of the women were in the kitchen putting away the food. The only reason she wasn't in there with them was because there wasn't enough room for all of them, and she got the feeling Ava knew she would be going back in there once everyone had gone to sleep.

"You seem to be holding your own as well," Mason said in a near whisper, though there was no chance of being overhead while the commentator's excited voice called out an interception on the television.

Paige looked at him to see if he was teasing, but his expression was sober. She must have been hiding her deeper anguish well. Just four more days to go. She shrugged. "Second by second, right?"

He gave her a shadow of a smile. "One breath at a time."

She tried to return his smile, but from the change in his expression, she could tell she'd failed. That was Mason. He wasn't easily fooled. One reason could be because they'd gotten to know each other around the same time she began getting to know Brandon. He'd been around for the most bizarre year of her life, but the memories attached to him didn't fill her with pain and sorrow. It was a welcome reprieve.

"You are blessed to have so much family around you. They seem loving and they adore you. When Rachel died, for months it was only Vivian and me until Victoria agreed to have Vivian in her life without

123

taking over custody. Having family around would have made things a little easier."

"One day would you tell me about your family?" Paige asked, watching him back.

"I told you about my dad, the traveling pastor with the second family. Well, we were the second family or other family. I guess it doesn't really matter how you state it. When he died we were treated like mud on the bottom of a soldier's shoe. It broke my mother and it left me to fend for both of us. The only time I saw my half-brother and sisters was when we found out about them at the reading of my father's will. There isn't much more than that."

Paige could tell he was skimming over the story and certainly didn't want to get into it while he was surrounded by so many unfamiliar people. She should have waited and brought it up when they were alone, but it had popped in her head, and it seemed a safer conversation than any other, at the moment.

Her heart and mind were like a minefield. She never knew when a conversation or thought would trigger a memory that would shake her to the core. Like the one that was skimming across the edge of her mind at that moment. She shook it off before it could fully form and turned her attention to the game.

"Have you heard from Mel recently?"

The question had her turning her head back to Mason. "No, I haven't. I'm starting to wonder if she will ever come back."

"Why would you say that?" Mason asked, looking startled by her words.

Paige thought his reaction was over the top but remembered that he didn't know what it was like to have family that would move mountains to come and help you when needed. "I needed my mother. I needed her here with me months ago, but she didn't come back. I don't know what could have been so important that she wouldn't be with me through such a hard time in my life."

"Are you angry with her?" Mason asked.

"I wouldn't say angry. I'm more hurt than anything. I forgave her after it came out that she wasn't my sister but my mother. She wouldn't reveal who my dad was, but I had hoped that she would come around." Paige spread her arms wide. "This makes me feel like we're going backward."

Paige placed her elbows on her knees and clasped her hands together before propping her cheek on them. "I want my mom, Mason. I want the bulldog you met at the hospital when I donated my kidney to Vivian. I need to know that there is a human being that can't be kept from me." She blinked up at him, trying to keep the tears from falling and failed.

"Oh, Paige." The words were so achingly sad; she bit her lip to keep it from trembling.

"I know you're feeling like a woman on an island with an ocean between you and those you love and who love you. It won't always feel this way. It won't always be this way. Melanie could have taken Gladys with her or left her with Brenda, but she placed her in your hands because your hands are not only the place she trusts for Gladys' well being, but she made sure both of her children were in one place and had each other. I have no doubt in my mind that she's coming back because she left her heart here." He gave her a look that said he expected her to believe him and that was that.

She snorted inelegantly before she responded. "Yes, sir." She pretended to consider something before speaking again. "You have gotten a lot smarter since you started listening to God."

The laugh that came from him seemed to surprise them both. He covered his mouth with his fist as he tried to regain his composure. She was about to sshh him but remembered this was Thanksgiving dinner, not a wake. The sound of his mirth seemed to dispel some of the heaviness that had been hovering over her apartment.

"Nah, it's just easier to see things when you are further away. Besides, with Antonio's antics this summer, I think it was smart for her to get out of Dodge. She obviously has information he wants." Paige thought about his words and wondered again what Melanie was doing.

Chapter 13

Melanie blinked away a fresh set of tears as she laid her head on her husband's shoulder. He rubbed her arm gently as he continued to stare out of the airplane window. They were close to the last leg of their trip back to Los Angeles. The two weeks of travel had worn on Melanie from the beginning because the excitement of seeing Brian and B.J. was now behind her. Of course, she anticipated seeing Paige and Gladys again especially after what both of her daughters had to endure since she'd been gone.

Saying "goodbye" to Brian and B.J. would have been unbearable if she thought she'd never see them again, but the conversation they had the last night she and Marc were at Brian's gave her the reassurance she needed to leave without a huge show of tears.

Melanie felt the landing gear release and peeked around Marc to watch the lights of Denver, Colorado draw closer. It was a bittersweet sight. Each moment that brought her closer to one half of her family, it took her farther away from the other half. From Denver they would catch a bus to Albuquerque, New Mexico and rent a car from there and drive into Los Angeles.

"Are you okay?" Marc asked her for what seemed like the thirtieth time.

"I'm a walking contradiction. You and God are my only comfort," Melanie said, wishing she had something more pleasant to think about, but all she could think of was the bomb Brian had dropped on her the second day of her and Marc's visit.

126

She'd woken up in Marc's arms the morning after they'd arrived which in itself wasn't new but something she thanked God for each day she was blessed to do so. The rest of the morning was less conventional.

B.J., who had his own home closer to the city, left before she and Marc left the comfort of Brian's guest bedroom. When they came downstairs, it was to the sound and smell of breakfast cooking. Brian had taken care of some early morning work with Luca since they were working on Eastern Standard Time and Luca's current time zone, which was twelve hours ahead.

"When do you sleep?" Melanie asked when they were first told of Brian's work hours.

"When Luca does. Otherwise, I take a lot of catnaps," Brian answered with a shrug.

Melanie thought that schedule was extremely hard on the body, but he was a grown man, and she knew her comments wouldn't be welcome.

They ate breakfast on the back porch under an overhang that provided some privacy from sailors coming into the bay. For the most part, it was quiet. Brian's home was only one of five on the bay, and since summer was well over those who used their home seasonally had long since vacated.

Melanie was at the end of her breakfast when she caught Brian shoot Marc a look before looking back at her. She set her fork down and wiped her mouth on a napkin, trying to prepare herself for what Brian was going to say.

With his elbows on the table, Brian looked into her eyes and began. "What I'm about to tell you may come as a shock, but I need you to trust and believe that I wouldn't share this with you if I didn't have to. It may sound wrong or selfish, but I only ever wanted for you to be happy and us being apart helped to aid in that."

Melanie followed his words around the imaginary bush and wanted to tell him to get on with it but reined in her curiosity so he wouldn't think she couldn't handle the news without getting emotional.

"As I told you yesterday, I work behind the scenes at Luca's company. I am privy to certain information while other information has been kept out of reach. When I chose to leave with B.J., I did it not only because I thought I could help save Paige, but because I no longer knew who to trust. It certainly wasn't my adopted parents. Luca never asked anything of me. He accepted me even though doing so put him and his wife under a lot of stress. He even changed his initial plan when I thought you wouldn't make it." Brian looked beyond them, and she could see his body relax a little.

"I took Luca at his word for many years because he was willing and able to do the things I wasn't, but over the last six or seven years, there has been a shift in the company. Luca has been dispersing more and more of his responsibilities, and I believe he is grooming a few people for his place. If I see this from where I work, others have definitely noticed, and it is making people restless. Restless enough to go looking for leverage.

Unfortunately, I found out something that could be used both in my favor or against me, and in turn, you, if it were discovered by the wrong people," Brian said, looking as though he wished he was anywhere but in front of her at that moment.

"I'm able to get an extraordinary amount of information using my computer skills. Since I am mostly incognito online, I'm used to taking certain precautions so that I don't leave a trail. I have used the curse or blessing, whichever way you wish to view my nonexistence on paper, to follow and gain information on Antonio."

"He's your father..." Melanie began, noting how naïve she sounded and let the sentence fade.

"Luca was more of a father than Antonio ever was. Antonio is swayed by money and what people think of him. He has no true north. No conviction about anything except money and how he can acquire more power." Brian said and Melanie saw the strain in the set of his mouth.

"A few months ago, Antonio began going through some warehouse files. I saw their designation in a monthly report from a file sweep I do of some of Antonio's less-than-discreet searches. He doesn't even try to hide some of the things he researches about Luca. I think he does it to get under Luca's skin, but he's sloppy and careless," Brian said, looking back and forth between the two of them.

"Brian, I know you are leading up to something, and by the way you're stalling. I realize it's bad, but this isn't helping. It's only making me more nervous about what you have to say," Melanie stated, her heartbeat accelerating.

Brian gave her a nod then swallowed hard. "Okay. I'm just going to preface what I'm about to say with this." He sighed. "I don't have all the information, but Antonio's searches caused me to wonder what he was after, so I backtracked and came face-to-face with a realization that involves you. The man you knew as your father, Colonel Wayne Morganson, wasn't your biological father," Brian said and breathed out.

Melanie heard what he said, but there must have been some kind of disconnect because she was sure she heard him wrong. She was so sure, she ran his words through her mind three times, waiting for her brain to rearrange the words in an order that made sense.

"Dramatic much?" Marc whispered next to her, sarcasm dripping from his voice as he squeezed her hand. She looked over to see him staring at Brian.

"If you could have done it in a gentler, yet more frank way, you should have," Brian said, leaning back in his chair.

"Man, *I* don't even know what you're talking about," Marc said, his words delivered sharp and clipped.

Melanie half listened to them as she tried to wrap her mind around what Brian had said. Of course, the colonel was her father. She'd seen pictures of him and her mom together before she was born. They were all in WITSEC together. There was part of her that knew both of those things didn't guarantee her certainty, but this was her reality Brian was talking about. This was her life.

"I don't understand," she finally gasped out, holding Marc's hand in a death grip.

Both men stopped talking and looked at her.

"I mean. I don't understand how I could not be aware of that at all, and how you could know…" Her mind left the sentence and jumped to another before she could finish speaking.

"What proof do you have?"

"Your blood type…"

"Really? The blood-type excuse? You know that only works in the movies," Melanie said, rolling her eyes. She was Wayne Morganson's daughter.

Brian stared at her for a moment, but she didn't see frustration or impatience in his eyes, just resolve, and it bothered her more than if she'd seen any other emotion in his eyes.

"Your blood type is AB positive. Your mother's blood type is O positive," Brian said.

"Okay," Melanie retorted.

"O-positive blood is recessive. When the mother has O-positive blood, the father would have to have AB blood for the child to have AB-type blood. Both your mother and Wayne Morganson have O-positive blood. Sadly, I think it's obvious that you're Brenda's daughter but one of your parents didn't contribute to your presence in this world, biologically anyway," Brian said almost apologetically.

"How does…" Melanie rearranged her thoughts trying to come up with a question that would help make all of this make sense. "Why would…" Yeah, that might work. She tried again. "Why would you or your family have that information?"

Brian rubbed his forehead. A sure sign the next bit of news was worse. "It looks like my family has an invested interest. My grandfather helped your mother relocate to Florida before you were born."

"Was it a job thing?" she asked but knew the answer before Brian shook his head to the negative.

"Maybe it was a wedding present, a send-off since she used to work for him. You know, a thank you?" she asked, trying again.

"That she repaid by turning into a state witness on his business partners?" Brian countered, making her feel a bit hysterical.

Melanie needed something she could hold on to. Why did it feel like this was coming out of left field? Wayne Morganson had treated her like a daughter in every way. He'd even adopted her daughter and treated her like a daughter instead of a granddaughter. Well, that didn't serve her case, but if she wasn't his then why?

Melanie tried to rein in her thoughts before they got completely out of hand. It wasn't like she could ask her father why he did the things he did, and she sure wasn't going to ask Brenda until all other options were no longer available.

"Did the files say who my real father was?" Melanie asked after going through another set of questions in her mind and choosing the most relevant.

"No, not directly, but as I said, I'm only following Antonio's movements," Brian said slowly.

"Oh my goodness, Brian. Spit it out! It's as if you don't..." She stopped midsentence. Everything stopped. The breeze coming off the bay died; Melanie's thoughts hit a wall, and she was pretty sure her lungs quit because she could barely pull in a breath. Then all at once, her senses came back online.

"No..." Heat flashed over her skin, and it was all she could do to swallow down the bile that rushed to her throat.

"Is it Luca? Are we..."? She choked on the rest of the thought. She looked toward Marc, whose grim expression showed her that he'd arrived at the same conclusion she had.

Brian's expression mirrored Marc's but was mixed with a little pity.

"But you're..." Melanie swallowed convulsively. "I'm... we..." She couldn't seem to finish a sentence, or was it the prospect of finishing a sentence made the horror of the moment real. Melanie closed her eyes against the thoughts and images that ran through her mind.

"They... Luca had an affair with my mom. They..." She needed one of them to dispute what she was saying. She needed Brian to tell her she'd jumped to conclusions, but when she turned to him he wasn't shaking his head.

Brian opened his mouth, but before he could speak Melanie jumped up from the table and rushed in the house toward the direction of the closest bathroom she could remember at the moment. She made a left through the living room to a door she prayed wasn't a closet. She threw the door open and with relief made it to the toilet with only a few seconds to spare.

As her breakfast made its reappearance, Melanie decided she would berate Brian about his timing.

"Baby, are you okay?" Marc asked from behind her. She heard the sink faucet turn on, and the sound warred with the ringing in her ears.

"No," she replied on a shaky exhale then heaved again as chills ran up and down her body, and tears came to her eyes. *Oh God... what are you doing? Why now? Why ever?* She couldn't do it. She couldn't tell Paige. This was too much. Melanie mentally put her foot down. She'd had enough.

White-hot anger rolled over Melanie replacing the nausea. She took the washcloth Marc placed in front of her and wiped her mouth. She wanted to scream out her pain and rage. Too much. There was no way she could go back to her daughter with this news. No way!

She knew she'd promised to tell Paige the truth from now on, but this was just cruel. It was bad enough that Paige had to work through the fact that her children weren't only conceived through a violent act but that the act had been done to her by her own cousin. Everything in Melanie rejected the idea of telling Paige that she too was born from incest.

"Melanie?" Marc's voice came from behind her. Melanie didn't respond. She couldn't if she wanted to. She heaved herself away from the commode and pressed the handle. Marc backed up but kept a steadying hand around her waist.

"Mel, you're shaking," Marc said quietly as she turned toward the basin in the now-too-tight space of the half bath. Melanie noticed that he was right as she held her hands under the stream of water coming from the faucet. She took in a deep breath and let it out slowly.

"I need a minute, Marc," she said before bringing water to her face.

"I just want to make..." Marc started, and Melanie's anger bubbled over.

"I'm not," she yelled. "I'm not okay. I'm so mad. I hate that woman so much right now. She's a life-sucking demon, and I'm sick of her." Melanie closed her eyes and grabbed the countertop to steady herself. She let her head fall forward as the door to the bathroom closed, and she thought she was alone. She growled low in her chest and let it out in a scream, and it felt so good she did it again and again until a pair of strong arms came around her. The feeling startled her into hiccupping sobs.

"It's going to be okay," Marc said in her ear.

"No, it's not. Not for her because I'm going to kill her!" Melanie said through her teeth.

Marc went quiet, and Melanie knew she'd scared him. She didn't care. She was tired of being her mother's emotional punching bag. It didn't occur to Melanie that even at that moment she was reeling from one well-placed jab.

It took ten minutes with Marc's arms around her for Melanie to feel composed enough to leave the bathroom. When they exited, they were met by Brian who was leaning against one of the sofa armchairs. She noticed the worry on his face and shrugged because she didn't know what else to do.

"You handled that a lot better than I did," Brian said, pushing away from the sofa and stepping forward to hug her. His comment and affection surprised her so much she couldn't respond right away.

The three of them were headed back toward the patio before some of the red haze of anger cleared. "I wish I could say that I'm not surprised. I thought nothing she did could surprise me anymore." She gave an unladylike snort. "It just goes to show you that you're never too old to be shocked." Melanie shook her head. "I'm just angry I didn't see it coming." Melanie sat down, noticing Marc's nearness right away. She glanced at him then bumped his shoulder with hers affectionately.

"So… just before you ran from the table I was trying to tell you that there is another possibility," Brian said, looking sheepish.

"Talk about burying the lead," Marc said out of the side of his mouth.

"Look, I tried, but Melanie guessed it was Luca and raced to the restroom. I don't blame her; I really did have much the same reaction." Brian squared his shoulders. "I'm not saying that Luca isn't your father, just that the information I have leads to him, but it leads to someone else as well. Until I can find proof of paternity, the files I have show that you are either Luca Sable or Angelo Mauro's daughter."

Marc gasped next to her. She took in his growing tension and told herself she would ask him about it before she turned back to Brian. "Angelo Mauro?"

"Marc mentioned him yesterday. He's Charles Mauro's son. The one Luca refused to work with directly until Charles passed away. He lives in Chicago," Brian said, looking at the palms he was rubbing together before looking up to watch her.

Melanie didn't know what he was looking for. She figured she'd reacted more than enough a few minutes ago, and now she felt like a quickly deflating balloon. If she considered Paige's reaction when she confronted Melanie about her parentage, she should at least feel betrayed. On some level, she felt that way but since the man who raised her was dead and her mother, lacking any moral character, wouldn't know the truth if it stepped out of her Ferragamo handbag, wouldn't tell her, she would have to find her answers elsewhere.

She let up on her death grip of Marc's hand since she could no longer feel her fingers and took a calming breath. "Do you think my mother was the reason for their inability to work with one another?"

Brian gave her a look that said he couldn't believe she voiced that question. She rolled her eyes at him much like she had when he said something that irked her when they were children. He smirked at her and winked, making her feel a little bit lighter.

"When my grandfather and Angelo worked together, Mauro was a whelp working his way up in one of the top crime families in

134

Chicago. Yes, the family was into illegal gambling, but they also had legit businesses with pharmaceuticals. Over the years, Mauro's been shifting their family businesses toward more legitimate ventures. When Charles died, giving him full rein of the business dealings, the Mauro family name was synonymous with legitimate drug manufacturing. Since Angelo never married or had children of his own, that he knows of, he began grooming his nephews Silas and Roman to take over." Brian looked between Marc and Melanie before continuing.

Melanie glanced at Marc again when his leg started bobbing up and down a mile a minute, showing his growing agitation. She placed her hand on his thigh to calm him.

"Silas and Roman are a different sort, but I will get back to that in a moment," Brian said, leaning back in, and Melanie followed his movement.

"When Angelo first began to sit in on meetings with Luca, he was known for his icy demeanor in the office and his merciless and somewhat unconscionable dealings with people who crossed his family."

Melanie was horrified by the description of this man and thanked God that she had a father who loved her. He'd lied to her about her parentage all her life, but it didn't erase the fact that he'd treated her and her daughter as though they were his own.

"As Marc stated before, the Mauro family was crippled when Brenda turned state's evidence. Their illegal gambling ring was almost wiped out, but their legitimate side kept the family from sliding into obscurity."

Melanie's mind worked to reconcile her mom's actions then with the woman she knew now. "Why would my mom put her life and the life of her child in jeopardy over a roll in the hay that didn't go her way. My mom is vengeful, but she's also very clever. Do you have any more information about her relationship with this Luca or Angelo?" Brian shook his head, a frown marring his features.

"Do you believe your grandfather would lie to you?" Marc asked Brian, drawing Melanie's attention to him again.

135

Brian stared at Marc for a few seconds and Melanie felt the tension in the room go up a few levels. She was about to step in, saying anything that came to mind, but Brian answered. "I've learned that Luca will give the answer as close to the truth that will serve him the most."

The staredown lasted a couple of seconds more before Marc nodded. "I agree, which is why I wonder, after all this time, why you wouldn't ask him what was between him and Brenda."

"I did early on," Brian replied on an exhale. "He told me he wouldn't tell me until I could do something with it."

"Do you think you can do something with the information now?" Marc asked.

"Where are you going with this?"

"You just revealed that Melanie is either an heir in the Sable family or the only heir of Angelo, the head of the Mauro family." The world slanted sideways then righted itself as Melanie finally grasped what Marc was saying.

"Luca doesn't strike me as a man who would let something like this go unfounded. It's too important. I asked Luca point-blank if he was Melanie's father when he asked me to watch her a year or two after the family was released from WITSEC," Marc said, glancing at Melanie before returning his gaze to Brian. "He told me he wasn't Melanie's father, but it was pretty obvious even at that time that they had shared something more intimate than the employer slash employee relationship shown in the file." Marc placed his hand on Melanie's back and began to rub it in a soothing fashion. It made Melanie wary instead of its intended purpose.

"I think you need to ask Luca again about his relationship with Brenda and why, after all of her vengeful acts against his family as well as other major organizations he had business with, she is still alive," Marc continued.

Melanie listened to most of the conversation between Brian and Marc as she tried to work out for the thousandth time what was driving her mother. It didn't take much to surmise that Brenda was seeking vengeance when she turned state's evidence and then brought

Melanie and Brian together for the specific purpose of gaining leverage over Luca. Melanie just didn't know who was the target of Brenda's retribution. Right now, it looked like it was both Angelo Mauro and Luca Sable.

"What does she have to be angry about..." She stopped, a horrible thought coming to her. "Do you think she was assaulted? It might account for why Luca refused to work with Angelo?"

Brian seemed at a loss at the idea at first, but then his features cleared before his jaw set in determination. I will check the hospital records around that time and a couple of other places. I'll let you know what I find out," he said before returning to their original conversation.

"To answer some of what you asked me, Marc, Luca agreed to help Charles and Angelo get through some of the backlash from what Brenda did, but only if Brenda and whatever family she gained remained alive and safe. Since Luca's money went far and his name went even further, they accepted the help, but I am sure no one in that family, or any of the other families Brenda betrayed, forgot about her. It was one of the reasons why I had to disappear. Of course, my grandfather hoped it could happen without staging my death." Brian glanced up at her, understanding passing between them. "But B.J. is worth it."

Brian paused for a moment as if deciding whether or not to share the next piece of information with them. "Luca set Brenda up." She watched Brian with more intensity, and he actually squirmed before clearing his throat. "When Luca found out that the Grossenbergs were paid by Brenda to put us together he was more than livid. He was ready to feed her to the wolves, but that would mean that anyone associated with her would suffer the same fate." Melanie's skin went clammy at the thought of how close she came to losing her life and her family because of her mother's need for vengeance.

"Your mother didn't hire someone to assassinate me, and if she did, I assume Luca set your mom up to take away some of her security, so she would be more reliant on him to protect her. If she couldn't move under the cover of the FBI, her movements against Luca would be easier to follow. It worked for a while. Brenda's movements didn't seem threatening, but as you know, no one should ever underestimate Brenda. Her new marriage to the homeland security contractor is a concern."

Melanie's mouth was so dry she couldn't talk if she wanted to. It was surreal. This was her life? Daughter of a vengeance-seeking woman and veritable iceman? No. This wasn't her life. This was Brenda's life, and it was leaking onto hers and her children's lives.

"As I said earlier, Luca doesn't know I've been digging into Antonio or him indirectly. If he knows what I do it's because he has his own hackers, and since I haven't been stopped or given a stern talking to yet, I don't believe he knows." Brian let out a long-suffering sigh. "Luca is a family man. Yes, he has made some transgressions that have hurt the people he loves, but I can't deny his acceptance, love, and safety when it comes to me and B.J."

"But Antonio didn't have the opportunity to show you love past the age you supposedly died," she said, hoping to get her point across.

"True, and I've considered that. It was the reason why I started watching him. I watch how he conducts business and how he treats his family. I think I received the better end of the deal," he said, not taking his eyes from hers.

"I'm sorry Brian," she said, feeling for the boy whose youth had been sold and the man who lived with an abbreviated family.

"No need to be sorry. In some ways, this is the life I chose," Brian said, his gaze hooded.

"What do you mean?" Melanie asked, catching the look between Brian and Marc. She wished they'd stop doing that.

Brian didn't look back at her but down at his hand. "Luca gave me a choice. Well, I can see it as a choice, now. Back then it seemed more like an ultimatum. As much as Luca loves his family, he was willing to disassociate himself from me and the Grossenbergs completely. He would have relocated us one last time, and then I would have been out of his life. After some point in time, I might have been able to see you and our children again. I thought we could have worked on maybe having a real relationship." Brian sent her a sheepish look, relaying a great deal in that one expression.

138

"When you told me what you overheard your mom say on the phone about getting rid of Paige, I thought you'd just taken what she'd said out of context. I also wasn't completely sure that it was only hormones that made it so we could hardly keep our hands off each other. Getting my grandfather involved saved our lives. Luca told me it was more than likely that your mother would have found a way to kill Briar... um... Paige."

Brian stopped and took a breath. He must have been feeling extremely emotional to slip like that. He'd only called their daughter Paige since Melanie and Marc had arrived. She reached out, placing her hand on his for a few seconds and squeezing before removing it. They were children. No adult, let alone child, should ever have to make the decisions he did, but his forthright nature was present even then. She was surrounded by good men. Her father, her children's father, her husband, and their extended family gave her plenty to thank God for. Most people got one, maybe two, great loves. She had been given three by the greatest love of her life.

"When I promised to take B.J. while you were in delivery, I hoped the decision I was about to make would also spare Paige's life. So, instead of staying with my adopted parents and constantly wondering how much B.J.'s life would be in jeopardy or how he would be used, I accepted my grandfather's offer and everything that went with it. Including the stipulation never to contact you again." Brian smiled ruefully.

"Luca may consider this a breach in our agreement, but technically you contacted me."

He did have a point, but Melanie knew Luca wouldn't see it that way. It was obvious Luca wanted Brian to stay hidden, and what was more obvious was that Luca was grooming Brian to take his place in the family business. Luca had four children. It was clear that only one of them was interested in taking over the family business, but what were the odds that both his son and *that* son's son would be in competition for the top spot. Both men had their advantages and disadvantages.

Antonio was the publicly recognized, legitimate heir. Brian, though invisible at the moment, had the advantage of knowing more about his opponent than Antonio knew about him, therefore giving Brian an advantage. From what Brian had shared, Luca's hesitance to sign over control to his son was the only sign Antonio had that the transition may not be as smooth as he once assumed. Melanie theorized that it might have been the reason why he was susceptible to Brenda's ploy to obtain proof of Brian's death.

"Your timing in reaching out to me couldn't have been riskier or more fortuitous. Sable Financial isn't the only company going through a transition. There is a power play going on in the Mauro family. Angelo's nephews, Silas and Roman Mauro are quietly working against him and slowly getting rid of any potential competition for head of *that* company. They are clever and leave next to no trail, but people talk and sometimes email and then I have a copy. More than that, I have a good guess of who will be next."

Silas and Roman have been using blackmail, extortion, and other forms of coercion to keep anyone else from stepping forward. They are also reviving the illegal side of the business, but this time it is drug trafficking, which is ideal with their main venture in pharmaceuticals."

"How do you know they aren't secretly doing their uncle's bidding?" Melanie asked.

"Why would Angelo have his nephews undo everything he's worked almost four decades to accomplish?" Brian asked her.

"Greed?" She let out a disgusted sigh. Have you talked to Luca about this?"

"I brought up the subject indirectly as a hypothesis. My grandfather doesn't believe in coincidences so if he has heard anything, he will look into it." Brian looked at both of them and Melanie dreaded what she saw in his eyes.

"Or if it turns out that you are Angelo Mauro's daughter, we could step forward, out in the open and take your mom's leverage away from her as well as possibly Silas' and Roman's," Brian said quietly as if his words could carry on the wind.

"Have you forgotten that my daughter just finished burying her husband? She needs peace and her family beside her, not whatever the fallout from this may cause," Melanie said, angry all over again at her mother and now Brian for suggesting she upend her life even more. "I came here to help keep our family safe, but you want us to throw on bull's-eye T-shirts and step into the fray. What do you get out of it?" Melanie meant the last as a barb. She had an irrational need to see him show some emotion beyond the surface concern. She got more than she bargained for in his response.

"Maybe a real life," Brian said, the mask gone. She was stunned into silence at the stark pain that flashed through them, and she was reminded once again of all of the things she'd had that he was cheated from. She felt selfish and angry on his behalf at the same time. Then those emotions were caught up in the whirlwind of all the other emotions vying for attention.

Afraid she would say something she might regret later, either in Brian's favor or not, Melanie held up her hands in surrender. "You know what? I need a moment," Melanie said as she got up and slowly walked to the edge of the lawn, taking deep breaths.

The beauty of the water was lost on her. All she could see was the past and a woman with eyes the same color as hers trying to destroy everything she held dear and had sacrificed to protect. Melanie swallowed down the anger, and it turned into a fire in her belly.

She wondered what more she might have to give up if she were to get involved. "Know your opponents; study them, and try to stay two steps ahead of them. If you are constantly on the defense, you've already lost," her father used to say when they played board games together. It frustrated her at first that he would never let her win, but the first time she won at chess, she knew she had beaten him fair and square. She recited his words back to him, and he smiled with pride. The game and the words had stuck.

She felt someone come up behind her, a breeze carrying their scent to her. She took a deep breath and allowed the dock and water to come into focus. "We didn't come here to pick a fight. I just

141

wanted to warn Brian about Antonio and Brenda, and avoid his presence for a while."

Strong arms came around her, and she sank into the familiar physique of her husband. "I think you are lying to yourself. You know I could have gotten a note to Luca about Antonio and Brenda," Marc whispered in her ear. "I think this was a long, overdue excuse to see the boy you shared a traumatic past with and your son. The situation with Antonio just gave you the courage to do it."

Melanie turned in his arms. "But Brian was right. By coming here we have put our family at risk, and now that we've found out about my parentage, there is no way to put that knowledge back in the box. If Brenda finds out that Brian is still alive, she still may try to hold it over our heads. Faking one's death comes with some unlawful companions, you know... like fraud," she said, her voice rising slightly in panic even after the resolve she had seconds before.

Marc placed his hands on either side of her face, cutting off her peripheral vision. All she could see was the warmth and love in his beautiful brown eyes. He read her now as he had been able to for years. "This civil war between your mom and these influential families has been going on for decades. I'm sure Luca has a plan if it is discovered that Brian is alive. I think he's had one in place for a long time in the event he has Brian take over for him. If you decide to join the fight"—he paused to kiss her right cheek then her left—"we not only have all the most important pieces of this game with you, Brian, B.J. and Paige being heirs to prestigious Italian families in Chicago, we have God." He kissed her nose before skimming his fingertips across her forehead and removing the bangs from her eyes. She sighed as he leaned in and placed his forehead against hers. "We will pray to see if it's time to step into the fray or sit back and watch them destroy themselves. Meanwhile, come back to the table, so Brian can finish telling you about Angelo Mauro's nephews, Tweedledee and Tweedledemon." She groaned at Marc's extremely bad joke but stopped him from pulling her back toward the table.

"Does it bother you that I might be Luca's daughter?" she asked, looking down at Marc's shoulder.

"That you may be heir to millions?" His voice sparkled with laughter.

"That I may have been manipulated into having children with my nephew." The words almost made her gag as they left her mouth.

Marc placed a finger under her chin to raise her face so her eyes would meet his. "That is on your mother." His eyes held hers while he wrapped his arms around her, pulling her in closer. "Whether or not you share DNA with Luca and Brian doesn't change the beautiful, intelligent, generous and loving person you are," Marc said, rubbing his hands up and down her back, slowly drawing her even farther into his space while he weaved a web of intimacy around them with his voice. "I was proud to call you mine when we first took our vows, and I am even more proud today," he said as his lips descended toward hers.

"Yeah?" she whispered, feeling his breath.

"Yeah, baby," he murmured against her lips before giving her one of the sweetest kisses she'd ever experienced, and Marc was good at delivering sweet kisses. Marc was good at all kinds of kissing. She immediately got lost in the feel of him, coming up on the balls of her feet and wrapping her arms around his neck as she usually did to keep him close and keep herself from melting to the ground.

The sound of a throat clearing reminded Melanie of her surroundings, and she lowered herself back down and began to unwrap her arms, but Marc placed a hand behind her head to keep her in place for a few more seconds. When he finally let her go, she was a little light-headed and leaned into him, her cheek resting on his chest. She opened her eyes to see Brian watching them, and she smiled, a little embarrassed by their display. Brian returned her smile but the longing in his eyes was clear. Her heart squeezed at the thought that he might never get to experience such happiness. It seemed her heart just made her decision for her.

She allowed Marc to turn her back to the deck. "I love you," she whispered in his ear after a few steps.

Marc looked at her, his eyes dark. "Good thing because I will stay just a little closer than usual while we are here."

Melanie stopped to look at him more carefully.

"Marcus Miller, are you jealous?" she asked, teasing him.

"There's no need for me to be jealous. He can make all the goo-goo eyes he wants at you. We are married and committed to one another. I know what I have, and I am not about to give it up." Marc punctuated the statement with a quick peck on her lips.

"Wait. He doesn't make goo-goo eyes," she denied.

"They follow you around whatever room the two of you are in. I, more than most, know how beautiful you are, added to that is the fact that he hasn't seen you since the two of you had a synthesized hormonally charged childhood affair. What man wouldn't be a little blown away by that? All I'm saying is I understand, but I don't have to enjoy it." Marc gave her a little squeeze, and she had to press her lips together to keep from smiling or laughing as they walked back to Brian.

Synthesized hormonally charged childhood affair? Oh yeah, he was jealous.

***

"Melanie, are you ready?"

Melanie looked around to see that they were one of the last to disembark. She raised up from Marc's chest. She didn't know she'd been so deep in thought.

"Um, yeah," she murmured as she stood and moved into the aisle. She shook off her thoughts. They had a few more days of travel before she could hold Gladys and Paige in her arms.

The pictures of Brian and B.J. were beginning to burn a hole in her proverbial pocket, and she was already rehearsing how she would tell Paige about her father and brother. If Melanie's trip taught her nothing else, it brought home the importance of being completely honest with her girls and being with her girls.

They took a cab to the bus station and sat eating breakfast across the street while they waited for the bus bound for Albuquerque, New Mexico to begin boarding.

"I know we've talked about it before, and I know being close to your family is important, but I was wondering, if Paige is averse to moving, would you reconsider putting in for a transfer?"

"To Los Angeles?" Marc asked, setting down his fork.

"Or anywhere close to the region," she said, trying to compromise.

He stared at her for a few seconds before speaking. "I would do anything for you. The only reason I was averse to moving before was because I felt you needed a mother figure, and you and my mother get along very well." He paused for a moment, not looking away from her. "On the other hand, Paige may want a change of scenery. Her church family is tight, but there's no harm in asking. I'm sure Mom would love another girl to love on," he said, going back to his plate.

"What about all of the stuff with the Sables and Mauros? I don't want that coming back on your family."

"If we decide to do something about the Mauros, we will be covered by God because we won't move without God," he said, eyebrows raised.

"Absolutely. Just feeling jittery now that we are so close to our girls, and I've decided to tell Paige about Brian," she said, going back to her breakfast.

"I think they will just be happy we're back," Marc replied.

"Do you think Paige will forgive me for not being there when she needed me most?"

"Yes. You never know. It may have been best that you weren't there to coddle her. It isn't how I would have planned it, but if she can embrace God during this then she can trust her relationship with Him even more."

"I don't understand." Melanie couldn't help the frown. She didn't like how it sounded so far.

"Do you think you might have questioned, even a little bit, whether you heard God right if you waited obediently to get married like she did and within four months you were burying your husband?" Marc looked at her. She knew he caught every nuance of her reaction which went from confusion to deep sorrow.

145

"I think it's good she got to spend some alone time with God before the Tatum family came back for Thanksgiving," Marc said before taking another bite.

"Maybe," she mumbled. She wasn't sure. "I still wish we could have made it back for Thanksgiving."

"I know, baby, but we will be there through Christmas, and you can spoil both of your girls rotten," Marc replied, not trying to hide his smile.

Her heart lightened, and she smiled back. "Yes, I can. Yes, I can."

Chapter 14

Grace touched the screen on her dash notifying her of the incoming call.

"Yes?"

"It looks like they're headed back." The male voice came through the speakers of her C- Class Mercedes AMG convertible, and she pressed the button to raise its roof.

"Hold." She used the one word, not comfortable with having to say too much on calls such as this. As soon as the top sealed, she spoke again, "Continue."

"Marc's credit card came up in a rental car company in Albuquerque, New Mexico this afternoon. As soon as they gas up I should be able to tell you where they're headed."

Grace smiled to herself and slowed for the light. She had a good idea where they were headed, and it was about time. This was the first good news in months. She'd very nicely asked her husband if he could make inquiries for her when Marc and Melanie crossed the border into Canada. He hadn't been able to come up with anything, which had grown into a point of contention between them.

Two days ago, Ross came home with what he called wonderful news and her favorite chocolates. Marc and Melanie had been detected crossing the Canadian border back into the United States from Winnipeg. She feigned a happy surprise since she'd gotten the news a couple of hours before. Her original response was one of disgust. On the maps she'd read over, Winnipeg didn't look as though it was

Eastern or Western Canada, though it was considered part of Western Canada to those familiar with the area. They'd masked their direction well.

If only Ross hadn't had to organize the presentation so he could bid on the former military project in Costa Rica. She could have convinced him to take her on a tour of the bigger cities in Canada. As it was, she'd spent a week in Costa Rica. It was a beautiful place, but she was unable to concentrate on the host's accommodations or the beach right outside of their villa. With suspect sightings of Melanie all over Canada, then nothing at all, Grace had become very cautious and more than a little paranoid.

So far, all she knew was that Marc and Mel stayed in Sandy Lake, Ontario for three days before catching their flight back to the States. Neither their passports nor their credit cards were used since they entered Canada the previous month.

Grace knew she was missing something. They had either been preparing a long time for the trip and didn't tell her what they were planning or they left on the fly and received some help from someone outside of her circle of influence. How did a teacher and an FBI agent have the cash to travel for months and why would they do so without staying in touch with their family? Unless, of course, the family was lying to her.

"Thank you. Continue to update me."

"Will do," the voice sounded one more time before the call ended.

Grace made a U-turn. She was originally headed home after a long morning of grooming and pampering. She would get takeout from Ross' favorite Italian restaurant, light a fire, and in the morning, she would ask her husband the tiny favor of flying them to Los Angeles for a few days. She had an overwhelming desire to see her girls. They could have an impromptu family reunion between holidays.

Grace's heart did a little skip of excitement, surprising her. She couldn't remember the last time she was excited about anything except maybe when Antonio agreed to help her get the information she wanted on Brian's remains.

Maybe she would even do some online Christmas shopping. Once Ross said yes, of course.

Oh yes, she was looking forward to this. She would finally get the answers she was looking for because none of her girls had learned to lie to her face successfully.

***

Grace slid home the zipper on her suitcase before reaching over for her ringing phone. She paused to check the caller ID   and blanched. She silenced the ringing but didn't connect the call. Ears alert, she stopped to track her husband's footsteps throughout the downstairs floor. Once she was certain that he was walking toward his study, she pulled her burner phone out of the purse in her closet and went into the bathroom.

Turning on the phone she saw that she had five missed calls and two texts. The first text from the number she was about to call read:

Are you having problems?

The second read:

Need more energy? Call now!

She didn't have to listen to the voicemails. She could tell from the number and texts that whatever Antonio needed to talk to her about wasn't good. The code they used was a simple one just in case her husband ever found her phone. The actual message was the last two words of the text and usually sounded like spam.

The phone rang only once. "You called?" Grace said, turning on the faucet and moving closer to the commode.

"I got blocked." Antonio's angry voice came over the line.

"I need you to elaborate, but you'll have to do it in one minute."

"I was denied in my request to receive any of my child's remains. I followed your instructions and used the back channels. I contacted the number you gave me, and the man said there shouldn't be an issue once I gave him proof of parentage."

"Yesterday I got a letter stating that I had no claim nor authority to Brian's remains. Due to the fact that I signed over my rights at the time

149

of his adoption, I could not be given access to Brian's remains unless it was authorized by Luca Sable."

"Do you know if they contacted your father?" Brenda asked, leaning against the bathroom wall farthest from the door.

"They did, and he denied me access," Antonio said in an angry hiss. She, on the other hand, could barely contain her glee. Luca was hiding something. Why would he deny his son access to his own grandson's remains unless there was a good chance they weren't Brian's remains.

"It's okay. I may have something better. I'll let you know in a couple of days. Meanwhile, chin up. By denying you the remains of your son, Luca is showing his hand. Why don't you go and ask him why he would do such a thing," Grace suggested, knowing it was exactly what Antonio wanted to do.

"I think I will," he said as if it weren't her idea.

"We'll talk in a few days," she said, hearing movement in the bedroom.

"Okay."

The line went dead, and she set the phone down before flushing the toilet and washing her hands. She couldn't walk out with the phone in her hand, but she didn't want to leave it in the restroom. She unbuttoned her wide-leg pants and slipped the phone in the elastic of her thigh high stockings.

She walked out of the bathroom rubbing lotion into her hands. Ross was sitting on the edge of the bed waiting for her. She blinked at him. "I think I got everything." She gestured to the piece of luggage still sitting on the bed. "How about you? Did you get the paperwork you were looking for?"

Ross merely nodded, giving her a speculative look. "Were you talking to someone in the bathroom?" He made a show of looking at her hands.

"Noooo." She drew out the one word giving him back a look of confusion before letting her features clear as though she'd just realized something. She hesitated for a moment before speaking, wanting to convince him that she was reluctant to tell him what she was doing.

"As you know, it's been a while since I've seen my girls. And though I thought I had a good relationship with Melanie and Gladys, Melanie up and left the country without giving me a call. With Paige, I'm not sure where I stand, especially after not being able to comfort her during the funeral. I need to see them to make sure they are all right and not in trouble, but I also know it might get tense, so I was, well…" She threw in a self-conscious shrug for good measure. "I was giving myself a pep talk. You know like, 'If things go wrong, it will just be a few days.'" She gave him a self-deprecating chuckle.

Her husband's eyes grew warm, and he got up to stand in front of her. He drew her into a hug. "A mother's love. There is nothing like it." He rubbed her back then grasped her waist before leaning back to give her a quick kiss. "You are adorable when you're self-conscious. But there is no need. Love always wins out," he said before giving her another quick kiss. He set her aside.

"I'm going to take care of a little business myself, then we can go," he said, pointedly looking behind her at the open bathroom door.

She smiled back at him wishing he hadn't just given her a very loving pat down and wasn't going into the bathroom to check for the phone he believed she was talking into. "Okay, I'll meet you downstairs." She turned and picked up her bag from the bed and made sure to keep the smile on her face until she cleared the landing between the flights of stairs.

Chapter 15

Paige took another deep breath because she could. Her home was quiet, and the space that felt almost claustrophobic, even a week before, was now quiet and once again more than enough space for her and Gladys to tromp around in.

It seemed, though, that Gladys had gotten used to being in constant proximity with others because she all but followed Paige around when she was home. At first, Paige thought it was because Gladys was still concerned about how heavily she was grieving. Soon it became apparent that Gladys missed the sound of a bigger family.

"Isn't it just you, Mel, and Marc most of the time?" Paige asked when Gladys bumped into her in the hall a couple of days before when Paige changed direction at the last minute.

"Yes, but they were always talking to me or each other or listening to music and dancing around or watching something on television. It was rarely quiet like it is here. It's not that I don't like the quiet here." Gladys hastened to say. "I am just used to there being more sound in the background," Gladys finished with a shrug.

Paige had felt a twinge of regret at how Gladys' life had been upended, but it wasn't her decision to separate Gladys from Melanie and Marc for months.

Even now as she sat snuggled up next to her daughter watching an action-adventure movie marathon, she hoped Mel and Marc would be back before Christmas. Not because she didn't know how to handle a child during the upcoming holiday season, but because Gladys had been so disappointed that Mel wasn't able to be back by Thanksgiving. Paige didn't know what spending Christmas without Mel and Marc would do to her. Paige was surprised the thought hadn't occurred to her before then stopped herself from stepping back into the guilt vortex that pulled her into a slump.

Richard and Victoria mentioned the possibility of coming to Los Angeles for Christmas. Maybe Paige could see what Mason and Vivian were doing for the holiday. Vivian always could make Gladys smile. Paige thought it would be fun to spend the day watching the girls open their presents. She looked around the living room that should probably already have a Christmas tree with a few presents underneath it and inwardly shivered at the thought of spending Christmas without Brandon in their home.

It was supposed to be a year of firsts. Well, it was in a way. It was her first Thanksgiving as a widow and it would be her first Christmas and New Year's Day as one too. Widow. What a strange word. Without knowing the description, one might think of window, which to her spoke of a possibility to be open to the outside world, an escape, a way of flying away from one's troubles. That was obviously the wrong train of thought because she couldn't escape. She couldn't fly, run, or walk away from her pain or the longing that constantly surrounded her. All she could do was face it and hope that some of the memories made her smile. For the more painful thoughts, she would imagine herself crawling onto her Heavenly Father's lap, placing her arms around his huge neck, and crying her heart out. It was so much more comforting than the anger.

Gladys shifted next to her, bringing Paige out of her thoughts. She looked down at her daughter and felt her heart grow another size. The big brown curls framing a heart-shaped face that currently held a rapt expression was the perfect package for the little girl with such a lovely heart. The possessive and protectiveness that swelled up in Paige startled her a little. She would hunt down anyone who dared to touch her daughters in any way except to show them loving kindness. In this one respect, Paige was thankful for how things had turned out with her sister, er, mother. It had given her the much-needed time to get to know her daughter, and she admitted that it would have been much harder to pull herself out of her depression if she didn't have Gladys to keep her on a routine.

Gladys shifted her pajamed feet, drawing Paige's eyes down to the blanket covering them. She hadn't spent a day purposed for lounging in her pajamas in a long time. It was more than nice. It was special. She hugged her child to her briefly because she just couldn't contain the love in her heart. Gladys looked up then smiled when it was clear that Paige didn't want anything more than to hold and snuggle closer.

"Can we make cookies after this one's over?" Gladys asked, staring at the screen.

Paige looked at the half-full plates and cups, displaying the remnants of their breakfast of French toast and bacon; the snack of grapes, apples, and cheese; and the lunch of chicken wings, coleslaw, and fries delivered from the restaurant a few blocks away. Paige would have laughed at the child's endless appetite if it didn't remind her of her metabolism at that age.

"Are you sure it won't make you sick? We still have dinner," Paige asked more as a warning than a question.

"We could treat it like dessert," Gladys said as if she'd just come up with a great idea.

Paige nodded her agreement. "Dessert, it is." She reached for her cup of apple cider just as the doorbell rang. Paige froze for a moment then looked down at Gladys, who had also stopped straightening her covers and looked between Paige and the direction of the door.

As Paige got up she didn't ask her daughter if she knew who it was. It was pretty obvious from Gladys' expression she wasn't expecting anyone. On the way to the door, Paige checked her phone laying on the kitchen counter to see if she had any missed calls or texts. There was one.

Mel: Open the door, please.

Paige's heart skipped a beat, but her feet suddenly grew roots. Mel was back. That brought with it so many changes, and not all of them good.

"Mati?" Gladys' voice pulled her out of her momentary stupor.

154

Paige hid her immediate feelings of panic behind a forced smile and turned to Gladys. "I think cookies might have to wait," she responded as she resumed walking to the door and looked through the peephole at Mel and Marc standing on her doorstep.

"Why?" Gladys asked, and Paige heard the girl get up from the couch as she opened the door.

Paige smiled at Mel and Marc and prepared herself for the squeal that would come from Gladys when she realized who was on the other side of the door. It came high and long as Gladys launched herself at the two. Paige stepped aside and back so the family didn't have to let go of one another as they came through the door. Paige was both happy and desolate. *How was that possible?* These warring emotions were getting old.

Mel looked up at her over Gladys' head and gave her a warm smile. It caused just a little bit of the panic from seconds before to recede. When Gladys finally let go of Mel, she walked over to Paige and wrapped her up in the embrace Paige had needed for months. Feeling the familiar weight against her as Mel's arms tightened around her, Paige wanted to give in to tears that had waited at the backs of her eyes and throat just for this moment. Paige couldn't give in to them though. If she did, they would take over like a tidal wave, and there was no telling how long it would take before they stopped. This was supposed to be a happy occasion. Mel and Marc were back safe and sound from wherever they had gone, and Gladys would get her wish for Christmas. This was good, and if Paige kept telling herself that, it may get easier to believe.

"Hey, baby girl. I'm so so sorry. I apologize for not being here when you needed me most. I will do whatever I can to make it up to you," Mel said quietly in her ear before squeezing her infinitesimally tighter. Paige wondered if this would be a good time to tell her that one way to make that happen was to leave Gladys with her, but when Mel finally loosened her grip and leaned back to look at Paige it was with such love in her tear-filled eyes Paige figured the request could wait.

When Mel finally let Paige go, Marc was right there to take her place. "Hiya, kid," Marc said, enveloping her in his strong arms, and she had to fight all over again to keep her composure. It slipped a little when he rubbed her back and said, "We got you now. You don't have to go through any more of this on your own."

Paige clamped down on the sob that wanted to escape but didn't slip from his arms without the liquid already pooling around her eyelids, spilling over. She quickly wiped her eyes and walked into the living room to start straightening up.

"Come, sit down. Gladys and I were having a movie marathon day," Paige said, removing the blankets from the couch and taking them to the bedroom where she folded them into tight squares while she regained some control. When she returned to the living room, the dirty dishes had been cleared from the coffee table, and Mel was in the kitchen at the sink. Marc was straightening the pillows and cushions while Gladys opened the curtains, and just like that, Paige's quiet Saturday was over.

As Gladys passed Paige on her way to the kitchen, she grabbed her hand and squeezed, her excitement palpable. Paige smiled at Gladys' happiness, but once Gladys looked away, she let it fall, not noticing that Marc was watching her. She could tell he witnessed her true feelings because his features became troubled. She gave him a sardonic smile. He would find out soon enough. There was no need to hide the fact that she was afraid that they would take one of her lifelines away.

He moved toward her, and she stepped back, not wanting to be touched. He stopped, holding up his hands. "I meant what I said. We won't leave you alone to deal with your pain and grieving anymore." She looked into his eyes and saw his determination. She wanted to believe him, but she didn't even know where he'd been up until ten minutes ago. Paige gave him what he wanted in the form of a nod then went in the kitchen to help Mel.

Paige stood next to Mel who was soaping dishes in the sink. "I have a dishwasher for that."

"I know. I just needed to do something with my hands otherwise I would still be hugging you and Gladys. No doubt we would probably be surrounded by a puddle of tears in your living room right now." Melanie lifted a soapy hand out of the water and clasped Paige's wrist.

156

"I missed you two so much. You have no idea. I have so much to tell you."

"Like where you've been for the last five months after practically dropping Gladys at Brandon's and my door while he fought and lost his bout with cancer?" Paige gave Mel an unwavering stare.

"Yes," Mel said, without looking away.

"Good," Paige said, picking up a cloth to dry the dishes with.

"And more," Mel said, and Paige could see from her peripheral vision that Melanie was still staring at her.

"Even better," Paige said quietly.

"Could I hug you again?" Mel asked.

"I'm not sure that would be a good idea." Paige's voice hitched as she dried a plate. "You were right about the puddle of tears. They are too close to the surface."

Mel was quiet for a moment causing Paige to look at her. "Fair enough, but later…"

"Later," Paige responded, feeling the lump in her throat grow to an uncomfortable size.

"Meanwhile, I was wondering what you would think of us spending Christmas and New Year's together. I didn't know if you already made plans with Brandon's family, Vivian, and Mason or any of the number of friends and adopted families you have," Mel said, sticking her hands back in the water.

Paige paused in the midst of drying a glass for a couple of seconds before resuming. Paige looked down at the glass in her hand and worked to bring her heart rate down. She concentrated on erasing any wet spots on the outside of the glass before taking a deep breath. She had been given a reprieve. She wouldn't have to spend Christmas by herself.

"I didn't have any concrete plans made. Vivian and Mason might come back this way, but we haven't discussed anything," Paige said, not trusting herself to say more without bursting into sobs.

"It would be nice to see Mason again. Is he still seeing that woman he was dating earlier this year?" Mel asked.

Paige was ashamed to admit that she hadn't given Mason's personal life much thought. She'd heard a passing comment from Vivian but nothing since Brandon's funeral or the weeks after they'd all returned from Victoria and Richard's. She found she was mildly curious about the woman, and if she was happy Mason had given his life to Christ, whoever she was, she would benefit from Mason's newfound relationship with God. She felt a small pang of emotion, but it was so fleeting, she didn't have enough time to analyze it.

"I don't know. I should ask him the next time we talk," Paige said distractedly.

"How's Vivian?" Mel asked, and Paige was grateful for the change of subject.

"I think she's good. She and Gladys are thick as thieves." Paige sent Mel a sheepish look. "I haven't had a chance to talk to her lately. She's been a little standoffish these last few weeks. I haven't really been available..." Paige trailed off not wanting to talk about the distance that had grown between her and Vivian.

Paige went back to concentrating on drying the dishes that had been placed in her drying rack, so she didn't notice when Mel wiped her hands and moved behind her. Her mother's arms came around her and Mel whispered in her ear. "I don't care if we end up using the towels to dry our eyes instead of the dishes. I need to hug you, baby."

Paige stiffened as she tried to fight the pull to sink into her mother's hold. She'd had to pull herself up so many times over the last few months. After Ava had left the first time, she'd had to talk herself into getting out of bed, making breakfast for herself and Gladys, take Gladys to school, muster up interest in her work, which didn't happen much, pick up Gladys, and listen with some type of comprehension to her child, then all she wanted to do was stay in that place of oblivion. She dug deep for the anger she'd felt even weeks before so she could stave off the tears but it was no use.

"Please," Paige pleaded as she tried to hold on to what little composure she had left. "I don't want Gladys to witness me breaking down again," she said in a rush, while she held on to Mel's forearms like a lifeline. "She's been..." Paige felt ashamed by the betrayal of her body that silently shook in her mother's arms. "Worried. She's been worried." Paige took a deep breath and forced her body to obey her.

Paige locked her knees to keep herself up. "To tell you the truth, I'm worried. It hurts so much to be away from him. I still wake up most mornings thinking he will be there lying on the pillow next to me, but once my eyes open it all comes flooding back, and there goes the first hour." She shook her head half in disgust and half in helplessness. "I know. I know it's only been a couple of months, but I want it to stop. I want him back." The last ended on a sob, and she turned in her mother's arms and let the dam open.

She heard Mel's soft shushing sounds as her arms enfolded her tighter. Mel began to rock her softly before her fierce prayer began to ring in Paige's ear.

Dear Heavenly Father, I'm counting on you to keep your promise. I can only do so much, but You—You can do all things. I need you to heal my baby girl. I need You to keep Your promise to give her peace and joy for her mourning. To make her whole again.

She is not some wayward soul who has denied you or lost their way. So if it grieves you that anyone would lose their soul, I know you have found a way to give even them an opportunity to come to You. What more would you do for a child of yours who is in such pain? She loves you, and she needs You so much now. I pray that you not only hear her and my cries, but that you give her the peace that she needs to heal. Give her the words she needs to hear, so she knows she will be all right. Give her Your joy so she has the strength to see this through and help others. She is my child, my heart, and it crushes me to see her this way. In Jesus' name. Amen.

Mel's words and the fierceness behind them moved Paige greatly. Realization came over her like a comfortable garment. She wasn't alone. She had family, and they were standing in the gap for her. She could lean on her mother. "I needed you, Mel. I needed you."

She lost what control she'd regained, for a moment, and held on to Mel as if her life depended on it. Her body shook, and the sobs weren't as quiet, but there was a hopefulness that began to fill up that desolate place, and as the tears of despair continued to flow out, she finally felt her heart begin to lift a little. She had her own family with her.

She didn't know when Marc's arms encircled her, but the warmth was a comfort she welcomed.

"We're here," Marc whispered.

"Yes," Paige choked out.

"It'll get easier," Mel said.

"It just did," Paige said and meant it.

Paige felt more weight join the arms already around her and opened her eyes to see Gladys peeking at her.

"Are you okay, Mati?" Gladys asked, her voice small and a little wary. The poor child had been through so much. She was probably afraid her mother would relapse and have to be sedated all over again.

"Yes. Just letting go of a little more pain," Paige said, trying to reassure her. She kissed Gladys' forehead and squeezed her with her free arm.

"I told Viv you would be okay. I told her God wouldn't let you down," Gladys said.

"I think He heard your prayers too," Paige said after sniffing with the remnants of the torrent of tears. Her body shuddered with a sigh.

"You do?" Gladys asked shyly.

"Of course. He sent just what I needed," Paige said, looking at Mel.

"Yeah. Ma is like a mother to everyone," Gladys said.

Paige and Mel shared a look, and Marc squeezed them both before letting them go.

"Marc and I've been traveling all day. I was wondering if we could call in some dinner," Mel said, letting go of Paige as well. Paige could see from the change in their demeanor that food would be the excuse used for them all to sit at the table where Mel and Marc could watch her and Gladys' reactions.

"Sure," Paige said in agreement. "I'm just going to shower and change. I'm good with anything you choose. Gladys knows where the menus are." Paige headed down the hall to her bedroom. She took some clothes from a drawer and glanced up when she heard her phone buzz where it lay on the corner of the dresser. She checked it, noticing she'd missed six calls. Two from Victoria, one from Carman. *Oh, she needed to call her back.* One from Ava, obviously checking up on her. One from Mason. Paige looked to see what time he called and considered delaying her shower to listen to his voicemail, but this was family time. She would listen to the voicemails as she got dressed. Then if there was nothing imperative, she promised herself she would call Mason before she went to sleep that night.

The last missed call was from a number she didn't recognize, so she gave it no mind before making her way into the bathroom.

Twenty minutes later, Paige exited the bathroom feeling lighter than she had in weeks. Even being surrounded by Brandon and her family for Thanksgiving hadn't brought her this level of comfort.

Paige pressed the button on her phone to play the voicemails through her phone's speaker while she finished drying and oiling her skin. The urgency in Victoria's voice made her pause briefly in toweling off.

"Hi, Paige. I hope you've recovered from the crowd that squeezed into your home for Thanksgiving. I still wish you'd taken me up on providing dinner for you all, so you weren't left with so much work. Anyhow." Paige could see Victoria waving her hand in dismissal of her last statement. "That's not what I was calling to discuss. It's a lot more important. I just learned that Melanie and Marc are headed back your way." *How did Victoria know before she did? Had she been tracking Mel?*

"I'll tell you how I know later, but that isn't the issue. Grace knows too. Grace has been tracking Mel too because she's headed to Los Angeles. Boy, I hope you get this message soon," Victoria said more to herself than over the line. "Flight 1077 from Washington will arrive in Los Angeles just past midnight. Knowing her, Grace, who looks to be accompanied by her husband Ross, might come straight to you if she thinks Melanie and Marc are there." There was a short pause before she continued. "Just give me a call so I know you got this before Grace arrives. Richard and I will be on the next flight if you need us… for support. I will keep my phone on, so call at any time."

161

Paige hadn't noticed she stopped moving until the phone prompted her to either save or delete the voicemail. She saved it and listened to the next couple of voicemails in a haze as she finished getting dressed, only coming out of it when Mason's voice came over the line.

"Hey, Paige, it's your friendly out-of-the-neighborhood pest. Just calling to see if you've recovered from Thanksgiving yet. I hope you haven't worn yourself out scrubbing the oven or stove. I know how you like things clean. Actually, whenever you are feeling like you need to clean up something you can come to Chicago. Just kidding... maybe.

"Anyway. I also called because I got a weird message from Richard asking me if you might have come here with Gladys after the holiday. He sounded like he was hoping that was the case. Do you know what's going on? Call me when you get this. Gladys told Vivian that you two might have an action-movie marathon day today. I hope so. I like the thought of you vegging out. Makes you sound human." Mason's chuckle came over the line letting her know that he was teasing her. He was so weird. "All right. I'll talk to you later, I hope." His voice sobered, and Paige found herself pausing again as she slipped her socks on.

"It was good to see you, Paige. Please take care of yourself. I'm praying for you. I will always pray. For you." There was a brief pause before he finished. "Talk to you later." Then the line disconnected.

Hmm, Paige thought to herself. *That was a different moment there.* She shrugged it off as the next thought came in. *What was he talking about regarding Richard? This was all too odd for her.* She hung up before the last voicemail message could play and took her phone with her into the kitchen.

"Mel, I just listened to a message from Victoria. She said Grace is on her way here with her husband." She held up her phone to the group sitting at the table, looking at Mel and Marc who had given each other a look. "She said they should arrive around midnight. Do you know anything about this? It sounded like they were coming here specifically for you and Marc. You said Grace's husband did something with Homeland Security." Paige stopped before what she was saying could sound like accusations.

162

Mel's shoulders visibly dropped. "Come, sit down." She waved Paige over.

Paige hesitated for a moment. Did she want to know what was going on? She was the one who had gotten on Melanie about keeping secrets, but was she ready to hear whatever just darkened Marc's eyes? She forced herself to move forward and sit at the table.

"Grandma's coming?" Gladys asked, and Paige couldn't tell if she was excited about the prospect or worried.

"What is going on?" Paige asked more as a demand for information than anything else.

"Grace is coming to ask us where we've been," Mel said after a long breath. "We aren't sure we want her to know just yet."

Paige looked between Mel and Marc, but Marc spoke before she could.

"Melanie and I want to tell you and Gladys where we've been. It's one of the reasons why we've come straight here."

"Besides the fact that we missed you so much," Mel said chiming in.

"The problem is, if we tell you before Grace gets here you won't have deniability, and please forgive me for saying this, but you, Paige, are a very bad liar."

Since Paige didn't have much recent experience, she wasn't insulted at all. "Why do we even have to see them? Why can't we just go somewhere until they give up and leave town?" Paige said, knowing the idea was a shot in the dark. Grace had never just given up on anything.

Marc just gave her a look. "If she is on her way here already, we know she's been tracking us since we came back into the country."

"So, she knows you left the country?" Paige asked, enthralled by the fact that they were able to evade Grace as long as they had. "What does Ross do again?"

"He's a contractor for Homeland Security. It wouldn't take much to get a favor or two," Marc said.

"So, you knew they could track you if you left the country?" Paige said.

163

"They tracked us inside of the country," Marc said.

"Was she the reason you left?"

"Most of it. Yes."

"Can you tell me where you went once you were out of the country? Grace knows *that* already, right?" Paige asked, trying to feel her way around the edges.

"We went to Canada," Mel said then shut her mouth. Paige watched her for a moment. She had a hard time containing her curiosity but knowing she would be given more information later helped.

"Victoria and Richard offered to come," Paige said and watched Mel and Marc exchange glances once again.

Mel placed her hands on the table before settling her gaze on Paige. "Do you trust Victoria?"

Paige gave the question the consideration it deserved before answering. The fact that Victoria didn't just hop on a plane as soon as she found out that Mel and Marc were heading her way, or Grace, for that matter, gave Paige the confidence she needed to say that Victoria was looking out for her best interests.

"Yes," Paige said without wavering.

"Do you know what the Branchetts were doing with Antonio Sable?" Mel asked.

"Victoria told me that she and Richard went to see Antonio Sable to see if he could answer some questions they had after finding files about Brian. Antonio told them that he had some questions about Brian's remains and wanted to talk to you. When you disappeared, he wanted to see me or Gladys, so they acted as buffers to make sure it happened in a controlled environment.

"By the end of the visit, though, Victoria told me that Antonio was being blackmailed by Grace, who has been pressuring him to inquire about Brian's remains," Paige said, hoping she hadn't forgotten anything through the haze of the summer.

"Blackmail? What does she have on him?" Mel asked.

Paige glanced over at Gladys, who was listening as intently as Mel and Marc were. She swallowed and looked back at Mel. "Um, we might need to talk about that later."

Gladys threw her arms up in the air. "Really? I'm thirteen. I'm not a little girl anymore. I can take it."

Paige looked at Mel and Marc who nodded their heads. She was surprised at their acquiescence but continued. "Victoria obtained copies of pictures of Antonio and Grace in compromising positions. Antonio confirmed their authenticity and the fact that Grace threatened to send them to his family if he didn't cooperate and help her find you," Paige said, noting the face both Mel and Marc made.

Gladys looked a little confused at first, but Mel's next exclamation cleared things up.

"Antonio and Grace?" Mel said as if she tasted something sour.

"But she's married," Gladys said, sounding both confused and dismayed by the thought. "I thought she loved Grandpa Ross."

Paige gave Gladys an apologetic look. She didn't want to be the one to cloud her idealism. It was too hard to come by. "We aren't sure when it happened. It could have happened way before Grace and Ross met. They just got married New Year's Day." Paige had to stop. She was starting to feel a little disgusted by her attempt to defend Grace. She wondered what put the look on Mel's face though.

She quirked a brow at Mel, but the woman shook her head slightly.

"She's getting desperate and a desperate Grace is a dangerous Grace. Do you think we should just tell her?"

"We haven't tried to figure out all of the repercussions. Most likely she already has a plan for what she will do if she finds out the truth, then we lose our advantage," Marc replied.

"So, why did we leave and stay gone so long?" Mel asked him.

Paige felt like she was sitting on the sidelines of a rehearsal for a play. Things weren't fully played out, but you could kind of see where things were going.

"We were looking for Brian as well," Mel suggested.

"Why? What personal reason would we have for trying to find out whether Brian is alive?"

Paige watched the two go back and forth for a moment before making a suggestion of her own.

"How about Brandon's sickness got you thinking about family medical history, and you wanted to check Brian's records and maybe with Brian himself to make sure that there wasn't anything that may come up later, but you couldn't."

"Wait." Gladys put her hand up as if she wanted to be called on in class. "Is Brian alive?"

Gladys asked the question that everyone had been avoiding. The kitchen went still and just like that, Paige knew. She knew what Mel and Marc had been doing for the last five months.

Paige made eye contact with Mel, and her mother's eyes widened slightly, showing that she realized they'd already said too much. Paige's heartbeat sped up. Brian was alive? Brian was alive. She wanted to know everything, and she was afraid of knowing anything. *What repercussions?*

"Paige." Mel placed a hand on hers, interrupting the torrent of thoughts taking over her mind. "I think you should call Victoria. We might need them to play interference."

Paige nodded before she was even up out of her chair. She was halfway to her bedroom when she remembered she'd brought the phone into the kitchen with her. She came back to the table, sat down, and gave Mel a ghost of a smile before picking up her phone to dial Victoria.

Chapter 16

"She sounded good," Victoria said to Richard, squeezing his hand again.

Richard squeezed her hand back. "You've said that a few times."

"I know. I'm just so relieved," Victoria said, taking in Richard's sardonic smile before looking away. She understood why he didn't get it, but to her, Paige's reaction was concerning. Victoria had seen the spirited woman still in her hospital bed, barely recovered from a life-threatening surgery defending God as if she were His champion. She'd never met anyone as close to God, not even her daughter—and Rachel had loved God. She didn't let a chance go by to share the message of God and Jesus.

Paige evangelized. To Victoria, her life and attitude was an example of a woman who loved God. She spoke with love and wisdom not to be honored as a woman of God but a woman who lived as she did because she didn't have a life without Him.

The widow that came to their home and spent days sleeping, crying, barely eating or talking was merely a shadow of that woman. She was a shell of herself, but what was more concerning was the dimness in her eyes and the lack of God's name on her lips the whole of her stay.

Victoria had tried to talk to her to assess her state of mind, but Paige had been guarded and unfeeling or given over to a deeper sorrow than Victoria first thought. It was as if Paige had disappeared

The night Paige had left, Richard had taken Victoria in his arms and just held her for a while. She didn't even try to hide her distress at not seeing any noticeable difference in Paige during her convalescence.

"You know our invitation to Paige to stay here wasn't so you could witness what a woman of God does in certain situations," Richard reminded her as he held her head to his chest. The feeling of his strong heartbeat dulled her senses, so he was well into the next sentence before she caught on to the change in topic. "The reason for Paige's stay was to give her time to rest, seek refuge from the pain and loss of her still-new husband without defending her actions or inaction."

He then let her know in no uncertain words, since Richard was not one to mince words when it came to God, anyway, that if Victoria had offered their home as anything other than a peaceful and safe haven for Paige to begin her healing, no matter what that looked like, then she was the one in the wrong.

Of course, she'd wanted to balk and get angry, but he wouldn't let her go, and Victoria knew it was futile to try and hold her anger when Richard's arms kept her from placing distance between them. She gave up when his hands kneaded the tense muscles of her back, and his voice spoke in a soothing cadence even if she didn't necessarily like what he was saying.

What finally caught her attention was the second-to-last thing Richard had said, and it would be a long time before she forgot because she recognized what God had been trying to do with her for years.

"It wasn't God's inability to comfort which had Paige suffering to the degree we witnessed," Richard had said even as he stroked Victoria's hair. "It was Paige's denial of that comfort due to her anger at God not healing Brandon as she wanted." The fight went out of Victoria, and she let her body go lax next to Richard's. She'd been there when she'd met Paige. She'd been there over and over again with each loss of her children. Victoria didn't want that for Paige.

"I'm glad she's doing better. I've been praying for her," Victoria said distractedly as she looked out the plane window.

"Well, don't stop now. It sounds like our family will need all the help they can get to deal with Grace."

"Do you think she's that formidable?" Victoria asked, turning back to her husband.

"I think she's that angry, that vengeful, and that desperate. She's so focused on getting revenge, especially now, that she doesn't care who gets hurt in the crossfire."

Victoria just nodded her agreement. She, more than most, knew what a motivator anger could be, but what was it about the Sable family that had Grace so bent on destroying them?

"Do you think Melanie and Marc found Brian?"

Richard gave her a long-suffering look before bringing her hand up to his lips and kissing the knuckles. "We've talked about this. I need you focused on what we planned, Victoria. I know you're close, but you can't get sidetracked with whether Brian is alive or not, right now. Our job is to protect Paige, Gladys, Melanie, and Marc against whatever Grace has devised. She leaves with what?" he prompted her.

"Nothing more than what she comes with," Victoria finished, repeating what Richard had told her earlier that day when Samuel informed them that Grace was headed to Los Angeles.

"Her words?" Richard prompted again.

"Can't hurt me unless I give them fuel to do so," Victoria finished, beginning to feel like she was at a pep rally.

"What is our main purpose for going?" Richard asked.

"To be a shield," Victoria responded.

"When do shields speak?" Richard asked touching her bottom lip with his thumb. Really? He was being all smooth and charming now? She needed to keep her head in the game. The whole seduction scene could wait. She grabbed his wrist and moved his hand away.

"Only when reflecting what the person says," Victoria replied, not taking her eyes from his.

He nodded his approval. "You're adorable when you get all riled up," he whispered, his brown eyes sparkling.

She pointed a finger in his face. "Not now. I need to focus."

Richard raised his hands in mock surrender. "By all means. I wouldn't want to distract you."

"Wouldn't you though," she said, giving him the side-eye.

169

Richard chuckled. "Yes. I would very much like to distract you." His voice took on a warm, rich quality she knew all too well. She had three-point-two seconds to escape.

"Richard," she said in warning.

"Yes?" he said, moving closer, making her heartbeat speed up. She glanced at his lips then turned to stare at the seat facing hers. She needed to concentrate on what they'd been discussing. She tried to recall Grace's knowing look. If she could just conjure the image, she could arrest the reaction Richard was evoking with his butter-soft baritone.

"Keep your lips to themselves," she said, not sparing him a glance even though she could feel his warm breath near her ear. She clenched her teeth against the shiver that ran up her spine and leaned away slightly as an attempt to salvage whatever resistance she could to his charms.

She adored Richard, and she felt truly blessed that he'd stuck by her through so many years when she'd buried her pain and retreated inside herself leaving Richard the only one actively participating in their marriage. She knew how close she was to living the rest of her life on her own and possibly dying without realizing God's forgiveness and the peace of a family that loved her.

She had lost so much and so many in her life, but she'd gained even more after she let go of the anger and desire to find someone to blame. She not only enjoyed her marriage again, she'd gained a granddaughter to go with her great-granddaughters. And what if her deepest desires came to pass, and Brian was alive? It was almost too much to hope for. *Almost*, she thought to herself, trying to keep her smile hidden so as not to give her still-lingering husband false encouragement.

"I think you are treating me very unfairly. First, you cut our second honeymoon short," he all but crooned.

"It was our fourth," Victoria bit out.

"Who's counting?" he responded just as quickly before resuming. "Then you have me take us home, so you can be closer to Paige. Just in case."

"I was right, wasn't I? She asked for our help. And might I add that if you hadn't told me what Samuel discovered in the first place, we wouldn't be here right now." She chanced a glance at him.

"Yes, but if I didn't tell you, I would have been in the doghouse when we got home," he said, shifting then turning away from her.

Victoria didn't like that, so she turned fully back to him. "How about, when all of this stuff with Grace is over, we take a trip someplace that gets very little reception and no WiFi?"

He turned back to her. "Will you keep the promise you made on the first day of our last trip?"

Since her mind was already on its way back to the potential confrontation at Paige's she drew a blank. "What promise?"

Richard whispered in her ear, and she was happy no one else was around to witness how quickly her face went from tanned to cherry-tomato red. She tried to feign nonchalance but knew it was in vain. "Did I actually promise, or did I just make a vague suggestion?" she asked to toy with him.

"Oh, it was a promise," he said, obviously ready to call her bluff. "Or would you like me to repeat what you said on our walk back to the villa?"

Victoria turned slightly, placing a couple of fingers on Richard's lips to silence him. "You have a deal. I'll be happy to keep my promise," she replied, unable to contain a chuckle.

"Then you're on." He leaned in and gave her a quick kiss but sighed almost immediately afterward.

"What?" she asked, seeing his exasperated expression.

"I have a feeling it will be a while before we get to take that trip. I've told you about her. This is Grace. She was manipulative when we were young. She hasn't gotten better with time," Richard mumbled, sounding reluctant to bring her up.

Richard had told her everything he'd remembered about the pampered heiress who'd learned how to bend unsuspecting men to her will from a very young age. She'd received all of her training from her mother who was as calculating as they came. Richard thought when he'd made it clear that they were not going to be a match that she took

171

the news rather well. Her subsequent move to Chicago even made him consider that he might have misunderstood her. That Brenda Lattimore, as he'd known her, had been a puppet wanting nothing more than to get out from under her mother's thumb. After realizing who she was earlier that year, he told Victoria that Brenda, aka Grace, would have done her mother proud.

What was with that woman? She collected enemies like other women collected shoes. Victoria wondered briefly if there was any place in Grace's heart that was open to God's love. He'd placed people in her life to get her attention even when her own daughter couldn't lead her to Him.

"I'm going to pray for her," Victoria said out loud. She felt more than saw Richard turn to her.

"What brought that on?"

"I was just thinking about myself and what God has done in our lives these last couple of years," she continued before Richard could speak. "There have been so many miracles, and I know He isn't done," Victoria said, warming to the idea of Grace giving her life to the Lord.

"Victoria, I'm not saying it's impossible, but this is the same woman who tried to blackmail you when she learned about your involvement in Vivian's adoption, who hired someone to kill your son after having him committed. She and Paige have a tumultuous past..."

Victoria lifted a hand to stop Richard's tirade. "So, what are you saying?"

Richard took a breath and blinked at Victoria. "I'm saying she's a woman in need of a hug."

Victoria burst out laughing. "Yes, I would say so."

***

Three hours later, the smile had been completely wiped from Victoria's face, and she was well on her way to wiping the smirk off Grace's face with her Fendi purse.

"We are here because I wanted to see how Paige was doing, and the next time you address my husband, it will be Mr. Branchett. We might be family, but we are not friends," Victoria said with a calm she did not possess. She was so hot she wouldn't be surprised if steam came out of her ears. Where did that woman get off questioning her and Richard's reason for coming to Paige's home and then ordering them to go back from where they came.

Richard leaned toward Victoria and whispered in her ear, "What is our job?"

Victoria wanted to tell her husband what he could do with their job speech but instead pasted on a very fake smile and stepped to the side to embrace Paige again. "You look so good. I'm so happy you let us stop in and see you. I know it's late, but I couldn't contain myself, and Richard is so indulgent."

"Thank you. I'm doing better. It's helped to have Mel and Marc back," Paige said, giving Victoria a tense but otherwise bright smile. Victoria cupped Paige's cheeks and looked into her eyes wanting to convey that she would do exactly what they discussed over the phone. She would not let Grace's words get to her again.

"Yes," Grace said with a bored tone from her seat on the living room couch. "I've heard that about him; funny that I never witnessed it for myself." She tipped her head to the side to look at Richard who just stared back at her, his face resembling that of carved mahogany.

Victoria followed Paige's gesture for her and Richard to sit on the love seat, which was the last piece of furniture available with Gladys sitting in one of the overstuffed chairs with Melanie and Marc sitting at the edge of Brandon's recliner. Paige perched herself on the armchair where Gladys and Melanie sat, and Victoria couldn't help marveling at the picture they made.

Three generations of beautiful young women. The two older with warm golden eyes that reminded her of a feline's. The younger with eyes that reminded her of liquid silver just before it was molded into something extraordinary. She felt a fierce possessiveness come over her at the knowledge that they were hers, and she would do whatever she could to keep them safe.

"Look, it was thoughtful of you two to... drop by," Grace said dismissively, pulling Victoria from her thoughts. "But this is a family matter." It was all Victoria could do not to point out that Grace was sitting in the very spot relegated for guests. She'd learned that Paige liked to sit at the kitchen table when discussing important matters.

"She *is* family," Gladys said, her chin going up as Victoria had seen Vivian's do when she was feeling defensive.

Grace scoffed. "Just because she considers your twin sister family doesn't make her your grandmother."

"No, but the fact that she is Brian's mother makes her more than family, especially since he was my biological father," Paige said, turning to look at Grace along with the rest of the occupants in the room. Victoria couldn't help but turn to gage Grace's reaction at the knowledge that Paige was aware of her true parentage.

The woman was good. Victoria barely saw the telltale sign of surprise in her eyes and reveled in that small feat.

"So, you told her who her father was," Grace said in what sounded like a calm voice to Melanie, but her usually cold golden eyes were sparking with anger.

"No, I did," Victoria said almost before she realized she was talking.

She felt the love seat shift as Richard sat back and lay his arm across the back. His thumb glided down the back of her neck from her hairline to the space between her shoulders. She took it as a warning and closed her mouth.

Grace's gaze landed on her with a calculating intensity that might have made her shiver if she hadn't just gotten the answer to a question that had been sitting at the back of her mind since summer. Grace might be blackmailing Antonio, but he hadn't been telling the whole truth. He was obviously still in communication with Grace, or the information Victoria just offered would have shown up more as a surprise than anger in Grace's eyes.

"And how did you come by such information?" Grace asked.

It was Victoria's turn to appear bored, so she let her features go slack. She set her Fendi purse down between her outer thigh and the arm of the sofa. "You'd be surprised at what you can find on the internet."

Melanie's cough could have been an attempt to disguise a laugh, but Victoria wasn't sure. Either way, it brought Grace's attention back to Melanie.

"Speaking of family. I find it very curious that you wouldn't be here to comfort Paige during what had to be the hardest time in her life. Then again, maybe you didn't approve of her marrying a man with a set expiration date, so you put the responsibility of helping Paige grieve on Gladys' and Brandon's family."

If Victoria hadn't previously experienced the crazy who was Grace, her mouth would have dropped open in shock. She could barely believe that a mother, biological or not, would say something so cruel to her daughter. As it was, the tension in the living room went up a few notches, but no one said anything. Victoria sent surreptitious glances around the room to evaluate everyone's emotions and found with surprise that Gladys looked upon Grace with pity.

"Where have you been for the last five months, Melanie?" Grace's voice was chilly.

"I'm not telling you any more than you already know. The fact that you arrived less than eight hours after I got here tells me that you know more than you are letting on," Melanie responded, not seeming to try to hide her anger at Grace's opinion.

"Why couldn't I have come here to comfort Paige and offer a truce while extending my services to take Gladys off her hands for winter break?" Grace glanced at Paige, giving her an exaggerated pitying look. "Since you didn't seem to be in a position to do so." Grace said the last as she shifted her gaze back to Melanie.

Victoria noticed that Melanie squeezed Gladys tighter and took a deep breath. The anger in her eyes radiated through her. Victoria could see it in her posture, the set of her mouth, and the narrowing of her eyes. She opened her mouth, but Paige beat her to it.

"What was it?" Paige asked, seeming truly baffled.

"What was what?" Grace asked Paige with an exasperated tone.

"What made you so hard and angry? For as long as I've known you, you have had the same attitude. It's like you repel love almost as if it hurts you to feel it, receive it, or even witness it." Grace rolled her eyes at Paige's words but didn't interrupt her. "When I was little, I wondered why you didn't show me love or comfort like my dad or Melanie did. When I got older, I could see that you couldn't because it wasn't in you, and I understand that. Not everyone should be a parent, but you were openly cruel. It's like you feed on hurting people," Paige finished, perplexity coating her words.

"Paige, I didn't come here for you to share your new revelations on my behavior and accuse me of being an unloving mother when I gave you your name, made sure you were fed, sheltered, educated, and let you remain with the woman child who had you in the first place."

Victoria saw Marc visibly stiffen and hoped he wouldn't take whatever bait she was fishing with. As Melanie had said, it was obvious that Grace knew more than she was letting on.

"Let me. Let me? You *let* me remain with my own mother? What were you going to do? Put me up for adoption? Sell me? Did you have someone lined up?" Paige blurted before getting up.

Grace raised her hands then made a shooing motion. "No need to get so riled up over nothing, Paige. It's not like we were going to leave you at the fire station."

Paige sat back down slowly, but Victoria could see she wasn't going to let the subject go. Grace, seeming to be on a roll, continued and by the way that Mel leaned back and wrapped her arm around Paige's lower back, Mel was getting ready for anything her mother might say.

"It was *godly* of you to forgive Melanie for keeping the fact that she was your mother from you. It made sense, what she did. She'd given over all rights to you when Wayne and I adopted you, so in essence, you weren't her daughter." A thoughtful expression took over Grace's features for a moment, and Victoria found herself reluctantly entranced by her act.

"I'm curious though. Did that forgiveness extend to anything else you might have been keeping from her?" Grace directed the last sentence at Melanie, and both curiosity and dread rose in Victoria.

The already tense room became unnaturally quiet. It was as if no one wanted to draw attention to themselves. Well, no one except Paige who was sitting up straight as a board.

"Grace, that's enough," Melanie said through clenched teeth.

Grace gave her back as innocent a look as was possible for a serpent. "I mean with how she responded to the news that you were her biological mother, you wouldn't begrudge her any more information about the day she was born," Grace said blinking overly fast. "It would be the only Christian thing to do. Don't you think?" Victoria watched while Grace stared at Melanie who, try though she might to keep her face blank, squeezed Paige's waist.

Why was the woman still talking? Why wasn't anyone, with dirt on this vicious creature, doing or saying anything to stop her? It took a couple of seconds for Victoria to stop warring in her mind over whether to stay quiet and find out what Grace was getting at or protect her girls.

"You know, as entertaining and suspenseful as this all is, it is late." Victoria moved to the edge of her seat and glanced at Richard while interrupting Grace's monologue. She could see Melanie visibly relax. Unfortunately, Grace saw it too and struck like a viper.

"It was so ridiculously ironic," Grace went on, waving the one manicured hand in the air like she'd shared this story many times. "Melanie had a thing for fairy tales when she had you, but then she was only twelve. There was still a lot of innocence in her mind, despite the fact that the father was nowhere to be found when she was in labor. She named you Briar Rose after that silly girl in the cartoon. I'd say your brother got the better end of the deal even though he didn't live long enough to hear it. Yeah, Brian Jr. was much better." Grace finished as if nodding to herself.

If it had been a car crash about to happen in slow motion in front of her, Victoria still would have been too shocked to look away in time to shield her eyes from the devastation brought on by the collision. Grace delivered the news like a Mack truck, and by the look on Paige's face, that truck had just run a red light and plowed through an intersection full of grade-school children. Melanie's face, on the other hand, became thunderous with rage.

177

Grace opened her mouth again, but Marc stopped her. "Enough, Grace. It's obvious why you came here, but we don't have to sit here and be assaulted by your words or your presence,"

Paige interrupted Marc. Her voice emotionless, and Victoria could see that she wasn't the only one shaken by the lack of tone in Paige's voice. "I don't accept your truce. I don't accept your story for why you are here, and you are no longer welcome in my home. You are a heartless woman whose surface beauty is wasted on a walking corpse. I've had enough of your caustic poison…"

"Blah, blah, blah," Grace interrupted, making no move to leave. "Before you send out pointless ultimatums and empty threats, I have one thing to say to Melanie, and she will listen." Grace focused her gaze on Melanie. "If I find out that you have been hiding Brian's existence from me, I will do everything in my power to see that you and your childhood lover are charged and prosecuted for conspiracy and fraud. I will also see that the person who helped you is also charged. Your chance for any leniency from me is to tell me while I am here in Los Angeles, and the clock is ticking because I will be back on a plane headed toward DC on Monday."

"Thank God for small favors," Victoria whispered but too loud not to be heard.

"The only person who should be prosecuted in here is you, Grace," Marc said, drawing Grace's ire.

"And why is that, Agent Miller?" Grace asked then feigned surprise as if she just realized something. "Oh yes, that's right. You aren't allowed to say unless you want to compromise your position, since that file is closed." Her features contorted into a look of disgust as if taunting him was beneath her.

"How's your mother, Grace?" The deep baritone rang through the room, gaining everyone's attention including her own. Victoria may not have even recognized his voice if she hadn't felt the vibration of it on the couch.

"Excuse me?" Grace said.

"No, I won't. I asked if you knew how your mother was doing?" Richard's voice had taken on a tone she hadn't heard in a long time and hoped it would be longer still before she heard it again.

Grace looked only a little uncomfortable for a few seconds before she veiled her feelings behind a frosty stare. "My mother is dead."

"No, she isn't," Richard responded almost instantly.

"She's dead to me, and I'm dead to her."

"Would you like to be dead to your daughter, granddaughter, and great-granddaughter as well? Because that's where you're headed right now. A nameless, faceless person we once had the misfortune to interact with."

Grace's lips twisted. "I've been threatened with worse."

"There's a conversation I'd be interested in hearing," Victoria said out of the side of her mouth. She didn't work too hard at keeping her voice low though.

"How about this?" Richard said, leaning forward. "You leave right now. Go find some manners, and meet us for brunch at a restaurant tomorrow with that successful Homeland Security contractor husband of yours. And when I say manners, I mean you don't ridicule, reveal hurtful information behind a fake show of concern, and you don't threaten anyone who doesn't answer your questions. You sit back, try to be as pleasant as you know how to be, and let Melanie, Paige, and Gladys get to know your latest husband. We will act cordial and put on a great show for him. Then you will get on a plane back to DC and thank him for giving you a chance to see your girls."

"And if I don't?" Grace murmured.

"I tell Ross Dillard, who, from what I hear, hates being made to look like a fool, and I assume that includes being the last one to learn personal information about his wife, that the current Mrs. Dillard uses his position to gain confidential information of her own." Startled by what her husband had just said, Victoria stilled at the news and so did Grace before she blinked at Richard and cleared her throat.

"Which restaurant?" Grace said, her voice wrapped in haughty disdain.

"You don't have to join us," Victoria said, angered by Grace's demeanor.

"Melanie will text it to you a few hours beforehand. Right now, I think we could all do with a good night's sleep," Richard said, smoothly talking over her.

Grace got up from her seat and started walking to the door without speaking or looking at anyone else. Marc got up and walked behind her. No one moved until the front door opened and closed, then everyone seemed to deflate.

Victoria was reminded of something she and Richard had discussed earlier and scoffed, drawing Richard's attention to her.

"I might be wrong, but I think she needs more than a hug," Victoria said wryly.

Richard chuckled at her statement, though she could tell it was the last thing he wanted to do. He leaned up against her and kissed her temple. "You never cease to amaze me, woman," he said fiercely into her hair.

"The feeling's mutual," Victoria murmured, breathing in his cologne. She knew she wouldn't have to say anything. Any second one of the other three adults in the room were going to ask him what he'd been talking about. She was just happy she was on his side.

Chapter 17

"Why did you do that?" Paige's voice was tired and hardly loud enough for everyone in the room to hear, but since Melanie was sitting next to her, she heard every nuance in her daughter's tone and was afraid that the one interaction with Grace was enough to set back their relationship.

Melanie only moved her eyes to follow Paige's gaze and saw Richard rubbing the thighs of his trousers. He took a deep breath before he began. "By now you've noticed that Grace is not one to back down, and when she gets cornered, she comes out fighting. If you cut all ties now, she will reinforce her efforts to keep tabs on all of you. Only you won't have a clue about when and how she is doing it. Giving her an ultimatum instead of throwing her out of your life gives you the upper hand."

"I don't want the upper hand. I don't want anything to do with her," Paige spat out, looking as though the day had taken a toll on her.

"I know, but that isn't going to happen during this visit. She needs to save face with her husband," Richard responded in a warm and cajoling tone.

"Which means we would be doing her a favor by inviting her to brunch tomorrow. We should warn him about her instead and cut her off from that source she uses to collect information on us," Paige argued.

"If we know some of the ways she gets her information, we can systematically cut her off before she gets destructive," Richard returned just as quickly but with less bite.

"That wasn't destructive? She's a walking cautionary tale," Melanie said in her daughter's defense. She didn't want the woman near her children any more than they wanted to be around her, especially after tonight. Melanie looked down into the wide eyes of Gladys.

"You okay? I know it was a lot," Melanie asked.

Gladys shrugged. "Vivian and I pray for her. She's on our list with all of you and a few others, but I guess Vivian was right. You can't make people do what is good for them. You can only pray and show love, but if they aren't willing to accept, you brush the dust off and keep going." Gladys cocked her head to the side. "I'm not sure what the brushing off of dust has to do with anything, but I get the gist."

"Well, you know, as long as she is alive, it is never too late, but yes, she will have to do her part if she doesn't want to live a life full of anger and pain," Melanie said, hugging Gladys to her and squeezing for a few seconds.

"In the early days of Christ, men would go to people's homes or villages to share the Gospel. If they encountered people who were not ready to believe, they wouldn't argue, just point out a few truths. If the gospel still wasn't accepted, they would wipe their feet or sandals outside of the person's door as a symbol of dusting off the experience and moving on. It didn't mean that if they were prompted to pray as they continued on, that they would ignore it. You never know what God has in store. So, if you feel led to continue to pray for Grace, do so, but don't feel obligated if you don't." Paige said the last sentence as she took Gladys' hand and squeezed.

Melanie smiled down at her beautiful girl that made her heart swell with pride and love. It also made her more determined to see this matter resolved. She looked at Richard who had been watching them with a wistful expression.

"You were saying... about Grace, Richard?" She addressed him with less antagonism in her voice than before.

It took him a moment to regroup, but he smiled at her. "Grace is getting desperate or she wouldn't have shown her hand by making it obvious that she'd been keeping tabs on your whereabouts. She's anxious to find out if your disappearance had anything to do with Brian. I don't know if his existence would be beneficial to her or put her at a disadvantage, but I do think it's at the core of all this. I also know that we can use the fact that she is using her husband's contacts or position to monitor you, against her. We can feed her false information and have her chasing her tail."

Melanie reluctantly nodded her agreement to what Richard was saying. He'd helped them immensely by keeping his head. She'd sat there looking at Grace while she, Richard, and Victoria went at it. Melanie had avoided staring at Grace for any length of time during her *surprise visit*; otherwise, Grace might have seen the knowledge in Melanie's eyes. The knowledge of who Wayne Morganson wasn't. It was all she could do to hold it in, but the callous way Grace had just revealed B.J.'s existence to Paige kept her silent. Melanie wouldn't contribute to that.

When Melanie opened the door to Grace, she knew the woman looked for her to be surprised and Melanie didn't disappoint. She'd played the game, giving her mother what she wanted to try and appease her before opening the door wide enough for Grace to enter.

Later Melanie had sat there letting Richard go head-to-head with Grace because she couldn't trust herself not to give away anything she'd learned from Brian. There were so many questions, and it frustrated her that she sat empty-handed in front of one of the few people who could give her answers. But she knew better than to hope for any help from Grace. The woman was as cunning and intelligent as she was cold and malicious.

Grace wasn't past using a few insults to make people angry enough to spill what they knew. Melanie went over the conversation in her head and knew she and Marc were right in their decision to keep their visit with Brian to themselves until after Grace was out of Los Angeles. She'd seen Grace's face after she dropped the bomb about Paige's brother. The woman had watched Paige's features like a hawk to assess

183

whether it was a surprise, and Paige didn't disappoint. Grace had gotten her answer, which was probably why she allowed Richard the last word for the evening.

Richard's next words, pulling her from her thoughts, said as much. "Don't be fooled by Grace's capitulation. I don't think she's as concerned about Mr. Dillard as it looked, by her actions. She is a woman with more than one way to get what she's after. You, Melanie, are just the easiest right now. Or you were until Victoria and I showed up. I don't think she was expecting you to include us in this little reunion," Richard said, taking his wife's hand.

"How did you know about what she's been doing with her husband's title?" Melanie asked, wanting to avoid the real elephant in the room for a little longer.

"If my daughter disappeared, and I thought she was hiding something that would have a profound effect on my present or future, I would use whatever resources I had at my fingertips to find them. In this case, it looks like you have more weapons in your arsenal than Grace does because she doesn't have enough to go on to track your whereabouts after you and Marc entered Canada.

"Speaking of that, how did you know I was back, and even more, that Grace was on her way here?"

"I have a man who watches passports. When you and Marc left the country, I was alerted as I'm sure Grace was. I just asked him to keep an eye out for you when you came back into the country and to see who else checked on those specific passports. Coincidences of coincidences or an act of God. My investigator went to school with one of the clerks in the Homeland Security Department in DC. They may have heard a thing or two about Ross Dillard's beautiful new wife."

"So you weren't bluffing. You really have something on her?" Melanie said, feeling a sense of relief and a pinch of guilt.

"Only if she cares about her husband. If not, it will mean nothing to her," Richard said with an apologetic look in his eyes.

Melanie let her shoulders fall. She wanted all of this to be over, but as she and Marc discussed, this could be just the beginning of an uphill battle to finding out the truth between Grace, Antonio Sable, Luca

Sable, and Angelo Mauro, and what that meant for Gladys, Paige, and her future.

"Do I have to wait until after we have brunch tomorrow?" Paige glanced at her watch. "Or later today for you to tell me about my brother? Better yet. Were you going to tell me about him at all?"

Melanie closed her eyes briefly. She didn't want to lie to Paige. Everything in her recoiled against the thought of keeping anything more from her daughter. She would tell her what she could until tomorrow.

"Gladys, it's way past everyone's bedtime, especially yours," Melanie said, kissing her girl on the top of her head. "Go ahead and get your bath out of the way. I will be in there soon to kiss you goodnight." She gave Gladys one more squeeze then helped her up out of the chair.

Gladys must have been tired because she didn't resist or complain before she got up. Melanie watched as she hugged and kissed Paige then went to Marc, Victoria, and Richard and repeated the actions, wishing them all a good night before walking down the hall to her room.

Melanie moved over in the chair to give Paige the option of sitting closer to her. When Paige accepted it, Melanie let out a breath she didn't know she'd been holding. Melanie wrapped her arm around Paige feeling contented for the first time in months. Images of Paige as a toddler passed through her mind, her infectious laugh ringing down the hall or in the kitchen when Melanie would come home from school. It made her a bit nostalgic, so she decided to used it to fill in some blanks for Paige, Victoria, and Richard.

"I'm sorry. I know it doesn't seem like there's any good reason to have kept it from you, but I was young, and I did everything I could to avoid Grace's wrath when I was living under her roof." When Paige opened her mouth, Melanie spoke faster. "I know. I know I haven't been under her rule for a long time, and yes, I could have told you about your twin, but it would just have been one more loss, one more person for you to mourn."

"But I would have known. I wouldn't have been blindsided again by that hateful woman." Paige leaned back, and Melanie removed her arm.

"Those petty wins mean nothing in the bigger scheme of things. The less she thinks you know, the less attention she will give you, allowing you freedom from her perpetual plotting," Melanie said, hoping Paige could understand how much Melanie had sacrificed for her.

"You don't see it, do you? By doing her bidding and 'staying under her radar,'" Paige said, standing up, turning to her, and placing the last of the statement in finger quotes, "you have given that woman power over your life. You have a loving husband. I gave you my daughter to protect. It's time for you to come out from under her thumb. She is a selfish, tyrannical piece of a human who gets more pleasure out of hurting people than she does loving them. Where is your holy boldness? Where is your faith and trust in God to make you victorious and free from her oppressive ways?"

"Paige. Enough." The firm voice from the other side of the room caught their attention.

"Everything she's done has been with you in mind. From the moment you were born, she has tried to protect you in any way she could. Keeping this from you was one of the ways she chose to protect you from all the mess Grace has been up to. If we could have kept certain parties from researching and digging into your past, we may have been able to avoid the trip we had to take this year," Marc said, leaning forward in his chair.

"The trip that you still haven't told me anything about, I might add," Paige said to Marc.

"And I had every right to find out more information about my family," Victoria chimed in, her indignation obvious from across the room.

"Yes," Marc countered. "And how did that work out for you when Grace blackmailed you for looking up information on Vivian?"

"I can take care of Grace," Victoria said with her chin going up in the air. "I'm not afraid of her."

"You don't even know who she is." Marc turned cool eyes on Victoria. "If you did, you would move with more caution. You're underestimating her. She never shows all her cards. She has built her life around manipulation and intimidation. She has people in some very high places watching over her, watching over Melanie and Paige as well."

"You seem knowledgeable. Why don't you share what you know?" Richard said to Marc.

"If we know more, we can band together. Richard and I have resources that can be used to help protect or come against her." Victoria's voice had changed from anger to imploring, and Melanie found herself at an impasse.

If what Brian shared with her had merit, her children's lives could be in danger if she trusted the wrong people. Melanie glanced at Marc who gave her a small shrug. He hadn't objected to Victoria and Richard coming to stand in as a buffer when Grace arrived, so he must have been somewhat appeased by what he'd learned about them so far.

"Have you known Ross Dillard long, Richard?" Marc asked, turning his focus on him.

Melanie turned to watch as Richard assessed her husband for a few seconds before his mouth tipped up in a reluctant but approving smile.

"Not long. I met him a few years ago. He aided the committee I serve on for my philanthropic efforts. He needed an introduction with one of the committee members for a contract he was bidding on." Richard shrugged. "He seemed like a decent fellow and extremely intelligent. I hate that he's with Grace. He deserves better," Richard finished solemnly.

Marc glanced at her as if to say, "It's up to you," before sitting back in the recliner.

Melanie took a breath, letting it out slowly. "Fine. We will share." She pointed her finger at the Branchetts then her daughter. "But tomorrow you can't give away what you know. Ross' presence will be of some help in that respect, but I'm trusting you to keep this to yourselves until we can find out what Grace is up to."

Melanie's gaze shifted back Richard and Victoria for their acceptance. When they each gave her a nod, she looked back over to Paige who seemed to hesitate before nodding as well and coming back to sit next to her instead of moving to the couch as Melanie assumed she would.

It took a moment for Melanie to get her bearings. She just wanted to take in the feel of her daughter's capitulation and closeness for a few seconds. "I met Brian when we were staying in Colorado." She paused briefly as she made a decision. "I was eleven before I went to school with other children. I had been homeschooled up to that year and I was terrified I wouldn't fit in. In some ways I did and in others I didn't, like being enrolled in a grade two years behind where I should have been. The day my mom finally trusted me to take the school bus on my own, I met Brian Grossenberg. He was the only one who made room for me on his seat and as it turned out we shared a backyard gate. He was a couple of years older, so he knew the ropes better than I did." Melanie took a breath before looking at Victoria.

"He had those deep-brown eyes that seemed to look right into you. They were intense but in a protective way. I guess even then I had a thing for heroes." She shared a smile with Brian's mother, forcing herself to look away before the tears came.

Melanie considered what she'd learned from Brian during their recent visit. She compared it to what she remembered and tried to be as truthful as possible. "Anyway, Brian and I grew closer both because of our constant proximity and subtle manipulation of my mother and the Grossenbergs. When my dad went on deployment it became less subtle. I found out later that she had been putting reproductive hormones in my food and doing just about everything she could to encourage Brian and me to spend time together." Melanie slipped back into one particular memory that filled her with bittersweet longing even at that moment.

"But why? I mean, it wasn't because she wanted another child. Why would she do such a thing to children?" Paige asked as if she hadn't been in the room to witness Grace herself a few minutes before.

"Because he was a Sable, and Grace has some kind of vendetta against the Sable family," Victoria answered.

188

"Because Brian was Luca Sable's grandson. The man Grace had an affair with while she worked for his company as an accountant," Melanie clarified and listened to the deep silence bounce off the walls. She considered dropping the bomb about her newly discovered knowledge about her parentage, but it would open up a whole new conversation.

"But she and Antonio..." Whatever else Victoria was going to say was lost with the breath that seemed to leave her chest. Melanie watched her look at Richard, her features going from confusion to dark and stormy anger. Melanie figured she'd just realized that Antonio was being more than just blackmailed or that there was a civil war brewing and Antonio was on Grace's side.

"Grace, as you can tell, is not the most nurturing person, but during the early days of my pregnancy, she was doting, affectionate, and loving. She was exactly what I'd always imagined a loving mother could be. I thought I had finally done something right by her even though after the winter break that year, I was relegated to being homeschooled again," Melanie said, shaking her head at her näiveté and foolishness. "When I was told that I couldn't see Brian anymore, I was more than confused. He was my best friend. He was the one I shared everything with, and then he was gone. I was wrecked and angry. Every moment I wasn't being watched, we would find a way to be together, even if it was just sitting at the fence on either side of our backyards and talking. We were careful, but inevitably we got caught, and we were grounded. Melanie paused as she weighed the consequences of bringing up some of the files that had been planted to lead people astray or discourage them from deepening their research. Victoria's thought must have aligned with her because the woman's next question brought them to one such plant.

"Do you know anything about Brian being placed in a..." Victoria's voice failed her for a moment, and Melanie saw Richard squeeze her hand. "In a mental ward?"

Melanie felt Paige go rigid at Victoria's question. She looked over at Marc for help.

"I saw a file referring to his stay at State General," Marc responded.

189

The small light of hope that showed in Victoria's eyes as she mustered up the courage to ask more questions, had Melanie let information slip because she couldn't take it anymore.

"It wasn't Brian. It wasn't Brian in the ward," she blurted before she could cover her mouth. She stared at Marc in horror. His features relayed his surprise for a split second before they relaxed and went blank. He lifted the left side of his mouth in something akin to a reassuring smile.

"What Melanie is saying—" Marc began, but Melanie interrupted him. It was past time for her to tell the whole truth.

"It was a setup," Melanie said, chancing a glance at her daughter.

"At the end of my seventh month, I overheard Grace confirming plans she'd made with someone for my babies. My children that she promised to help me raise." Melanie ran a hand down the side of her face. "Up until then she'd told me that she and my dad would adopt the twins as their own, but she'd planned on only keeping my son— probably to use against Luca Sable. I couldn't let her do it." Melanie rubbed her forehead trying to organize everything in her head. When she felt Paige's hand squeeze hers, she looked over into a pair of eyes that mirrored her own. She could do this. They had each other and maybe even more than that.

Melanie took a deep breath and shared how she got in touch with Brian almost the moment her mother left for a business trip a week later to see if he could help her keep their children together. "Brian had called his grandfather from a payphone around the corner from school, telling him everything the week before when his parents had started watching him even more closely and acting skittish. He told me he shared everything that had transpired since we'd met and Brian's parents' part in it. I'm not sure where his grandfather was when he and I spoke that day, but before it was over, I was examined by an obstetrician and deemed healthy and far enough along for labor to be induced. I was taken by ambulance to State General where the delivery and labor were overseen by a group of medical professionals who were more than likely given a hefty sum to keep my age, name, and relationship to Luca a secret."

190

"Brian Jr. was born first, but I was having a lot of trouble delivering Paige because she hadn't turned, and I was so tired and scared. When another hour went by without any movement or change and both my body and Paige began to go into distress, I made the nurse call Brian in, and I begged him to take Brian Jr. with him."

"Wait, you said Brian Jr. didn't live. I assumed he was stillborn. Did he live long enough for Brian to take him?" Paige asked, her hand on Melanie's arm forgotten, her eyes wide.

Melanie blinked at her daughter and licked her lips before answering. "Yes, he did. I convinced Brian to take him that night." Melanie heard a gasp come from Victoria and Richard's direction. She looked up to see that Victoria had a vice grip on her husband's hand and gave them an apologetic smile, not that it would mean anything after she finished.

"Originally, Luca was just going to take Brian from the Grossenbergs and charge them with child endangerment, but once I convinced Brian to take B.J., Luca made other plans. He gave the Grossenbergs one chance to redeem themselves. They were to check Brian, well actually his look-alike, into the mental ward of the hospital. It was supposed to be a seventy-two-hour stay, but Grace pulled some strings on the day Brian's look-alike was to be released, and he was transferred to a more permanent asylum. Paperwork was doctored to make it look like he stayed in the State General mental wing for an exaggerated period. It was placed where people researching for Brian could find it.

"So you're saying Brian wasn't left in a mental ward?" Victoria's voice barely reached Melanie's ears; her tone sounded like pure hope. When Melanie looked at Victoria, her heart tripped. Tears were streaming down Victoria's cheeks, and she didn't even know it. The picture of such abject fear and hope closed up Melanie's throat, so she nodded that Victoria's words were correct.

Victoria let out a sob. She seemed just as startled as Melanie but was unable to stop. When Richard put his arms around her they came in earnest for a few seconds while everyone else in the room remained quiet.

191

Once Victoria had gained control of herself, Richard nodded for Melanie to continue.

"Grace would check in every so often but never visited Brian, so it was easy enough to deceive her. It also made setting Grace up for the assassination attempt on Brian easy for Luca. It was what he used to get Grace kicked out of WITSEC even though the case was thrown out of court since the evidence was tampered with. Luca wanted Grace beholden to him for her safety."

"I appreciate you being so forthcoming with all of this information. It's more than we ever could have hoped for when we made the trip here," Richard spoke, interrupting Melanie, "but I'm sure you know that we are anxious for one piece of information above all else. Is Brian alive?"

Melanie swallowed more to stall for a moment than for any sort of dramatic effect. "Yes."

A short cry came from Victoria before she spoke. "Where is he?"

"I can't tell you. The fact that you know he's alive places him and my son's life in danger," Melanie said vehemently.

"Brian Jr.?" The small voice came from Paige, and Melanie turned to her.

"Brian Jr. is with his father," Melanie said and watched a myriad of expressions cross Paige's face before her daughter got up and walked out of the room.

"Paige," Melanie called, but her daughter didn't turn around or respond.

Melanie sent a helpless look Marc's way, but he gave her a reassuring nod.

She turned back to the Branchetts.

"When can I see my son?" Victoria stated more than asked.

Melanie stared at her for a moment. "I don't know," she said before turning to Marc for assistance. He nodded, and she got up to follow her daughter out of the room. They would have to finish in the morning. Right now, she needed to be with Paige.

192

Chapter 18

Paige sat at the edge of Gladys' bed watching the sleeping child. It was amazing how watching her child sleep could ground her. Quiet the restlessness within her. Gladys was so peaceful and young looking in sleep. Gladys was thirteen in age, but in so many ways she was wise beyond her time. Her way of communicating was mature, though Paige knew that had more to do with her mom's teaching than anything else. Her spiritual life was also mature, and Paige credited that to both God and Vivian whom Paige was sure worried about her. The look of concern on Vivian's face when she arrived for Thanksgiving pulled at Paige's heart and let her know that her girls hadn't missed a thing when it came to her grief over Brandon. It also made her work that much harder to remain in the present. Not that the present was any better at this particular moment.

The feelings of betrayal were always close to the surface, and with them came the anger Paige had tried so hard to eradicate. It was funny how it was always that emotion that put up the strongest fight. She had no issues with jealousy or envy. She'd never coveted what other people had. Sure, she wanted something of her own, but as her relationship with God grew, she understood He had a special plan for her life. It made her feel honored and extremely important all the way up to Brandon's death.

At that point, she felt more like a martyr than a soldier in the army of the Lord. She felt as though she'd been set up to take a fall rather than set up to receive a blessing. She felt foolish, like a court jester who didn't get the fact that people were laughing at her instead of laughing with her. She felt a sense of shame for being so happy when Brandon asked her out, then courted her, then asked her to marry him. he'd even toyed with the thought that God had set her up as an example of what happened when His children waited on Him for their mate. Instead, she felt like she'd been set up as an example of how not to place anyone or anything above her relationship with Him.

It was true. She'd sought God first, but not only. God came before everything else until she received the second thing she'd been desiring more than anything. A husband who would love her as Jesus loved the Church.

Now she was a former. A former wife, former daughter, and sister-in-law and formerly thought of as a blessed woman. She knew some of the women of her church thought and talked about her. She could imagine their pity, concern, and in some cases, curiosity as to what she'd done to deserve what had happened. It might have fleetingly crossed her mind as well, if it had happened to someone else. If she were in someone else's shoes, she might think the sins of her past caught up to her. That she received exactly what she deserved thinking she could change God's mind by marrying a man who had already been diagnosed with a terminal illness. Had she? Had she thought her relationship with God gave her such favor and authority. Had she overstepped in her zealousness to see the man she loved healed? She couldn't deal with that answer at the moment. It was disturbing enough that the question entered her mind.

Paige took a deep breath and pulled the blanket up on Gladys' shoulder. She leaned in and kissed the side of Gladys' head before getting up to head for her office. She knew it was extremely late, but she also knew, selfishly, that Lady Menagerie would take her call no matter what the time. Paige was sure she wouldn't sleep with most of the thoughts running through her head about all the secrets that were kept from her, let alone the revelations crisscrossing her mind at the moment.

As she stepped out of the room, she came face-to-face with Melanie.

"Hi, do you want to talk?" Mel asked, looking all types of uncertain.

Paige wanted to ask her where she was when Paige wanted to talk about Brian months ago, but she didn't. It wouldn't be productive, and she didn't feel like wasting their time. There was very little Melanie could say that would make the secrets and betrayal better, and Paige figured if her own life and safety wasn't a good enough reason at the moment, nothing would be.

Paige shook her head. "No, not right now. I'm just trying to absorb it all," Paige hedged.

Melanie visibly swallowed and nodded her head in acquiescence.

"I changed the sheets on my bed for you and Marc," Paige said, moving away from the door and heading toward her office. "I will sleep in Vivian's bed for the time being. It's just easier that way," Paige added when Melanie opened her mouth.

Paige stepped out of Melanie's reach just in case her mother had an overwhelming urge to touch her.

"I'm sorry, Paige. I'm so sorry about how all of this information was revealed," Melanie started but Paige interrupted her.

"I'm not. Because of Victoria and Richard, I learned why Grace never felt like a mother to me, even with her obvious disdain for motherhood. I found out why you were so possessive and protective, and I ultimately found out that I have a twin brother. I have more family," Paige whispered a little louder than she intended as her emotions got the better of her.

"Tell me something, Mel. Would you have ever told me about my father and brother if no one interfered?"

Paige watched as Melanie's eyes lost a little of their softness in the presence of steely resolve. Melanie's shoulders flexed, and Paige had her answer before Melanie spoke.

"Until I find out what Grace has to gain, even now with the knowledge of Brian or Brian Jr.'s existence they have to remain dead to everyone," Melanie said, her voice flat.

"That's not what I asked," Paige countered.

"As long as their existence put your life or their lives in danger, I wasn't going to tell anyone. Nor was I going to check for myself until I needed to do so," Mel said, her eyes softening again.

"You didn't trust me," Paige whispered. The words came out unbidden but were no less true.

Melanie opened her mouth then shut it. "If keeping Vivian's existence from Gladys meant keeping Gladys safe and alive, wouldn't you do the same?"

"I'm not thirteen years old anymore, Mel. I haven't been for a long time, and I don't believe I have displayed the type of emotional instability over the last few years that would cause you to think I wouldn't be able to handle that information," Paige came back without hesitation.

"Paige, until a few weeks ago, I wasn't sure they were both alive," Melanie said before shifting her stance. "Let me ask you something. Do you want to meet your biological father and Brian Jr.?"

"Of course, why wouldn't I?"

"What if you can't? What if you can never meet them?" Melanie leaned in as she asked the questions.

Paige balked at the thought of knowing her twin and biological father were out there but never being able to meet them. Paige didn't have a ready answer for Melanie so she just shrugged.

"I love you, Paige, and it is my greatest hope that the four of us can be in the same room together, but I can't take back what I did, and I won't apologize for trying to keep you from harm, both physically and emotionally. The circumstances around your conception may be muddied, but I loved you from the moment I felt you move inside me and even more so when I held you in my arms for the first time. You may have their name, but you are mine, and I will do whatever's in my power to keep you safe. I hope it can be done with you still talking to me and wanting to have me as part of your life, but I will take what I can get," Melanie said, looking at Paige in earnest.

"What about Gladys?" Paige asked more as a test than anything else.

"You are Gladys' mother. You've built a bond with her. It would crush me to let her go, but if that was your wish, I would do it," Melanie said with a sincerity Paige wasn't expecting. It went a long way to convincing her that Melanie only meant to do what was best for her. It also warmed a part of her heart she'd been withholding in fear of Melanie's continued deception.

Paige nodded her head in acceptance and continued down the hall to her office. She needed to talk to Lady Menagerie more than ever.

Ten minutes later, Paige sat at her desk staring at her phone. She glanced at the clock which read two-thirty a.m. and debated whether or not to give her mentor a couple more hours. Paige decided to text Lady Menagerie first to see if it woke her or if she felt like responding. If she did, Paige would call her.

She typed out a quick message then waited. There was no immediate reply, and she bit her lip in consternation. She could email Lady Menagerie some of her thoughts so her mentor could read them when she woke up. Paige rejected that idea as soon as it formed.

Paige jumped when her phone vibrated in her hand signaling a call. She glanced down at the screen before answering even though she knew who it was. Her heart sped up at the sight of Lady Menagerie's name, and she answered the call.

"Hello," Paige whispered even though there was no chance of her anyone hearing her.

"Paige, my love," came Lady Menagerie's concerned voice over the line. "It's good to hear from you. Are you okay? You're whispering. Can you talk?"

The love she felt from the woman's voice settled over her, and she had to swallow to keep her throat clear.

"Hi. Yes, sorry for whispering. It was just an automatic response to the lateness," Paige responded.

"Oh, okay. How are you doing?" Lady Menagerie replied.

"I'm better in some ways and worse in others," Paige said, knowing her answer was ambiguous but it was true.

"Well, the fact that you reached out to me gives me hope that something is better. Sorry for the delay in my response. When I read your text I thought it would be best to just call you when I got downstairs."

Paige smiled at the upbeat of her mentor's voice. If she didn't know better Paige would have thought it was twenty minutes to three in the afternoon instead of the wee hours of the morning.

"I apologize for the early hour—" Paige began but was interrupted.

"I know if it wasn't important, you would have waited. I also know there have been plenty of times when I think things are important enough to merit an early morning call but you still wait." Lady Menagerie paused, but Paige only nodded her head even though she knew her mentor couldn't see her.

"So what's going on?"

"Melanie's back," Paige said, knowing it would surprise Lady Menagerie as much as it surprised her.

"What? When?"

"This afternoon," Paige said, then had to calculate the hours. Had it really only been hours since Melanie and Marc arrived? She should be exhausted and probably would have been if she hadn't spent the morning and early afternoon on the couch.

"Oh my. Did she tell you where she's been?" Lady Menagerie asked, her voice just above a whisper.

"Yes, but I'm afraid I can't say yet what it is even though it is some of the reason for why I called," Paige said, feeling dumb for calling before thinking about what she could and couldn't say.

"Well, just tell me what you can, and we can start with why you felt the need to call me," Lady Menagerie said.

She loved this woman. She was willing to be there for her, no matter what.

Paige didn't want to waste her mentor's time, so she organized her thoughts so she didn't reveal something she wasn't supposed to. "Okay. My thoughts and emotions are ping-ponging all over the place, but I need to have a clear head later on this morning because we are having brunch with Grace and her husband."

The line was silent for a full three seconds before Lady Menagerie responded. "Okay, start at the beginning, and tell me as much or as little as you can."

Paige began haltingly, wanting to make sure she didn't give away any information that could harm her or her family if it went beyond Lady Menagerie, which wasn't a fear, but the exercise in restraint was needed. By the time Paige had brought Lady Menagerie up to speed an hour had past and she could see some of the reasons behind Melanie's decisions more clearly.

"I have some questions," Lady Menagerie said after another long pause. "I figure you left out some obvious pieces like where Melanie ended up after traveling out of the country, who she saw, and why Grace can't know, but how are you dealing with this new information, and do you feel like what she did justified not being there for you when Brandon passed?"

It was just like Lady Menagerie to get straight to the point.

"Melanie said she left when she did because she felt my life could be indirectly and negatively affected. She said she was trying to interrupt a plan she thought Grace and Antonio were devising. I believe her, but right now it doesn't make me want to trust her more with my feelings."

"I understand. Well, at least you haven't completely shut the door. You are listening and absorbing all of this drama well, especially considering your emotional state," Lady Menagerie said matter-of-factly.

Paige wanted to defend her family and tell Lady Menagerie that it wasn't drama, but she didn't have another name for it. Grace seemed to be the queen of drama, and she had just flounced back into her life with all the subtlety of a skunk at a wedding.

Paige sighed. "Yes, well, I don't know if I'm handling it all that well. I want to scream and yell and tell everyone to get out of my house except Gladys. We were having such a peaceful day before all of this. I was finally getting control over some of my thoughts and feelings."

"Already?"

"What do you mean, 'already'?" It's been a mess in here for a while."

"Honey, it's only been two months since Brandon passed. Before his death, you two dealt with his illness for months. I would be

199

surprised if you had half of your thoughts and feelings under control. Then there was the reason behind tonight's call. It wasn't solely about what happened today. I think your family landing on your doorstep was just the last straw."

Paige couldn't deny it. She had called Lady Menagerie for this very reason, but now she was wondering if she dared to let go of all the thoughts in her head.

As if reading her mind, Lady Menagerie continued, "Unless you aren't ready to have that conversation."

Paige exhaled slowly. This was Lady Menagerie. Paige could be honest with her. Her mentor didn't judge, but Paige felt ashamed for having the thoughts she was about to voice. Why not go with the hardest first?

"Why didn't you tell me not to marry Brandon? You knew how I felt about him. Why didn't you warn me against being with him?"

Lady Menagerie didn't miss a beat in her response and it made Paige wonder if her mentor had expected her questions.

"I think you have overestimated my clairvoyant skills," Lady Menagerie said with more than a touch of sarcasm before clearing her throat and addressing Paige's questions more seriously.

"I'm going to purposely address your questions in a very objective fashion because I know you didn't truly mean for them to sound accusatory," Lady Menagerie said and paused for effect. Paige went over her words and winced. Though they expressed her yearning for answers to questions she didn't think had an answer, they could have sounded judgmental and accusatory.

"I'm sorry…" Paige began, but Lady Menagerie spoke over her as if she hadn't said anything.

"When Brandon broke up with you because he learned that his treatments weren't having the effect he hoped for on his tumor, and he wanted to save you from the very pain you are going through right now, you challenged him to live life as though he would be healed. Even then I asked you if you knew what you were doing. If you were making sure you were preparing yourself in the event that he might die. You told me with all the confidence of an intercessor with God's ear,

200

that your faith didn't allow for 'ifs' or living with doubt." Lady Menagerie spoke with a quiet but firm authority that quickly got under Paige's skin.

"But faith is the substance of things hoped for and the evidence of things unseen," Paige responded, knowing that Lady Menagerie couldn't nor would argue with the Scripture she'd lived by since learning of Brandon's illness.

"Yes it is," Lady Menagerie readily agreed. "And you had substance but no evidence. You can't take God's answer out of the equation." Paige opened her mouth, a response quick on her tongue, but something inside her told her to be still. She wrestled with the urge to defend herself against what Lady Menagerie was trying to say even before she fully understood the allegation.

"You pray until you receive an answer from God then you move in the faith of the answer you heard, but if you come to Him with your own answer you can't expect Him to just cosign so you can put your faith in *that* answer," Lady Menagerie said with just enough love to keep Paige from getting angry. Paige filtered through all the fear, pain, feelings of failure, and hope and saw her on her knees praying to God about Brandon and sincerely asking if he were to be her husband. She'd been sure at the time that she had recognized God's voice, felt the peace that accompanied the answer and the love that opened her heart to Brandon as more than a friend.

Had she somehow placed her desires in front of her objective inquiry about Brandon? Had she convinced herself that she'd heard God's voice? It was her constant internal struggle and very close to the root of what kept her bound by shame. Paige forced herself to voice the question that lay in the darkest part of her mind. This was safe ground after all. Wasn't it?

"Then why would God bring us together? Unless I got it wrong from the beginning, and we weren't supposed to go beyond friendship?" There it was. She'd said it even as she braced herself for Lady Menagerie's confirmation.

"Is that what you really think? That because your love didn't last past your ideal timeline, it wasn't meant to be? Is it so hard for you to believe that God put you and Brandon together not only for your enjoyment but to fulfill part of His perfect will?" Lady Menagerie asked after a couple of seconds and Paige wondered if she weren't bias and blind to Paige's fault by their friendship.

"I'm not even talking about enjoyment. I would settle for less than devastating heartache," Paige said, moving the conversation along.

"Did you think you were exempt from pain, sorrow or struggles?" Lady Menagerie asked, the lovingly soft lilt of her voice going firm again.

"No. Especially not after the year I've had where I discovered that both of the daughters I conceived through rape were alive. Learning that *I* was conceived through manipulation and deceit by the woman I thought was my sister. Thank goodness she's not. Let's see, I almost died on the operating table while donating a kidney to the daughter I just met whose great-grandmother was about to try and take her from the only father she knew. The same great-grandmother who tuned out to be my biological paternal grandmother." Paige took a breath before continuing. "I figured I was due a little happily ever after or a few years of bliss with the man I married."

"Who's to say you won't get that?" Lady Menagerie said, and Paige's mind revolted against the thought. She'd gotten her chance.

"Because the choice was made. I put everything into loving Brandon because he was mine. He was supposed to live. I didn't think God would put us together knowing that we only had a little time together. He knows me better than anyone. He saw me at my worst. He knows what I struggle with." As soon as it came out of her mouth, Paige knew it sounded whiny and selfish, but it was how she felt.

We will get back to your last statement in a moment. First I'd like to ask you how much time would have been enough?" Lady Menagerie asked. Twenty, maybe thirty or fifty years?"

"Not a few months," Paige replied

"But why?"

"What do you mean, why? Because I didn't have enough time to fully get to know him. I didn't get to make more memories with him. I didn't get to have and raise children with him. We didn't get to argue and compromise and learn to stretch around each other."

"Did you have enough time to tell him how much you loved him?" Page didn't want to answer the question. She pressed her lips together.

"I asked you a question, Paige," Lady Menagerie said.

"Yes. Yes, I did," Paige finally answered.

"Did you take the opportunity to show him how much you loved him?" *Every day,* Paige's heart whispered before her mind could think of a response. She closed her eyes as if the action could stave off the tears in her throat.

"Yes," Paige finally whispered.

"Do you think he questioned your love for him?" Lady Menagerie kept on like an insistent rain eroding rock.

"No. I don't believe he questioned my love for him," Paige said but instead of feeling vindicated she felt cheated.

"You know better than I do that life can change in a blink. Yours has several times. Many people fall in love and don't even get to realize what it is like to be married to the one they love for many reasons. You know this too. So, what bothers you so much about the fact that God may have put you and Brandon together knowing that you two had a short amount of time together?"

"If God put us together then He also knew how much it would hurt me to be without Brandon. God knew what state I would be in, and He still allowed it to happen," Paige almost hissed through the phone.

"God also knows what state you'll be in this time next year and the year after that," Lady Menagerie said just as fervently, shaking some of Paige's resolve.

"What if I don't recover?" Paige whispered, truly fearful that she would be one of the exceptions and live with this level of heartache for the rest of her life.

"What if you do?" Lady Menagerie answered just as quickly.

"What do you mean by that?" Paige asked, not expecting the question.

"I've come to know how you think, Paige. You hold on to your relationship with God with a vice grip. It is beautiful and scary to watch.

203

We talked about this when you first started coming to our church, and you would be the first to arrive and the last one to leave. I thought you needed balance and told my husband so. I wondered if you were trying to prove your worth by your obedience, your good stewardship, your humbleness. I even suggested that maybe you were using the church as a refuge to get away from your past," Lady Menagerie said.

She hadn't been far off the mark, Paige thought. The church had been a form of refuge for her. The peace she'd found in the presence of God before she understood that He remained with her was a balm, but she had already talked to the pastor about that.

"My husband told me that you fell in love with God. You were thankful and full of praise and when I watched you with that new understanding I saw it. I saw a woman that was wholly and unabashedly in love with God. You went through the courses for eldership but was happy to sit in the back, preferred it even. You were just happy to learn and absorb everything you could about God. It was inspiring, and your relationship sometimes made me a little envious.

"Last year, though, I noticed an air of desperation around you, and I wondered if your volunteering, your obedience, and prayers weren't a form of payment." Lady Menagerie's voice got quiet and a little high.

"No, no, it wasn't. I love what I do. I love God. Payment for what? For Brandon's healing? The Scripture states..." Paige stopped speaking. Her mind was like a runaway train. How could Lady Menagerie think she would consider trying to pay for Brandon's health with good works when only supplication and God's will would do. "No, I wouldn't do that."

"Okay, I'm sorry. It was an inquiry, not an accusation. I may not have even worded it right. I know I had a lot of things to deal with on my own, but I would still watch you and sense things when I prayed for you. It was as if you were struggling with surrendering, but it didn't make sense to me. You never challenged authority and always seemed so willing to be open to both learning and chastisement."

Paige had an idea of what Lady Menagerie might have felt. It had been hard admitting that she needed help with her obsessive behavior and need for control. It made her feel as though she wasn't as close to

God as she thought. It was true that she spent more time reeling over new revelations, family health issues, and her new marriage than praying. It was also true that she spent less time with God than she had been and allowed Brandon to take the lead for their prayer and study time. *She'd put Brandon between her and God.*

"Which brings me back to the subject at hand," Lady Menagerie continued. "What if this wasn't punishment? What if you weren't martyred? What if your love with Brandon was meant to be a gift? Something you could take with you for the rest of your life. Something that would speak to other young men and women who have been tempted by television and society to do everything but wait on God for their spouse."

"Really?" Paige interrupted Lady Menagerie, her voice incredulous. "I would think it would say just the opposite to those who are waiting for their spouse."

Paige heard the sucking of teeth on the other side of the line, a sure sign that she was trying Lady Menagerie's patience. The sternness in Lady Menagerie's voice when she spoke her next words only confirmed Paige's thoughts.

"Then you've missed more than I thought," Lady Menagerie said with such sadness in her voice, it got Paige's attention. "You do know, beyond the fact that it is Scripture, that God will never leave you or forsake you, right? I mean, you know deep within you that there is no distance that God will allow between you and Him. He will work harder than you will to stay where you need Him."

At those words, swallowing was useless against the emotion looking for release. If it were true, she hadn't made it all up in her mind. God's drawing of her spirit, the constant words of love and adoration with acts of devotions she saw in people He used, passages in His Word that He drew her attention to, and situations He taught her to look at from different perspectives. If it were true, God didn't do this *to* her.

Paige tuned back into Lady Menagerie who was speaking with a quiet fervor that Paige could finally witness as truth.

"I will not now, nor will I ever tell you how long you have to grieve over Brandon and your marriage, but I will tell you to get over this pity

205

party that you are having because you believe you either heard God wrong or are being punished by God for loving Brandon. Neither one is true. You listened to God. Brandon listened to God. You did not let fear keep you from being together, and you loved one another until death parted you physically. It just came sooner than you wanted." Lady Menagerie seemed to be picking the words out of Paige's spirit and spoon-feeding them to her. Paige remained silent and let Lady Menagerie's words reverberate through her.

"Love heals, Paige. It heals, mends rifts, uplifts, teaches, calms, comforts, makes forgiveness possible, creates life, builds hope, obliterates confusion, breathes peace, saves souls—just to name a few. Love doesn't just find a way, it creates a way. A way to do all of those things I just listed and more because God is love, which makes it impossible for you to be the exception."

Paige was not only speechless after Lady Menagerie finished, she was breathless. Her mind was quiet. No, it was clear. It felt funny to think that she could have wept with relief from the realization because she was already crying. Crying as a person did after a long and grueling run where laughing and shouting wasn't enough because the knowledge that the challenge was over was bone-deep and any sound made just didn't reverberate to the core.

"Paige? You still there?" Lady Menagerie asked after a minute of silence went by.

"Yes," Paige responded when she could trust her voice not to give away how much Lady Menagerie's words had shaken her. "Yes," Paige repeated, and the word rippled through her as if her spirit were confirming unspoken questions: Yes, she was going to be all right? Yes, she believed God would never leave her? Yes, she was loved?

"Yes."

His voice warmed and sent a chill through her at the same time, but there was no word to describe the well-being she experienced. It was as if a niche had been perfectly formed for her at that moment and she slipped in effortlessly and just breathed.

"Yes," his voice repeated, and she smiled inside and out.

"Are you all right?" Lady Menagerie's voice was back to concern.

"Yes," Paige said, "I really am."

She heard Lady Menagerie sigh over the phone. "Oh good because that was all Holy Spirit," Lady Menagerie said with a small chuckle. "I just have one thing to say."

"Uh."

"Sshh, listen."

Paige giggled. She wasn't sure if it was due to her mentor's high-handedness or the weight that seemed to have lifted.

"No one is guaranteed tomorrow. No one. Are you listening?"

"Yep," Paige responded before forcing her lips together to stifle another giggle.

"We *are* all given the opportunity to love. It may come in different forms, but we have the opportunity to love. You got to love Brandon deeply, and he loved you the same. The amount of time has nothing to do with the depth of your love, and time also has little to do with what it will take to heal so that maybe you can love again."

Paige shied away from the last statement. It seemed like a betrayal.

"Not now. Certainly not now, but just don't go getting a whole bunch of cats and holing up in your apartment."

"That's not going to happen," Paige said with all sincerity, but she got the feeling that Lady Menagerie misunderstood her seriousness.

"That's good to hear," Lady Menagerie said.

"I'm not a cat person," Paige deadpanned.

"Don't sass me, girl," Lady Menagerie said in a voice that brooked no argument or sass.

I grieve for you and with you, but don't compound your pain by projecting your pain and loneliness into the future," Lady Menagerie said.

What Paige wanted to say was, "Do you think I can get that sewn on a pillow?" but she was sure she would get some type of reprimand. What she did say was, "I will try not to, Lady Menagerie."

"Good, now what are you going to do about your... well, Grace tomorrow? Do you want me to come?"

Paige could see it now, and in light of everything was tempted to accept Lady Menagerie's offer, but she was feeling more calm and secure than she had in a while. She would deal with Grace, her husband and their questions, God's way.

"No thank you, Lady Menagerie. You have given me and reminded me of all the weapons I will need for tomorrow's showdown. Besides, the more reinforcements I bring, the more it will look like I'm hiding something."

"Okay, I understand, but I can be ready at a moment's notice—or close to it—tomorrow morning, so if you change your mind, I will make sure I'm free until one o'clock in the afternoon," Lady Menagerie reiterated. Paige smiled at her willingness to jump into the fray that was her family's feud at the moment.

Lady Menagerie's voice lost its playfulness with the next question. "What about you and Melanie?"

"It hurts," Paige said honestly. "She was the one who always looked out for me. Even when I was being a brat I could go to her with anything. She knows almost all there is to know about me, but with each layer of secrets that get revealed, I feel like the woman I once knew as a sister doesn't exist. It's hard to have a relationship with someone you're not sure is real."

"Did she tell you what she revealed from her trip was the last of the secrets?" Lady Menagerie asked.

Paige thought back to her conversations with Mel that day. "Not in so many words. The last piece of information she shared made me walk out of the room because I just couldn't absorb any more. Everything was so jumbled, and my emotions were ready to take over, so I stopped taking anything else in. She tried to talk to me right before I called you, but I shut her down because nothing that came out of my mouth at that moment would be beneficial to our relationship." Paige felt a little bad about how she'd handled the situation, but it was still better than screaming and yelling like she'd wanted to.

"Did she at least explain why she made some of the decisions she's made over the last year?"

"Yes," Paige responded, while she recalled the last conversation she'd had with Melanie. "She said she'd done it all for me. She'd sacrificed our mother-daughter relationship to keep me alive and safe.

She did it because I was the most important person in her life," Paige said more to herself than Lady Menagerie, staring into space above her desk.

"Do you believe her?"

"I'm not sure," Paige whispered, hoping her heart might not hear.

"Well then, I think that is as good a place to start as any," Lady Menagerie said succinctly. "Be open and let her prove her words. It's on her to earn back your trust, not the other way around. But..." Lady Menagerie paused, getting Paige's attention. "But don't make her pay for your hurt."

"Okay."

"Okay, you will get to the other side of this. I have no doubt about that," Lady Menagerie said, and it warmed Paige's heart that her mentor had so much confidence in her.

"Just don't forget to learn all you can from the process, and when it doesn't hurt so much, begin to enjoy it."

Paige thought enjoying the process was going to be much harder than just getting through, but one thing Paige knew was that Lady Menagerie didn't tell people to do things she hadn't done herself.

"I will, Lady Menagerie."

"Good. Now you need to go and get some sleep so you don't look like you've been up all night planning what you're going to say tomorrow... I mean today."

"Lady Menagerie?" Paige said, fingering the edge of her shirt.

"Yes, sweetie?"

"I love you."

There was a short pause before her mentor's gruff voice came over the phone line.

"I love you too, sweetie. We're going to get through this. I think you have amazing strength and one of the biggest hearts I've ever seen." Lady Menagerie's voice broke on the last few words.

"Goodnight," Paige said in response.

"Good morning, love," Lady Menagerie answered back, making Paige chuckle before she took the phone from her ear and stared at the screen for a moment before pressing the end button.

Chapter 19

Paige woke up slowly. It took her a few moments to realize the ache in her heart wasn't so sharp. It was like a wound that had once been angry and festering that finally scabbed over, making it less likely to get infected again. *Huh. How about that?* She might heal after all.

She turned to see that Gladys' bed was not only empty, but it had also been made. Bless that sweet child. *What time was it?* Paige turned over to look at the small radio clock Vivian used when she visited. It read nine-thirty. She squinted to double-check that she was reading the clock correctly even as her heart sped up. Why didn't anyone wake her up? She threw off the covers, stood and turned to straighten the covers as the door opened.

"Good," Melanie said. "I was just coming in to wake you." Paige glanced up briefly before returning to her task. *Was it lighter in the room this morning?* Melanie walked to the other side of the bed and spread the bedclothes out evenly.

"How are you feeling?" Mel asked as they straightened from the task.

Paige looked at her mom. Really looked at her for the first time in months. Mel looked tired and a little haggard. Paige couldn't remember what time Melanie had retired to her room, but it was before she'd finished her call with Lady Menagerie. "You look tired. Didn't you sleep?" Paige asked.

Mel shrugged. "Some." Paige watched Mel's eyes flit back and forth, taking in Paige's features. Whatever she'd been looking for, Mel seemed to have found because she visibly relaxed. "You look... better."

Paige gave Mel half a smile. "Yes, I feel better."

Melanie blinked rapidly as if stemming a tide of tears. "Good, good." She let out a long breath. "Well, Gladys was hungry, so she's having a bowl of cereal. Marc spoke to Grace and the Branchetts. We will be meeting at the Journey restaurant at eleven-thirty. I wanted to give you as much time to sleep as possible." Melanie added the last sentence in response to the frown she must have seen on Paige's face.

Question answered, Paige waited for Melanie to go on. She knew they had a lot to talk about, and she realized that the overwhelming confusion and pain from the night before had subsided. There was a clarity to her thoughts that hadn't been noticeable in months. Had she put this all on herself with her insecurity regarding God's intentions toward her. Her spirit was no longer at odds with her soul though they both mourned.

Paige's internal evaluation was cut short by the sound of Melanie's slow exhale as she turned to walk out of the room. "Mel, we need to talk."

Melanie turned in the doorway, her eyes moist. "We have time. Go ahead and get yourself ready. The coffee is on, and I found some fruit in the refrigerator. We can talk while Gladys showers and gets dressed. I tell you, that child takes more and more time to get ready every day.

Paige smiled. "It's because she goes over her wardrobe choices with Vivian online, but this being Sunday she might be on her own. Vivian is in church until eleven our time."

"We are blessed to have two beautiful girls, aren't we?" Melanie said with her hand on the door.

"Yes, we are," Paige confirmed and watched the ghost of a smile on Melanie's lips deepen into something more believable before she walked out of the room.

Paige turned to gather her toiletries when her phone notified of her of an incoming text.

Mason: *I spoke to Richard this morning. He's very concerned about you.*

She bet. Last night wasn't one of her finest moments.

Mason: *If you need to talk, I have two very good ears.*

Paige didn't know she was smiling until she caught her reflection in her phone's display. She didn't force it away. It felt good to give in to it and not feel ashamed for even having a pleasant moment.

Paige: *Aren't you in church?*

Mason: *I couldn't concentrate so I stepped out. Needed to ask. Are you okay?*

The text reminded her of the restriction she'd placed on him, and it squeezed her heart that he would try and honor her unreasonable request even as he broke it.

Paige: *Thank you for asking, Mason. I am all right.*

She paused for a moment, testing the feel of her next sentence before pressing the send button.

Paige: *We'll talk later today. Okay?*

She promised herself that no matter what happened at the brunch that she would talk to Mason. If his text could make her smile then she was sure his call could help relieve some of the tension she was sure to feel at brunch.

Mason: *Looking forward to it.*

The wording jogged Paige's memory, and she wondered if she should ask Mason about his woman friend on their call this evening. She shrugged at herself as she walked to her bathroom. If it came to mind while they were talking, she would ask; otherwise, she would stick to whatever topics came up. Given what lay ahead, she was sure they would have more than enough to talk about.

Two hours later, Paige walked through the plush dining room of the Journey alongside Gladys, who had slipped her hand in Paige's, as they exited the car and refused to let go. She could only imagine the excitement and nervousness Gladys was feeling. Paige was feeling nervous herself though a great deal more composed than the night before.

She gave Gladys' hand another squeeze then made a cross-eyed face at the girl when she looked at her. Gladys let out a surprised giggle, drawing Melanie's stormy gaze to them. Paige gave her the same look and watched Mel's features ease before her mother nodded her thanks.

This didn't have to be difficult. It wasn't like they were going to war. This could be treated like diplomatic talks between three countries wanting to avoid conflict. They could be cordial... Paige's mind stuttered at the word. Well, they could be civilized. It was a nice restaurant after all.

Paige took a deep, fortifying breath and rounded the corner to a more intimate setting of the restaurant and saw that Victoria, Richard, Grace, and Ross were already seated. Richard and Ross sat next to one another, in deep discussion, while Victoria and Grace looked to be purposely ignoring each other.

Victoria stood and came around the table when she saw them approach. She greeted and hugged Marc and Melanie then Gladys, saving Paige for last.

"I apologize for last night," Victoria whispered as she extended her hug with Paige. "All the excitement and anticipation had me a little stir crazy."

"You are no longer excited?" Paige asked when Victoria drew back, feeling a little like her old self.

"Oh yes. I'm definitely still excited, just a little less crazy," Victoria said, making Paige chuckle before she was delivered into Richard's arms.

"Paige," Richard said on an exhale as he held her to him. When he released her, she saw the unvoiced question in his eyes.

"Richard," she mimicked, trying to get as close to his baritone as possible. She could see from his expression that she startled him, but after a couple of seconds his features cleared, and he kissed her cheek in affection and obvious relief. His reaction gave her pause. She knew she'd been caught up in her grief, and as Lady Menagerie had so eloquently put it "having a pity party," but people were acting as if she had been on the edge of death herself.

Richard stepped aside, and Paige came around the table to meet Ross Dillard.

She reached out to shake Grace's husband's hand. His eyes were clear and gentle, and his grip was warm and firm, especially when he added his other hand. She watched him only to find that he was watching her. She smiled sheepishly before addressing him. "Hello, Mr. Dillard."

"Paige, it's a pleasure to finally meet you. Please call me Ross." She nodded her head in concession. "My condolences on the passing of your husband. I certainly would have attended the funeral, but I was out of the country on business. Was Grace able to extend my sympathies?"

Paige's mind blanked for a moment. It was obvious Grace showed her husband a different side of herself. One that didn't actually exist.

"Um, I wasn't really in a state of mind to remember much from that day. Brandon's family came in and took over, allowing me to just be," she finished apologetically. It was as close as she could get to the truth.

"Thank you for your thoughts, Ross. That's really nice of you. It's a pleasure to meet you too." She found that she meant it and didn't know whether to be happy for her mother or sad for him.

He stepped aside revealing Grace who hadn't gained her feet. Paige came to her, placing a hand on the woman's shoulder as she walked behind her chair on her way to the seats on the other side of the round table.

"Grace."

"Paige," Grace responded, obviously unhappy with Paige's cool greeting. Grace's practiced look of disdain might have ruffled Paige before learning what she had this weekend, but since her greeting wouldn't have been any different, Paige wasn't going to let it bother her. Grace had long ago lost any claims to warm welcomes.

Gladys, who had been following Paige, didn't seem phased by Paige's response to Grace either way. She bent down and hugged her great-grandmother after greeting Ross in the same manner.

There was small talk and light discussion after they gave their drink orders and took turns visiting the expansive buffet. When everyone was finally back at the table, Ross inadvertently brought up the subject most of them wanted to avoid.

"That's sweet that Gladys calls you Papa Richard," Ross said, looking back and forth between Gladys and Richard.

Richard chuckled. "Yeah, it's much easier than Great-Granddad Richard.

"Yeah, Grace told me what a year your family has been having with all the discoveries and revelations. It's almost unreal."

Paige thought Ross had a gift for understatement but just smiled along with everyone else as he continued. It seemed Ross liked to hear himself speak.

"After all this time you find out that your adopted granddaughter is actually your biological great-granddaughter and has a twin. That must have been a day," Ross said, directing his last sentence toward the Branchetts. "To go from such a tentative beginning to this." Ross spread his hands out wide to include the table as a whole. "It's a blessing."

Paige sent Melanie a covert glance, wondering if she was mirroring her thoughts. *Tentative beginnings? What was that?* Paige wondered what Grace had told him regarding her and the twins' conception. Melanie returned her glance for a couple of seconds, sharing a look that said she was just as clueless as Paige.

"And you, Melanie." Paige watched Melanie's gaze snap to Ross. Her expression guarded.

"Yes?" Melanie answered, her voice sweeter than honey. Paige looked to Marc beside her. His features had morphed from indulgent to impassive. It put Paige on alert, and she worked on keeping her expression openly curious.

"Where have you been?" Ross asked as if his question wasn't the opening to a hot topic.

It took all of Paige's concentration to pretend mild interest when all she wanted to do was ask the man if he knew what his wife was really up to.

Melanie looked at Ross and then looked at Grace whom Paige noticed was having a hard time keeping her smirk from showing.

Paige's gaze shifted back to Melanie, and the look that crossed her features made Paige shiver.

"From what I know about you, Ross, you are a very nice man, so I say this with respect for your position in Grace's life." Melanie blinked once before continuing. "I'm not sure if that is any of your business."

"I disagree, Melanie. I believe anything you do to cause my wife concern or distress is my business. You have been traversing this country for the last five months, obviously trying to avoid any surveillance which could have served only to aid you in the event of an emergency." Paige watched the man's facial features as well as his body language and found no deception or guile. It struck her again that he might really care for Grace.

His response seemed to take the wind out of Melanie's sails, and she slowly pushed her plate away from her.

"I think thwarting surveillance was never really a possibility for me and Marc. If it were, Grace wouldn't have shown up on my daughter's doorstep for the first time, only hours after Marc and I arrived in Los Angeles."

"Do you deny that your mother might have been worried about you after her calls to you went unanswered for months?" Ross asked, leaning toward Melanie as though he was afraid of missing anything.

"I don't deny that she was worried, but I think it was more about *what I would find* rather than for my safety, which is in no more danger than it was when I turned twelve," Melanie replied.

Paige could barely remember the last time Melanie went against her mother's wishes, let alone being openly antagonistic. This was like looking at a woman she'd never met before. She was proud to know this woman.

Paige looked down at her drink while watching Ross with her peripheral vision. He looked upset, and rightly so, if his feelings were genuine, but he didn't bluster or get puffed up. In fact, just the opposite happened. A calm seemed to come over him. The reaction startled Paige enough to look up at him right along with everyone else at the table.

"What do you think it is my wife is afraid of you finding?" Ross asked quietly. His tone didn't give anything away, but Paige saw a challenge in his eyes. He was daring Melanie.

Why?

"Whom would be more precise, and the person I am speaking of is Brian Grossenberg, Paige's father."

216

"Is that what you were doing? Looking for Brian?" Ross asked, looking no more invested in the answer than in starting brunch all over again.

Melanie didn't flinch or look away. "Yes."

"Baby..." Marc began, his face showing his confusion, but Melanie turned to him, placing her hand on his cheek briefly before turning back to Ross.

"And did—" Grace murmured

Melanie shifted her gaze to Grace. "No, we didn't."

"Why now? Why go looking for Brian now after believing he was dead all these years?" Grace asked.

"I should ask you the same question," Melanie responded, and Paige watched Grace's brow furrow. "Why would you be interested in Brian after all this time?"

"I don't know what you're talking about," Grace retorted.

"You didn't approach Antonio Sable?" Melanie began, and though her voice sounded curious, her eyes were cunning. "You didn't convince him that it would be in his best interest to test Brian's remains against the DNA he obtained when he had a paternity test done?"

Grace opened her mouth then shut it as if it just occurred to her where Melanie was going with her comments.

Paige watched it all unfold like an orchestrated nightmare. Melanie talked to her that morning about what was discussed between her, Marc, and the Branchetts the night before after Paige had left the room. Paige listened to Melanie's explanation again for why she decided to keep Brian Jr.'s existence to herself, and Paige listened with an open mind. She couldn't even imagine what she would have done had she been in the same situation at twelve. She barely got through her own situation with her sanity in tact, and she had been two years older.

"What is it you were hoping to discover?" Melanie prompted when Grace didn't answer. "I mean if you were to find Brian alive, what would you do with the information? What would you have to gain?"

Grace glowered at Melanie. "You're so quick to see me as the villain. Have these people so easily brainwashed you?" Grace swept a hand in Victoria and Richard's direction. "What else could explain your reason for leaving like you did while your daughter was mourning her husband?"

Melanie breathed deeply, and Paige could see the struggle she was having in keeping her emotions in control. Paige was having problems herself and was happy she wasn't in Melanie's shoes. There was no telling what would escape her mouth after finding out that her grandmother had plotted to get rid of her as a baby.

"There was no brainwashing needed. All I had to do was look back on my childhood to see that any theory the Branchetts came up with after their research, was plausible where you are concerned." Melanie closed her eyes briefly, and Paige wished she could help but was relegated to supportive looks and soothing pats to Gladys' thigh. The child had grown unnaturally quiet, and it only took one look to see that she wanted to crawl over everyone to get to Melanie but was also torn.

"It wouldn't take much convincing for me to believe that you were plotting and scheming with Antonio Sable against his father when Luca Sable was the very same man who brought charges against you for your assassination attempt against Brian. With that one move, you put all our lives in jeopardy. The fact that we are still here is nothing short of a miracle," Melanie said.

Grace stared at Melanie for a few seconds. Paige wondered if she were trying to assess whether Melanie was telling the truth or calculating how far to push the subject. When Grace blinked and sat back against the booth's cushion, Paige took her first deep breath. When she nodded, Paige took another.

"Is this true?" Ross asked, gaining everyone's attention.

Grace turned to her husband, her face and voice were cajoling. "Antonio contacted me when he found some documents in their company's warehouse with my signature. On occasion I authorized wire transfers from Luca Sable's personal account to the Grossenbergs, not knowing the relationship between the two at the time. It was none of my business, and my digression was one of the reasons why I was so good at my job. Antonio has been looking for answers regarding his son's death for years. He wanted to know just how far back my knowledge of his father's influence went."

Paige watched Ross's eyes take in Grace's features and her cultured lie. She could tell he wanted to believe her, but there was that one moment between the time he broke their gaze and looked back at Melanie that Paige saw doubt and hurt.

"Okay, but why now?" Ross asked.

Paige's attention was jerked toward Victoria as was everyone else's when Victoria began speaking. Paige had been so caught up in the conversation between Grace and Melanie she had almost forgotten the Branchetts were there.

"There's talk that Luca is ready to retire, and Antonio isn't altogether confident about the loyalty of the men he works with. Also, I think Antonio is feeling a bit overwhelmed because none of his other children have an interest in the business." Which Paige knew wasn't true at all. Antonio would happily take the reins from his father then adopt some children who were already interested in the business, if that was what was called for.

"Antonio is looking for a business prodigy, and I'm looking for my son. The only common denominator was Luca," Victoria finished.

"And?" Grace asked, sounding impatient.

"And so are you?" Victoria replied. Her voice, devoid of emotion.

"What are you saying?" Ross asked, visibly disturbed by what he thought Victoria was implying.

"She is just reiterating that I used to work for Luca Sable and have also been in contact with Antonio Sable," Grace said before Victoria could answer.

Victoria openly watched Grace and Paige and looked back and forth between the three.

"Is that what you meant?" Ross asked Victoria.

Victoria stared at Grace for another second before turning back to her husband and responding. "Yes, exactly."

Ross's color seemed high behind his bronze complexion. Paige could tell he was not happy but he remained civil. She didn't know if that made him just a good businessman or a dangerous man.

"And this business about Antonio looking for a prodigy?" he asked.

219

Victoria gave him a slow smile, and it made Paige shiver. These people were communicating on a whole other level.

"He is trying to weed out any possible opposition, and he is just paranoid enough to think that his own son, who has been buried for over twenty years, might be one of them."

"So, you believe your son is dead?" Ross asked, watching Victoria intently.

Paige continued to watch their interaction, entranced.

Victoria, who had emanated confidence just seconds before, now looked crestfallen. "There's nothing to prove otherwise."

"Every place we thought Luca might have visited or taken Brian to over the last twenty-seven years came up with little to no leads. Either he is extremely clever, or Brian really is dead," Melanie responded, looking as despondent as one would expect from someone who had traipsed across the country only to come back empty-handed."

The table grew quiet, and Paige began to pray that the conversation was over. That Grace and Ross would let it go, even if it was only for the moment. She prayed for peace, knowing no one but God could heal what had transpired.

Grace took inhaled deeply and Paige looked up to see her open her mouth, but Ross squeezed Grace's hand and shook his head to dissuade her and she closed it.

He went on instead. "You know, when Grace asked me to accompany her here to see how her children were doing, I didn't know what to expect. I knew there was some tension between her and Paige, and I hoped with everything that happened recently, it would allow you all to see that life is short and that you would work to come together, instead of widen the gap in your relationship. I can see there is a lot more here than I was told or suspected, but it isn't something that can't be overcome.

"It sounds like my wife has made some mistakes in where she put her trust, but there's been nothing said today that would make me think that her intentions were purposefully hurtful. If anything, she has been seeking answers and resolution for the harm that has come upon this family from the Sable grandfather."

Paige fought the temptation to look at Melanie and instead listened to Ross with a discerning ear.

"I know I'm new to this family, but I believe you could band together for a solution. If one doesn't present itself, your efforts may bring you together rather than divide you. Those are my two cents." He raised his hands in surrender. "Do with them as you will."

Paige wondered what side of herself Grace showed Ross when they were alone for him not to see that she wasn't on the same side as the solution.

Everyone at the table looked at everyone else and seemed to decide that the conversation was best abandoned where it was.

Grace cleared her throat, and dread stiffened Paige's spine.

"I want to apologize for my heavy-handedness this morning, but it was more from my anxiousness to see my daughter and judge her well-being for myself," Grace said with more humility than Paige ever thought she'd see the woman display. Even if it were just for show.

Paige was ready to go home, and by the feel of Gladys, who just laid her head on Paige's arm, she was too.

Paige knew this wasn't the last word from Grace regarding Melanie and Marc's trip because no one, except maybe Ross, believed Grace was really sorry for her impromptu early morning interrogation. Paige just hoped it would be a few days before she, her mother, or daughter heard from Grace.

Paige glanced at her watch and was happy to see that it only felt like they'd been at the restaurant for most of the day. She had more than enough time to call Mason as she'd promised when they got back to her apartment. It would be good to talk to someone who wasn't keeping secrets, scheming, or holding alternative motives. She was more than done with all of that.

221

Chapter 20

Guilt was racking Mason. He would have given anything for another word or message from Rachel when she first passed. He'd so wanted something to look forward to. Something he could take with him. To keep a letter from Brandon meant for Paige seemed like the ultimate betrayal, but as much as he wanted to give Brandon's mother the go-ahead, there was something in him that told him giving her the letter would do more harm than good at that moment.

For days he pondered over the decision, asking himself if he was doing it more for himself or for Paige, but Vivian with one well-timed comment helped answer that question.

Vivian came over and sat at the kitchen table, placing her head in her hands in a dramatic fashion while he was preparing dinner the night before.

"I'm not sure what to get Mati, Daddy. I was thinking something for authors, like a lap desk, some pretty flash drives or custom-made bookmarks with her books on them." She sighed. "But now I'm thinking that she might like something with all of our pictures on it."

He looked up from the recipe he was reading on his tablet. "Why don't you get her both?" Vivian seemed to consider it. "I could, but I don't want to give her anything that would sadden her. I'm trying to be sensitive to the spirit."

"Sensitive to the spirit. What do you mean by that?" Mason had an idea but wanted to see if Vivian could clarify what she felt.

"Well, I wanted to get Paige something that wasn't too personal. I was thinking of getting her useful things surrounding her books, so I didn't remind her of the bad things that happened and make her any sadder than she is." She stopped speaking for a moment, and Mason turned, giving her his full attention.

Vivian sighed again. "But even though I don't think it would be a good idea, I keep getting a feeling right here." She splayed her hand high across her stomach. "That the more personal gift would be better."

Mason nodded his head in understanding. "So, what are you going to do?"

"I guess I'm going to have to let go of what I think is right and listen to the Holy Spirit," Vivian said, not looking pleased but resigned. "I will also pray that Mati feels the love I put in my gift to her. That should help, right?"

"I think you are wiser than you know," Mason said to his daughter.

She tipped her head to the side as if she were trying to read more into his compliment. He wanted to tell her that she just helped him resolve an issue he'd been wrestling with, but he couldn't chance her pressing him for details regarding his situation.

"You've listened so far, and you haven't been steered wrong. Don't second-guess yourself now."

He watched his daughter swallow a few times before answering. "Thank you."

He nodded again. "You're welcome," he said before turning back to the recipe he'd been reading. Just to double-check that she'd understood him, he asked her another question.

"So, what are you going with? I don't want to duplicate your present," Mason said with as much nonchalance as he could manage with a throat constricting with emotion.

"There is this really nice travel mug you can personalize with pictures and an electronic frame that will show all of your pictures as a slide show. It is on one continuous loop. Gladys and I have a whole bunch of pictures of everyone from last Thanksgiving, the wedding, and our birthdays," Vivian said, starting to sound more invested in the idea.

Mason wondered what pictures Vivian and Gladys had taken of him the Thanksgiving before. He was curious to see if he'd successfully hidden his feelings from the camera. Maybe he could talk Vivian out of using the ones that caught him with his thoughts on his sleeve since he knew better than most that it took only a few times in her presence to fall in love with her.

"Hey, could I see some of the pictures before you give them to her or use them in the gift?"

Vivian went quiet behind him, and he glanced over his shoulder to see her staring at him. "What?"

"Are you going to tell me not to use certain pictures?" Vivian asked as if plucking the thoughts from his mind.

He shrugged.

"It's not like she didn't know how you felt at the time," Vivian murmured.

He didn't turn around that time.

"Dad."

"Yes?"

"Do you still love her?"

Mason played dumb. "Who?" He began going through the cabinets in search of the spices needed for the beef sliders he'd chosen to make for dinner. When there was no response from his daughter after a full minute, he glanced toward the table to see her sitting there with an expectant look on her face.

"What?" he asked in reaction to her expression.

"Do you still love Paige?" Vivian asked when he went back to preparing their dinner.

Knowing she wouldn't let it go, Mason washed his hands and took his time drying them before giving his daughter his undivided attention again. He crossed his arms over his chest and stared back at her.

"Is that why you're not seeing Tabitha anymore?" Vivian asked, obviously expecting an answer.

"I know that I've been pretty open with you about my feeling for Paige in the past," he began, but she interrupted him.

"No, you haven't. You rarely talk about your feelings for Paige or any other woman, for that matter," Vivian said matter-of-factly.

"Then what makes you think I would start sharing now?" he asked, baffled.

"Nothing. I just thought it was worth a try since you were distracted with dinner." She shrugged, her mouth tipping up in a mischievous grin.

"You little rascal," he said before shaking his head and returning to face the counter.

"Yeah, but I'm *your* little rascal," she returned, seeming undaunted by his words.

"That you are, and don't you ever forget it."

He heard her laugh and it warmed his heart.

"Well, whomever you choose, they will be extremely blessed," Vivian said. A few seconds later, he heard the chair she'd been sitting in scrape against the floor as she got up and left the kitchen. He didn't even try to fight the smile that took over his face. It would have been in vain considering that his heart had just grown two sizes to hold the emotion Vivian's comment brought and it still wasn't enough. His daughter thought he was a blessing.

He considered her words right then and later that evening. It was a hard compliment to take. He'd made so many mistakes—in his life and his marriage. He loved Rachel. That could hardly be questioned. He gave her everything he believed he had in his power to give. From the moment he met her in school he'd made room in his heart and his life for her.

She'd made his life more meaningful from the day she agreed to go out with him for the first time. If he were honest, she still was through her influence and teachings to Vivian. Three years after her last breath Rachel was still causing an impact on his life. He just hoped that he made half as much of one on hers.

There was no doubt in his mind that she knew he loved her, but over the last few months, he discovered there was a whole level of love that he had kept from her just because he was angry and bitter and refused to forgive a man God allowed to misrepresent Him.

Not until recently did he consider that the sum of his father's whole worth wasn't measured in his failure as a family man or more specifically, Mason's father. He had been a traveling preacher for years, and when he was home, he was a good father and husband. He'd introduced Mason to God in Bible stories for children and slowly taught Mason to admire God by crediting Him for all his most profound thoughts and sayings.

Being a recipient of God's gift of redemption through an event that most would struggle to find a bright side to, Mason could now see that though his father destroyed his mother with his deception, there was another side. It was the side of his father that was used to usher many, many souls to Christ.

Did it relieve Mason of the burden of anger he felt toward his father for his weak acts? No, but it showed him the greatness of God and His ability to use the destructive acts of a situation or person, to fulfill His perfect plan. A plan that brought Mason back to Christ even as his newfound friend transitioned to heaven.

Mason also found it ironic that as much as he'd vowed to be unlike his father, in some ways he'd fallen short of that pledge.

He took his marriage vows seriously and looked forward to spending decades with Rachel. He'd imagined her belly growing with their children and the years they'd spend teaching and raising them. He saw him and Rachel marrying their children off to almost worthy prospects and growing old, surrounded by grandchildren and great-grandchildren.

He didn't get most of the latter, but the years he did get with Rachel were full of beauty and wonder until they weren't, and he still would have taken those last few months over the pain of not waking to her fragrance every morning or knowing at some point in the day she would gift him with a smile.

When Rachel became bedridden and their friends stopped coming around as often, Mason would get the occasional call, card, or look from a colleague or acquaintance offering help and praising him for sticking around. They wouldn't use those words exactly, but it was implied. At first, the platitudes incited anger and indignation. He didn't understand what the praise was for. He'd made a vow before everyone and he'd meant every one of them. He'd promised to love Rachel. He'd promised to cherish her, take care of her, and allow her to take care of him. He'd promised himself that he would do his best to make her happy and give her everything her heart desired. Everything except accepting the fact that God wasn't tyrannical. Admit that God was a gentleman and didn't force men to love or serve Him. He didn't crucify men like Mason's father for what they thought they were doing in the dark, but He didn't let the victims of those transgressions go without some type of redemption back to Himself.

Mason had sat back and watched, thinking it was enough not to discourage Rachel from praising her God and teaching Vivian to love and praise Him too. That he was being generous to allow his wife and daughter to love and serve a God he was angry with. Even before he walked to the front of the church and kneeled beside Brandon's coffin, he knew that he'd been nothing but selfish and spiteful not to encourage Rachel and Vivian to express their ever-growing love for God.

Mason wished every day that Brandon was still alive so they could talk about all the thoughts and ideas he had and what the Holy Spirit had shared with him. He was continually excited and astounded at all the ways God showed him how to love, how to see life, how to give more, and how to forgive. Well, the last one was still a work in progress. Either way, it was hard to keep it to himself, and he began to enjoy conversations with Vivian that he wouldn't have had the tolerance to hold before.

He had smothered Rachel and Vivian's enthusiasm and need to express their happiness and thankfulness for even having the desire to acknowledge God in their lives. Even now, he understood what Paige had meant when she'd told him what she could and couldn't abide in a husband. Though Mason thought they had a great deal in common when he'd first gotten to know Paige, she'd made the fact that she couldn't openly discuss God with Mason a deal-breaker. It was just one more reason why Mason admired Paige. It sounded crazy and there was no way he would share with anyone, including Dr. Seagrate.

Mason hadn't known until recently how upset he'd been at Rachel for "choosing God over him." It was real. Six months ago he would have denied it even though he felt it true enough. It just sounded insane. It didn't sound much better now, but knowing without a doubt that God was real made it less so. Up until Rachel, Mason had managed to diminish God in his life and mind enough to render Him as minute as an excuse for why men did peculiar things. In Rachel's presence, the awareness of God had grown to the degree that Mason could justify being hostile toward Him and blaming Him for not stopping Mason's father from destroying his mother's life.

Mason had openly spoken to God twice since the beginning of his relationship with Rachel. Once when he'd pleaded for Rachel to be healed and not die and once when Vivian was in the hospital. Neither were lengthy conversations by any stretch of the imagination. He didn't doubt that they were both one-sided with him uttering no more than a paragraph each time.

"Please, God, she believes in You. Please heal her," were spoken on behalf of Rachel as she struggled to breathe a couple of nights before she passed. It was much the same for his daughter, and still, in this moment, he didn't know why God spared Vivian and not his wife or Brandon for that matter.

True, there was a level of distrust between him and God. He had some questions, but he also knew that God was the only one who could answer those questions, and Mason hoped that He would do so, sooner rather than later.

Meanwhile, Mason had some work of his own. Forgiveness had come surprisingly easy for Mason when it came to tearing up the pamphlet worth of transgressions he felt Victoria and Richard made against him. It was almost disconcerting how quickly he let go of his desire to see Victoria pay for all her hurtful words and deeds toward Rachel and Vivian as well as his anger at Richard for allowing his wife to treat their family as she had.

He wanted Vivian to feel free to call her grand- and great-grandparents without asking him for permission because something she might say could be used against him in court. He wanted her to be able to spend holidays with her whole family instead of having to pick and choose which week she wanted to stay with him and which one she would be with them.

He knew from the moment he met Victoria she was less than thrilled about her daughter dating a man with next to no history. At first, he thought it was because he was a darker shade of brown compared to Rachel's extremely fair complexion, but when Richard walked into the room with his mahogany-hued features, Mason put that assumption to rest.

Still, there was a certain condescension Victoria spoke with when addressing him that put his teeth on edge. When he'd mentioned it to Rachel, she admitted she'd noticed it and had spoken to her mother about it, but it wasn't until they had graduated from college and were married that Victoria's attitude lessened. When she stepped in and assisted them in the adoption of Vivian, he thought everything had worked itself out.

They had many more civil and sometimes pleasurable interactions with Victoria and Richard until Rachel became ill. Then it all went south.

No one was more shocked or dismayed to find out Paige was Victoria's granddaughter than him. Mason had spent the last three years trying to put as much distance between him and Victoria without completely severing her relationship with Vivian. It was hard letting his child go visit a woman whose disdain for him was so obvious. Mason's relationship with Richard was much more cordial, but his lack of influence on his wife's behavior worked against their relationship the first few months after Rachel's death.

Over the last year, Richard had taken it upon himself to keep Mason in the loop regarding Vivian and her parentage. After Paige came into the picture, the information Richard shared with Mason extended to Paige and her family. It was both welcome and uncomfortable for Mason.

He still remembered the moment he'd looked into Paige's captivating eyes. It was like a beautiful dance gone wrong. He'd miscalculated the steps it would take to breach their distance, and she ended up bouncing off his chest. Though he'd been able to keep *her* from falling to the ground, her belongings were not so fortunate. He took in her petite frame, graceful movements, and nervous energy all in the few seconds she was in his space, and it triggered a longing in him that he thought had been turned to ash.

He'd had little to no desire to have any woman close to him, let alone have her in his environment, but that was exactly where he saw Paige at that moment. It only reinforced itself each time he spoke to her until she was embedded in his skin. He knew he would have sounded demented if he'd chosen to speak those thoughts so he filed them away, going back to them only in the very loneliest of times.

There was no doubt that there had been a mutual physical awareness and electric chemistry between them. It all but short-circuited him when their eyes met and had reintroduced him to his long-lost libido, which after a while became more of a burden.

Some of his physical passion toward Paige had been cooled by her rejection, even as sweet and logical as it was. It cooled even more with her engagement and marriage to Brandon. What had not ended was his love for Paige, though he'd done everything he could think of to kill it or dampen the feeling.

His drunken interaction with Tabitha's sister months before they'd met had been proof of that. Though it triggered Tabitha's breakup with him, hurting her was the last thing he'd wanted to do. He'd wanted to at least salvage their friendship because he cared for Tabitha, and she'd already been through more than enough in her life. Once he realized what his drinking and irresponsible behavior had done to an innocent woman, let alone his daughter, it bothered him enough to stop drinking altogether.

Thankfully, after months, Tabitha had finally begun to return his words of greeting at church. He'd hoped she wouldn't go as far as leaving the church to stay away from him and she hadn't. It showed him that her faith was stronger than he first suspected, and she was stronger as a person. Mason happily bore the brunt of the shame and awkwardness whenever their eyes met or they ended up in close proximity, today included.

***

After church, Mason took Vivian to breakfast. He couldn't escape the fact that Paige, Gladys, Melanie, Marc, and the Branchetts were having brunch together. What he wouldn't give to be a fly on the wall in the establishment they were all in at that moment.

"Daddy, yes or no?" Vivian's voice brought him out of his thoughts.

"I'm sorry, sweetie. What did you say?" He forced himself to give her his complete attention.

"Samantha invited me to her house on New Year's Eve. There will only be girls because it's going to be a slumber party. May I go?" Vivian asked, watching him.

"You don't want to spend it in Los Angeles with Gladys?"

"Yes, but Gladys told me Melanie and Marc are back, so she'll probably want to spend it with them," Vivian said before placing a forkful of pancakes in her mouth.

"I'm sorry. I assumed you would want to spend some time with your sister, so I bought our tickets." He watched her face fall and considered a compromise. "I'll look up how much it will cost to change our return date."

He watched her face brighten. "Are you all right with that?" he asked.

She nodded her head and took another bite then chewed quickly and swallowed before speaking again. "I had some things planned that we could do, but we can do them another time. I'm happy her parents are back because she missed them so much, but they want to stay in Los Angeles to be with Paige for a while. With everyone there, I'm not sure she will have time for me."

The sadness in his daughter's eyes pulled at his heart. "Are any of the things you've planned something that we can do together?"

Vivian's eyes bugged out for a second, then she tried to mask her expression with her cup of hot chocolate. It only made him curious as to what she had planned. When she still didn't say anything, he needed to know what his daughter was trying to get up to.

"Vivian?" he asked.

"Um, do you like skateboarding?" She finally spoke up. A small smile on her lips.

"I've never tried. I think, though, if I were to try and start now, I might break something that can't be unbroken," Mason said, returning her smile.

Vivian laughed. "No, Daddy. I didn't mean to actually skateboard but to watch."

"Why would you want to watch people skateboard?"

"If you have to ask, then it isn't for you," Vivian replied, shaking her head solemnly before going back to her meal.

"All right. What else?" he prompted, wondering if there was really something on her list they could do together.

He watched her silver eyes cloud over in concentration and hoped she would always be so easy to read.

"What about angel wings?" she asked, her eyes lightening again.

"Angel wings," he repeated, hoping it wasn't something that one painted on themselves.

"Yeah, you know, the murals of angels' wings people paint on the sides of buildings all over the country. You can get your picture taken with them, and you look like you have wings." Vivian smiled.

He had no concerns about his masculinity, but he drew the line at taking pictures of himself wearing angel wings.

"Do they have these wings in Chicago?" he asked.

"Yes, really cool ones." She took out her phone and tapped twice then swiped her thumb across the screen a few times before turning the screen of her phone toward him. It was a picture of Vivian sometime during the last year standing in front of a pair of huge black and white intricately sketched designs that created wings with feathers at the top. They were too high for her, looking as if they were coming out of the upper part of her shoulders, but the picture was beautiful.

He passed back the phone and looked at her expectedly. She looked back at him for a few seconds then heaved a sigh.

"Okay, I will save the list for another time."

"You don't have to. I'll talk to Paige and the others and be your and Gladys' chauffeur for the day. I will drive you two wherever you want to go. I would feel a lot better doing it myself than allowing you to hop around on buses since you aren't old enough to utilize the rideshare in California."

Vivian was quiet so long he thought she would reject his offer. "Could you rent an expensive-looking car for the day? It doesn't have to be a top of the line luxury model."

He laughed to himself. His little girl was definitely not little anymore. "I think that can be arranged."

"And could you wear a black suit and open the door for us?" she added just as he finished his sentence.

"Now, you're pushing it," he said, pointing his fork at her.

"How about, if you wear the suit, we all go play laser a couple of days later," Vivian bargained.

"How about I rent a nice car and chauffeur you and Gladys around for the day, then we all go play laser tag a few days later," Mason replied.

"The suit?" Vivian asked, obviously trying to look innocent.

"Not gonna happen," he responded without hesitation.

Vivian's grin turned into a smile that warmed his soul. "Okay, Daddy. You've got a deal."

He nodded, and they went back to eating their breakfast in silence for a few minutes before Vivian spoke again.

"Thank you, Daddy."

Grateful as he was that Vivian was thoughtful enough to offer up the gratitude, he wondered what it was for and asked her.

"Thank you for listening to me, really listening. Even if you can't get a good deal on changing the tickets, I'll be okay. I can just tell Samantha what happened, and I would try to make it back." She shrugged during the last part of the sentence.

"Why are you thanking me for listening to you? Don't I always?" he asked, confused.

"Oh, yes. It's just, some of my friends have parents who don't listen. They're either too busy, too impatient, too tired, or just don't seem to care. You should hear what some of my friends do for attention, but it doesn't seem to work. Plus, if the answer is 'no,' there's no compromise—ever."

"Well, don't paint me with the wrong brush. There are sometimes when a 'no' is a 'no,' but I will always try to give you a reason," Mason said, watching his daughter carefully.

"See? That's what I mean. You listen. You give your answer, and you give a reason for it. Not just "Because I said so.""

"Well, if I think you can understand the reason for my answer I will give it to you. It didn't work so well when you were five. You wanted what you wanted when you wanted it." He chuckled as he shook his head and reached for his orange juice. "It was those times when I handed you to your mother." He took a drink.

"So, if I said I liked this guy, and I wanted to start dating? What would you say?" Vivian asked with a straight face. It took a moment for him to truly comprehend what she was saying due to her innocent expression. The orange juice he hadn't yet swallowed spewed forth covering most of the table near him and part of his plate since he also began to gag on the liquid that got caught in his windpipe. He coughed and heaved, trying to bring in enough air to think about, let alone answer, her question.

He looked around for a napkin, which she produced, so he could wipe up his mess.

After expelling the last bit of liquid from his windpipe Mason sat back exhausted. His left eye twitched. He was sure he had a ministroke or heart attack. Maybe he broke a blood vessel while he was coughing. He put his hand to his forehead. How did you check if you popped a blood vessel? What were the symptoms because he was sure he had them all, whatever they were.

She'd said the "B" word. He didn't even know she knew boys. Well, of course she knew boys. She had them in her class. It was logical they would talk to one another, but she was only thirteen. Boys should still be cootie-infested, upright-walking mammals.

Mason took a deep breath and let it out slowly before finally glancing back up at Vivian who looked contrite.

"Sorry, it was a joke. Haha?" she said meekly. He breathed a sigh of relief. He still had his little girl.

"Not funny," he said and kept his face stern until she bent back over her food.

Lord, please don't allow her to *discover* boys are human beings until she graduates from college. Unless she goes into the medical profession. Amen.

Chapter 21

Mason set the car keys in the bowl on the table by the door and pulled his vibrating phone out of his back pocket. Vivian bumped him hard enough to cause him to lose his grip on his phone. He juggled it a little before he regained control over it, but it gave Vivian a good look at the screen.

"Mati's calling you?" Vivian asked.

"It's not unheard of," Mason replied before answering the phone. He felt a little put out by her comment and watched her as he put the phone to his ear. Before he could say anything, Vivian yelled out. "Hi, Mati!"

The gesture was rude and took him aback. He frowned at her, and she took a small step back. He placed the call on speaker for a second, so Vivian could hear Paige's response.

"Hi, honey. How are you?"

Vivian glanced up at him before leaning toward the phone. "Good. I miss you."

"I miss you too. Why don't I give you a call before you go to school in the morning, like we used to." Paige's voice was melodic, and he did his best not to send Vivian any cues to hurry up.

"Really?" Vivian's face lit up.

"Really. I'm sorry I disappeared like that, but things are better now." Paige's apology startled him just as much as the knowledge that she hadn't been communicating with Vivian daily. He wondered why

Vivian didn't say anything, then the conversation they'd had on the way to Paige's for Thanksgiving came back to him. He thought Vivian was upset because she noticed the changes in Paige during their morning talks with Gladys. Come to find out, there were no morning talks.

He wondered if that disrespectful display just a moment ago was Vivian's way of getting a little attention from Mati. He also wondered, yet again, if he would have noticed this before he surrendered his life over to Christ.

Mason silently chastised himself. *You were a good father before. You had some work to do and you still do, but now you have more knowledge and understanding. Stop beating yourself up.*

"I'm being rude, and I will probably get an earful once he gets off the phone with you, but I'm looking forward to praying with you in the morning. It hasn't been the same," Vivian said as she backed away, her voice getting louder to compensate.

Paige must have heard it because she spoke louder too. "I'm sorry again, baby. Thank you for being patient with me."

"I can't help it. You're the only Mati I've got," Vivian said with a smile on her lips and in her voice. "Talk to you in the morning."

"Okay, Baby Doll," Paige responded, making Vivian laugh before she turned to go down the hall to her bedroom.

The choice of her direction made Mason pause. He had intended to go to his room, but now that Vivian was headed to her room, he decided to go in the opposite direction.

"Mason?" Paige's voice shook him out of his thoughts, and he made a beeline for the couch.

"Hi. Sorry. We just walked through the door when you called so I'm getting situated." He made himself comfortable and leaned back against the cushions.

"Do you want me to call back, maybe—"

He cut her off. "No, I'm good. I just sat down on the couch. I am full. I am hydrated." *I am an idiot that doesn't know when to shut his mouth.*

"Okay, good to know. I am the same, but probably a lot less relaxed than you are right now," she replied, and he concentrated on the sound of her voice. She sounded tired. Very tired.

"Richard called me this morning. He said you all would be having brunch with Grace and her husband," he prompted because he wanted to know but also because he believed she needed to talk about it.

"What did Richard tell you?" she asked.

"Not much. It was a quick call because I had to get ready for church." He fingered the throw resting on the back of the couch. "He just said that he and Victoria learned that Melanie and Marc were headed back to you in Los Angeles. They were going to give you all some time to settle in and do the family bonding thing, but they found out that Grace and her husband were also headed to Los Angeles, possibly to intersect Melanie and Marc."

"Family bonding thing?" she asked, her voice sounding a little lighter.

"Yes, that's a technical term. It's really complicated and hard to explain," he teased.

"Oh, really? Give it a try. I'm intrigued," she retorted.

"You know what. I don't want to interrupt. You called, and I get the feeling that the brunch wasn't full of all the feels. You go ahead." He unlaced his dress shoes and freed his feet from the confines of the dense leather.

"I see what you're doing," Paige said through her chuckles.

"Really? What is that?" he hedged.

"You are trying to amuse me with all of your technical jargon and using verbs like 'feels' as nouns."

"Hey, 'feels' is legit. All the kids are using it these days."

"Really. Well, if it's Vivian, don't encourage her. We need someone from that generation we can still communicate with when we get older. At the rate the English language is falling apart with texts and emailing, we will be back to communicating with grunts and groans in fifty years."

"You plan on being around in fifty years?" he asked.

"Of course. I'm only twenty-seven now. I will be a lively and sprite seventy-seven-year-old traveling the world in search of the most beautiful place to do Pilates," she said with more energy in her voice than he'd heard in a long time.

"You do Pilates?" Was that why she was always in such great shape?

"No, but I've been thinking about giving it a try."

"What do you do to keep fit?" he asked, really curious.

"As little as possible. I might walk around the park now and then when I need to filter through information in my mind but not too much more than that. I feel better when it comes naturally."

"You do know it's natural to move, right?"

"Yes, yes, yes. You sound just like Brandon," she said before going quiet and he winced.

"Okay, we have surmised that you have been gifted with every other person's dream. You eat what you want, and you look like you just walked out of a fashion magazine."

"That is highly exaggerated. One, I'm not tall enough to be a model, and two, I am definitely not that thin. I'm just fortunate."

"Yes, you are, but what do you do to work off frustration or anger? You know, before you pray," he asked, wanting to see if she would shut down the conversation.

"I clean. I clean the kitchen floor, the baseboards, the bathroom grout, any place that takes some elbow grease to come clean."

"How clean is your place these days?" he asked by way of gauging her well-being.

"I haven't needed my housekeeper to come by for months, but I'm not sure I would eat off the kitchen floor today even with seeing Grace last night and this morning, which is saying a lot."

It did his heart good to hear her laugh at herself. She sounded so much better than the last time they spoke. He wondered at the reason for a moment but decided it wasn't a pressing need. He just thanked God for it and hoped she continued to heal.

There was no doubt in his mind now that he would give Ava permission to send her Brandon's letter. He just didn't know how long it would take him to tell her that he knew about it. He shook off the thought and rejoined the conversation.

"Good. I'm glad she didn't get to you."

"Oh, she did. I hate the way she jabs at all the people I love and is constantly condescending and straight-out mean. I got angry on behalf of my other family members, but something happened that made me think the brunch might have been worth all the backhanded compliments." Her voice was filled with wonder, causing him to hold the phone closer to his ears to keep from missing a word.

"Really. What was that?"

"Melanie got angry and not only that, she showed her anger and got in a few dibs herself. For a moment I thought she was going to give away the fact that she knew Grace had an affair with Antonio in front of Grace's husband. To tell you the truth, I secretly wished she had, but then it may have left Grace with nowhere to go and even more anger and vengeance in her heart, and that is just not something we need right now."

"It sounds like Melanie and Marc's getaway served them well," he said.

"More than you know," Paige murmured.

"Don't do that. Don't tease me. You know how I feel about secrets," he said.

"You love dispelling them?"

"I don't like having them between me and the people I care about," he returned, wanting to make sure she understood his reasoning.

"Well said," she responded, and without another breath, dropped the bomb on him. "Melanie and Marc found Brian, my biological father."

At first, he wasn't sure he heard her correctly. There had been a lot of speculation and hearsay that covered the spectrum from Brian taking his life to Antonio questioning the authenticity of his remains, but this was concrete. "Um, wow. I'm not sure what to say. You're sure, right?"

"Yes, Melanie confirmed it last night," Paige said.

Mason wondered why Richard hadn't said anything. Was there a security issue?

"Why were Victoria and Richard originally told something different?" he asked even as he wondered if they should be talking about it over the phone.

"No one is supposed to know he's alive," Paige answered.

"Are you sure it's okay for us to be talking about this over the phone?" he asked, feeling uneasy on her behalf.

"Why? Do you think someone is listening in on this call?" she asked, beginning to sound hesitant.

"I don't know. What did Melanie say about you sharing the information?"

"I didn't think to ask her. I figured it was now my information to share with someone I trusted and I trust you. You won't tell anyone, will you?"

"Everyone I would tell already knows," he replied honestly. "Where are you? Are you home?"

"No, I decided to get some fresh air, and I wanted to be able to speak openly. I'm at the park," she answered in a stage whisper.

"I'm sorry. I didn't mean to alarm you, and you don't have to speak in whispers. Besides, if I can hear you anyone else listening in can hear you too. We'll just be careful."

"How? I just blurted out the most detrimental part," she retorted.

"Let's pretend I'm paranoid and have seen too many spy movies. You're not a spy, are you?" he asked, trying to ease her tension.

"Yes, I am, but I am one of the bumbling ones who get lucky by bumping into my target instead of strategizing," she responded.

"You are my favorite kind. You always come out on top in the end," he said, working hard to bring more levity into the conversation but she took a hammer to that endeavor.

"Do I?" she asked, and he heard the underlying question loud and clear. So he answered it.

"Yes, you do," he said with as much sincerity as he could put in his voice because he believed she would. She was already on her way up. Talking to her today compared to the sparse conversations they'd had over the last few months made it apparent that she had decided to receive God's healing.

"How do you know?" Her somber question tore a hole in his heart.

"Because you are a child of the Most High God. The one and only living God, who *was* before the beginning that we know of, *is* even now, and *will always be*. You are an heir to the One who created everything you see and much, much more. The one being who knows not only how your story ends but how it all ends, and He has told us time and time again that now that we have accepted Him into our hearts and adopted into the family of Christ, we are on the winning side. He is the great I Am, the beginning and the end, and next to Him, there is no other." Mason took a breath, knowing that he had gone beyond answering the question, but it was hard to stop once he got started talking about God.

"I know that and I'm grateful. I really am. I mean, I am at the point that what I think sometimes makes me feel selfish, but I need to talk to someone, and with everything you've been through in life, I trust that you won't judge me."

Mason heard everything up to the moment she said she trusted him not to judge her. She trusted him. Paige trusted him, a man who used to be... *Used to be. Not anymore.* He listened, and his heart swelled to twice the size it was when they first got on the phone. Could it be that he might be worthy? He needed to think about that another time. Paige seemed to be pouring her heart out and he was stuck on himself. He thought back to her last words.

"So, you're grateful, but..." he prompted.

He heard her exhale deeply. "But I want to know if *I* get a happy ending."

Oh. He didn't know why he was surprised by her comment. He'd been there... in a way. He'd wanted to know if the deep-seated pain of losing Rachel would ever let up enough for him to get in one good deep breath, or as impossible as it sounded at the time, if he could go more than a few minutes without wishing he could be with her.

He stopped himself again. He was assuming she meant the romantic happy ending she may have felt cheated from.

"There are many types of happy endings. You told me about one just a few minutes ago. Who could have imagined *that* after all these years?" he said, hoping she could follow him without him spelling it out.

"Yeah, *that* is definitely a happy ending, but it is more of a new beginning in a lot of ways," she said as if she were in deep thought.

"So what kind of happy ending are you speaking of?" he asked and waited a few seconds in silence before she answered.

"It's hard to form into words because it isn't as simple as finding love again. Not that I'm looking or can even stomach the thought of being with someone else right now. I just... I just want to know that if I ever do take the chance of getting close to someone again, it will last... like years."

"Are you looking for a guarantee? An absolute?"

"I guess I am," she said slowly.

He could remind her that there was no such thing, but he was pretty sure that wasn't what she needed or wanted to hear right now.

"I think I understand. You just want the hope of having the highs of love again. The promise of a "one day," he said.

"Yes, I knew you would understand," she said, sounding relieved.

As much as he wanted to, though, he couldn't leave it there. He felt compelled to do more than just cosign on an unrealistic desire. He wanted to give her truth to hold on to as well.

"So, as I said, you are a child of God. You are treasured and adored by the very being who has the ability to be anywhere and do anything, yet He chose to sacrifice His only begotten son so that on a dark almost helpless night many years ago He could speak a word into an older woman's spirit. A word that answered your question on whether or not you were truly as alone as you felt. A word that would convince you that He was with you though you couldn't feel Him through your pain. A word that would convince you to delay giving up, just one more day so He could win your trust and your heart and kept drawing you day by day until you did."

The line was quiet for a moment, and he was content to let the words sink in.

"You remembered that? You remembered that conversation?" Her voice held a little bit of wonder.

"Of course. It was profound and I was struck by your transparency. It was the first time I let myself acknowledge that I felt envious of the attention God paid to someone," he said, then wondered if it was too revealing.

"The way you tell it, it sounds like I already got my happy ending," she said, and Mason couldn't read her voice.

"Well, at least one of them. A pretty big one, in fact. Why does there only have to be one? Does a loving relationship not have a happy ending? Listen for a second before you interrupt." Mason said when he heard Paige inhale.

"Our God created a relationship with us that would never ever end. Once we leave this earth, we don't disappear, we just take on a new form. You know that just because we leave these bodies our relationships with God don't end. It just transitions to a new level. Just the same, your relationship with Brandon didn't end, it only shifted and took on a different type of relationship. He didn't stop loving you because he transitioned to heaven and took on a new form. He takes that love with him. It's a part of him, just as his love for God is a part of him.

"But I can't hold a Brandon who transitioned."

"No, but you can still love him and know that his love for you didn't leave just because the body he shared that physical love with you died," he said, hoping the thought was as profound for her as it was for him at that moment. He could have saved himself a lot of heartache and struggling if he'd even considered that Rachel's love for him hadn't died with her body.

"Really think about it. We say, 'To be absent from the body is to be present with the Lord,' Why would God stress developing a personal relationship with Him while we're here or at least accepting Jesus into our heart if we would forget it all and basically start all over again when we got to heaven.

"I understand the enemy's play is to separate souls from God forever, but if we were to buy into his seductive line of crap, we would be left to bathe in fire for eternity. I don't know about you, but I'm not ready to go through that type of torture forever.

"I never thought of it like that," she said, her voice thoughtful. He was pretty sure he hadn't either until that moment. He wondered to himself if God hadn't just dropped a word in his spirit for her. Well, there was nothing that said he couldn't hold the nugget of wisdom for himself as well. Mason thought and reveled in what God continued to do for Paige. He didn't think she truly understood just how much God loved her. He caught a glimpse of it and it was brilliant. The line remained quiet. Mason figured Paige was contemplating his question.

"This discussion brings me to the other reason why I called you," Paige said, but he heard the hesitancy in her voice which made him very curious.

"Okay." He tried prompting with the one word.

"I found out last night that I had an older brother."

"What?" Mason's mind got stuck on one word. *What?*

"He was about two hours older than me," she continued, unaware that he was still trying to absorb the first part of her news. *A brother?*

"And you didn't know? Your mother, Melanie, never told you?" he asked, baffled. *What was with this family and their secrets?*

"No, Melanie said she wanted to spare my feelings. She didn't want me to mourn him," she replied.

"Yes, but still. Didn't you have that right?"

"I thought the exact same thing," Paige confirmed.

"Why now? I mean I'm glad she finally told you, but why would Melanie tell you now?" he asked.

"Melanie didn't tell me; Grace did," she responded.

"Are you sure she was telling the truth? Why would Grace tell you anything?"

"To hurt me, to divide Melanie and me, to see if Melanie shared anything with me about my biological father or brother. Take your pick," Paige said, her voice filled with disgust.

"Wow, just when I think that woman can't do anything to make me dislike her more," Mason said more to himself than Paige.

"I wish that was all," Paige murmured. Mason noticed the change in her voice, and the hairs on the back of his neck stood up.

"Maybe we should talk about something else," Mason suggested.

"No, I need to talk about it. I need to get it out of my mind. I don't understand her reasoning."

"Evil doesn't need a reason," Mason retorted.

"I know, but everyone has a beginning. I just wonder what happened in hers to make her so destructive," Paige said. "If she knew my brother lived, Melanie said Grace would have gotten rid of me."

"Rid of you? What do you mean?" Mason asked, hoping it wasn't what he thought and grateful it hadn't come to that.

"I'm not sure, but the knowledge made me wonder what Grace is after."

Paige told him what Melanie shared with her and the Branchetts the night before as well as what went on in the restaurant that morning.

He was sickened on Melanie's behalf and knew that he would have had a great deal less restraint than Melanie had that morning. He would have told Ross what type of woman he married. Desperate or not, he would have liked to see Grace get a little of what she dished out.

He wondered how Richard had convinced Victoria not to climb over the table at the restaurant. Maybe she really had changed. Hearing that your son had been manipulated that way would test anyone.

"So there must be a plan if you all didn't put her in her place at brunch," Mason said, his head in his hands and elbows on knees, the position he'd moved into during Paige's summary of the last twelve hours.

"I'm not sure, but I think it's to find out why she wants to know if Brian is alive and where he is," she answered, sounding weary.

"How are you really doing? I mean you sound better, but this is all a lot to deal with," he said, hoping she would share.

"It is, and a part of me is angry on behalf of Melanie, that Grace would throw away her family like this, but she hasn't been in my life since I had the twins. Unless you count the rare calls where she tries to belittle and berate me for choosing God instead of the anger she believes I have the right to feel," Paige said.

He laughed at that. He couldn't help it. It came forth like an avalanche.

246

"Why are you laughing?" Paige asked, sounding baffled and he tried to rein it in.

"It just struck me funny that I had the same thought, and I thought it made me feel privileged to be able to hold on to my anger at God, at my dad, at Victoria, even at Rachel. I wore it proudly because I felt I had earned the right to hold it close and wield it over anyone I wanted. When all I was doing was shooting myself in the foot and using it as an excuse to be mean and rude to people that didn't agree with me.

"Feeling anger and constantly giving in to it is not a privilege; it's a crutch in the best of times and a dagger that you use on yourself at the worst of times. I have the privilege of hurting myself over and over again. Aren't I a strong one?" He expected to hear laughter on the other side of the line, but there was a two-second span of silence before she spoke so quietly he almost missed it.

"I was angry with God."

"I'm sure you were," he said without judgment.

"It wasn't because I didn't get my way," Paige said quickly as if she knew where his thoughts were going. "Well, maybe in the beginning, but that wasn't the main reason," she conceded.

"Do you want to tell me what the main reason was?"

"Not right now, okay?" Her voice was still low as if she didn't want the world to overhear.

"Never an issue," he replied.

"May I ask you a question?" Her voice was hesitant and he rushed to answer.

"Sure."

"Do you think the reason why I felt so alone when I was a child is because my brother and I were separated at birth?"

"That could be a reason. The other is that the woman you identified as your mother when you were a child wasn't one to you."

"Yes." She drew out the word slowly. "But I had Melanie."

"Who you identified with as your sister. The expectations of a sibling are different from the expectations of a mother. A mother's love is beyond compare unless you don't get it, then you will take whatever is closest."

"Do you do counseling as a side hustle or something?" she said with a little awe in her voice. He liked that.

"No, I just spent a lot of time with one over the last year. It tends to stick," he said with a chuckle.

"Does he do long-distance counseling?"

Mason considered her question for a moment. "I'm not sure."

"Huh. Oh well. It's probably for the best if he doesn't," Paige said.

"Why?" Mason asked.

"I don't know if it would be a good idea if we saw the same counselor," Paige responded hesitantly.

"It's not like he would say anything," Mason said, wondering what she was getting at.

"No. Of course not, but he would still remember what you said, especially if you talked about me," Paige elaborated.

"Why would you think I would talk about you?" Mason hedged. The silence that met him on the other end of the line was deafening. He decided to relent. "Okay. Maybe I talked about you a little," He said lightheartedly.

"I'm sorry that was presumptuous and self-centered of me." Paige responded in a small voice.

"Maybe just a little, but you did come up once or twice." He said. More like twenty or thirty times, he thought.

"Did you search out a counselor?" Paige asked.

"No, I was given his card. I figured if he could help me get some of the heaviness off my chest, I would continue to see him."

"I'm glad you did. I didn't want to see you lose Vivian," Paige said then went quiet.

"So, some of my less-than-stellar moments made it all the way to Los Angeles," Mason said, feeling a twinge of regret. He hadn't been anyone he would have wanted her to date back then. He just hoped that one day she could see the difference between the man he used to be and the man he was now.

"Yeah." It was the only word she said, but he heard a whole sentence behind it.

"What else did you hear?" he asked, prompting her to speak her mind.

"It's none of my business, so if you don't want to confirm it, you don't have to."

"Yep," he answered a little sharper than he meant because he was momentarily frustrated by the fact that he couldn't spell it out to her that any and everything he did was her business.

"Well, um…" She stopped.

"Sorry, I didn't mean to sound short. I'm just curious."

"I heard you were seeing someone earlier this year," Paige said.

"Ahhh, a little birdy was talking near your ear, were they?" He chuckled.

"Yes, I was seeing a woman for a few months around the time you got married. It didn't work out."

"I'm sorry."

"I'm not. She deserved a man who could love her without distraction or hesitation."

"And you couldn't do that?" Paige asked.

"No, not with her," Mason answered honestly then changed the subject to something safer. "Vivian and I will be there in a couple of weeks for Christmas. I'll have the same setup as Thanksgiving, so if Vivian and Gladys want to bunk together they can. Vivian told me Marc and Melanie were staying for Christmas and maybe beyond."

"I think it's going to be beyond," Paige replied.

"And how do you feel about that?"

"Honestly, I thought I would do anything to get the apartment to myself again, but it's really nice having them around. I didn't know how much I missed Mel until she came back. Even though it has only been a little over twenty-four hours, it feels like a week and I'm loving it. I'll tell you if I feel the same by Christmas." She laughed and he joined in.

"Speaking of Christmas. Is there anything special you'd like that you can think of?"

"You don't have to give me any special gift. You and Vivian coming for Christmas is more than enough," she answered, and he could tell she meant every word.

"All right."

"All right?"

"Yes, all right. Since you won't tell me, I will just have to lean in the little birdy's direction to find out."

"Mason…" she began sternly then paused. "What's your middle name?"

"Michael," he answered.

"Mason Michael Jenson, you better not go all out like you did last year. That's just too much."

"Hey, hey, Briar Rose Paige Morganson. I will decide what is too much."

"You did not just use my full birth name?" She sounded astonished and mildly annoyed.

"You used mine. Besides, I think Briar Rose is sweet."

"It's a fairy-tale name," she said, sounding perturbed.

"It's a great pen name if you decide to write children's books."

The line went quiet again for a few seconds.

"That might not be a bad idea."

"See? It's a good name," he said, trying to work his way back into her good graces.

"Just don't call me by it again. My name is Paige."

"Okay, Paige," he said, glancing over at the window and watching the sun dip low on the horizon. He was two hours ahead of her but he still didn't like the idea of her in the park in the late afternoon.

"Are you still in the park?" Mason asked, getting concerned.

"No, I started walking back. I don't want to be there when it gets even close to dark."

"I'll stay on the line until you're in the house."

"How gallant of you."

"Not really. I am still sitting on my couch." He chuckled.

"Yeah, well, that's technology for you," she quipped.

He could hear her breaths coming faster as she walked and tried to think of something to pass the time between then and her getting inside her apartment.

"Will you all be having a family debriefing?" he asked as the day's events came to mind.

"Um... yeah... Victoria and Richard are supposed to come back around dinnertime. I was surprised they suggested it. None of us got much sleep, but I think they want to... discuss some things... before they go back." She sounded winded.

"Slow down," he said. "You can hardly talk."

"I didn't want to keep you waiting on me."

It was as if the world of irony was using her to bait him. "Slow down. I'm in no more of a hurry to get off this couch than I was when we first got on the phone. If I didn't like talking to you, I wouldn't have called you every week whether you picked up the phone or not."

He heard her shoes scuff the sidewalk then stop. "Really? I thought... never mind." He heard her start walking again.

"Oh no. No, you don't get to do that. Finish that sentence," he said almost forcefully. He stood up from the couch. Had he said too much? Given something away?

"You promise not to get upset or annoyed?" she asked and he relaxed.

"No," he answered then spoiled the stern reply with a chuckle.

"I thought you were calling me so much because you were concerned."

"I was concerned."

"And because you might have promised Brandon you would check in on me."

He was annoyed.

"You remember I knew you first," he said, trying to keep the annoyance out of his voice.

"Yeah, but you and Brandon grew really close," she volleyed.

"I thought you and I were close."

"We were... we are," she corrected before he could speak. "It's just that you became distant when I started dating Brandon, and I barely

251

heard from you when I got engaged and I'm not playing dumb. I know why, but I thought we were better friends than that," she finished quietly.

"You're right. I was a lousy friend, but I aim to change that," he said, trying to sound gung ho when she had just dealt him a serious blow. Not that he didn't deserve it, but it still stung.

"You already are. You didn't disappear with the rest," Paige said.

"I can't. You're the mother of my child."

She laughed, and it rang through the phone, clear and full of humor like he remembered.

"If you can't make me laugh, you can at least make me smile. Though I didn't always pick up the phone, I did listen to your voicemails, and they made me feel better," Paige said quietly.

"Well, good. That's why I left them." His response sounded lame to his ears, but he couldn't think of a better reply.

"And now... I... am.... up... the... stairs." She panted.

"Good. Now get inside and lock the door."

"Yes, sir."

He sat listening to her select a key and place it into the lock. He heard the door open and chatter coming from inside, and he felt a small pang of disappointment that their call would be over soon.

"I'm in," she exclaimed, and he heard her drop her keys.

"Very good." He exhaled. "Well, you have a good evening—" he began, but she interrupted him.

"Wait. I wanted to tell you something." He heard her footsteps go down the hall, and he tried to imagine where she was headed. He heard a door close softly.

"Where are you?"

"In my office. Marc is in the living room alone. So I figured Melanie was in my bedroom, and I wanted to say this away from prying ears before we got off the phone."

Oh, okay," he said because he couldn't even begin to imagine what she needed to say to him in the privacy of her office.

"I just wanted to tell you that the woman you choose will be very blessed to have you," Paige said. Mason wasn't sure if he was more happy or disturbed by her comment.

"You know Vivian said something similar to that yesterday," he murmured, not wanting to give away his conflicting feelings.

"She is a very bright girl, and who would know better?"

"Who would indeed."

"Goodnight Mason."

"Goodnight Paige. Talk to you soon?"

"Yep. Oh, and thank you... you know about reminding me that Brandon's love for me is still with Brandon. That helped."

"I'm glad." And he was. "Bye, Paige."

"Bye."

He listened until she ended the call and tried to feel more encouraged by her parting words than melancholy at the fact that he may have to wait a whole week before they could talk like that again.

He would just have to keep himself busy. He leaned into the couch and decided to replay their phone call in his head before going to look up return flights that would get him and Vivian back to Chicago by New Year's Eve without paying for the price of the tickets all over again.

Melanie and Marc had found Paige's biological father. Wow, that must have been surreal. Mason checked the time. He was pretty sure Richard would have enough time to talk to him before he and Victoria left for dinner. He would see if he could get a few more answers if he could be assured that no one was listening.

Chapter 22

Richard lay there on the bed watching his wife sleep. It had been a long night and an even longer day, but he was too keyed up to take a nap as had been the intention when he and Victoria went back to their hotel room after brunch.

He'd lain there staring at the ceiling with his hand cradling the back of his head, allowing his body to rest while his mind ran over one scenario after another on how he could keep his wife, granddaughter, and great-granddaughter safe. He knew it was ultimately up to God, but he needed to feel like he was doing his part.

Each and every clue, lead, or document led to either Grace, Antonio, or Luca as if they were leading him and Victoria somewhere they didn't want to go. It could be Grace. She was just twisted enough to lead their investigators down a rabbit hole when it came to getting any more answers about Brian and why he was hiding. On the other hand, Melanie and Marc seemed to think Luca was behind everything and he could neither agree nor deny it because he simply didn't know enough about the man.

It didn't sit well with Richard that a man could have so much influence over some of the most important parts of the lives of the people he held dear without coming out from the background. He didn't know whether the man was a detriment or a saint. He so badly wanted to believe that Luca had everyone's well-being in mind, but most men with Luca's money, power, and authority were only concerned about themselves. Sometimes even family took a back seat to what they were trying to build and preserve for said family.

Richard had read everything he could get his hands on regarding the finance titan and so-called family man. What kind of man would hide his grandson away from the world, from his own mother and father?

What Richard was afraid of was that Luca's behavior was warranted. What danger was he hiding Brian from, and what would he say when Richard went to see him because he wasn't going to wait for his wife to grow impatient then desperate and step into chaos.

Richard would do anything for Victoria, short of sell his soul or take another person's life, and even the latter was debatable given the right circumstances. He would not allow her to run headlong into some ongoing feud, as quiet as it had been kept, just to put her and her son's life in peril.

Feeling Victoria shift beside him, he turned to look at her, recognizing the signs of her slowly drifting toward consciousness. He loved to watch her when she was sleeping. There were many years when he lay in bed at night and watched her long after she'd surrendered to slumber. He suspected she knew he watched her, which is why she would sometimes try to out wait him.

She was a beautiful woman, and time had only etched more character into her features. When her eyes were open and that new-penny stare caught him, he found it hard to break away, but while she slept, there was a peace that lay across her features that he suspected not too many people experienced in life. Lashes fanning her still-smooth cheeks and lips slightly parted. If he was a painter, he would decorate a canvas with her image and hide it away.

It didn't matter whether she was blissfully happy or simmering with anger, once Victoria gave in to sleep, he would see the gift God gave her in spades. No matter how long she slumbered, when she gave in to sleep she rested deeply.

She sighed, and he turned the rest of his body toward her. He didn't even consider resisting the temptation of tracing her jawline with his finger. After all these years he was still fascinated by her fairness and the contrast between their coloring despite the fact that both of her parents were African American. He removed his hand slowly but let it fall in the middle of the gap between them.

"Are you staring at me again?" Victoria's sleepy murmur was light and playful. She stretched, and he continued to watch silently, waiting for her to open her eyes.

She didn't disappoint. Her eyelids came slowly open then blinked to adjust to the light still left in the day. She breathed in deep and exhaled as her lips tipped up into a smile. And there it was. The second most beautiful sight in his entire life. The first being his daughter Rachel's eyes when she looked up at him for the first time. He didn't know if it had been like that for most fathers but for him it was unequivocally love at first sight.

"Hi."

"Hi."

"Did you sleep?" Victoria asked, moving one hand under her pillow and the other underneath his. It was a simple movement, but she had begun doing it soon after their renewal of vows and he never tired of it. He took it as her desire to be close to him. Connect to him after being away from him during sleep. He wouldn't ask her why she did it. He was fine with his assumption.

He did what he always did next. He brought her hand up to his lips, pressing the back of it to them for a few seconds before slowly removing it.

"No, but I rested," he finally responded.

A small line formed between her brows. "Are you worried?"

"Concerned," he replied.

"Don't be," she whispered, then her eyes lit up. "Brian's alive," she whispered excitedly.

He couldn't help but smile back. "Yes."

She shifted toward him. "No," she said as if reading his thoughts. "If he's alive, there is someone looking after him. He isn't alone."

"Just because he is still alive and hidden away doesn't necessarily mean that the person that has been taking care of him has his best interest at heart. It's easier to manipulate someone who can only rely on you for their survival," Richard returned.

"We're going to see him soon. I just know it." She went back to a whisper as if she didn't want any naysayers to catch wind of her hope.

He remained quiet, not wanting to dampen her mood. He would deal with the reality and still try to give her her dreams. It was what he'd done from the day he said "I do" while staring down into those tawny-colored eyes.

She shifted forward again, subtracting more of the distance between them. He watched her. Out of his peripheral vision, he saw her leg move and half a second later felt her socked foot lay upon his calf. He still watched, never losing her gaze.

"Come here," she whispered.

He shifted close enough to feel her breath on his lips but stayed far enough away to focus on her eyes.

"Closer," she prompted, with a small smile playing at her lips. He obeyed, removing whatever space there was left between them. He felt her hands move to his T-shirt-covered chest as their lips met, and he let the worry go for the moment.

He wrapped one arm around her torso and brought the other hand up to cup her jaw to keep her right where he wanted her. He turned his head slightly to deepen the kiss when his phone began to vibrate on the nightstand followed by an all-too-familiar ringtone. He growled his annoyance but continued to kiss Victoria, putting effort into keeping their romantic cocoon in place.

After what seemed like an interminable amount of time, the vibrating stopped and the ringtone quieted. Victoria sighed, and Richard chuckled, moving his lips to the edge of hers then along her jawline. He was on his way to her neck when his phone began shaking and ringing again. He wondered how much it would cost him if he threw it out the hotel window.

"Aren't you going to get that?" Victoria asked on an exhale.

"No," he whispered into her neck.

"What if it's Vivian?" Victoria said.

"It's not," he responded between small pecks, knowing he'd already lost the battle.

"Richard," Victoria said, pushing at him gently.

"Okay, but someone better be on their way to the hospital," he grumbled as he turned away from the warmth of his wife to answer his phone.

"Hello." He didn't even try to mask his irritation.

"Richard?" Mason's voice came through the line relaxed and even.

"Yes."

"Are you all right? You sound funny."

Richard didn't bother to answer but asked a question of his own. "Are you hurt, Mason?"

"Huh? No."

"Is Vivian hurt?" Richard asked and snaked a hand around Victoria's arm when he felt her shift away.

"No, we're both good. What are the questions for?"

"My wife needed me to ease her mind before I hung up on you," Richard said.

"What? Why are you hanging…" Richard interrupted Mason before he could finish.

"Two guesses," he replied before disconnecting the call.

Richard rolled back toward Victoria. She looked at him with an apologetic smile. Then started laughing.

"Really. You find this funny?"

She nodded then laughed harder and tried to get away from his fingers that skimmed the inside of her upper arm. He pulled her back into an embrace and kissed her quiet.

***

Richard lounged in the sitting room while he waited for Victoria to finish getting ready for dinner. He glanced at his watch. They were going to be late if her usual pace prevailed but muttering any word of warning would be the equivalent of shooting himself in the foot.

He retrieved his phone from his pocket and pressed the button to return Mason's call who picked it up on the third ring.

258

"Good evening," Mason greeted.

"Mason," Richard returned, wondering what Mason was so chipper about. He waited for a beat, but when Mason failed to speak, Richard prompted him. "You called."

"Ah yes, but before I begin, I just want to say one thing."

"Yes," Richard said, prompting Mason to continue.

"You are an inspiration, and I'm proud to know you."

Richard shook his head, smiled at Mason's antics and audacity, but made sure Mason didn't hear it in his voice when he spoke again.

"Let's get to the reason for your call. Victoria and I will be leaving soon to have dinner with Paige and the family."

"I spoke to Paige earlier today. She sounds good."

"I agree," Richard responded.

"She told me about Melanie and Marc's trip, but I asked her to be cautious because I didn't know who might be listening. Do you know if anyone is listening?"

Mason's question sparked something in Richard's mind, and he couldn't believe he hadn't already taken precautions. Grace had been in Paige's home. He tried to think of everywhere she was during her short visit. The living room couch.

He wondered if Marc considered the same possibility. Being part of the bureau, Richard wondered if Marc's thoughts leaned toward conspiracy and threats.

And he wouldn't put it past Grace to bug Paige's house or belongings in some manner. He was surprised he missed it.

"Richard?" Mason called from the other side of the line.

"Did she say anything to you in particular about Melanie and Marc's trip?"

"She mentioned who Marc and Melanie were looking for but not where they went," Mason responded, beginning to sound a little concerned. "Is there anything you need me to do?"

"As a matter of fact, there is. I'm going to make a call. Could you call Paige back and let her know that Victoria and I will be taking everyone out to dinner."

"Okay. Anything else?"

259

"Yes. Tell them to stop talking about Melanie and Marc's trip. What's been said can't be undone, but we might be able to distract someone if they're listening."

"Okay, will do," Mason replied.

"Was there another reason for your call?" Richard asked, feeling some remorse for how he'd treated Mason even up to a few minutes ago.

"Nothing that can't wait."

"All right. I'll call you back when we get to the restaurant."

"Sure."

Richard disconnected the call then picked up the hotel phone and started dialing. This time it only took two rings for the person on the other line to answer.

"This is Marc."

"Hi, I hope I'm not interrupting anything."

"No, just resting. The women are standing around the kitchen debating recipes."

"Still?"

"Mmm-hmm."

"Well, they may not need to bother depending on your answers."

"Okay, that was only a little mysterious."

"Do me a favor and move to the back of the apartment. Somewhere Grace wasn't last night."

"Okay," Marc said. Richard could hear him moving around. A few seconds went by before he responded again.

"I'm in Paige's bedroom," Marc said.

"I know this is your lane, but I was wondering if there was anything to be concerned about regarding listening devices in the apartment?"

"I did a cursory sweep with a piece of equipment I keep on me for emergencies, but if Grace planted something more sophisticated, then I am going to want you to tell me what this call is about," Marc said with a smile in his voice.

Ten minutes later, Richard hung up with Marc and made another call.

"Good evening."

"Good evening, Sam. I need a favor."

"Sure, boss," Samuel replied, making Richard smile. It didn't matter what time he called; Sam was always available.

"I need you to get in touch with your best guy in security tech. I need a sweep of Paige Morganson's home and a new security unit but nothing that will draw the apartment manager's eye." Richard glanced up when Victoria came out of the bedroom in a pair of black wide-legged trousers and a tailored black top that emphasized her small waist. She was sliding her arms into a cropped suit jacket that accentuated the flare of her hips and Richard momentarily lost his train of thought.

"Sure, I know someone." Samuel's response pulled him back to their conversation.

"Oh, and I'll need all new phones, unlocked, and untraceable for..." He counted off his family members in his mind. "Seven... no, you better make it eight." Even though he looked away, he saw Victoria pause at his words. After a couple of seconds, she stood in front of his line of sight, obviously refusing to be ignored. He looked up at her but kept talking.

"Tell them there will be a bonus in it for them if they can make it happen this evening. I'm taking my family to dinner, and I would like to make sure everything is clear before we get back. Oh, and Samuel, the fewer who know about this the better. So just two that you trust in her home. I don't need to tell you what she's been through."

"You have my word. They will be in and out within an hour."

"Thank you, Sam.

"Welcome," Sam replied right before he hung up.

Because he hadn't taken his eye off Victoria since she'd walked through the door, it didn't take much to see that she wasn't happy. He continued to watch not sure which way her emotions would swing.

"Since I don't see steam coming out of your ears, I'm going to guess that you are taking some preventative measures where Paige is concerned."

He shrugged before getting up from the chair. "Mason, of all people, brought it to my attention that Grace's 'surprise' visit may have served more than one purpose. I didn't expect her to give up, but she was still way too civil for the woman we've gotten to know on paper." Richard took her coat from her and held it as she turned to slip her arms in the sleeves.

"You and I did catch her off guard," she said, turning back to him.

"Or she wanted us to think that we did," he said, straightening her collar then resting his hands on her shoulders.

Victoria looked up at him, her eyes wide. "Do you really think that?"

Richard ran his hands down her arms until his fingers met hers. He opened her coat and glided his hands along her hips and skimmed her pockets. Victoria leaned into him, but he moved back before she could tempt him. He pulled her phone from her pocket and set it on the side table next to his.

Victoria started chuckling. "You could have just asked me to leave it here."

"What would be the fun in that?" He gave her a sly grin and began pulling her toward the door. They now had a timetable. "I'm not taking any more chances than I already have. I should have considered that Grace may have bugged Paige's home and could be recording our phone calls, but I was too concerned about how Grace's appearance would upset her, which it turns out I didn't really have to worry about. It's almost like Paige has done a one-eighty."

Victoria stepped to the side as Richard opened the door for her. "I know. At first, I didn't know whether to ask her or to just thank God for what He's done. I'm all right with leaving it in His hands." Richard paused, surprised by her response. He looked at her.

"What? You don't think I can leave it in His hands?" she said, sounding indignant, and he found himself with nothing clever to say, so he kept his mouth closed as he shut the door behind them, making sure it locked.

Richard placed a hand on her back to guide her along.

"Just watch. I won't say a word," Victoria continued.

"Honey, I'm not trying to change you. You are a passionate person. You love with everything you are, and you protect the ones you love just the same. I stopped trying to pick and choose a long time ago." He wrapped his arm around her shoulder and leaned down to kiss her temple.

"So you are telling me I should ask Paige?" Victoria looked up at him.

He laughed. "I said no such thing." He laughed even harder at her pout.

"Come on." He spurred her on. "I need you to come up with a restaurant that you would like to treat everyone to."

"Really?"

He watched her eyes light up. "Of course, but nothing too fancy because they won't have time to change." She frowned slightly at his words.

"Yes, I figured we didn't have too much time by the way you are practically dragging me out of this hotel."

He slowed his steps. "Sorry. Now that it's been brought to my attention, I'm even more wary about them saying something Grace can use.

"But after last night, wouldn't she have plenty of information to cause problems?"

"Maybe, but she still wouldn't have the most important information if Melanie hasn't told Paige where Brian is," he said, glancing down at her, her introspective expression drawing his attention as they reached the car. "You have another concern?"

"What does she have to gain? I understand the need for vengeance better than most, but she moves like she has an end game. Anger and revenge are messy and unfocused. There is a huge circumference of fallout surrounding the target and lines get blurred. This woman has focus."

Richard opened the door for Victoria as he considered her words. His wife was intelligent, but even more than that, she had a way of deconstructing information, which for many years had made it hard to hide anything from her. He liked that they were on the same side again.

Victoria was never satisfied with waiting for information to come to her. Nor did she take the person's next step at face value. She was always looking for step five or six.

"What does that mean to you?" Richard asked as he slipped behind the driver's seat. He made sure they both had their seat belts on before pulling out of the parking space.

"Grace has obviously spent decades with her anger, for her to devise a situation where she could manipulate two young children into having a sexual relationship. Let's say the end game was to have a grandchild. She isn't exactly Mother Teresa as we've stated before, so it's easy to assume she wanted to use the child." Richard glanced over at Victoria. He'd come to much of the same conclusion.

He pulled out from the parking garage onto the street in the direction of Paige's apartment.

Victoria continued "If Brenda truly considered Paige expendable, as Melanie said, then it was Brian Jr. she was after, the one she believed she could use as leverage. Leverage over Luca Sable Sr. It makes sense, but why not hurt him when she put everyone else's businesses under a microscope for the FBI? Why wait then form a plan that had no more than a fifty-fifty chance of working?"

"I don't know, but then I don't know why after everything she's done, she is still breathing. Those weren't saints she betrayed," Richard said, adding his thoughts.

"No. Which means someone is protecting her." Victoria interjected.

"Or she has an 'in case I die' card that she'd been holding over someone's head," Richard replied.

"Which still means someone is protecting her, only reluctantly."

"I know last night Melanie was holding some things back to keep us from accidentally giving something away when we were with Grace and Ross. Maybe what she tells us tonight will give us a better understanding," Victoria said as she looked out of the passenger's window.

He could feel the energy radiating off her.

"This isn't just some family squabble Victoria." He stopped to look her in the eye at the red light. "These people are dangerous."

264

"My son..." Victoria began but Richard interrupted her.

"Your granddaughter, her mother, your great-granddaughters... what do *they* mean to you?" he asked before moving forward.

"That isn't fair."

"No, it's not. It isn't fair to them or yourself. You finally have your family. Everything you thought was taken from you is within your grasp. Your son is alive and has been taken care of all this time without your knowledge. You coming into the knowledge of Brian's existence won't change his life unless you interfere."

Victoria went quiet, but he could feel her mind working. She was ridged.

He turned the corner and found exactly what he'd hoped for on the way to Paige's place. Richard maneuvered the vehicle across a lane and into the parking of a small plaza. He parked and to Victoria's credit, she didn't ask why he was stopping, nor did she make a move to exit the passenger's side

"Will you be quick?" she asked but he couldn't read her voice so he glanced over at her. Her face was blank but he could see in her eyes what she had only recently begun to show him again: her vulnerability.

He nodded, tipping his lips up to the right. He reached out and grazed her jaw with his forefinger before exiting. He walked into the mobile store no more wide than it was deep. He recognized the small pay-as-you-go devices sitting off in the corner. He pulled six off the display rack and carried them to the counter where he handed the cashier enough cash to take care of the six phones. He gave the woman a polite smile as she handed him change then averted his gaze quickly so he didn't stand out in her mind.

He shook his head at himself and his fanciful thoughts as he walked out. He was getting in way over his head. When he got in the car he handed Victoria the phones.

"I thought you asked Sam for replacements," Victoria said looking at the phones in her lap.

"I did, but meanwhile we will need to communicate," he replied, starting the car and putting it in gear.

265

He drove in silence until they reached Paige's apartment. When he parked he took Victoria's hand. "I'm sorry if I hurt your feelings and I know this is something that you've wanted desperately for a long time, but I can't risk it putting the rest of the family in danger."

"I know what you're saying is right." She heaved a sigh, sounding defeated. He should have known better. Victoria was never so easily defeated and even when she was, she wouldn't show it.

"And I would say that you were exactly right if I knew for a fact that you wouldn't go and try to see Luca without me." She looked him straight in the eye when she delivered that sentence, and try as he might to hide his surprise at her correct guess, he couldn't keep his eyes from giving himself away.

"I'm coming with you," she said before he could speak again.

"No," he said without hesitation, which he could see surprised her.

"Why?"

"I don't know this man. I don't know what he will do to protect his grandson. Just by me having knowledge that Brian is alive, I am a threat to him. Someone created Brian and Brian Jr.'s new identities, and I'm pretty sure it wasn't the government. That's fraud."

"But you wouldn't... I wouldn't," Victoria said.

"But Luca Sable doesn't know that, and we don't know if he would want to take that chance. Only one of us can chance this in case he doesn't want to be allies. He is obviously a very smart man."

Richard was about to exit the car but changed his mind. "Did you notice that neither Melanie nor Marc mentioned Brian's new name? They stayed with him for more than a day and it never came up?" Richard shook his head. "He's hiding something. Why? I don't know but if he won't trust Melanie and Marc with his secret, I would be a fool to trust his grandfather with you." He looked back at her so she could see his determination. "I am going alone," he said before exiting the car and walked around the front to open Victoria's door.

"It's been over twenty-five years since they've seen each other," Victoria said as he helped her from the car and began walking up the steps to Paige's apartment building.

"That doesn't help your case, darling," he said, tucking her arm in his.

"I'm just saying, that could be a reason why he wasn't quick to disclose all his secrets," Victoria said in exasperation.

"I agree, but with it being over twenty-five years, it could be something else entirely. Please, honey... please don't fight me on this. I need to make sure you are safe while I do this. It's just what I need." He stopped to look at her, letting his eyes convey his desperation.

Victoria didn't look happy, but she nodded her agreement.

Knowing how hard it was for her, Richard hugged her to him. "Thank you. Really. Thank you. This means a lot to me."

"You're welcome," she said as he turned them back toward the doors.

They were in front of Paige's door before Victoria spoke again. He wished he could say with certainty that she hadn't timed it, but he just didn't know. He knocked as she turned to him.

"What about wearing a wire? No one has to know except the two of us..." Victoria said quietly out of the side of her mouth.

"What?" He looked at her perfectly impassive face, but before he could say any more the door opened, and there stood Melanie, Marc, Paige, and Gladys dressed and ready to go. Obviously, Mason has been able to relay the importance of Richard's message as well as the message itself.

He looked back at Victoria to give her a warning look, but she had shifted into full grandmother mode.

She quietly gestured for everyone to come out, giving them a hug and fussing over them quietly. Even Marc took it with a graciousness that caused Richard's respect for him to deepen.

Once the door was closed again Victoria spoke in a more even tone. "Did everyone leave their phones and other devices in view?

"Yeah," Paige replied sounding skeptical. She was justified. He would feel the same unease about having people he didn't know going through his home, no matter the reason.

Richard placed a reassuring hand on her shoulder. "They are professional, thorough, and efficient. You won't even know they were there."

"Not altogether reassuring, but since you know them, I will trust your judgment," Paige said looking up at him.

Victoria took Paige in her arms and cooed at her. Actually cooed at her before hugging Paige again and ushering everyone away from the door. "I thought of the sweetest little place we could have dinner. It's relaxing, but the food is good and served in abundance."

Victoria continued to describe the restaurant and some of her favorite items on the menu in detail. Melanie glanced back at him with a wide-eyed look before she smiled and returned her attention back to Victoria who continued to prattle on.

Lord please, this woman you gave me. Amen.

Chapter 23

Richard watched as his family enjoyed themselves in the back room of the Italian family-style restaurant Victoria had elected. She called ahead as he'd suggested and worked her charm on the maître d' and the poor unsuspecting hostess that answered the phone.

He could tell just by the gleam in Victoria's eye that she was hyped up on the energy she'd stored from the brunch earlier in the day, her excitement over uncovering more about Brian and her nap. He was fine with it since the alternative, a grumpy Victoria, was not something he even wanted to consider entertaining. To her credit, she hadn't begun interrogating Melanie and Marc from the moment they were all seated. She'd sat back at his right and watched everyone else go over the menus. Well almost everyone. Gladys was still engrossed in what could and couldn't be done with a burner phone. Richard could tell that she was fascinated with the concept more than the obviously limited abilities of the phone.

When she opened her backpack and took out what looked like scrapbook embellishments, he cautioned her. "You know this isn't going to be your permanent phone. You will get a new one with all the bells and whistles in a few days."

"I know, but it doesn't mean I can't trick out this one in the meantime," she said before adding a purple rhinestone to the outer edge. Richard shrugged to himself and opened his menu.

***

An hour later the table was quiet except for the occasional scraping of an utensil against a plate or a glass being set back down. Richard breathed in slowly, taking in the aroma of the foods, the relaxed moods of his family members and the deep satisfaction of knowing he'd been able to make a measurable difference in their safety. He observed Marc's perusal around the table catching the same expression of watchfulness in his gaze as it swept over his wife, Gladys, and then Paige. Richard felt a kinship with Marc and knew after this trip, they would become close friends.

Richard was pulled away from his thoughts by the vibration of the cell at his hip. He pulled the phone out of his pocket and answered. He didn't need to check for any ID since Sam was the only person who had his number besides those sitting at the table.

"Yes," he said in as low a tone as he could. He suspected that everyone was waiting for this call, but if the food could distract them for a little longer, the better.

"We found something," came the quick reply.

Richard exhaled slowly but resisted the urge to close his eyes.

"What do you have?" Richard asked.

"It's a low signal device which made it hard to detect, but that also means the feed isn't that strong. You would need an amplifier to lengthen the signal or sit outside of the apartment to get anything worth listening to," Samuel said, sounding like he was reading over a report.

Richard's heart dipped into his stomach. They had planned for this. He reminded himself. There were contingencies made. Sam went on and Richard thought about their next moves.

One of the guys is looking for it now. Suffice it to say, if it was from Grace, she got the information she was looking for, but only if it was said in the living. Oh, and there didn't seem to be a delay so I doubt it was able to record unless she did it through a speaker on her side. Everything was relayed in real-time," Sam finished with a sigh.

"Thank you, Sam. Great work as usual. I'll wait for your update," Richard responded before hanging up. He stared down at the device in his hand for a few seconds before looking up to find everyone at the table staring at him expectantly.

270

He blinked a couple of times before answering. "Well, Brenda, sorry, Grace planted a device. There's no telling how much information she received but we need to plan for the worst."

"What can she do?" Gladys asked looking confused. He felt for her. This wasn't something any child should have to deal with.

Richard shook his head. "We aren't sure," he said, for the benefit of the table. "It depends on why she wanted to know if Brian was alive." His eyes went unbidden to Melanie before he forced himself to look at everyone at the table. "We need to know who, besides Antonio, she's working with."

Richard took a deep breath before continuing. His food was forgotten as he pondered whether or not to share the next bit of information. He glanced at Victoria before speaking and found only open curiosity in her gaze.

"I have decided to go see Luca Sable," Richard pronounced and watched the myriad of expressions around the table. From his gaze, he detected everything from horror to confusion. Richard decided to address the person with the most intense of the reactions first.

"Melanie. Is there a particular reason why this alarms you?" Richard asked and watched Melanie try to school her features before turning to Marc.

"You might as well say it now. It's as good a time as any," Marc replied to Melanie's gaze. She turned back to Richard.

"I don't know if that would be the best plan." Melanie swallowed before she continued. Out of the corner of his eye, he saw Victoria glance at him before placing her fork and knife down and turning back to Melanie.

"Although Brian was able to share some information with us about his life and his grandfather Luca, it was limited, due in part to the fact that Luca gave him most of the information and he could only obtain so much background without giving himself away." Melanie took another breath before looking at Paige and then Gladys, her eyes growing moist and Marc took her hand.

Richard grew still.

"Like I told you last night." Melanie paused. "Was it only last night. Oh my God, this day is lasting forever." Melanie said more to herself than anyone else at the table.

"Baby," Marc said, pulling her away from her vocalized thoughts. Melanie looked up at him and the pain in her expression shook Richard. He watched as she nodded her head and visibly gained control of her emotions.

"As I told you last night," Melanie repeated. "Grace and Luca had an affair. What I didn't share was that Brian gave me proof that Colonel Wayne Morganson wasn't my biological father."

The gasp that came from Victoria mirrored Richard's own inner turmoil. He glanced at Paige, wondering what her reaction was to this news. Surprisingly her expression was resigned. He shifted his gaze back to Melanie when she started speaking again.

"But there is another man. One Angelo Mauro."

Richard's breath caught at the mention of the name and he went even more still. He knew the use of that name along with Luca Sable was no coincidence. There was only one man Melanie could be speaking of and the mere thought that she would be connected to that family sent chills racing down his spine.

Richard was sure the mere whisper of the Mauro name on certain streets of Chicago would cause people to hold their breath to keep from bringing attention to themselves. Though Angelo Mauro hadn't been recently linked to deaths, disappearances, dismemberment or crime for that matter, business or otherwise, some of his family members were spoken of in only the dark and quiet places.

Richard had the unpleasant experience of learning about Angelo's nephews during one of his earlier philanthropic projects. They had shown interest in investing in the building of a well near one of the orphanages Richard designed in Uganda. When he made it clear that it was a purely altruistic venture they pulled back, with the expressed interest of investing in something at a later date that could see a return. Richard had no clue how they'd learned about his foundation or the work he did, but he hoped their interest would wane quickly.

"Was Brian hinting that you could be Luca Sable's daughter?" Victoria asked, her voice breaking on the last word.

Melanie smiled wanly, "There was no hinting. He suspects that I am either Luca Sable's daughter or Angelo Mauro's daughter."

Richard weighed the magnitude of either possibility and was no less shaken by either. Once again he looked to Paige and she wore much the same expression but he could tell she was present and listening to the conversation. From Melanie's reaction, he would have guessed this was the first time that anyone at the table other than Marc had heard her speak of this.

His wife's voice pulled his attention away from Paige.

"Would Grace really do that? Put you and Brian together knowing you were…that you and he were…" Victoria seemed to struggle with the last of the sentence.

Melanie's voice was solemn. "That is the question right now isn't it."

"On the other hand." Marc broke in. "It could be the motive behind Grace wanting to confirm Brian's existence. If Luca is actually grooming him to take over, the scandal the proof of his identity would bring could cripple the firm and place Antonio in a position of power. With Grace blackmailing Antonio, it would then give her the leverage she has been working for all of these years.

But if Melanie is Angelo Mauro's daughter then Paige and B.J. are the heirs of two of the top Italian mob families in Chicago. That will not be well received by the other families especially since they were raised outside of the influence of both houses and are related to Grace." Marc finished grimly.

Victoria let go of a sob, startling everyone at the table. She put her napkin to her mouth and seemed to work desperately to gain some composure. She stood up and Richard got up with her. He laid a hand on her back, wanting to take her in his arms, but she stepped away.

"I'm going to the ladies' room," Victoria said brokenly.

"I'll take you," he said, wanting to do whatever he could to help.

"I'll take her," Paige said, getting up from the table and walking around to place a hand around Victoria's waist. When he hesitated

Paige said just so the three of them could hear. "If she has to cry this out you can't go into the ladies' room with her."

Richard double-checked to make sure Paige was able to console his wife after the shock everyone had just received, but she looked oddly calm. He nodded his consent and watched them walk out of the room.

With his concern for Victoria now overriding his emotions, his anger came to the forefront and he turned to Mel and Marc. He opened his mouth then spotted Gladys sitting quietly in her chair, watching him. He sat down heavily in his chair and finally gave in to the temptation to place his elbows on the table and place his head in his hands.

He was a mess. The confidence he had just a few moments before had evaporated and now he didn't know which direction to go. A small arm came around his neck, startling him and he looked up into liquid silver eyes. Gladys pulled his head in for a hug and he was horrified to feel his own tears close to the surface. Wasn't it supposed to be the other way around?

He was so tired. His wife, all of them, had gone through so much over the last few months. He didn't know how much more of this she could take. How much more he could carry her through.

Gladys pulled back and peered into his eyes much as her sister would do on occasion. "Your job is not to have all the answers, just to continue to point to the *one* who does."

Richard blinked at her, taken aback by the words and her mannerisms that seemed decades beyond her.

"What?" he said for lack of anything else to say.

"Sunday school. I spoke to Vivian today and she shared the Sunday school lesson," Gladys said with a small smile. *This is what they taught in children's Sunday school?*

"You are the head of the home. If you trust God, then the rest of the family can trust that you will make the right decisions." She looked at him as though that was supposed to solve everything. When he continued to blink up at her, she giggled before sobering again. She kept her hands at his neck and he saw his reflection in her silver gaze.

"When you trust in God, you don't have to come up with the answers yourself. You get them from God. So, when you think about it, you don't have to worry about coming up with all of the answers. You just have to look to Him and let Him be the head of your home," she said the last part of her sentence with a shrug and it was that movement that allowed him to absorb the words she was saying. He inhaled, catching the scent of bubblegum and realized it was the fragrance of her shampoo. *Bubble gum.* He just got schooled by a child.

All of a sudden, he wanted to laugh. He smiled at her and she nodded as if satisfied that he'd understood her. She placed a small palm on his cheek and seemed to look into his soul before she spoke again. "You're my Papa Richard too."

He reached out, smoothing back a stray curl before wrapping his hand around the back of her head and bringing her forehead to his lips. "Always," he said before enveloping her in a hug.

Over her shoulder, he met Melanie's teary gaze and had to look away before his waterworks started. After one more squeeze, he let her go and she smiled at him before going back to her seat. "Thank you again for the neat phone."

He wouldn't have been able to hold back the laugh even if he'd known it was coming. "You're welcome," he said before righting himself at the table.

Richard looked up at Marc feeling a good fifty pounds lighter. "So, do either of you have any ideas?"

"I'm going to go have a talk with my mother," Melanie said, determination flashing in her golden eyes. He saw Marc look at her in surprise.

"Do you think that's wise? No telling what she has up her sleeve and from what I can tell she has no problem tracking you." Richard stated.

"Not if you and Victoria give me a ride," Melanie responded and Richard saw Marc stiffened.

"I don't like the thought of you being in that women's house, in that city," Marc said, sounding cautious.

Melanie looked at her husband. Her voice sugary sweet. "That's why you are going to send a few men to watch her for a day or two to make sure her calendar is pretty much the same. Then you and I are going to Washington." She looked back at Richard.

Richard threw up his hands in surrender. "I have no qualms with taking you and Marc to Washington, but are you sure you want to approach her? No telling what she knows. It could have devastating repercussions on Paige, Brian, and B.J."

Melanie searched Richard's face for a second. "I'm doing it for her, Brian and Brian Jr."

"Did you tell Paige about you possibly being Luca's daughter before you shared it with all of us today?" Richard asked.

"No, I didn't. Why?" Melanie asked with a frown, seeming to lock on his concern.

"She seemed very calm. I didn't notice any distress or see surprise register on her face. She's been through a great deal, and I looked to see if this shook her. Instead, it seemed like she was…" He searched for the right word again. If all of this was wearing on him, he couldn't truly understand the effect it was having on his wife and Paige. "Resigned," he said, looking up at Melanie.

He watched sorrow wash over her expression. She reached for her glass, but her hand shook too much to bring it to her lips. She gave up and set it down hard with a huge exhale. Melanie began to shake her head as if warring with herself.

Melanie finally looked up at Richard, her gaze steely. "This is actually a blessing. I have sat in limbo for too long, staying quiet, playing it safe. For what? So Grace can continue to go around ruining people's lives? I'm through playing the docile daughter. I want some answers and she has them.

"What makes you think she will tell you?" Richard asked, a little stunned by her about-face.

"Nothing, but she also doesn't know that I won't go to Mr. Mauro or Mr. Sable for the answers." Melanie's eyes were fierce. Richard looked to Marc for some kind of reassurance that Melanie knew what she was about to get into.

276

"What if she tries to corner you about Brian being alive?"

"I think that horse has left the barn. If she received anything from bugging the apartment the other night, she is already looking for him. If not, now that I have decided to move against her and whatever she has been planning, there's no need to hide him. But I will let Brian make the decision on how he comes forth."

"She's proven that she's an unpredictable and dangerous woman, Mel," Marc said. "You have no real idea who she's working with. What if this goes deeper than her using Antonio as her puppet? What if it's Angelo Mauro against Luca Sable? You would be putting more than your life in jeopardy."

Melanie's anger seemed to deflate under Marc's questions, but her voice was firm. "Do what you have to do to keep me safe, but I'm going to see her," Melanie said, crossing her arms over her chest.

Richard looked at Marc whose complexion had darkened with exasperation then at Gladys who was staring at her mother openmouthed. She closed it then looked at him as if he had the answer.

Richard started praying silently to himself. *Lord, please. I need an answer. You've done so much to expose and reveal over the last few months. Is this you? If so, I know you will keep us safe, but I have to know it's you before I move.*

Chapter 24

Victoria worked hard to get her tears under control, but Paige's warm arms and soothing voice were working against her efforts to regain her composure. *Crying in a restaurant bathroom. Get ahold of yourself.*

"It's fine to let it go. You have to get it out. It's healthier this way," Paige murmured.

It wasn't what Victoria expected to hear, but it soothed her and gave her the permission she needed to give in to the grief just a little bit longer. The grief from the loss of so many years with her son, the loss of having *this* loving soul in her life.

The thought that Grace would use the time and potential love of her children as a weapon instead of treasuring and holding them close, turned Victoria's blood cold and allowed her to get a hold of her tears. Victoria pulled back and a tissue appeared in front of her eyes. She dabbed at her eyes and cheeks before looking up at Paige.

"I'm sorry," she said, looking at the young woman, once again tempted to seek out similarities between their features, but Paige held a great deal of her mother's genes.

"For what? For crying?" Paige asked, shaking her head.

"No, no," Victoria repeated Paige's movement then took a deep breath before continuing. "For a lot of things. For the way I treated you when we first met. I didn't even know you, but I was afraid you would step in and take away more of my family. A family I hadn't treated right up to that moment."

Paige took her hands. "We've been through this," Paige said, obviously trying to stop her.

"Please, let me finish," Victoria said, feeling an urgency to get out what she was thinking. "I'm sorry that I keep underestimating you and your love for God. I keep projecting my reactions, thoughts, and experiences on you, and you keep coming back more resilient, but more than that, you forgive me." She didn't even try to stop the tears that returned to her eyes. She continued on, looking at Paige through the watery blur.

"I can't imagine what type of effect the revelations of the last couple of days have had. I just need you to know that I recognize it was wrong of me to push as I did when you came to visit us a couple of months ago. You came seeking refuge, and I was looking for someone unrealistic. I kept thinking back to you in that hospital and put that expectation on you." Paige tried to stop her again but Victoria pulled her hands out of Paige's grasp and held them up.

"Please, I need to say this," she said before continuing. "I looked up to you and your ability to keep your hold on your faith, despite what you went through when you found out about Vivian... and how much you almost gave up for her. I held you up on a pedestal, and I tried to put you in a position not made for you. That position was created by God so that I could take a step toward Him even as He took two to me." Victoria reached out and cupped Paige's cheek. "You are an amazing woman of God. You made loving the Lord look effortless, tempting, irresistible, but it wasn't enough until I chose to surrender my anger and the fortress I had worked so hard to construct around my heart. I get it. Thank you," Victoria ended sheepishly.

Paige hugged her again, and though Victoria was able to pull back the emotion before giving in to sobs again, it was close.

"It's still hard though," Victoria said after a moment. "I want to reach out and yank Grace back to the past by her neck and undo everything she did to my son and your mother."

"And as much as I would love to see you try out that theory, if you proved successful, I wouldn't be here," Paige replied.

Victoria stared at her for a moment trying to think of a way around that scenario. Finally, she just shrugged and Paige smiled.

"How are you doing? I mean, I know this has all been a lot, but today, finding out that your mom and dad may be related." Victoria winced at how crass she sounded.

"It doesn't make me think any less of myself. I'm the same person I was when I thought my parents were Grace and Wayne Morganson. I think Melanie may have a harder time with it. There is the guilt of what you might have inadvertently done to your children and whether there are physical or mental consequences to bringing children conceived from incest to term," Paige said, giving her an apologetic smile.

At first, Victoria didn't follow Paige and was about to ask her why she thought Melanie would feel guilty then she remembered how Vivian and Gladys were conceived.

"Oh. Yes." Victoria said on an exhale. "One day when we have time, would you be willing to share that with me? If you want to, of course." Victoria stopped before her mouth made things more awkward than it already had.

Paige blinked at her, looking surprised by her request. "Yeah, sure I can. One day when all of this mess is cleared up, we will sit down with some tissue and tea, and I will tell you how God used the enemy's plans against me to bless me."

"Well said," Victoria responded. "Nice. May I use that?"

"Of course. It isn't even mine. I got it from the Bible," Paige said with a giggle before turning toward the mirror. "Let's get cleaned up. I'm afraid if we stay in here much longer, your husband will come banging on the door and I like this restaurant. I would like to be able to come back."

Victoria followed Paige's lead and went about restoring her makeup. They were almost ready to leave when Victoria thought about what might come from everything that was revealed during dinner. "What do you think Melanie might do now?"

Paige had leaned against the wall a few minutes before while she waited for Victoria. Their gazes met in the mirror.

"I think she's going to want to confront Grace," Paige said after a moment of thought.

Victoria turned toward Paige. "You think so? Why didn't she do it this morning?"

"Melanie doesn't like confrontation, but more than that I think she was hoping that at some point, even with everything Grace has done against her, there would be a chance for reconciliation. I think seeing how Grace acted today, along with the realization that she would bug my place, Melanie is done hoping. I've never seen her as angry and combative against Grace as I did at brunch.

"Whatever Brian shared with her and Marc has her seeing things differently," Paige said, moving away from the wall.

"What do you think she's looking to get from Grace at her home that we didn't get during brunch?"

"I think Mel likes Ross and didn't want to embarrass him in front of us, but when she gets Grace alone, she will confront her and demand answers," Paige said before adjusting her purse. Victoria could tell she was about to turn to open the door, so Victoria reached out and caught her hand.

"How do you know?" Victoria asked.

"Because that's what I did when I found out she lied to me," Paige said before pulling open the door and stepping aside to let her exit.

Victoria nodded before preceding her through the door.

***

"So, we are going to Washington," Victoria said while dabbing night cream under her eyes. She really needed to get some sleep. There was no hiding the half-moons under her eyes if they got any darker. Well, at least with the change of plans, they would be able to sleep in tomorrow. She was looking forward to a leisurely morning with room service.

"That's what it looks like," Richard replied, turning off the bathroom light and walking toward the bed.

She rubbed cream on her hands and turned toward him from the desk-vanity table in their hotel room.

281

"Do you actually think Melanie and Marc will wait until after Christmas?"

"I believe so. Even though Melanie is angry, she isn't a hot head and Marc is good at looking at a situation from all angles. With all of the potential Christmas and holiday parties, it would be almost impossible to get Grace alone. Plus, I pointed out that they had only just arrived and maybe leaving so soon, even if it was just for a day, wouldn't help their relationship with Paige."

Victoria felt a little deflated at Richard's success. She'd been looking forward to giving Grace a piece of her mind immediately. It looked like she would have to wait.

"I was thinking we could go after the holiday rush. The skies would be quieter, and the spas would be starting their offseason. It was my plan to do a turnaround. Six hours there and six hours back plus four to six hours for refueling. We could pamper ourselves while Melanie and Marc confronted Grace."

Richard pulled back the covers on the bed as if that were all to the conversation. Victoria waited, but when Richard slipped into bed without another word, she grew tense.

"You mean we are supposed to wait for them? I know what you said to them at the restaurant, but I didn't think you really meant we weren't going to go in with them," Victoria said, staring at Richard.

Richard blinked at her. "We won't just be waiting." Excitement rolled through Victoria at what he might be saying.

"We will be *getting pampered*," he said as he slid under the covers and closed his eyes briefly, a look of sheer bliss on his face. Victoria stared at him until he opened his eyes.

"Vickie, when have you known me to be a man of subterfuge? I say what I mean, and I mean for us to stay out of this," Richard said before closing his eyes again.

Victoria understood the need for Melanie to confront Grace alone. If they were all there, it would undermine the stance Melanie was trying to make, but she felt cheated. She wanted to look the woman in the eyes and ask her how she could purposefully manipulate her child… an actual child into a sexual relationship with another child?

282

She was sure the statute of limitations had expired but wasn't that illegal? It should be negligence at the least. Melanie could have died giving birth.

"I can feel your mind buzzing, and it is too late for your mind to be so busy. There is nothing you can do about it tonight, or tomorrow for that matter. It has been an extremely long weekend, and I don't know about you, but I am ready to see it come to an end.

Victoria watched her husband for a moment and knew he was right, but she planned to have her time with Grace. It might not happen during this trip, but she would have her say soon. She got up and turned the corner lamp off before removing her robe and slipping into bed.

As her body relaxed and began to entice her mind into slowing down she ran over a couple of scenarios where she confronted Grace and her lips tipped up unbidden.

"Stop dreaming of beating Grace up. It's not how you share the love of Jesus," Richard said, and Victoria opened her eyes to see her husband staring at her with a grin on his face.

"Not once did any of my conversations with her lead to an altercation with fists," she said, but his expression didn't change. "How did you know I was thinking about her in that way anyway?"

"You had this impish smile on your face, but your brows would crease every now and then like when you get into a heated debate with our foreman," he replied.

"I haven't gotten into a debate with Nathan... in a long time," she amended when he raised a brow. She shrugged her shoulders then turned to look at him. "He's the foreman. It was an authority thing," Victoria said ruefully.

"I'll let you tell it," he said before leaning over and giving her a quick peck on the mouth. He turned and shut off the bedside lamp, dousing the room into darkness.

She relaxed back into the pillow, but before sleep claimed her, Victoria whispered a prayer of thanks for her family and everything God had done. "I'm not sure I would have done it all the way you have, what with all the secrets you've been unraveling and lately, but I am grateful for everything and everyone you have given back to me. I'm feeling full, Lord. I'm feeling loved. Amen."

A chuckle came from Richard's side of the bed, startling Victoria.

"I thought you were sleep," she said.

"I'm sure." She heard him shift in the bed just far enough to be out of her sight in the darkness of the room. "I wouldn't have whispered that prayer out loud if I knew someone was listening either."

"It wasn't wrong," she said, feeling suddenly vulnerable.

"No, it wasn't wrong. It was very honest, in fact. I just find it funny that you talk to God like you talk to me about my work, which I have been accredited to be great in," he said with amusement.

Victoria shrugged but didn't say anything. She gave no apology for missing Rachel or any of her unborn children. People thought heartbreak was reserved for those who breathed outside of the womb, but she knew more than most the wreckage left from the death of an unborn child.

There was so much love poured into each of their children, not only at conception but while they grew in her womb. If she could have breathed for them each moment until they were ready to be born, she would have. She spoke to them from the moment she found out they were growing inside of her. Her love grew to encompass every hope for the life they would live and the impact they would have on humanity, all the way down to whose features they would share, but it didn't die with them. She did whatever she could think of that might cajole, lure, and persuade them to grow to full term so she could hold them in her arms.

Victoria used to wonder what happened to that love that she'd stored up for each one of her children. It didn't just get transferred over to the next baby. She knew this because each baby had a different personality or characteristics—if not name—in her mind due to when, where, and how they were conceived or the type of effect they had on her body.

The love didn't just dissipate with the death of her child. She kept loving them long after they were gone. She loved them now, but with an aching longing.

284

It took coming out of a haze of anger to realize the love never left her heart, it just grew to hold more.

"What are you thinking about?" Richard asked.

"Our children," she responded without hesitating.

"All of them?" His voice was cautious, and she smiled.

"Yes," she answered.

"What are you thinking about regarding our children?" he asked.

A moment before, his voice made him sound as though he were on the verge of sleep, and now she could tell he was alert. She loved this man. He never referred to them as *her* children even though he wasn't aware a few of them existed a year ago.

She yawned and snuggled under the cover a little more, feeling safe in voicing her thoughts. "I was thinking about my love for each of our children and how that love is still there, in my heart, even after the hope that some of them would be more, has died."

She heard him move among the sheets and knew he was seeking out any part of her to connect with. "I'm fine," she said, in case he thought she was in need of comfort. "It was just a thought."

His hand found hers and he squeezed it and rubbed her knuckles with his thumb. Well, maybe she had needed a little comforting.

"I love them too, and I grieve for the ones who aren't with us anymore," he said before moving close enough in the dark for her to make out the outline of his face.

She didn't know why she was surprised by his statement. He was shocked when he found out she'd been keeping her miscarriages from him, but he was nearly undone when she brought out her baby journal and mapped out where their ashes lay in the garden.

The fact that he stayed, knowing she'd kept so much from him still had her down on her knees at night sometimes thanking God for His mercy and the love of a man who also showed mercy.

"You're quiet," he said.

"Yes," she responded, not sure if she should voice her surprise.

"And what are you thinking?" he asked, his breath sweeping over her face.

285

"That I am sorry I didn't realize that you still grieved, but otherwise you would not be the man I married. I'm also thankful for the grace God has shown me through you," Victoria said, then gave his hand a squeeze back.

He was quiet for a moment. "How long do you think it will be before you trust that you aren't alone?"

"I'm almost there," she said, feeling it in her heart.

"Good," he said with an exhale.

"Richard?" she asked.

"Mmmm?" His sleepy voice was back.

"I love you," she said before closing her eyes.

"I love you too, Vickie," he replied, warming her soul with his words.

"Richard?" she called out.

"Yes," he answered, sounding no less patient.

"I changed my mind. I wouldn't change a thing," she whispered.

The silence that followed her words was thicker than the darkness of the room. Then she heard Richard move. She expected him to come closer and wrap his arms around her. Instead, the lamp on the nightstand on his side of the bed turned on. She squinted in the light, waiting for her eyes to adjust.

"What are you doing? Why did you turn the light on?"

"I was just making sure I was in bed with the right woman," he said before turning the light back off.

She would have swatted him if she could have reached him.

"Whatever," she murmured before turning over and shifting to the edge of her side of the bed. He had just ruined a perfectly good moment and mocked a realization it had taken years for her to get to.

"Where did you go?" he asked. He must have gotten to the middle of the bed.

She felt him come up behind her and wrap an arm around her waist. She didn't try to get away—she couldn't—but she didn't snuggle into his hold as she usually did.

"Come on. I'm sorry, sweetie. I was just joking around," he said, kissing the back of her neck.

"It wasn't funny," she said in a quiet voice.

"Okay, it wasn't funny. I apologize," he said.

"Why are you apologizing? It was a joke," she said, trying and failing to keep the pout out of her voice.

"I'm apologizing because my response was insensitive," he said.

She smiled to herself. She had such a good husband. Victoria closed her eyes and had nearly dropped off to sleep when Richard spoke again. "Do you forgive me?"

Victoria thought about going to sleep without answering, but with the last breath before unconsciousness she whispered, "Yes."

PART THREE

Chapter 25

Luca Sable stepped from the jet slowly, his long legs feeling a little heavy after the long flight. Even the most comfortable flights these days were a bit of a bother, but as long as his family was scattered across the country he didn't have a choice. He didn't even bother with an umbrella but instead chose to hold on to the rails. The last thing he needed to do was slip and fall, forcing his son Antonio into position before he was ready. If nothing else, Antonio had shown, over the last six months, that he was not ready to take over the family business.

Luca hated to see his son repeat his own mistakes, but Brenda was hard to resist as an innocent and determined young woman. He probably wouldn't have stood a chance against her now either if she set her sights on him. Antonio definitely hadn't. He'd fallen prey to her machinations even after Luca had warned him from her the year before when he'd seen hard inquiries into Antonio's position at Sable Financial and Brian's health records only to find out they came from Brenda's husband's computer IP address.

It put Luca on alert, making him very careful what he said around his son and others in the family. He didn't feel the need to say anything to Helena since she'd successfully kept the secret of Brian and B.J.'s existence for decades and would be the last person Brenda would approach for any reason. He couldn't think about the two of them without wincing to this day. If he'd known the destruction that two weeks with Brenda would reap upon his family, he would have tried harder to resist her. Right now, it looked like she was retracing her steps, which didn't bode well for anyone.

Luca covered the ground, between the jet and car waiting near the hangar, with a few long strides. The rain was moderate but expected this time of year in this region. It had been months since he'd visited the boys. He originally planned to visit them right after his birthday party. Their presence had been missed as it always had been during family get-togethers, but he'd been thrown by the report he received one night as they cruised around the Mediterranean.

He couldn't even recall all the emotions that ran through him at the news that Melanie and Marc had visited Brian. His only consolation was that Brian met them at the Sable summer home, and they had only stayed three days and left in a way even he couldn't track. He knew his grandson had planned everything, just by the way Melanie and Marc appeared and disappeared across the country. Brian was good at playing hide-and-seek with Luca's blind spots, which was the only reason why Luca hadn't headed toward Maine the moment his birthday trip was finished.

He followed Marc and Melanie when their legal passports showed up in customs and headed straight to Paige, which made sense with Gladys staying with Melanie's daughter. He also watched as Brenda and her new husband tracked them and knew nothing good would come of it.

Luca slipped into the back seat of the Town Car and relaxed with a sigh into the heated leather cushions. The cold rain that wet his hair was a forgotten discomfort as he slipped off his shoes and coat. December in Oregon was simply an irritation. He didn't understand why Brian would want to live in such a climate. The East Coast was so much more beautiful in the winter.

When Brian had asked to head up the project of renovating the Sable summer home off Sebago Lake in Standish, ME twelve years ago, he obliged him. Brian came in as if he were a hired foreman and did an incredible job of bringing the house into the twenty-first century.

It had been a birthday present of sorts. Brian had proven himself to be an extremely intelligent, practical, and wise man for a then thirty-year old. Luca knew he'd held on to the reins too tightly for most of his grandson's life, but he had never lied or kept important information from him about his birth and his value, both as Luca's grandson and the invisible man behind a couple of the greatest business deals Luca had made in the last decade.

Antonio was also an excellent businessman. He'd made Luca proud with his keen eye for both details in the lines of numbers representing other companies' true bottom line and for the people who ran those businesses. It was why Luca wanted so desperately to place Antonio over the firm, but Antonio's ambition and emotions had a way of getting the best of him and his judgment when it came to women, and he could not be trusted, even now.

Luca glanced out the window. He could see lights from the city through the ever-growing copse of trees, and it calmed him some. Though he'd argued with Brian on constructing another home on the West Coast and being so far away from the rest of the family—Helena in Chicago—Brian had made some very valid points as to why a home situated off the Northwest Coast was worth the investment. It was secured by two private roads and a driveway that seemed to lead into a hedge until said hedge, which was really a foliage-covered remote-controlled gate, moved. All this was extra security since the home had been purchased by a Shell company in Brian's alias name and wasn't found on any GPS map because B.J. made sure of it. The whiz kid had also made sure the surrounding area received no cell reception for a mile. Within the confines of the house though, the WiFi worked perfectly with the software to boost and conceal outgoing signals. Maybe "conceal" was the wrong word since B.J. had explained it as more of a hide-and-seek trail rather than a cloak-and-dagger trail for the IP address.

This meant no one came to the house unless, one, they knew it was there, and two, were given access. It was all mostly above Luca's head, but he still expected a report from Brian weekly on any upgrades.

The fact that Brian had Melanie and Marc come to the home in Maine let Luca know they had not been in contact before that weekend almost six weeks ago. Brian would out Melanie and Marc just like that even in an emergency. It was obvious to Luca that Brian had wanted Luca to know that he'd met with them, but that concerned Luca more than it eased his mind.

Brian, Brian Jr., and Luca had always been close. It had been out of necessity, sure, but it was also out of love and respect. Luca always knew Brian wouldn't stay hidden forever. Honestly, he hadn't expected him to stay hidden as long as he had.

Over ten years ago, when Brian had met Leslie Caine, a marketing agent in Portland, Oregon, Luca both quietly wished for and dreaded their relationship getting serious. It meant Brian would not only have to come out from under the cover of his alias but Brian Jr. with him. It was impossible to build a successful relationship on lies, and with Brian keeping his true identity to himself, he and Leslie weren't going to prosper.

In the end, Brian chose to step away for the security of his son. As far as Luca knew, Brian and Leslie still spoke from time to time, but Brian Jr. said it always sounded painful.

At first, Luca took Brian's visit with Melanie and Marc to mean that he was ready to stop living in the shadows, but he hadn't reached out to Luca, which was unlike Brian and the real reason why Luca was on the West Coast.

Luca pulled out his electronic tablet from his inside suit coat pocket. It had been a couple of days since he'd last checked up on Brenda. The thought of her brought warmth and then chills to his body even after all this time.

When Luca first met Brenda he was arrogant, immature, knew more about success than loss, and thought himself entitled to nothing but more success. The earth was his to do what he wanted with it until one beautiful African American woman with golden eyes and a heart full of longing taught him differently.

By the time he'd sent Brenda to Florida, possibly with his child in her belly, he'd lost his wife's trust, respect within certain circles of his business organization, and some self-respect. What he didn't know was that it was only the beginning of the destruction Brenda would bring upon him, but his guilt for what he believed he'd turned her into wouldn't allow him to hand her over to the mob when she was done giving over state's evidence.

It wasn't until more than a decade later when she threatened the most vulnerable part of his family—his legacy that he chose to retaliate. On the surface, it had cost him, Luca, nothing, but it had cost his grandson and great-grandson their freedom. Every day he second-guessed his decisions on that fateful night twenty-seven years ago, but he had not been willing to live with the repercussions of what Brenda would have done if she'd had access to Brian and Brian Jr.

Luca checked his watch. He had another forty-minute drive, so Luca sunk even farther into the leather and closed his eyes but didn't sleep. He'd lowered the floodgates where his thoughts on Brenda were concerned. He would let them play out, and hopefully by the time he reached Brian's house, Brenda would be exorcised for a while.

Luca had sworn to himself that once Brenda married Wilson, he wouldn't contact her for her sake. What his wife had done showed him that as ruthless as men could be, women, when crossed, could rein devastation.

He had to break that oath to himself when Charles Mauro called him asking if he should be concerned about the men in his office going through all his files. Luca was confused at first, wondering if Angelo, perchance, wasn't as interested in going legit as he'd claimed months before. It was when the other Chicago business leaders began calling him that Luca's blood ran cold in his veins, and the feelings of apprehension turned into full-blown panic.

When the FBI came into his office with a warrant he wasn't at all surprised. When they told him of the documents they were looking for, any doubt he'd harbored that Brenda had taken files with her and turned state's evidence were dashed.

Luca dared not call Brenda from his office or home phone, so he had Patrick drop him off at the house, and he took the roadster out for a drive to the next city where he used a payphone. The phone number he called was no longer in service, and it only served to heat his blood more. He spent twenty minutes in the cold being run around in circles at Wilson's base until he ran out of change. He went home but was in such a foul mood he could barely be civil to his family.

He wasn't surprised when Helena came in while he was getting changed for bed and told him that she'd gotten a call from Charles Mauro's wife, Camila.

"What did Camila have to say?" he'd asked while taking off his socks.

"She was wondering if she and her family's life had been turned upside down by the woman you had an affair with?" Helena asked as she sat down at her vanity and began to remove her earrings, her gaze on him through the mirror.

Luca glanced up at her reflection to check her expression since she'd delivered the sentence as if they were discussing the idea of a new Jacuzzi. Her dark eyes were cold, and if her opening sentence hadn't hinted to the fight she was trying to start, the glint in her eyes made clear her intent.

"So you spoke to Camila about my affair too. How many others do I have the honor of getting the evil eye from?" he said, feeling indulgent where her wish for a fight was concerned.

"If the least of the consequences for your infidelity is that a friend or two of mine know what you've done, then you should consider yourself fortunate."

"That is inconsequential. The consequence of my infidelity is the loss of your trust and that is huge. Their looks or name-calling behind my back can't do more to me than I've already done to myself," Luca returned as he removed his other sock.

Clapping from across the room drew his attention. "Bravo. Well said, but after my call today it doesn't look as though losing my trust is the only result from your fling with that..." Helena looked at him before voicing her slur on Brenda's character, and he didn't even try to hide his ire.

He considered his frame of mind and took back the decision to engage in a full-fledged fight with Helena. She knew what buttons to press, and after his day she could provoke him into divulging information that would put Brenda's life in even more danger than it was today.

He began to put his socks back on because after they finished, he was sure he wouldn't want to sleep next to her, let alone spend the night under the same roof. She went quiet, and he knew she was taking note of his movements.

"You have nothing to say?" Helena spat out.

"To what, Helena? About the fact that a woman who obviously felt wronged may be striking out at the family of the man that beat and raped her?" he replied without looking up, the words raising bile his throat.

"Are you saying she is justified in her actions?" Helena asked, sounding incredulous.

"I am saying nothing that you don't already agree to. That every action has an equal and opposite reaction," he said, unbuttoning his nightshirt.

Helena looked startled for a moment. "Did *you* get a visit today?"

"Yes. I'm surprised that wasn't your first question, Helena," he said, taking off his nightshirt and walking to the closet for a T-shirt and sweater.

"Who?" Helena asked, sounding ill.

"Why, the FBI my dear," he returned snidely before pulling the sweater over his head.

"How bad is it?" Helena had turned to him with her last question.

"Since the Sable Financial Firm is not a front for laundering money and has worked hard to maintain an integral viable business, it wasn't bad."

Helena blinked at him. "She's not coming after you?"

Luca slipped his feet into a pair of loafers before going to the dresser to pick up his wallet. "Not financially."

"What does that mean?"

"It means that the subpoena asks for the company's financial records for years after we'd already gone fully legit. We may get a tap on the hand for our association, or older business deals, with some of

294

the other organizations now being scrutinized, but it won't be more than a light fine. If the Sable Firm walked away without a scratch it would have looked suspicious," he said as he took a bag from the top of his closet and brought it back to the bed. He began to transfer clothing from the dresser to the bag, not stopping to count. He had no clue how long it would take for him to calm down or find Brenda since she was probably already in witness protection.

"Are you going to give her up?" Helena asked without emotion.

"To whom, Helena? Maybe to more men than last time? Was five not enough? What is a good enough number for you? What amount of punishment would satisfy you?" She winced at the graphic picture he drew about the form of justice Helena had served Brenda, but she rallied quickly.

"Whatever happened to an eye for an eye?" Helena stood up, coming to stand between him and the dresser.

"That was not what was served," he said slowly, losing his grip on his control. "*I* wronged you. *I* hurt you. *I* was the one who did not keep my vow to you or God. ME! If someone had to pay, it should only have been me," he finished, pointing at himself as he towered over her.

Her eyes had grown wide. Not in fright, but pain, and once again he was reminded of what he had done. He continued in a quieter tone, hoping she would understand that he wasn't trying to defend Brenda, but protect her.

"Speaking of an eye for an eye, I hope Brenda's mother never gets wind of what you set in motion for her daughter. I can't imagine what you would go through to avenge your daughter if she were beaten and defiled that way."

Helena began to wring her hands. A sure sign that she'd started to think of what she'd done. The distress that crossed her features pulled at his heart. He opened his arms, and for the first time in almost a year, she walked into them and allowed him to comfort her.

"How are we going to get past this?" Helena murmured into his sweater.

"One day, one hour, one moment at a time," he answered.

"I don't think we will be able to survive any more of these," she said without censure, just pure honesty.

"There won't be," he said and meant it, but he didn't plan on giving up his search for Brenda. They had some things to discuss.

***

It had taken two days and the use of a long-held favor to find Brenda. To say that Luca was frustrated and annoyed was an understatement. He had been irritated two days before. Now he was peeved and at the end of his tether.

He decided to make his call from his hotel room in Detroit while on a business trip. He checked the time to make sure that if she was home, she would be there alone. He was so angry his hands shook as he began to press the buttons to her new number.

"Hello," Brenda answered the phone as if she were expecting his call. She hadn't said his name. That would have been nothing short of suicide for both of them, but he could tell by her tone that she knew it was him.

"Brenda," he said.

"Grace," she said.

Was she asking for Grace? "What?"

"It's Grace Morganson now," she said.

"What have you done?" Luca asked, and try as he might, couldn't keep his voice from shaking with rage.

"It's so nice to hear from you, Luca. How's the weather?" Brenda replied in a calm and almost silky voice.

"This is not a courtesy call."

"I didn't expect it would be since you didn't have the courtesy to reach out to me after you married me off and sent me to Timbuktu or have the decency to even ask if I had a boy or a girl. Florida, Luca? Florida? You couldn't find a state farther from you? It's hot here, Luca," Brenda bit out.

"So is hell, Brenda, but you seem determined to get there in a hurry," he replied and was met with silence.

"Why, Brenda?"

"Will you please respect the bureau, and call me by my government name. I worked on it for nine months," she said frostily.

"You've been planning this for nine months?" Luca asked, feeling the heat rise up his neck to his head.

The phone was silent for a good fifteen seconds before she spoke again.

"Don't you want to know what I named my child?" Brenda asked.

Luca took a deep breath. He didn't see himself getting any information from her unless he played along.

"What's her name?" Luca asked.

When the phone grew quiet again, he knew he had her attention. He'd kept in touch with Wilson until Brenda gave birth. They arranged an exchange of DNA, and three months later Luca Sable received the report stating that his DNA was not a match for Brenda's. He had been both relieved and distressed at knowing the obvious truth. Angelo Mauro was the father of Brenda's child. That knowledge alone was the innocent baby girl's death warrant, and Brenda just made it so much worse with her stunt.

"It's Grace Melanie Morganson," Brenda answered.

This child would need all the grace God was willing to give her.

"And do you know what you just did to Grace Melanie?" Luca asked, trying hard to keep his voice even.

"Absolutely nothing, but for myself, I took something that was owed to me."

"What is that?" Luca asked even though he had an idea what it was.

"What you refused to do. Get revenge for what was done to me," she said.

"They will kill you and your child," Luca whispered over the line.

"They can try, but you can either live with our deaths on your hands, or you can keep them off us," Brenda whispered back.

"And why would I do that?" Luca asked.

"Because it's your turn to pay. I've paid many times over."

"You aren't giving me much incentive," Luca said.

"Really. The possibility that she could be yours isn't incentive enough?"

"I had a DNA test done right after she was born. She isn't mine," Luca said quietly, his heart squeezing at the words.

297

The only reason he knew Brenda was still on the line was because he heard her heavy breathing.

"Have you shared this with anyone?" Brenda asked.

"No."

"Are you going to?"

"Never."

"I kept the records of your meetings with the other top four crime families in Chicago a secret. Call it a good-faith gesture," Brenda said, seeming to have regained her equilibrium.

"And?"

"And because they listen to you. If you tell everyone that I am off-limits, then they will obey you or suffer even more."

"You could have just left everything alone and built a new life for yourself. You would have been free. Brenda, if I found you, so will they," Luca said desperate to have her understand her predicament.

"Yes."

"That's all you have to say?" Luca was incredulous.

"I was hoping you would do this out of the kindness of your heart. That maybe our time meant something more to you." Brenda's voice lost all emotion, and it sent chills down his spine. "I knew I could never have you. That's why I fought what was between us for so long. I just hoped that those two weeks would get you out of my system, give me some wonderful memories of the man who could have loved me if we had the freedom to do so."

He heard her huge intake of breath but waited knowing there was more.

"I know who set Angelo Mauro and his men on me," Brenda said with a little more emotion, but it chilled him so much he would have preferred that she went back to sounding dejected. "If I die of anything but natural causes, or if anything happens to Grace Melanie, everyone in this country will know too. Goodbye, Luca. Don't call me again."

Luca barely heard the phone click disconnecting their call. His mind was still on Brenda's threat. She was right. It was his turn to pay, and he would be doing so for the rest of his life.

Chapter 26

Luca opened his eyes as the ground under the Town Car went from smooth asphalt to gravel. He pressed the small fob in his breast pocket to ensure that when they turned the corner, the hedges would already be open to the edges of the road leading to the driveway. The gate would remain open until the driver left the premises and the gravel lane leading to the main road.

He unfolded himself from the car, taking the overnight bag from the driver as the front door opened. He shook the driver's hand and headed for Brian Jr. who met him halfway up the wide and shallow stairs leading to the house.

"Hi, Nonno. This is a surprise," B.J. said, giving him a warm hug.

Luca draped his arm over his great-grandson's shoulder as B.J. took his bag.

"Yes, well, I hope it's a welcome surprise," Luca said, continuing up the stairs.

"Always, Nonno, always," B.J. responded without hesitation.

"Have you been behaving yourself, Nipote," Luca asked, using the Italian word for grandson.

"Nope," B.J. replied, "but I promise there is no proof," he added as part of their usual greeting.

They walked into the house, and Luca heard familiar footsteps coming from the left. He looked over to watch Brian striding toward him. His heart warmed as it always did for this gentle giant of a man who he'd had the opportunity to see grow up, in part anyway.

"Hey, Nonno. I've been expecting you," Brian said, giving Luca a hug as well.

Luca hugged him back. "I suspect you have," Luca replied stoically.

Brian looked him over. "You look tired. Have you been sleeping?"

"Enough," he replied.

"Hungry?" Brian asked. "B.J. and I were going to sit down to dinner in fifteen minutes."

Brian's greeting reminded Luca so much of his wife's he had to smile, and he realized that he was hungry. "Yes, I can eat something," he answered as he followed Brian through the living room and into the kitchen. He glanced behind him to see if B.J. was with them but spied him walking up the stairs with his bag.

It was always the same. His boys never failed to take care of him. It was the assurance he needed in his advancing age. Luca pulled out one of the island barstools and leaned into it. He loved the higher chair that made it easy for him to slip off and on. He also noted how his thoughts had shifted from how he could help prepare dinner as they had all done in the past, to his comfort in getting in and out a chair. Getting old was not for the faint of heart.

He watched as Brian donned an apron and went back to slicing bread and smearing garlic butter on them.

"How was the party?" Brian asked, referring to his eightieth birthday celebration, and passed him an unbuttered slice of the aromatic bread.

Brian had practically grown up with his wife. There were many times when Helena would pretend to disappear on shopping trips to Milan, Italy; Rodeo Drive; South of France; Barcelona, Spain; or New York, but spend a few weeks in Maine or at a smaller home in Rockford. Since her children were out of the house, it wasn't unheard of for her to leave for a few days now and then.

The boys loved cooking with her and had become really good. So good that eating their cooking even now was like eating his wife's cooking. He would not be the one to share that with her though.

"What are we having?" Luca said by way of conversation though he had a good idea from the scents coming from the oven.

"Spinach manicotti," Brian said with one of his boyish smiles.

Luca nodded. He wondered if he should wait until after dinner to broach the subject of Melanie and Marc or just come out and say it.

"I thought you would have come right after your party, especially after Roarke told you about our visit with Melanie and Marc," Brian said, continuing to cut from the baguette.

"It wasn't Roarke's job to tell me that you invited Marc and Melanie to come to see you. It was yours."

Brian nodded. "True, but I wanted to make sure that it was only the four of us."

"Why?" Luca asked around a bite of bread.

"Well, for one, she reached out to me to let me know that Antonio and her mother, Brenda, had retrieved an old sample of my DNA and wanted to test it against the remains in the grave you claimed was mine."

The news didn't surprise Luca. Antonio was easily manipulated and Brenda was the best. Besides, he'd been told before he left for his trip that Antonio had been making inquiries.

Seeing that the news hadn't fazed Luca, Brian narrowed his eyes in realization. "You could have said something."

"Since when have I failed to take care of you, to keep you out of harm's way?" Luca asked.

Brian set the knife aside and focused on Luca. "Never. Which is why I don't understand you hiding the fact that Melanie Miller might be your daughter."

Ah, the real reason for all the secrets. He had to hand it to Brian; he did his research. Luca rubbed his hands together to get rid of the crumbs. *Well, it looked like they would be discussing it now.*

"Melanie is not my daughter," he said, looking Brian square in the eyes.

"What about Angelo Mauro?" Brian asked and Luca stilled. He handled billion-dollar deals with men who prided themselves on having the best poker face. His was always unreadable, but right now in front of his grandson, he could barely pull together a blank mask.

"What are you going to do with this information?" he asked Brian because there was no use hedging.

"Ease Melanie's mind," Brian said.

Luca's appetite fled along with the blood from his head. He stared at Brian in horror.

"You told her?"

"You don't think she had the right to know?"

"Her father was Colonel Wayne Morganson."

"You don't think it's important for her peace of mind to know whether or not the twins were conceived through an incestuous relationship?"

"She wouldn't need that peace of mind if you hadn't told her about her father in the first place," Luca chastised quietly. He'd rarely had to raise his voice to Brian even when he was disciplining him.

"How do you know she wouldn't have found out on her own? The FBI agent of hers is very sharp."

"How did you?" Luca asked, wondering if it would be logical even if he took Brian's actions out of the equation.

Seeming to feel that Luca's initial ire had passed, Brian went back to spreading garlic butter on the bread and explained to him what he'd found out about Col. Wayne himself and his suspicions, given Luca's ultimate refusal to work with Angelo until Charles Mauro's death.

When Brian was done, Luca just shook his head. After all of these years, something as simple as a blood test could be his family's undoing. He decided to play devil's advocate to see how sure Brian was about his assessment.

"I'm afraid I'm going to need something more substantial than you suspecting it is Angelo Mauro because I wouldn't work with him, Brian." Luca held up his hand at his grandson's scowl. "I'm not saying I don't believe what you are saying is true. I just need you to walk me through how you connected the dots," Luca said to Brian. *So I can see if there are any holes that could lead anyone to you.*

"After all these years, why were you poking into Melanie's medical history?" Luca asked, watching his grandson's expressions intently. Brian had mastered his ability to hide his feelings when he wanted to, except Brian had a tale or two.

Brian blew out a breath and set the knife back down.

"Last year when Paige donated her kidney to Vivian and ended up in the ICU, I was tempted to go to see her." He looked Luca square in the eye. His look wasn't one of defiance. Neither was it apologetic. "My daughter is twenty-seven, and I've never met her. She could have died in that hospital never knowing I existed." Brian dropped his head and rested his hands on the island. When he finally looked up, Luca saw both pain and determination in his gaze. "I know what I promised you, but this isn't enough anymore. I don't want to sit on the sidelines of my life."

Brian transferred the bread to a cookie sheet and placed it in the oven. Luca watched him silently, knowing there was more; otherwise, Brian wouldn't have been so quick to admit that he'd been watching his daughter.

"The whole incident with Paige, Vivian, and Gladys got me thinking. I wanted to make sure I knew all there was to know about the family I wanted to reunite with, including medical history. I went back to the records from when Paige was born. As B.J., her blood type is O positive. It's a perfect match for Brenda and Wayne's blood types which are also O positive. The obvious conclusion is that Melanie's blood type would be O positive as well, but it isn't. It's A positive. So I went on a little hunt. I had my suspicions for a while, but I'm happy to say that they were unfounded. Really happy, actually."

"What suspicions?" Luca asked, feeling a knot forming in his stomach, but Brian continued on as if he hadn't spoken.

"I found an agreement between you and Angelo Mauro just before Melanie and Marc arrived"—now it was Luca's turn to mask his features—"stating that you wouldn't do any business with him until after his father put him in charge. And here's the kicker: if no harm came to Brenda by his hand or anyone else's that he might have hired."

Luca remembered the agreement and knew it had rankled both Charles and Angelo to give Brenda a pass, but there was no way around it for Luca. He could barely stomach to look at Angelo, let alone deal with him directly, no matter what Helena requested.

"What suspicions?" he asked his grandson again.

Brian finished checking the manicotti before turning back to him. "The suspicion that you were Melanie's father." Brian walked back to the island and began cleaning up the crumbs from the bread. "Believe me. That wasn't an easy time for me. I might have found it hard to look you in the face if you had come to visit before I obtained the proof I needed." The boy was purposefully needling him. *He must have really been upset,* Luca thought. Luca went along with the conversation.

"What proof?"

"I had Melanie give me a swab sample of her saliva before they left. I had it 'quietly' matched against Angelo Mauro's. Did you know the whole family had their DNA studied? I think it was more to test that their investment in that industry was safe. Who would have thought DNA kits would become a common Christmas gift?" Brian finished up his cleaning and came back to lean on the island.

Luca had underestimated his grandson, but could this information get out without leading back to his grandson and ultimately his wife?

Brian frowned at Luca. "I have a question though."

"Really? It sounds to me like you have figured everything out," Luca said, unable to keep the sarcasm out of his voice.

"Why the agreement? Did Angelo's and Brenda's affair go bad at the end? Is that why she turned state's evidence against them? Is that why you set her up with Wilson Ellis?"

Luca was tempted to allow Brian to continue on with his misinterpretation of Brenda and Angelo's association, but he didn't see where it would help.

"After dinner you, B.J., and I will have a talk. What you decide to do with the information is up to you, but you need to know the ramifications of your actions if you want to move forward with this." Luca took a deep breath.

"And Victoria Branchett, formerly Langston. Can we talk about her as well?" Brian asked. Luca's heart dropped to somewhere south of his knees.

Luca didn't deny knowing what Brian was talking about. He just nodded and watched a light dim in Brian's eyes. He knew he should have told Brian the truth about his mother years ago, but he couldn't trust that Brian's presence would help Victoria turn off the destructive path she was on. It was pure irony that Brian's daughter had been able to help even before Victoria knew she was family. He stood by his decision and still felt that it was the only recourse at the time. He had given the boys a grandmother in Helena, and she doted on the boys as if they were her very own sun and moon. He may have overlooked the need a boy had to know his mother: the woman who birthed him, but he wouldn't have jeopardized his grandson's life for it.

Luca sighed. It was time to let go of some of the secrets and trust his grandson's judgment.

"May I ask why you had Melanie and Marc meet you at the family home and not this one?"

"I didn't know how much of an influence Grace had over Melanie over the last twenty-seven years. I didn't understand after everything that has happened why she still allows that woman in her life.

Well, Grace has a way of digging her claws into people that makes it very hard for them to extricate themselves from her."

Brian seemed to think about his last sentence for a moment. "Does she still have her claws in you?"

"No, she doesn't, but we are connected by blood whether I like it or not," Luca said.

Brian nodded but didn't say anything.

"What was your impression of Melanie?" Luca asked, remembering the beautiful young woman and her selfless defense of one of her friends who had been drugged at a party.

"She is still very possessive of her family. She's a great mother, and I believe I'm the reason why Brenda is still in her life. I would say

305

she's stayed close to Grace to keep an eye on her. Melanie never believed that Grace was convinced I died. It isn't fair for her to continue to shoulder that part of the responsibility."

"Have you spoken to B.J. about your decision?"

"Yes."

"And?"

"He's been wanting to meet his sister for some time, but more than that I have sensed a restlessness in him. I don't know if it has more to do with Simone or his need to step out on his own, but he has voiced dissatisfaction in both areas."

Luca wasn't surprised. B.J. didn't make waves, but he had voiced his desire to step from under Brian and himself. He didn't mention Simone, his on and off—mostly off—girlfriend since high school, but Luca felt that had something to do with his unease as well.

"If you're sure. I can set things in motion during the holidays," Luca said, thinking of the contingency plan he had in place for the day Brian was discovered or wanted to come out of hiding."

"Really?" Brian said, obviously surprised by Luca's quick acceptance.

"It was never meant to be forever. Just until you all could fend for yourselves. I think B.J. and Paige are well past that, but what was essential became convenient to your grandmother and me over the years and I apologize for that. I have one warning though."

"Oh, I can handle Brenda," Brian said, misunderstanding Luca's words.

"No, not Brenda. Silas and Roman, his nephews. They won't take to kindly to being challenged."

"Why? I doubt Melanie would want to have anything to do with the Mauros even if Angelo wants to claim her."

"Do you think she has a say?" Luca asked.

Brian's eyes flashed with the realization that Angelo's desire to meet and bring Melanie into the family may outweigh Melanie's wish, whichever that may be. He also realized that sharing the information about her parentage with her may have in turn compromised some of her own freedom.

Brian opened his mouth. Maybe to offer an apology, but Luca wouldn't know since Brian then closed his mouth without speaking.

"What was your plan?" Luca asked Brian.

Brian stared at him for a moment before answering, and Luca saw secrets in his eyes. "I had many plans, but none of them were any good without your help."

"What do you want, Brian?" Luca asked.

"I want to be free to give my daughter her Christmas present... in person," Brian said, his gaze not wavering.

"And B.J.?"

Brian nodded. "We talked about it. He and Melanie hit it off, especially the second night she and Marc were here. They gave each other a run for their money while playing Monopoly. It turns out they are both very competitive and creative with ways to make money." Brian chuckled. "We had to call it a draw after Marc and I were out, and they each still owned half of everything on the board two hours later.

It was bittersweet news, but Luca smiled before forming his next question. "What about the firm?"

"Does that have to change? I mean, I still want to work for the company. I guess it wouldn't be in the same capacity," Brian said, reminding Luca of his fifteen-year-old self when he was unsure of his place in the family.

"Same capacity, only now you will get credit for your own work under your real name. No more Marco Sanza," Luca said, and his heart skipped a beat like it would miss Marco Sanza. Well, more the thought of who Marco represented rather than the name itself. As long as there was a Marco Sanza, his grandson was less than a phone call away.

Brian exhaled long and loud. "Nope." He cocked a bittersweet grin at Luca, but when he sobered, his eyes held sincere gratitude. "It has always been my dream to work at your side. Thank you, Nonno, for everything. You gave me two lives when most people only get one... and I owe them both to you."

"No you don't," Luca said before trying to clear some of the emotion from his throat. "It's just what family does. From now on live for you. No more hiding."

"No more hiding," Brian repeated.

The timer went off on the oven, and Brian gave him a soggy grin before turning to take the delicious-smelling manicotti out of the oven.

When Brian turned back from laying the hot plate down, Luca was up and standing in front of him. He gave his grandson a fierce hug then took him by the shoulders. "After dinner, we will also discuss how and what you know about Angelo Mauro's nephews. It will help when I go to Angelo Mauro with news of Brian Jr. and Paige and what this means for our two houses." Brian frowned in concentration at his statement and nodded his acceptance.

Maybe by his next birthday, Luca would have his whole family sitting at his table.

Chapter 27

Christmas Day dawned bright and quiet with the sun filtering through the white curtains decorated with silver snowflakes in the twin's room. Paige lay there half-asleep holding on tight to the last vestiges of her dream. Brandon's face flashed before her eyes again.

"Merry Christmas, honey." Brandon's brown eyes twinkled as he handed her the pretty red velvet box. Paige held tight to the box, more interested in committing his eyes, beveled lips, strong chin, and high cheekbones to her memory.

"I miss you, babe," she whispered as she leaned in close enough to feel his warmth.

A shadow crossed over his eyes before he smiled at her again. "I'm right here, Paige. I'm not going anywhere." Brandon drew closer until his lips met and pressed against hers in a kiss that warmed her all over. The familiarity of his touch and fragrance enveloped her, and a part of her wept at the thought that this would not, could not last, but the other part of her shut her eyes tight and reveled in the feel and taste of him until he wasn't there anymore.

Paige blinked to clear her vision. Remembering the gift, she looked down at her closed hand and took a deep breath before uncurling her fingers. It was empty. She turned over and burrowed deep under the covers. She would try again later.

***

309

Three hours later, Paige stepped from the shower feeling a little more tethered to reality and less like a balloon drifting in the wind. She shook her shoulders as if to dislodge any remnants of the heaviness that followed her from her first dream. She would hold on to the small gift she'd been given in the early morning. A chance to spend a few moments of Christmas morning with Brandon.

Paige got dressed and put her hair up in a ponytail. It was Christmas with her family. They'd seen her at her best and at her worst. Still, she glanced at the mirror before leaving the bathroom and decided to put a little concealer under her eyes to hide her rough night and morning. There was no way she would be able to explain to anyone the bittersweet visit from a few hours before and them not be concerned about her mood.

Paige pasted a bright smile on her face before walking down the hall toward the sounds of breakfast cooking and Melanie and Marc whispering.

"I'm not forbidding you to go. I'm not even saying you shouldn't go. I just don't like the thought of you being in that woman's presence. We don't really know what she's capable of and to think for a minute that she wouldn't hurt you if it meant getting what she wanted, would be naïve. She's already proven that much," Marc said.

"I know. I will be safe. I won't move without you, but it's time I confronted her. I know there is very little hope in it turning out as I want, but at least I will be able to get this off my chest and maybe get some closure," Melanie replied just as quietly.

Paige felt bad about eavesdropping but was relieved to hear that Melanie saw her mother for who she was.

She continued around the corner into the kitchen to find Marc holding Melanie. Paige leaned against the doorjamb happy that Melanie had Marc to hold, love, and protect her and a little envious.

Paige crossed her arms. "So, you're going to see her."

Melanie's eyes popped open, and she stared at Paige, obviously trying to assess her mood.

Paige shrugged then crossed the room. She leaned in and gave Melanie a kiss on the cheek. "Do what you feel you must to get free

310

from her," Paige said before she rubbed Marc's back. "I'm glad she has you," she said close to Marc's ear before turning toward the stove.

"I'm hungry. Are you two making breakfast? When is everyone else getting here?" Paige inhaled the numerous scents while she picked up lids and took a peek at what was in the oven. Paige reached out to snag a cinnamon roll when her hand was slapped. She pulled back quickly and rubbed the offended body part. She turned to see Melanie standing next to her.

"Those aren't iced yet. Mason and the girls will be here in fifteen minutes, then I will start the eggs. Marc has finished the bacon and has started setting the table. You can get out the milk and orange juice and set them on the table. Everyone will make their plates at the table and take them into the living room. TV trays have already been set up." Melanie took Paige by the shoulders.

"And Paige..." Melanie said, getting Paige's undivided attention.

"Yes."

"Merry Christmas, sweetie," Melanie said before pulling her in for a hug.

"Merry Christmas, Mel." Even though Melanie had pretty much fulfilled the role in Paige's life as her mother, it would take time for Paige to get used to thinking of her as anything other than Mel. She wondered at times if it pained Melanie that she didn't call her mom or mommy as Gladys did. She would have to bring that up one day when they weren't in the middle of a holiday, wedding, funeral, or a situation that could bring them harm. The way things were right now, that talk might not happen for years.

Melanie let her go, and Marc took her in his arms and gave her a squeeze. "Merry Christmas, Paige."

"Merry Christmas, man," Paige said, squeezing him back.

"Oh, I almost forgot," Melanie said over her shoulder after going back to the stove. "Ava sent you something. I placed it on the side table next to the couch against the wall. She called about a half an hour ago to wish you a Merry Christmas, but you were sleeping so deep I told her you would call her back. Was that okay?"

Brandon's mom decided to stay close to home for the holiday, and Paige couldn't blame her with all the traveling and time she'd spent away this year.

"Yeah, sure," Paige said before going into the living room to retrieve the mail.

Spying the gold mailing envelope, Paige picked it up and was surprised by the weight. She didn't know what she was expecting but this was bigger. She hoped Ava hadn't gotten her a big present when Paige had only sent her a scarf Ava had shown interest in one day when she had practically dragged Paige out of the house.

Paige sat on the couch and carefully opened the envelope then turned it upside down so the contents could spill out on her lap. Three envelopes landed on her thighs. Two were obvious greeting cards with their square shapes. The third looked more like a business envelope, so she figured she would get the business out of the way first. She turned it over in her hands and stilled after seeing the writing on the front. It was addressed to her in Brandon's very clean and precise hand.

She considered for a beat of her heart to set it aside and open the other two envelopes, but she knew she wouldn't be able to concentrate on anything else until she opened this envelope. Paige's fingers shook slightly as she unsealed the envelope. Once she finally opened the flap, her heart gave a small leap. She brought her nose to the folded papers. It smelled like Brandon. She stared at it knowing she may never get another chance to experience this again.

After one more huge breath, Paige pulled the papers from their enclosure. She counted the pages, her heart growing lighter with each number. She brought the pages close in an unconscious possessive gesture and began to read:

Hey Baby,

It's late, but I couldn't sleep. I'm watching you lying here next to me. You're so beautiful, even if you snore. Now, let's not debate this. I still have more proof than you do.

Paige laughed then looked up to make sure she hadn't drawn Mel or Marc's attention. She and Brandon had debated the fact that she snored during their honeymoon, and every now and then Brandon would bring it up just to tease her.

Anyway, today we got some bad news regarding the 'C.' Paige could imagine him whispering the letter as he usually had and her mouth tipped up in another smile.

It felt like I'd been hit with a sledgehammer after finally getting to my knees. I think I hid it well, but man did it cost me. I wanted to cry, wail and get down on the floor of the doctor's office and throw a tantrum until he or God changed the results. Instead, I walked out of the office with your hand holding mine so tight, I could imagine you telling God yourself that you wouldn't let me go. So much fire. How did I get so blessed?

You ordered all of my favorite foods which we gorged on in front of the television while we watched something I couldn't keep my attention on for longer than a few minutes at a time. I had trouble concentrating because one, you sat behind me on the couch with me stretched out in front of you, my feet propped up on the opposite arm, feeding me hand-to-mouth. I can't tell you how decadent it felt. Two, after dinner you rubbed my head, neck, shoulders, arms and any other part you could reach until I was so relaxed I could have poured off the couch into a puddle on the floor. You were the epitome of comfort to me tonight and I want to be the same for you.

Paige heard the sob come from her throat and covered her mouth. She knew it would be misunderstood if anyone saw her right now so she picked up all the papers and envelopes and went to her office for some privacy.

First. Congratulations! I'm proud of you. I had no doubt that my transition would be extremely hard on you and you would be angry with God. Maybe even angry with me. I understand. You know I understand, and I wouldn't say anything to belittle your feelings. Like you said. I get to go to heaven, but you have to stay here without me.

He was listening, Paige thought

Yeah. I was listening, and you could not have made your suffering plainer.

313

This may sound odd since you are already reading this but go with me here.

I'm going to ask my mom to hold this letter until she thinks you will be in the presence of mind to receive it. It's not my intention to have her read it but to just look in on you from time to time and to see if it looks as though you are coping, i.e. not taking out my absence from you on God or your family. You know what I mean. (One eyebrow raised)

Paige smiled again, unable to stop the action and no longer trying.

So, my love. Here we are. You, hopefully accepting the fact we had an extraordinary marriage and think of me fondly, without too many tears, and me also hopefully in heaven singing my soul out, also remembering you fondly as one of the favorite parts of my life on earth.

Now, as hard as it is for me to write with you breathing heavily beside me (smile) and as hard as it may be for you to even consider at this moment, life will go on for you. You will write more awesome books, visit more of the sick and shut-in (a-hem), return to your Elder duties, fall in love again, grow even closer to Mel when she comes back, start that young women's group you've been talking about, and forgive Grace.

Yes. I know it isn't the easiest thing to imagine, but you deserve happiness in all its ways. You have to let go of what you have been holding onto so tightly nothing else can get in.

I bet you think I'm talking about you forgiving Grace. Well, I am a little. You should let go of the disappointment, anger, and offense you hold up between you two like a wall. I'm not saying welcome her with open arms. From what I've witnessed, she's a piece of work. But you do have to forgive her so you can stop feeding energy into that emotional abyss. You deserve more.

Speaking of more… If I'd been given the time, I would have given you more kisses (sounds good—hold on for a second while I kiss your cheek) more hugs, more children, more date nights, more quiet nights in and more moments where we communicated only with our eyes. You deserve more and I pray you will have more even after I'm gone. And you know how God answers my prayers so there is no need to fight it.

There is nothing about us that was a waste, a mistake, an accident, or a coincidence. We were ordained by God. He placed us together on purpose for many purposes, including bringing me to the realization that living a very safe life on the sidelines was not living at all.

I love you... so much. It's impossible to consider that I won't take it with me. So, know that I am loving you from heaven even as I am loving you in this moment and that will never change, neither will the love we shared.

I'm finally getting tired so I'm going to call it a night and snuggle up next to you.

I'm wondering if you will find this whole present tense from the past language, bizarre. If I find another way to do this, I will give it a try. Meanwhile, if this is your second time reading through this letter, put it away and go live your life and tell Pastor Lawrence and Lady Menagerie, I said "Hi." Give Dominy, Robin, and Nicky a hug and kiss for me. And tell Vivian and Gladys to never stop praying.

Goodnight Sweetheart.

Sweet dreams,

Brandon

Paige read the letter again before Melanie stuck her head in the door. "Everyone is here and breakfast..." Melanie stopped, her expression morphing into one of concern. "What's wrong?"

"Nothing. Absolutely nothing," Paige replied through her tears. She held up Brandon's letter. "Brandon wrote me a letter. It was beautiful and sad and funny and I'm not sure how to feel." Paige laughed because it just felt right to do so.

She got up and hugged Melanie, wanting to share some of the love pressing at the seams of her heart, trying to get out. She laughed again through the tears.

"I had the best. God gave me the best husband," Paige said, hoping the two sentences would be enough to convey her happiness at the realization that God had given her so much more than she'd seen even an hour before.

"I had the best," Paige whispered fervently to Melanie before putting the letter in her desk drawer and leading a bewildered-looking Melanie out the door.

Paige listened to the indistinguishable chatter coming from the kitchen and living room. She put her arm through Melanie's and placed her head on her shoulder as they walked down the hall. She felt Melanie turn and plant a kiss on her head. "And you deserve nothing but the best, my love." Paige's already misty eyes began to water. Paige blinked them back, but she didn't have to paste a smile on her face because it was already there.

They rounded the corner, and she saw Vivian and Gladys filling their plates with food. "Merry Christmas, lovelies."

Vivian and Gladys set down their plates and came over to envelop Paige in a hug. "Merry Christmas, Mati. They singsonged in unison.

"Uh, ugh, so sweet. I think I'm getting a cavity," Melanie said, and Paige gave her arm a push. The girls let go of Paige and surrounded Melanie, covering her with kisses until she squealed with laughter. Paige stepped over to the serving table and picked up a well-iced cinnamon roll and bit into it as she left the kitchen.

"Looks like someone started breakfast without us," Marc said when Paige appeared in the living room.

"Sshh, the kitchen warden will hear you," Paige said before turning to Mason. "Merry Christmas, Mason.

"Merry Christmas, Paige. You're looking sweet," he said, gesturing to the roll.

Paige giggled. "Yeah, well, I'd give you a hug, but I'm pretty sure you would not come away unscathed.

Mason shrugged. "That's okay. I will collect later."

Paige nodded. "Okay, come on, you two. It's time for breakfast and I'm starving."

"I couldn't tell," Marc said sarcastically.

Paige curved the temptation to stick her tongue out at him but still yelled as she watched his expression. "Melanie, Marc is being mean to me on Christmas Day."

"Marc, Mason, and Paige, come into the kitchen. It's time to eat."

Paige stuck her chin out at Marc before taking the last two bites of her roll. She chewed hard and fast to get rid of the evidence.

"You missed some, Brat," Marc said, pointing to the side of his mouth before moving toward the kitchen.

Paige giggled at the old nickname and chewed faster. She glanced at Mason when he walked around her, giving him a close-mouthed smile that froze when he reached out and wiped the icing from the side of her mouth. A small jolt of electricity crossed over her lips, and she had the urge to touch them to see if there was any damage.

"Got it," Mason said as he backed up. "You might want to finish chewing before you join us in the kitchen. One look at your cheeks and Melanie will know where the missing roll went." He continued to back up until he reached the threshold then turned and walked out of sight. Only then did Paige remember how to chew.

Paige took her time as she thought about what just happened. Mason didn't seem to be aware of it so maybe it was all in her mind. It had already been an emotionally charged morning, and they were only just about to sit down to breakfast. That was it. The dream, the letter, and her excitement in realizing that her love life hadn't just been used to serve as a witness of faith, but God had truly given her the desire of her heart, the one she'd dreamed of, not just the one He'd placed in her heart for her to desire.

Brandon had been right in his request for his mother to wait to give her this letter. If she'd received it a month ago she would have been sorely tempted to build a shrine around it. The letter also would have delayed the conversation she had with God because she would have been less inclined to be completely honest with Him.

Paige didn't want to look a gift horse in the mouth, but she did wonder how Ava knew she was ready to receive Brandon's letter. His mother did pray, and often while she stayed with Brandon and Paige. That was as good an explanation as any. Paige swallowed the rest of her roll then swiped her tongue along her lips to make sure she hadn't missed any.

When she finally walked back into the kitchen, everyone was gathered around the serving table holding hands. They turned to her with expressions ranging from impatience to amusement, the latter worn by Mason and Marc. She stepped forward clasping Melanie's hand and listened while Marc said grace and a blessing over their first Christmas spent together. Inexplicably, Paige wanted to cry again. She was surrounded by her family. At one time or another she'd given half of them up, and even two years ago she didn't even know the other half of them existed. She smiled to herself, taking in the moment. She didn't have words for how blessed she was.

***

A few hours later, everyone, including Victoria and Richard, sat in the living room exchanging gifts and reveling in Vivian and Gladys' excitement over their presents. Paige knew all the parents and grandparents had gone overboard with the gifts, but seeing the twins' smiles and hearing their laughter was like a balm to Paige's soul. As it was, Vivian would need an extra suitcase for the new boots, jeans, jacket, tablet case, and purse Victoria and Richard had given each of the girls in their favorite colors. At least the electronic books and money for music that Paige gave the girls didn't take up more than just virtual space.

Mason leaned forward from his place on the couch opposite Paige, handing her another present. He and Vivian had already gotten her a pair of beautifully monogrammed pens and stationery for the notes she could take at the Christian Writer's Conference they'd bought her a week's pass to. It touched her heart that they would take such an interest in her career and craft.

"What's this for?" Paige asked, taking the brightly wrapped package from him. She looked into his hazel-green eyes for answers but only saw nervous excitement and...

"For you to open," Vivian answered, drawing her attention away from Mason and whatever else he'd been trying to convey. Paige smiled into Vivian's eyes while she placed a finger on her shoulder and pushed the girl until she lost balance from her precarious perch on her knees in front of Paige.

318

"Behave," Paige said, laughing with everyone else as Vivian landed on her behind.

She slowly unwrapped the box glancing at Mason a couple of times, but his eyes were on what was in her hands. When she got to the box she hesitated. The room had grown quiet, and she looked up to see everyone watching.

Paige opened the box and took out the folded pages. Curiosity took over, and she straightened them out and read the title to what looked like legal forms. She read it again and one more time as she tried to absorb the significance of what was in her hands. She stared at it a moment longer before looking up at Mason's. She knew her shock registered on her face, but what registered on Mason's was hope and no small amount of anxiousness.

"Really? You're sure?" Paige asked as she looked between Mason and Vivian.

"Of course. If you ask me, it's overdue," Vivian said. Paige smiled down at her with burning eyes. *How many times would she be brought to tears today?* Paige looked up at Mason.

"This is an application for adoption," Paige whispered, afraid if she spoke the words louder the papers would disappear.

Mason nodded his head.

"You're sure?" she repeated. "I mean, what if you get married and want to give your wife that honor?" Paige didn't know why the thought made her nauseous. It was probably because she finally had her family with her, and she wanted this so bad, so bad.

Mason shook his head. "We talked about it. Vivian wants you to adopt her. No one else will be her mother."

Paige smiled at Vivian whose form had become blurry from her tears. Paige blinked to clear them but didn't try to wipe them away as they coursed down her cheeks.

"And you?" she asked Mason.

He gave her an indulgent smile. "I'm a little old for adoption."

Paige laughed then began nodding because no words could express the size of the "yes" in her heart. She got up and pulled Vivian from the floor. Paige hugged her little girl tightly and rested her cheek on her daughter's head. She had just been given a second chance to claim her daughter as her own. Paige felt Vivian begin to shake in her arms right before she heard the sobs, and she held on tighter, trying to soothe her as much as take comfort from Vivian being in her arms.

When Paige looked up, everyone in the room had moist or tear-filled eyes. Vivian leaned back and gave her one of those heart-stopping smiles. Paige leaned back in and kissed Vivian on the forehead. "Oh, I love you so much," Paige said, cupping her cheeks.

Paige looked over at Gladys, who was leaning against Melanie and gestured for her to come join their circle, and the girl mimicked Vivian's smile before stepping into the hug.

Paige, with her arms and heart full, gave God a silent prayer of thanks and praise for bringing them all back together as only He could do. She hugged her children just a little closer and buried her head in the curls on their heads.

Chapter 28

It could have been five or fifteen minutes before Marc spoke up. "Okay, if we don't stop, we will flood this apartment, and I will have to find another place to present you and Melanie with your surprise."

"Who?" Paige asked. When Marc pointed at her she took a deep breath. "Marc, really, I don't know if I can take another surprise. I'm already overflowing with emotion. Any more and I might explode."

"Well then, Vivian and Gladys, I'm going to need you to keep your arms around Paige so she stays together," Marc said, just before a knock sounded at the door.

Paige glanced at Melanie, who shrugged, looking just as mystified. She looked at Mason then Victoria and Richard who gave her similar looks. She felt Vivian and Gladys squeeze her just as Marc opened the door and two men walked in.

They looked familiar somehow, but she knew she hadn't seen them before. She could tell they were related, but the difference in their ages...

"Oh my goodness." Melanie gasped, breaking into Paige's thoughts, her eyes going as wide as saucers. "How? Who? Ahhh, I don't care." Melanie walked quickly over to them, hugging the younger then the older of the two tall and handsome men.

When Melanie turned back, Paige looked the older gentleman in the eyes and she knew.

"Hi, Paige. I'm..."

"Brian?" His name was carried on a gasp from across the room.

Paige followed the sound to Victoria whose face had lost all color, but her eyes were brighter than Paige had ever seen them. Richard's arms were around Victoria as though he were holding her up, but he looked like a feather could have knocked him over.

Paige looked back at Brian who gazed at Victoria in confusion for a few heartbeats before his brows straightened, and his eyes also widened in incredulity. His body went rigid, and Paige watched along with everyone else as Victoria walked toward him slowly, as if she were afraid he would bolt if she moved any faster. She came within touching distance then stopped. Paige watched as Victoria with bottom lip trembling, scanned his face from his hairline to his chin then smiled and reached up a hand to touch his cheek, which Brian leaned into and covered with his own hand.

Victoria sucked her teeth before drawing Brian into a hug. "My baby boy," she whispered. "My beautiful baby boy."

If Paige hadn't already been crying, she definitely would have started then. Matter of fact, she was sure a fresh bout of tears had just started as she witnessed a reunion that was forty years in the making.

When their hug looked like it would go on for minutes more Paige wiped her eyes and turned back to the other gentleman still standing at the door. "Hi," Paige mouthed, not wanting to interrupt the moment. Her heart beat so hard in her chest she wasn't sure if he mimicked her greeting or actually spoke.

They began walking toward each other at the same time. *Huh. That's what that feels like.* When they were a step away from one another they whispered over one another.

"Hi, Brian."

"Hi, Briar Rose."

Paige raised her hand. "Paige."

"B.J.," he said.

They laughed out of nervousness and due to the absurdity of the moment.

"You go ahead," he said.

"It's nice to meet you, B.J.," Paige said, looking up at him. He definitely got all the height. He had to be at least six feet, two inches. Their coloring was similar, but where her eyes were golden, his were fathomlessly dark. She stared at him as she noticed what he was doing, taking in subtle differences and similarities in their faces.

After a moment she felt awkward and rude. "Sorry."

"No need. I was staring too. I have a beautiful sister who takes after our mom," he said.

Paige smiled, warming all over. "Thank you. You are too: handsome I mean. Wow. This feels so surreal."

B.J. laughed. "Yeah." He looked over her shoulder and smiled.

Paige turned around to see Mason. She took his hand, excited about sharing this moment with him. "Mason, this is B.J., my brother." She looked back at B.J. "B.J., this is Mason, Vivian's father and my friend."

Paige looked between the two men wondering why it felt so important that they like each other.

"I thought you said he died soon after birth," Mason said with confusion marring his features.

Paige felt instantly contrite and now even more awkward. "Oh... uh... yes... about that." She winced. "I'm really sorry for making it sound like that. We were on the phone. You told me to be careful, so I only told you only part of it. I was going to tell you when you got here a couple of days ago, but with the girls, and, well, everything else, I never got a chance to get you alone."

Paige watched Mason's expression, hoping he would see the sincerity in her eyes. She squeezed the hand she still held and saw his eyes lose their wariness before he gave her a smile.

Mason's shoulders visibly relaxed, and he extended his hand to B.J. "Welcome to our hodgepodge of a family."

B.J. laughed. "Thank you?"

"Exactly," Mason responded.

Paige was darn near giddy and was about to call Vivian and Gladys forward to meet their uncle when there was a light tap on her shoulder. She turned and looked up into the eyes of her... Brian.

"Hi, Paige," Brian greeted, question and hope in his still wet eyes. Her heart made the decision to propel her body forward, and Paige walked into Brian's arms and hugged him tightly.

When they finally parted, she saw that Brian's eyes were even wetter and his smile was bright. "You look just like your mom. So beautiful."

Paige tried not to let the words penetrate too deeply. After all, she just met this man. Just because they shared DNA didn't mean he was honest and had good intentions. Paige smiled, but she could sense that he noticed her hesitation. He nodded once.

"There are a lot of years between us. Hopefully, you will allow me and your brother to get to know you better," he said before swallowing a couple of times.

Her throat, full of emotion, wouldn't let her speak so she nodded.

"Good," he said before his eyes shifted to someone behind her. She turned to see Vivian and Gladys and made the introductions.

It was another twenty minutes before they were all seated again in the living room. Brian sat next to Victoria and Richard on the couch. Paige noticed that Victoria could barely keep her hands off him, whether it was patting his hand, laying a hand on his shoulder or just resting her head against his arm. Brian seemed to be reveling in it. B.J. sat between Melanie and Marc, resting his head on Melanie's shoulder while he shared looks with Paige, who sat in the chair behind Mason, Vivian, and Gladys, who were on the floor opening even more presents.

This beautiful Christmas had turned into something sublimely surreal. She wished Brandon could have been there to witness what could only be called a miracle. He would have looked at her and smiled, letting her know without words that he saw what she saw.

There was no way she could have guessed at all the twists and turns her life would have taken in such a short time. When she stood outside the small church where she was preparing herself to give her cousin's eulogy, she felt empty. As though *her* decisions and the decisions made for her had taken more from her than most people ever even hoped to possess. Her hands had been full of the dust of her dreams, and she was hoping to close the door to the past. Instead, she was forced to face the unresolved issues of her past at every turn. She'd wanted to run. How she'd wanted to run from the anger and failures and continue to pretend they'd never existed, but if she had she would have been calling God a liar. Paige would have said with her own actions that she didn't believe He would keep His promise to restore her and what she had lost.

As she looked around the room, Paige admitted to herself that God had done more than restored what she had lost. He had multiplied her family. She had a mother who had always been there for her, two beautiful daughters that hadn't been emotionally crippled by her abandonment, a grandmother who was as close to a best friend as her first lady and book agent, a father and brother to become reacquainted with, and... Mason. Paige looked down at Mason as she tried to put her feelings for him into words. There was gratitude for how he treated and loved on Vivian. He was a wonderful father before but there were no limits now that he'd surrendered to God and let go of the anger.

There were bittersweet feelings for the things they wouldn't share. Sometimes she wondered what might have happened if God had chosen Mason for her but quickly shied away from the thoughts. She would never regret or wish for anything other than her time with Brandon, except for more of it, of course.

Yet there was the curiosity that had been there from the beginning. The careful attention Mason had given her when she was recovering from the surgery and the attentiveness he showed her when he gave her a tour around Chicago. It seemed like a lifetime ago. Their talk where he'd showed her more of himself than he had before or since, and his disappointment then disappearance when she made it clear that she was going to be with Brandon. When she saw him again, there was a firm reservation about him, as though he'd covered up the parts of him he'd once showed her. He had relegated her to distant relative and acquaintance, and she'd let him because she wasn't sure what part he played in her life outside of the father of her daughter. Had it hurt? Yes, but with everything else going on, she'd been unable to emotionally juggle anything else. Whether it was cowardice or acceptance, she wasn't sure, and now she wondered if she had been unfair and maybe just a little too happy to be set away.

Only recently had they begun to speak again, to really converse. She didn't count the numerous calls that went unanswered while she was still trying to wrap her mind around the fact that she was a widow.

She wondered from Mason's perspective if it looked as though she'd made her choice and he wasn't it. Though she couldn't blame him.

Mason looked up at her as though waiting for her answer. Paige startled, wondering if she'd whispered any of the thoughts in her head. She swallowed.

"Sorry, I must have been daydreaming. What did you say?" she asked, blinking.

"I was just saying that you looked far away," Mason replied. "Gladys wants to update the new phones Richard gave us. She wants to make sure you have all the communication apps the twins use."

"Oh yeah, sure," Paige said, trying to remember where she'd last used her phone while fighting the blush that was slowly rising to the tips of her ears.

He watched her for a moment too long and Paige ducked her head. She had been taking pictures of the girls as they opened their presents before Brian and B.J. arrived. Paige felt around the cushions, her fingers brushing up against the hard plastic. She handed the phone to Gladys.

She watched Gladys fiddle with her phone, avoiding Mason's gaze until he bumped up against her leg. "You okay?"

"Yes, why?" she asked.

"You just seemed a little, I don't know... melancholy?"

"How can I be melancholy? I just met my biological father and twin brother for the first time. I am sharing Christmas with Melanie and Marc, which hasn't happened in I don't know when. My grandparents are here, and I'm surrounded by my girls and you. It may be a little overwhelming, but none of this makes me melancholy," Paige said sincerely, smiling down at him.

Mason smiled, his features morphing into an expression she couldn't read. He opened his mouth, and she found herself holding her breath to hear what he would say. Almost as quickly as the look came, it left, and he closed his mouth.

She leaned forward. "What were you about to say?"

"Later. I'll ask you later." He smiled, but it didn't reach his eyes.

"Dad, I want a picture with you and Mati to put on my screen," Vivian exclaimed, holding up her new phone complete with its rhinestone-encrusted back and flip-over cover, which she'd received as one of her many Christmas gifts from Victoria and Richard.

"Sure," Mason replied before he shifted a little closer to Paige's leg. Paige leaned forward so their faces were close together feeling a little awkward.

"Come down to the floor," Vivian commanded after looking at the picture she'd taken. It was obviously lacking.

Paige watched Mason shoot Vivian a look.

"Please," Vivian said to Paige.

Paige smiled at Mason's influence on their child and moved down to the floor to sit beside him. She looked up catching Melanie's eye. Her mother raised an eyebrow making her want to giggle. Marc and B.J. watched with equally curious expressions.

Mason nudged her shoulder to draw her attention back to Vivian and Paige bumped him back. "Yeah, yeah, yeah. Stop pushin'," she said with her version of a New York accent then drew her knees close and leaned into Mason and smiled.

"Me next," Gladys called out and scooted to the other side of Paige. Mason turned slightly, his heat warming her right side. Paige smiled through another round of pictures.

When Vivian handed the camera to B.J., Paige moved away from Mason to make room for Vivian and Gladys between them, needing some space and questioning that need. Paige took a deep breath then forced her heart to stop racing. *What was going on?*

Vivian joined them, and what was supposed to be two maybe three pictures at the most became a family photo session with everyone alternating between having their pictures taken with each other and taking the picture.

It was another hour before they were all dressed to leave for dinner at the restaurant where Richard had made reservations. Paige rode with Melanie, Marc, and B.J. They chatted on the way, and Paige was surprised to learn that Brian and B.J. both worked for the Sable Financial Firm but in two completely different departments. Brian researched and found new clients but handed over the contact and face-to-face portion to an acquisition team. B.J. worked in the digital programming department, creating new code and formulating algorithms to help better assess the risks of taking on new clients.

Paige, unfamiliar with financial algorithms, had little understanding of what they were talking about, but she did know something about writing code and was fascinated that her brother's mind worked that way.

"How long are you going to be in town?" Paige asked.

"We only planned to be here for a few days, but with the surprise of Victoria and Richard, I think Dad's going to want to stay a little longer."

"Well, stay as long as you'd like. I'd love to have you stay for weeks, but I don't want there to be any trouble with the two of you staying under the radar," Paige said, running her fingers over the rose-gold leaves raised from the white, yellow, and rose-gold bracelet with embossed roses that Brian had given her as a present. She never would have bought something so expensive for herself, but it was exquisite. She hadn't taken it off after he placed it on her wrist, choosing to wear it to dinner. She would probably wear it to breakfast too. Paige was beginning to feel uncomfortable about not knowing when she would see them again.

"I'm pretty sure Dad is telling Victoria and Richard right now that we will be visiting you and them quite a bit in the future. We talked with Nonno, uh, Granddad Luca a few days ago. Nonno is going to talk to Antonio during the Christmas break and let him know that Brian is alive."

"Really?" Paige gasped.

"What?" Melanie asked from the front passenger seat.

"I thought that was dangerous, that you and my mom could be charged with fraud for falsifying your death certificates and other records plus taking on a new identity?" Paige continued, unable to keep the astonishment out of her voice or stop talking. "I thought that was the reason why you were in hiding from Grace all this time, why we were kept apart. And then there's Antonio. He and Grace teamed up to look for Brian, though I'm not really sure if that is because he is more of a threat to Brian or Brian to him." Paige finally got her rambling mouth under control.

B.J. chuckled before answering. "Luca has a contingency plan in place to handle any charges of fraud that may occur due to our existence. Dad said it has to do with something he charged Grace with years ago, but he didn't go into detail."

Paige saw B.J. glance at the rearview mirror before quickly shifting his gaze around the car. "Regarding Grace: she has nothing to worry about if she cooperates," B.J. continued.

"Wait, what do you mean by that?" Melanie asked.

"I'm sorry. I don't know all the details. Dad said he would talk to all of us about it because it will affect the family, but it has something to do with the Mauros."

"Marc, do you know about any of this?" Melanie looked at her husband.

"Yes," Marc responded after making a left turn.

Paige strained to keep up with the conversation. How long had Marc known that Brian and B.J. were coming for Christmas or about what that really entailed?

"What part?" Melanie asked

"Enough to feel secure in letting Brian and B.J. come for Christmas. Luca and Brian gave me an overall understanding and Brian promised to share the particulars." Marc glanced at Melanie and took her hand while they sat at a red light.

Paige sat back and glanced at B.J. who looked over at her and smiled. "So, sis, do you mind showing me some sights while we're out here? Vivian, Gladys, and… Mason can come along."

"Sure. Mason and Vivian will be going back to Chicago in a couple of days, but I'm sure Gladys will love playing tourist and tour guide. Brandon and I took them around earlier this year," Paige replied, starting to get excited about sharing her town with B.J. It was weird to think of him as her brother when she'd just met him a few hours before but she felt comfortable with him. He didn't press or prod. He just observed her and gave her the same opportunity to watch him.

"You don't have to answer this if you don't want to," B.J. began, and Paige wondered if her assessment about B.J. not prodding was premature. Paige nodded, giving him permission to ask his question.

"How are you doing? I mean, regarding Brandon? Is it still very hard?" B.J. looked at her intently, reminding her of Melanie when she wanted to make sure Paige was telling her the truth.

Paige thought about his question for a moment. "You know, if you'd asked me that yesterday I'm not sure how I would have answered. It's been hard, but instead of crying for most of the day, I have been crying less and less, and when Melanie and Marc got back it was better."

"What happened between yesterday and now?" B.J. asked, and she was actually grateful to be able to share.

"I received a letter from Brandon."

Paige saw the sharp look that passed between Melanie and Marc but she didn't comment on it. Paige just looked back at B.J. who was beginning to look uncomfortable.

"Brandon wrote to me one of the nights he couldn't sleep. He had trouble staying asleep for a while. His sleep pattern was all off, but he didn't want to take anything for it. It wasn't until the last few weeks that he began to sleep more," Paige said, getting lost in those last days.

"What did he say?" Marc asked, bringing Paige back to the present.

Melanie gave her a look as if asking if she were okay. Paige focused on her mom, grateful for her intuitiveness. She thought about Brandon's words, not wanting to share anything too private. "He said I snored."

"Well, I could have told you that," Melanie said.

"Whatever," Paige said, dismissing Melanie's comment with a small smile. "He wrote it the day we received some not-so-good news about his diagnosis. I know he had a great deal on his mind, but instead, he wrote me a letter he knew I wouldn't get until after he passed and told me he loved me so much he was sure he would take it with him." Paige didn't even try to fight the tears.

"I had a very good man," Paige said.

"I could have told you that too. You did say God blessed you with the best earlier." Melanie said.

Paige didn't say anything. She just smiled at Melanie.

"Did you doubt it?" B.J. asked, watching her.

"That he was a good man? No," Paige replied.

"That God had blessed you with the best," B.J. clarified, causing Paige to pause. She stared at him for a few seconds before nodding.

"Why?" he asked.

She wasn't sure she could put it into words so she shrugged.

He continued to look at her expectantly as if she hadn't tried to brush off the question.

She sighed, seeing he wouldn't let it go. "I took it personally."

"What?" B.J. asked.

"Brandon dying."

B.J. looked confused. "In what way?"

She smiled at him sadly. Normally she held something as personal as what she went through with God and Brandon close. She was used to keeping her thoughts hidden, especially after making the mistake early on in her walk with God. She'd assumed everyone who called themselves a "child of God" spoke to Him and had a relationship much like hers. She was wrong, and their blank looks or frowns told her so when she would talk about some of the things He revealed to her. With B.J., it was different. She felt a spiritual kinship with him which should have been weird considering they'd just met.

"The wrong way. I thought I was being put in my place. I took it as a slap instead of what it really was."

"Oh, I'm really going to need you to explain," B.J. said, looking lost and she couldn't blame him. It had taken her months to get to

331

where she was with God. She tried to keep her explanation as clear and concise as possible. Paige talked about her belief that she could pray Brandon well and that the wedding was also her way of walking in the faith of her belief. She told him about the betrayal she felt when Brandon died and turning away from God's comfort. She shared the rebuke she'd been given which got her attention but didn't pacify her. She told him about her talk with her spiritual mother that opened her eyes to the fact she was angry because she thought God was punishing her, but just because she was in error about Brandon being healed on earth instead of heaven didn't mean that they weren't to be married, weren't to take advantage of every moment of happiness they were given and weren't to love each other a lifetime's worth.

"Brandon's letter just reminded me that we did take advantage of every moment of happiness we could get, and we loved each other deeper than most. I had the best. Brandon even tried to hint that I would have that kind of love again, but it's a hard concept to wrap my mind around," Paige said with a flourish of hand gestures. "So there you have it. My three hundred and sixty-degree turn. What about you?" Paige asked.

"Ahhh, I'm going to need more than the last five minutes of a thirty-minute car ride to tell you about my love life, but maybe in the upcoming days," B.J. said with a warm smile she knew was meant to distract her, but the hurt in his eyes spoke volumes. Paige sensed a kind of kinship with him that went beyond physics. She wondered who put that hurt in his eyes.

"I'll take you up on that," Paige said, smiling at him. "Melanie told me you've known about me for a while. I don't think it's fair that you know so much about me, and I know so little about you."

He shrugged at her much as she had a few minutes before. "I'm an open book, so it's nothing time can't solve." He grinned at her but his eyes were shadowed. "I have another question," B.J. said.

Paige nodded even as she said a short prayer that God would place His comforting and healing hand upon B.J.'s heart.

"Mason," B.J. said, and Paige prepared herself for the question. She looked at him and waited. When he didn't continue, Paige couldn't help herself from commenting, even though she had a feeling of where he was headed. "Is there a question there?"

"Mason is Vivian's adopted father."

"Yes."

"You met him when you donated a kidney to Vivian?"

"Yes," she replied without hesitation.

"Has he always..." B.J. faltered and started again. "Do you know?" B.J.'s gaze flicked to the front seat, and Paige followed it in time to see Melanie give him a look she couldn't decipher.

"How did you feel about the present he and Vivian gave you regarding adopting her?" B.J. finally asked. Paige could tell that wasn't the question he originally meant to ask her and paused while she decided whether to confront him right away or wait until they were alone. Paige felt it might be easier without Melanie or Marc refereeing so she would wait.

"It was one of the best presents I've ever gotten. Not too many people get a second chance," Paige said, feeling the excitement of the moment all over again.

"I think you deserve it," B.J. said sincerely.

"You barely know me," Paige said, feeling his compliment hit home even as she tried to render it meaningless.

"From what you've shared just during this car ride, I know you to be a powerful woman of God, filled with prayer and the anointing to heal."

"I'm not sure you were listening very well," Paige said, not even trying to keep the skepticism out of her voice.

"I was," B.J. insisted, his dark eyes growing even softer. "It wasn't Brandon who I was talking of you healing. God did that when He had him transition to heaven or from the beginning of time, whichever way you wish to look at it." Paige barely grasped what he was saying and laughed, delighted by his reference to God not being governed by time. His next words sobered her though.

"It was you. You healed yourself," he said as if he'd known her for the entirety of their lives. "You could have given in to the anger or given up on receiving any kind of peace or happiness, but you didn't even though you had to continuously surrender and let go of the things that made you heartsick. God has the cure, yes, but it does you no good if you don't take it, no matter how hard the process is." B.J. sat back when he was done as if he hadn't just summed up her life and spoken a word in her heart so profound, she'd never forgotten it.

Paige stared at her brother—her twin brother—for a couple of seconds as he looked out the front window then sat back herself.

Pastor Lawrence and Lady Menagerie were going to love him.

Chapter 29

"So why didn't he use it? I mean, I understand why Luca took you both away when B.J. was a baby and the need for secrecy, especially until you were eighteen, but why not before now? It's not like both of you aren't old enough to take care of yourselves," Mason said, confused about Brian's explanation for why he and his son were only now coming out of hiding.

Brian raised his hands to waylay Melanie and Paige's questions as well. "Let me start from the beginning, and then I will answer any questions you have.

Mason leaned against a counter in Paige's kitchen next to Marc musing about the semi-quiet Christmas he'd anticipated with Paige and her immediate family growing into this revolt against Grace. He wouldn't have chosen to spend his last day in Los Angeles talking about Grace period, but he understood the importance of them all knowing what to expect now that Brian and B.J.'s existence had been shared with Antonio.

From what Brian had shared a few minutes before, Antonio's reaction had gone from shock to disbelief to anger. He hadn't even asked to see Brian. He had just handed the car keys to his wife and left the house.

"As I shared with Melanie last night, Luca confirmed the results of the DNA match I made between Angelo Mauro and Melanie. When I first discovered the connection between Grace and Luca and then Grace and Angelo Mauro, I did some research on the Mauro family's history and holdings. Angelo Mauro has spent the majority of the last four decades turning the Mauro family business legit. That was helped along by Grace reporting some of their less-savory business practices to the FBI," Brian stated, and Mason, relying only on what he'd seen in documentaries or movies about the Chicago crime families, wondered if or how much danger this would bring to his child.

"Luca won't tell me why Grace has such a vendetta against the family, but it has taken favors and threats to keep them from going after her for what she did. When I asked him why he protected her and continues to do so, he only said that she was a monster of his making. That he had sinned against his family and would have to carry the weight of that."

Cryptic much? Mason thought as he glanced at Marc who just shook his head.

"I'm assuming that Grace had an affair with Luca since he only denied that Melanie was his daughter, and he's taking a lot of responsibility for Grace's actions. I'm not completely sure about her interaction with Mauro, but since he is Melanie's biological father, and she has tried to destroy him, it's not good." Brian said the last as he sent Melanie an apologetic look.

"Even as the firm's assistant accountant, Grace failed to turn over information to the FBI that would bring down the Sable family financially. I think she also knew she could only go so far before Luca handed her over to the other families.

"What she seemed to want was some type of leverage over him. Something no one could touch and family was untouchable. So she devised a plan to cultivate a hormone-based relationship between Melanie and myself and manipulate us into actions that resulted in Melanie's pregnancy," Brian said, sounding a whole heck of a lot more comfortable with the words than he could have. Mason was just happy the girls were out showing B.J. their favorite parts of Universal City Walk and Hollywood Boulevard.

"My relationship with Antonio was nonexistent. Luca said Antonio's new wife at the time had no intention of playing stepmom. And I saw Luca maybe three times before the night Melanie called me and told me she overheard Grace talking to someone about getting rid of Paige and letting them know that B.J. would be the one to make Luca finally choose between what was right and his family," Brian said.

"What was right?" Mason asked, curious that it wouldn't be one and the same.

Brian shrugged his shoulders. "Getting information out of my nonno about that period in his life is like pulling teeth. I was fortunate to get what I did. My guess is at some point Grace expected Luca to choose her over his family," Brian said, looking up at him.

Mason knew he still had a long way to go in dealing with his anger and abandonment issues, but they were nothing compared to the rage burning in Grace. His insecurities regarding his upbringing still caused him to be impulsive and possessive about certain things or people if he were being honest. It was one of the reasons for his very possessive feelings when Brian and B.J. walked in.

Mason had just been thinking about his and Paige's relationship before they arrived. She looked at him in the most peculiar way and he considered for a moment that maybe one day their relationship might revolve around more than Vivian.

Mason was happy Vivian had latched on to his idea of gifting Paige with an application for adoption. He couldn't deny how much he wanted to bind himself to Paige in any way possible, but honestly, it felt right giving Paige back the child that had been stolen from her. When Paige had asked him if he was sure he didn't want to save the honor for the woman he might someday marry, it was all he could do to keep his mouth shut and his face blank because there would be no one but her.

When Brian and B.J. walked in, Mason was instantly on alert, especially when both their eyes came to rest on Paige. All he could think of was that they had come to take her away then had to reprimand and remind himself of who *he* was in Paige's life. The knowledge that he was looking at her biological father and twin brother didn't dispel all his unease, but after spending the afternoon and most of the evening getting to know them, he was happy Paige had even more support.

"Luca had given me his personal number years before, and when I called to tell him what had been going on, he came out and organized everything from an OBGYN to look at Melanie and assess whether she could be induced to what he would put in place if I wished to leave with him. It's a lot to get into, but by the time I left Colorado with him a few weeks later, Luca had found a nanny for B.J., and prepared one of the family's lesser-used homes for us.

He had even framed Grace for a fictitious hit on my life when she convinced the Grossenbergs to place me under a 5150 in State General's psychiatric wing when she got back from her business trip to find that B.J. was out of her clutches. She tried to have me transferred to a state mental institution, but Luca circumvented her plan and made sure Grace was charged with attempted murder which got her kicked out of WITSEC.

Luca let her know that her life and safety was then at his mercy. He paid off the Grossenbergs who leaked the story about my so-called suicide to the media sometime later, per his instructions. In the end, he had the adoption dissolved and had the Grossenbergs sign a non-disclosure and paperwork stating that they believed staging my death was the only way to keep me safe."

Mason's head was buzzing after the last bit of information. And he thought his mother-in-law's moral compass had been stuck on sadistic. Grace couldn't have picked a less fitting name. The fact that she "borrowed" it from her daughter to be able to use her identification was proof enough.

"And now what? You and B.J. will just show up at Sunday night's family dinner?" Paige asked, brows furrowed.

"No, not necessarily. Though we have spent a lot of time with Nonna Helena, we aren't really family. The letters will back up the need for new identities as well as other contingencies that Luca has in place that I would rather not know about," Brian said, looking uncomfortable and rubbing his hands together.

"So what's to keep Grace from trying to use you or B.J. as leverage now? I mean, I wouldn't put it past her to threaten your lives to gain the

338

upper hand or get the revenge she's been seeking all this time?" Paige asked what had been on Mason's mind.

"One of my talents is research. I seem to have the ability to find threads and clues that others overlook. When Melanie and Marc came to Portland, I told them that Angelo Mauro has two nephews who he's been grooming to take over the pharmaceutical business. One of my jobs is to do background searches and dig further into any companies and their leaders during a transition.

"I have proof that Roman and Silas have quietly re-established the company's initial illegal drug trade, using some of the drugs manufactured by their plant in the Western Region of India. The opioid crisis in the United States has provided the cloak they need to move the product in smaller units, and their silent partner has helped open a corridor in the black market, subsequently washing the identity of the makers from the drugs before it enters the United States."

"Really? How long have you been working on this?" Marc asked, his attention completely focused on Brian.

"A couple of months. I can't take all the credit for this one. I found out they had buyers lined up before you came to visit me, but when you told me about Grace and Antonio and who Grace was married to, I couldn't let go of it as a coincidence. I shifted my search and found a DC phone number that Roman called from one of his personal phones more than a few times, along with a piece of correspondence forwarded read from Ross Dillard's home computer. Two guesses on who the phone number belongs to," Brian said, wearing a somber expression.

"Grace," Melanie said through gritted teeth.

Mason looked between Melanie and Brian, the realization of what they were saying hitting him between the eyes.

"What does this mean for us?" Mason asked, a sense of dread crawling up his spine.

"If Grace is looking to set up Angelo Mauro by using his nephews to run an illegal drug ring with Mauro's pharmaceuticals the repercussions will reverberate throughout this family. I'm not sure what type of contingencies Grace has in place or if she thinks she can continue to use my grandfather as a form of shield, but if she succeeds in her plan, Luca may not be able to help us.

"We could get the authorities involved but I wouldn't put it past her to have set her husband up to take the fall. We could confront her, but if Grace has been plotting and scheming for almost four decades, I don't think threatening to expose what she's been doing will stop her. I think we are at the point where we tip off Angelo Mauro or Luca removes his protection," Brian said, glancing at Marc then Melanie.

Was he really saying what Mason thought he was saying? He wanted to ask how a person like Brian's grandfather removed his protection but stopped himself, knowing the answer would bother him even more. How did he end up in a kitchen a few days after Christmas listening to a conversation where words such as black market, illegal drugs, crime families, and removal of protection were used? He wanted to take Paige's hand, remove her from the room, and take her back with him to Chicago, swooping up Vivian and Gladys on the way.

"Marc, I need a flight to DC."

"Melanie, I'm not sure that's a good idea..."

Melanie turned and shot Marc a look that made Mason cringe. "You and I both know that threats won't work with her." Melanie turned back to Brian. "Have you already talked to Luca about this? Is he going to go see her? I want to go first."

"You don't know what Luca has planned for her. I don't want you caught in the middle of it." He sighed before continuing. Maybe it's time she..." Melanie put up a hand, halting Marc's sentence.

"I have no delusions of who she is and what she's done, Marc, but I can't let this go without giving it one last try. Brian can get a word to his grandfather." She looked toward Brian. "Right?"

Brian gave her a reluctant nod, which Mason could see had Marc gritting his teeth.

"If this is you being the good Christian daughter..." Marc began, but Melanie shook her head.

"This is just what it will take for me to let go, so I can live with the fact that she will no longer be in my life," Melanie said, her voice barely above a whisper, but her words still rang through the room with the clarity of a bell.

"If Luca will wait a week we can go with the original plan and you can use my company jet after the New Year's holiday. It's only a few days more. Grace won't know you're coming unless she starts looking up private fights," Richard offered.

"See? She won't even see us coming," Melanie said to Marc.

"That isn't necessarily a good thing. Grace in the know is unpredictable. Grace caught off guard can be dangerous," Marc said.

"Well then, I guess you better stay glued to me," Melanie said, a little sass entering her voice. Mason saw Paige wince and smiled to himself.

"I hadn't planned on being anywhere else," Marc replied.

"Very good. I will reconfirm the arrangements for the third of January. Things should have died down by then."

"DC is so lovely in the winter," Victoria said wistfully.

"Victoria..." Richard said her name in warning.

"What?"

Richard sent her a meaningful look that Mason bet everyone in the room could read. It said *I will not be taking you to DC to start trouble.*

Victoria let out an exasperated breath. "We will accompany Melanie and Marc to DC. They will take care of their business, and we will all have a lovely dinner followed by an early evening and fly back the next morning. The plane can let us off in Oklahoma City, and they can come back to Los Angeles."

Richard watched her for a few seconds before turning to look between Marc and Melanie who nodded their agreement.

He shrugged. "Okay."

"What's next?" Melanie asked Brian.

"Angelo Mauro may want to meet you," Brian said, looking as uncomfortable as the thought left Mason, and he was on the outskirts of this conversation.

"Why?"

"I'm almost certain he doesn't know you exist. When he finds out about Roman, Silas, and Grace, he is going to feel vulnerable." Brian

341

raised his hands as if to surrender his responsibility for his next statement. "I have only seen Luca openly vulnerable one time, and it made him very possessive and cautious. Finding out about his nephew's betrayal and learning about you after all these years will definitely make him cautious and possessive. It will also make him skeptical, and he will want to look upon you with his own eyes to make sure you weren't part of Grace's deception."

Mason could not only see Marc go rigid through his peripheral vision, he could feel the tension emanating from him. To his credit, Marc didn't come right out and forbid Melanie from going near Angelo Mauro. After learning what he had about the top five Italian families in Chicago even during this meeting, Mason would have had to bite his tongue to keep from making his opinion clear about what he would do to keep his family away from them.

Mason saw the indecision and concern in Melanie's eyes when she looked at Marc, and he held his breath, not wanting to influence Marc's response in any way.

"If I had my choice, you would never go near that man, but I will have to defer to Brian on this for your future safety," Marc said quietly.

Brian watched him for a moment then nodded. "I understand your wariness and it is warranted. Angelo Mauro isn't known for his gentle nature, but he has grown wise, and he *is* known for his fairness. This means he listens to those he trusts, and he surrounds himself with men who are more strategic than bloodthirsty. If he invites her to meet him I think she should go and assuage his curiosity." Brian turned to Melanie at the table. "It could be done at a public place. He will probably insist on that to make you feel more at ease. Marc, myself, and B.J. would accompany you."

"What about me?" Paige asked, and Mason couldn't help the flexing of his hands. Marc glanced at him before returning his attention to Paige.

"My presence is a given. I'm her husband and protector. Brian's research uncovered the deception," Marc said in defense of Brian.

"And B.J. is his first male blood heir," Brian said.

Paige rolled her eyes, and Mason relaxed back against the counter.

The conversation went on for a few more minutes, but Mason just replayed the last few minutes. He had been included in the conversation as a whole only because he was Vivian's adopted father, but he was so emotionally invested he could barely keep his mouth shut and his reactions tempered. Mason knew it wouldn't be easy, loving Paige from afar after he gave himself permission to hope again, but he didn't know how much he would have to fight himself. If he was wrong, he would ask God to forgive him, but he was looking forward to getting on the plane in the morning and putting some distance between them.

***

Mason sat on the couch in Paige's living room staring at the television while he waited for Vivian, Gladys, and B.J. to return. He looked up when Paige handed him a cup of hot apple cider.

"Thank you," he said, then took a sip of the warm liquid.

"You're welcome," Paige replied. She'd sat down facing him with one leg curled underneath her. "I bet you've never had a holiday like this one."

Mason glanced at Paige to see her eyes bright. She was teasing him.

"Nope." He shook his head. "I honestly can't say I've ever had any type of holiday or family gathering like this." He grinned at her.

"It's a lot," Paige said, but he could somehow tell that she was looking for his opinion.

"It definitely wasn't a quiet week, but you can't deny that it wasn't also entertaining. Who gets surprised by not one but two family members they've never met?"

"Mmmm, people who've just won the lottery?" she said with her impish grin.

He laughed. "There is that, but I think your family reunion was much more genuine."

"Yeah, I do too," Paige agreed. "I'm blessed."

Mason watched as she took a sip of her drink. "Yes, you are," he said before forcing himself to look away.

"We haven't had a chance to just sit and talk since you arrived. I hoped we would have had some time Christmas night, but well..." Paige spread her hands out in front of her.

Mason watched her hands then looked up into her golden eyes hoping she couldn't see his heart in his.

"I wanted you to know how much your presence means to me." He watched her eyes go big and moist, and he had to work not to allow it to affect him.

"You gave me the second chance I didn't deserve, but I want to let you know that I will not take it for granted nor will I abuse it," she said so ardently, he had to reach out to her to get her attention and calm her before she started listing all the ways she could prove herself worthy.

He placed a hand on hers, ignoring its warmth and softness for the moment. "I know. I didn't make the decision lightly. You are already a good mother to Vivian, and she adores you."

He watched as she looked down to avoid his stare, her ears growing red. Paige took his hand, running her fingers over his knuckles in an absentminded way. She had no clue how many times he'd wished she'd touch him in any way and now that she was, she wasn't even paying attention. As good as it felt, it also hurt.

"How're you doing, Mason?"

He looked up to see her watching him again. He needed all his wits about him to converse with her, so he slowly removed his hand from hers.

"Work has been good lately. In fact, I'm up for a promotion," he said, trying to work up the same anticipation he felt about the advancement two weeks before. "Vivian is sharing with everyone who will listen that I should start teaching Bible study."

"Really? Is that something you have been asked to do?" He saw no judgment, just interest.

"No, it's just a proud and excited Vivian. I answered a couple of questions she had and she overreacted."

"She's happy to be able to share that with you," Paige said, her face softening.

He shrugged, feeling a little embarrassed by the attention. "Yes, well I learned a lot in some of my conversations with Brandon. He really knew his Scripture."

"Yes, I was always comfortable, not satisfied, but comfortable with my knowledge of the Word. I felt like I was right on track with what I knew compared to others around my age. The first time Brandon and I studied together I felt like a first-year student. I studied more just to keep up."

"Huh," he said before he could stop himself.

"What?" Paige asked, looking at him with open curiosity, and he considered where he had just placed himself—between a rock and a hard place. He could refuse to answer or hedge, but neither felt right to him.

"Brandon said much the same about you," Mason said, watching her expression close a little.

"You two talked about me?"

"Well, yeah. But not often. We had our own subjects, but you can't blame him for mentioning you every now and then," he said as matter-of-factly as possible.

"Yeah, I guess," she said, not sounding convinced.

"Anyway…" he said, trying to move the conversation forward. "Brandon said the first time the two of you studied a Scripture he was fascinated by how your mind worked. He saw he had to sharpen up his game just to keep up with you."

"Really?" she said, the uncertainty fading in place of a thoughtful smile. "What do you know?" Mason watched her puff up a little and exhaled. He was happy he'd chosen to tell her the truth.

"Did you talk a lot?" Paige asked, causing Mason to reconsider his last thought.

"Um, when we all first came back from Victoria and Richard's it was probably a couple of times a week but it grew to almost daily," he said, watching her carefully to see her reaction.

Paige grew quiet. He watched her eyes cloud over and wanted to comfort her but didn't know what to say.

"I'm happy he had you," she finally said, giving him a shadow of a smile.

"I got stuck in my head so much those last weeks. I constantly struggled with what I saw and what I thought I should be. I was there physically, but the sicker he became the more I was convinced I had failed him," she confessed, blowing his mind. He sat there blinking at her as he absorbed what she'd said.

"I never got the feeling he thought any less of you than amazing," he said, trying to reconcile what she'd just admitted about herself with what he knew. His heart squeezed at the thought of her beating up on herself on top of the grief.

"Do you still feel that way? That you failed him?" he asked, turning his body toward her and leaning against the back of the couch.

She frowned slightly, but her eyes didn't show any self-incrimination. "I wish I had been present more during those last weeks, but I've done a lot of soul searching. I've been scolded, cajoled, reprimanded, and held during the time I've spent with God these past two months. I've even gotten a few lashes with a wet noodle from my spiritual mom and grandmother…" She gave him a sardonic smile that made him chuckle. "All so I could pull my head out of the sand."

He thought she was being entirely too hard on herself. "But you've been grieving. Everyone does it differently. Who's to say how you should grieve," he said, feeling indignant on her behalf.

"Um… God," she said with a shrug and a nod.

"Well, okay. I guess," he said, pretending to give in grudgingly all the while fascinated by her ability to put her interactions with God in such simple terms. He wondered as time went on if he would grow to have such an understanding of his relationship with God.

"So, with all of that, what did He tell you?"

"The very short answer was that I needed to stop pouting because I didn't get my way and focus on the beauty of what Brandon showed me," Paige said without sorrow or guilt, and Mason knew it was the Holy Spirit that prompted him to tell Ava to hold back Brandon's letter.

"Can you share what that was?" he asked, almost needing to know.

"That even when Brandon had everything he'd wanted in life, he wanted God more because God is more. God is everything." Paige's smile grew from a grin to something so brilliant it lit up her whole face, and Mason was helpless to do anything but stare.

"Isn't that wonderful? It's not like I didn't know it, but if you aren't willing to live it, do you really believe?"

"Amazing," he said, losing the ability to filter his thoughts.

"Right?" she said, thinking he'd agreed with what she'd said. He had, but he was also astounded.

"No, I mean you're amazing." The quirk of her brow had him backpedaling.

"What I'm trying to say is, I absolutely agree with what you are saying. The amazing part is that it only took you two months to sort through all of that when I wasn't even that far after two years with my counselor."

Paige leaned forward as if she were about to share a secret with him. Her eyes danced, and her hair, secured in a low ponytail came to rest on her shoulder. "Maybe it was the counselor."

Her whispered words wrapped around him, sealing themselves in his heart.

Maybe it was the counselor.

"How hard was your first Christmas without Rachel?" Paige asked, and he automatically caught his breath but when only a distant pang registered in his heart, he let it go.

"I was a wreck. I don't even know how I functioned enough to give Vivian gifts, not that she was really interested. She grieved just as hard. I bought new frames for all her favorite pictures of Rachel, and we ended up spending most of the day looking through photo albums. We ordered takeout from a family restaurant because Vivian didn't want to change out of her pajamas, and I wasn't going to make her. I would say the fact that you got dressed this Christmas means you are doing better than me and Vivian," Mason said.

Paige gave him a small, secret grin. "I had a little help. Ava sent me a letter from Brandon she'd been holding. It was rather perfect timing." She nodded her head as she finished the last sentence.

"You're going to be all right, Paige," Mason said, feeling compelled to encourage her even though she sounded good. Maybe it would be something that could help during the harder moments.

He watched as she took in her living room before her gaze landed back on him. Her eyes were a little sad, but he could still see her light shining through them. "Yes, I believe I will.

"So, what do you think of Brian and B.J.?" he asked out of curiosity and because he wanted to see her eyes sparkle again.

"I know it's weird since I just met them a few days ago and didn't know they even existed until a few weeks ago," Her gaze shifted to the ground and he leaned in closer. He got the feeling that what she was about to say was extremely important.

"But they make me feel... safe." Paige looked at him, her eyes asking him if he understood and he did. Paige hadn't just lost her friend and husband; she'd lost a tangible covering. It was something he wasn't sure he would have understood a couple of months ago. He would probably have asked her why, with her relationship with God, did she feel unsafe at all? Ha, who was he kidding? They wouldn't have even had this conversation two months ago and the fact that he had the opportunity to do so now left him feeling conflicted.

It seemed too high a price—his salvation—the friendship he now shared with Paige. The conundrum was that even as Mason gave into those thoughts, he felt like he was betraying everything he and Brandon had shared, as well as what God chose to do through *that* friendship. Mason just hoped he would be able to resolve the conflict soon; otherwise, he didn't think he would be able to move forward if an opportunity presented itself for his relationship to grow into something more with Paige.

"I understand," he said as sincerely as he could and was rewarded with a relieved smile from Paige.

"I thought you would," she said, not losing eye contact even when she took a sip from her cup. He clamped down hard on the warmth he felt at her words. It unfurled something within him that he'd been carrying since their dinner in Chicago when she'd told him that she couldn't be with a man she couldn't share God with. The space between the lines of her words seemed vast, but there was nothing in her countenance that spoke of any awareness she could have of him as a man.

Mason smiled at her even as he blinked and gazed down at his drink to veil his thoughts.

"I'm going to be in your neck of the woods the third week of April," Paige said, and Mason said a silent prayer of thanks to God for the subject change. "The author circuit Carmen has me participating in next year starts in Salt Lake City, Utah the second week of January. We will hit Tucson, Arizona and Colorado Springs then take a small break before going north to Billings, Montana, Minneapolis, Minnesota and Madison, Wisconsin. I'm going to come back home for a few weeks before we start up again in Chicago.

"That sounds hectic. How long are you at each venue?" Mason wondered if Paige accepted the seemingly grueling schedule so she could stay away from her home, but then remembered the time he'd met her and Carmen in New York and considered that it was just something Paige enjoyed doing.

Paige shrugged. "Usually about a week. It's a lot of traveling, but I think I'm more focused when I'm on the road. It's me, God, speaking engagements, book signings, and writing. I actually think it's my most productive season. The work of the Holy Spirit is so prevalent in some of the forums that it takes a couple of days for me to recoup. I love it." Her eyes sparkled, and he could see how her touring fed her spirit more than took from it.

"I have plenty of breaks in between as do all the other authors on the circuit and there is such a comradery. After Chicago we go east, hitting Atlanta, Georgia; Savannah, South Carolina; Raleigh, North Carolina; Richmond, Virginia; DC; and finally New York in time for the Christian Writer's Symposium in July. The reason why I first agreed to it was because the circuit travels through Chicago and Atlanta. I thought I could spend time with you and Vivian and then Melanie and Marc, but Melanie told me she wanted to stay close to me."

Mason was completely surprised by the news, but he didn't know why. If he could have picked up and moved Vivian to Los Angeles or somehow convinced Paige to move to Chicago, he would have just to make sure she wasn't alone.

"They're moving to Los Angeles?" he asked, searching her face, which was moving while she scanned her living room again.

"She said they would if I didn't take her up on her offer to move to Atlanta." She finally looked at him again.

He took a good look around the room that still held so much of Brandon. "Are you thinking of moving?"

"I'm giving it some consideration," Paige said with a small shrug.

"What about your church, Pastor Lawrence, and Lady Menagerie?" Mason asked, wondering why he was so surprised by her words.

"They are the main reason why I'm not jumping at the chance. These last few weeks have shown me that I need my family. I prided myself on being on my own for so long. It felt like a right of passage after my dad... the colonel died. Shifting over to a career as a writer means a lot of hours by myself and I enjoy the peace that brings me. Still, I love having my family with me. I missed them and I'm one person. It would be easier for me to move in with them, and Atlanta is less expensive..."

"And more humid," he volleyed with a grin.

"And more humid," she repeated with a grin.

"Do you need to make a decision soon?" Mason asked, hoping Mel and Marc wouldn't pressure her.

"No, but Marc has to go back to work in a couple of weeks. He'll put out some feelers to see if there's anything at the office in Los Angeles. They've been talking to a realtor about options but haven't decided on selling the house or renting it out if I decide to stay here. They aren't pressing me, which actually makes me want to make a decision quicker."

"Just make sure you don't dismiss your own feelings or happiness. This move should be what's best for you," Mason said, feeling free to speak his mind.

"I will." She nodded, seeming to take his words with the seriousness in which they were meant. Then just as quickly shifted the conversation back to her previous topic.

"So would you be willing to see me again in April? Maybe you could show me the other half of Chicago?" Paige asked, and Mason had to clear his throat to keep the words he really wanted to say behind his lips.

"You are family, Paige. Not just Vivian's family, but my family as well," he said, meaning it from the bottom of his heart.

He saw Paige's breath catch and her lip tremble ever so slightly before she pressed them together. She blinked rapidly, but her initial reaction had already affected him profoundly.

"Yeah," she said through a watery smile.

"Yeah," he repeated, pretty sure his smile was just as wet.

She reached out and lightly pushed his shoulder before shifting her position on the couch to face the television. She swiped at her eyes and brought her cup to her lips again, but the smile didn't fade, and he couldn't help glancing at her from time to time to see how long it lingered.

By the time Vivian, Gladys, and B.J. dragged themselves through the door, Paige was asleep on the couch next to him and even knowing that waking up for their early flight in the morning would be a challenge, he was reluctant to leave. Mason hadn't woken Paige up or tried to send her off to bed but considered the last half-hour his very own Christmas present. One moment she was watching the really bad Christmas-themed action movie with him and the next, she was snoring. Initially, he had to work to keep from laughing at the ironic picture she made, but just like everything else that was Paige, it was adorable.

"Wow, she wasn't kidding," B.J. said, taking off his hat.

"What?" Mason half whispered.

"She said Brandon told her she snored. He was right," B.J. elaborated.

"That's nothing," Gladys said through a giggle. "She sleeps in my room. Let's just say, I always try to go to sleep before her."

Feeling bad, Mason shook Paige so she could go to bed after they left.

The snoring stopped, and a few seconds later Paige opened her eyes. She stared at him for a moment or two before her lips tipped up into a smile that turned his heart over.

"Hey, sleepyhead. It's time for Vivian and me to go." He watched her stretch and look past him.

"Ahhh, already?" She straightened and pushed herself up from the couch. She crossed in front of him to get to Vivian, giving her a long hug. "Safe travels. I'll miss you." Paige continued whispering words of love until she released Vivian.

Mason donned his jacket while he waited for Paige to let go of their daughter. He said goodbye to Gladys and B.J. "It was good to meet you," he said after giving the young man a half hug.

"You too. I'm glad to know Paige has you in her life," B.J. said, surprising Mason.

"Thank you for that, B.J. I'm glad she has you too. I look forward to seeing you again," Mason said.

"You will. We're family," B.J. said matter-of-factly, and Mason was momentarily taken aback by the words that were so similar to his own.

He nodded and smiled. "True."

Mason turned and found himself in front of Paige. He felt a half-second of awkwardness before she stepped into his embrace and hugged him tight. "Be safe," she whispered.

"Will do," he said on an exhale after inhaling her scent and taking a full body picture of how she felt in his arms, to capture and keep for his memories.

"Thank you again for my present," she said before giving him one more squeeze and letting go.

"You're welcome," he responded automatically, looking down into her eyes and trying not to lose himself in front of his daughter and B.J.

"Call me when you get home?" she asked, taking a couple of steps back.

"Consider it done," he said before forcing his gaze away from her to his daughter.

"You have everything?" he asked her.

"Yes, Dad," Vivian responded in a monotone.

He quirked a smile at Paige. "This is your daughter."

Paige looked at Vivian adoringly. "Yes, she is."

He chuckled and shook hands with B.J. one more time before ushering Vivian out the door, leaving yet another piece of his heart on the other side.

Chapter 30

Melanie felt the squeeze of her hand and looked over at her husband's profile as he drove them down yet another wide, tree-lined street with red-and-gray-bricked brownstones on both sides.

"I can't promise this will be the last time I ask you this question tonight, but then you know me, so I won't apologize. How are you doing?"

Melanie checked her emotions. After the first kaleidoscope of butterflies left her stomach, somewhere in the middle of the flight she thought she had overcome her nerves, but it felt like a new set had just come out of their cocoons, and the closer they got to the dot on the navigation map on the rental car dash, the more active they became.

Melanie knew in her heart that she was doing the right thing. She couldn't allow Grace to continue to put her family in jeopardy, but to know that when she left her mother's home, it could be the last time she laid eyes on her, made her physically ill.

Part of her was still ashamed it had taken so many lies, schemes, and threats for them to get to this moment. She should have put her foot down more firmly when Grace stopped allowing Paige to visit with her and Marc's family. She should have told Paige then that she was her mother, but she hadn't, and Paige had suffered for it.

But her fierce and courageous daughter had faced her fears and past and pulled through. It was Melanie's turn now.

354

She glanced over at Marc's profile again. "I'm good. I have God, you, my children, my grandchildren, and heaven help us all, Victoria and Richard on my side."

"Don't forget Brian," Marc said.

"I didn't. I just didn't mention him because you get all weird when I do," Melanie said with a snicker.

"I don't get weird. Rico Suave has nothing on me," Marc said as he made a turn. Melanie laughed.

"He looks nothing like Rico Suave," she said through her mirth.

"What about when he was fourteen?"

Melanie thought about it for a moment and conceded. "Maybe a little. Rico Suave with a tan."

"Told you," Marc said with a smile.

"You're right though," Melanie said. "Rico Suave doesn't have anything on you." She leaned over and kissed him on the cheek.

"Right. Wait. We are talking about Brian, right?" Marc said, glancing at her quickly.

"Are we? Huh," Melanie said and turned to the passenger window, working hard to keep the smile off her face.

Your destination is on the right. The computerized voice rang through the car's cabin, and Melanie's nerves spiked again. Melanie scanned the numbers, not having been to Grace's and her husband's new home. It was no less than what she expected with gray brick, white shutters, and a red-brick walkway from the six-foot, black wrought-iron gate to the bottom of the steps leading to the porch.

Her body trembled with nerves before she shut them down but not before Marc noticed.

"Melanie?"

"Yes."

"I won't leave you two alone at any time."

"I know."

"I said that more for my benefit than yours," Marc said.

Melanie looked into his eyes and saw both concern and love radiating from them. She leaned in and gave him a slow, warm kiss.

"Brian doesn't have anything on you either, honey," Melanie said as she pulled back. She looked into his overly bright, slightly unfocused eyes and smiled.

"I love you, Melanie Grace, and I wouldn't change you for anything, but I'm proud of you for doing this even though I would rather you not be anywhere near Grace," he said, holding her gaze.

"I love you too," she said, then took a deep breath. "Let's do this."

Melanie looked back up at the brownstone. It had grown dark on the drive from the airport to Grace's address, but it was still only five in the afternoon.

Marc parked a couple of cars ahead and got out. He came around and opened her door, taking her hand and helping her from the car.

Melanie gave him a quick hug before taking his hand again and walking back to the house Grace shared with Ross. They walked up the steps to the front door, and Melanie stretched her hand out to ring the doorbell. It was like she subconsciously had been going back and forth in her mind until that very moment. *Well, there's no going back now.*

It took a whole minute before Grace came to the door. She was dressed smartly in a pair of plum-colored slacks and a white top. Melanie realized that though they'd been keeping track of Ross' whereabouts, they had just assumed Grace would have been at home or close to it while her husband was out of town. As Melanie took in Grace's appearance, she could see that her mother had recently arrived home.

Grace's expression of surprise gave her away for a fraction of a second before she schooled her features. "Well, to what do I owe the pleasure of this visit?"

"We need to tell you something," Melanie said, taking in her mother's demeanor. Melanie would have thought Grace was expecting them if it weren't for her initial reaction.

Grace stepped aside giving them room to enter then shut and locked the door before preceding them through the entryway and into a room to the left.

It reminded Melanie of a drawing room or parlor, a place where guests would be invited to come, sit, and communicate without being invited into the rest of the home because it was understood they weren't staying long.

It was comfortable looking with its leather club chairs and hard-backed sofa, but it was pretty clear that this was more of a holding station. There were pictures and paintings on the walls. The colors were nice but nothing made the space personal. It looked more like a sitting room in a hotel than a room you would find in a home.

Melanie took a step down into the room and stood in front of the sofa next to Marc.

"Can I get you something to drink or eat? I have no clue what's in the kitchen, but I could probably scare something up."

Melanie wanted to clap at Grace's ability to get the sentence out without grimacing or laughing. Before Melanie left for college, she and her dad did most of the cooking.

"No thank you." Melanie's reply was seconded by Marc.

They all sat down opposite one another before Grace spoke.

"Well, I'm sorry Ross isn't here right now. He would have enjoyed this visit," Grace said, crossing her legs. "He so much wants us all to get along."

Melanie tried not to let her thoughts on that subject show on her face. She wasn't buying Grace's little show of domesticity.

"Yes, well, please give him our greetings," Melanie said looking at Grace then at Marc to see if she should begin. He nodded, so she took a deep breath.

Grace looked between Melanie and Marc. "I will. What did you want to say that you couldn't over the phone?" Grace leaned back in her chair and crossed her legs.

Melanie figured the only way to get started was to jump in the deep end and work her way back. "First, I wanted to tell you that Brian and B.J. are alive. I believe you understand why I denied knowing this before, and though I will not apologize for the deception, I am sorry that there was a need for it." Melanie took another deep breath and let it out gradually to slow her racing heart.

Grace stared at her for a few seconds, and Melanie saw the wheels turning before she spoke. "Why, I wonder, would you come all this way to tell me this now? What has changed?"

"Brian and B.J. spent Christmas with Paige and me. I figured it was only a matter of time before you found out, and I thought it should come from me," Melanie answered, gaining a modicum of control over her emotions.

"It should have come from you twenty-seven years ago when you participated in this scheme to commit fraud by pretending that your little boyfriend was dead," Grace said, leaning forward in her seat. She shook her head solemnly, but there was no real emotion in her voice.

"I'm disappointed in you, Melanie. You always portray yourself like such the good little Christian girl, but you really aren't any better than the rest of us."

"It was deception. There is no need calling it anything else, but so was your plan to get rid of Paige when you promised me you would keep my children together. Then there was your scheme to use B.J. as leverage against Luca and I couldn't let you do that," Melanie said, keeping her voice calm even though her pulse was jack-rabbiting.

"Like I said. Just like me. You can put any reason on it. Set any motivation behind it. It is still deception. Actually, I should applaud you. I didn't think you had it in you. I thought you only grew something like a spine when you met him," Grace said, glancing over at Marc. "I'm surprised you haven't come to her rescue yet, Marc. That is why you're here, correct?"

"I'm here to support her. If that means I have to keep quiet when I want to tell you what I think of you, escort her out of here, and order her to never come within two miles of you again, so be it," Marc said without batting an eye or shifting his position.

Grace blinked at him then turned back to Melanie. "From your husband's tone, I take it there is more."

Melanie watched Grace. There was still no show of emotion. The news of Brian and B.J. should have at least caused an eye flutter unless she already knew.

"When did you find out?" Melanie asked Grace.

358

Grace pursed her lips and glanced at her fingernails before looking back up at Melanie. "I found out the day after Christmas."

"Good. Now that we have that out of the way. I came here to tell you that Luca will be coming to you to present you with an offer, and I want you to accept it," Melanie said, trying hard not to squirm at the hardness that entered Grace's eyes.

"So, you're his lackey now delivering his messages?" Grace asked, her voice taking on a controlled note that used to grate against Melanie's nerves when she was younger.

"No, I'm actually here to warn you so you aren't caught off guard," Melanie said, feeling the conversation slip from her hands.

"Like you did with the news of Brian and B.J.?" Grace asked.

Melanie took a couple of seconds to get her bearings. "Whatever you are planning with Antonio Sable, please stop. If you have any other plans to gain revenge against the Sable family or any of the other five top Italian families in Chicago, please stop. Put your anger and vengeful plans aside and enjoy your life with your husband. In a few years it could even be possible for all of us to have a family reunion," Melanie said, knowing from Grace's reaction that her words had fallen on deaf ears.

"Is that all you have? Is the thought of a family reunion supposed to coax me into an enlightened existence where church services and Sunday dinners surrounded by people who smile in my face and talk behind my back are something I look forward to? No thank you," Grace said, leaning back against her sofa again.

"You are continuing down a road that will make it impossible for me to allow Gladys to be near you. I will not put her in danger because your need for vengeance supersedes your self-preservation. Don't do this to her."

Anger flashed in Grace's eyes, but her voice was still just as controlled. "There you go. That's what I've been waiting for. See how easy it is? You find something the person you are negotiating with cares about and you use it against them to get what you want."

"I would never use Gladys as a bargaining chip. She is a person, your great-granddaughter, and she loves you as I believe you love her, but I am not going to put her life in danger so she can spend time with you." Melanie took a deep breath to temper her words. "Is it so bad to want to have you in our lives? To know that you are safe, comfortable, and loved?" Melanie asked, hearing her voice climb as she tried to reason with her mother.

"Why? Why would you want these things for me? I won't win any awards for mother of the year, any year. Why is this so important to you?" Grace asked as if she were asking what colors a luxury car came in.

Melanie was almost at a loss for words. Grace had taken the reasons for her argument away with one statement. "I love you. You're my mom."

"Wow, I can honestly say that I didn't see that coming." Grace looked at Melanie with open curiosity. The bitterness and angry lines lessened for a moment.

"How do you do that?" Grace asked.

"Do what?" Melanie replied, confused by Grace's question.

"How do you let yourself forget? Forget everything I've done to you. Everything that has happened to you because of me?" Grace asked in a rare moment of candor.

"I haven't forgotten. I just chose to focus on the good that came from those things instead of what I lost. If it weren't for you I might not have Paige. I may not have come under the scrutiny of the FBI and then Marc. I certainly wouldn't have had the opportunity to raise Gladys for the first thirteen years of her life. I would hope that either way, I would have come to know the Lord and have a relationship with Him, but He more than anyone else is the reason why I can forgive and love you.

Grace scoffed. "You and your daughter both. There must have been something in the water."

"I would drink it again and again because He gives me peace. I can plan ways to show my love to those I care about instead of how I will hurt them, and they do the same for me. I am happy. Don't you want to be happy, have peace?"

Grace looked at Melanie and began to laugh. She actually laughed, great guffaws of laughter as if Melanie had just told her the funniest joke she'd ever heard.

When she finally got herself under control, Grace wiped the tears from her cheeks and looked Melanie square in the eye. "I had a chance to be happy with your father, with you, with Paige and Gladys. I even had the chance to be happy with Ross." Grace opened her mouth to continue but Melanie, her heart breaking one beat at a time, spoke before her.

"Which father?"

Grace blinked. "What?"

"You said you had a chance to be happy with my father. Which father? My biological father or the colonel?"

Grace's eyes looked like glass; they were so cold and hard. Her mouth formed a line dividing her nose and chin, and color rose so deep in her cheeks Melanie feared just for a moment that she might have a stroke.

"Who are you talking about?" Grace asked. Her voice holding fewer inflections than the navigational system in Marc's rental.

That was emotion. Melanie thought to herself before she answered, "Angelo Mauro."

"He's not your father. He's nothing but a dog sent to do a dirty errand. My happiness will come when he's put down," Grace said, her mouth coming just short of a snarl.

Melanie felt Marc's hand squeeze hers ever so slightly as if warning her to tread carefully, but she'd been walking on eggshells all her life and was tired of it.

"What do you mean by dirty errand?" Melanie asked just before her mind made the connection then wanted to back up, cover her ears, or somehow reverse time before her mother spoke.

"What do you think? He raped me. If it wasn't for Luca's driver, there would have been more." The sneer on Grace's face transformed her beauty into a composition of bitterness and pain that tore at Melanie, and out of instinct she tensed to move forward but Marc held her hand tighter, keeping her in place.

Melanie opened her mouth then closed it. What did one say to this? She skirted around the reality of her creation not even wanting to touch on that until she was in a safe place. Her mother had been raped, almost gang-raped and had sought revenge all this time. So many pieces of the puzzle came rushing together at once, and Melanie could see what her mother had been hiding for so long.

"Why?" Melanie asked, barely noticing the emotion that made her voice rough.

Grace laughed again, but this time there was no humor in it. It was a mocking sound that swept away what warmth there was left in the room.

"Why? Because I dared to be beautiful, intelligent, clever and black. Because I dared to fall in love with the wrong man." Grace's eyes glazed over slightly as they lost her to her memories. "I wasn't naïve about it, you know. I didn't expect him to leave his family or even feel the same way I felt, but he did, and we had two weeks. Two weeks and I let him go. I had prepared myself to move on and to go back to climbing as high up the corporate ladder as I could."

Melanie knew the moment Grace came back to the present because her eyes focused back on them with an intensity that caused Marc to stiffen even more beside her.

"But he broke his word. He went back on his promise and sent me to a conference in Nevada and met me there. It was wonderful and precious, and it sealed my fate." Grace got up and walked over to a small liquor cart in the corner of the room. Melanie had overlooked it in her perusal but could see that it held a few decanters of clear and brown liquids. Grace took a glass from a lower shelf of the cart and poured herself two fingers from one of the darker liquids.

Melanie had seen her mother drink wine on occasion when she was younger, but it was usually when they had company and it was only ever the one glass. Melanie assumed it was Grace's controlling nature that kept her from imbibing substances that could cloud her judgment.

Grace took a sip and shuddered before continuing. "His wife had him followed. Had a private investigator take pictures of us through one of the windows that last week." Grace turned back to Melanie and

Marc. "I believe we would have gotten away with it if it wasn't for that week in Nevada." Grace took another sip of her drink but didn't come back and sit down. Instead, she walked to the window and Melanie's gaze followed her.

"I was kidnapped from in front of a restaurant and taken to a warehouse on the outskirts of town. The plan was for me to be gang-raped then..." She shrugged off the last of the sentence, not turning back to them. "I was saved from the worst fate, but that flea-bitten mongrel did his deed before I was found and taken out of there, beaten, battered, and violated." Grace waved her hand as if to disperse the cloud of memories then turned back to them.

"I was cared for by a private physician, and within two weeks I was back at work. I never searched out the man, I planned to continue my climb as far as Luca's firm would let me before I found someplace that I could afford so I could go into business for myself. I asked him for one thing—one thing," Grace said, lifting her forefinger in the air. "I asked that he avenge me, and not even with the person who ordered the act, but that beast who carried it out. I told him I would keep my head down and let him take care of it." Grace chuckled. "I was just as naïve as you."

"Grace..." Marc said her name in warning, and Grace narrowed her eyes at him before lifting both her free hand and the one holding the glass in surrender.

"I got nothing but sent away when I found out I was pregnant. He told me to forget about everything. Live my life. Be happy." Grace practically spit out the last sentence.

"But you turned state's evidence. You nearly brought down the family," Melanie said, too caught up with Grace's story to watch her words.

"You've been doing a lot of research. Good for you." Grace finally went back to the couch.

"Why are you really here, Melanie?"

"I wanted to convince you to give up on your quest for revenge," Melanie said as firmly as she could, feeling the futility of her visit rest across her shoulders.

"Why should I?"

"Because Luca is willing to remove his hand of protection if you don't," Melanie said, hoping at least this would get her mother's attention." She saw the hurt flash through Grace's eyes before she dropped the veil and hid her emotions.

"No."

It was Melanie's turn to blink. "No? Just no?" Melanie gave in to her anger. "No, I will think about it for your sake, Melanie, the sake of Ross, and to have the family and love I deserve?"

"No, I want more," Grace said, and Melanie saw the truth of it in her eyes.

"Why couldn't it have been enough?" Melanie asked, seeing Marc shift out of the corner of her eye. She'd promised him and herself that she wouldn't plead.

"What?" Grace asked, her defenses beginning to slide back up.

"Why wasn't my daughter's or my love enough? Why wasn't your husband's love enough?" Melanie asked.

"Enough for what?" Grace asked. Melanie could see from her eyes that the wall was almost closed.

"Enough to make you happy," Melanie said, continuing to watch Grace intensely. Instead of nostalgia or softness taking over her features, Grace's eyes hardened. Melanie wouldn't have thought the color of fire could freeze over, but Grace had mastered it.

"Love makes you weak. It leaves you vulnerable to predators and those who would use that love against you," Grace said without hesitation or remorse.

"That isn't true," Melanie replied without thinking and knew she'd made a mistake by opening up this part of the conversation again. She had already been shredded by her mother's reaction.

"Yes it is. You've shown me so at every turn. I used your love for me to manipulate you into a relationship that you knew had no chance at a happy ending. Your daughter's need for love and approval had her seeking attention from a woman who raised a rapist. For twelve years you raised someone else's daughter because you wanted the love only a child could give. How do you think that will work out? Someone will lose. They always do," Grace said as she slowly uncrossed her legs and sat forward in the chair. By the time she was done, her eyes were gleaming.

"You're right," Melanie said, glad her voice was steady even though her emotions weren't. "My love for you kept my mouth shut when I should have rescued my daughter from you and sought out Brian years ago, but I will have to live with that."

Grace nodded her head again. "See? As I said, love makes you soft. Like tonight. You delivered your message, but your love told you that if you gave it one more try, I might what... see what I've been missing and desire what you have? Ask forgiveness, change my ways, and hope you have room left in your heart for me? I chose what I wanted years ago, and love is not it."

The room was quiet after Grace's diatribe, and Melanie saw that she truly had underestimated the woman's hatred.

Melanie looked at her mother, Grace-Brenda and conceded defeat. She nodded because there was nothing more she could think of to say. *God, please take control. I have nothing left but my forgiveness.*

Melanie looked over at Marc. He stood to his feet and pulled her up after him.

Melanie took one more look at Grace, suspecting it would be but hoping against hope that it wouldn't be the last time she saw her. "Goodbye," Melanie whispered, not using any of her names on purpose because she was leaving them all behind.

Marc pulled her forward without a word.

"Bye, Grace Melanie," Grace said, not bothering to get up. Melanie knew it was her mother's way of reminding her of where she came from and the tears that were nowhere in sight seconds before threatened to overtake her. She followed close behind Marc, not daring to breathe until they were outside.

Melanie didn't give in to the tears until they were back in the car.

"I'm sorry, honey. I know you wanted that to go differently. He held her through the worst of the sobs that wracked her as she cried out her sorrow for all the years of pain that woman had caused her, but when they dried, she felt peace in letting Grace go.

Chapter 31

Luca wouldn't say he was a masochist, but given the fact that he'd endured a verbal lashing from his grandson for not disclosing one of the reasons behind Brenda's vengeful plight and taking the blame in the board meeting for the security threat his son's incompetence caused by dealing with Grace, Luca had no business walking up to Brenda's door that evening. He could have waited another day, but he'd already waited three decades plus three more days beyond what he'd intended. And all so Melanie could try to convince her mother to abandon a goal she'd made her life's pursuit to accomplish.

He hadn't held out much hope, but he'd wished for Melanie's sake that she would be successful. When Brian called him with the news the night before after speaking to a somber Marc, he wanted to hop on a plane right then and take Brenda by the arms and shake some sense into her.

It didn't make it any easier knowing that he could keep the inevitable from happening by pretending Angelo Mauro knew what his nephews were planning, but there was already enough blood on Luca's hands, and he was tired.

Luca pressed his finger to the bell, releasing it when he heard the chimes from the inside.

He watched as the peephole darkened and lightened again, and still it took another five seconds before Brenda opened the door.

Her expression was smooth as if she hadn't a care in the world, but her eyes were wary. "Luca."

"Brenda," he said.

"Grace," she responded through gritted teeth.

"Grace. May I come in?" he asked, beginning to feel the cold wind of the night through the back of his coat.

"Are you here to kill me?" she asked with the same fire in her eyes that had caught his eye years before and he remembered why he had allowed this to go on for so long. It was hard to imagine that light going out.

"No, I am not," Luca said, making his tone indifferent.

Brenda watched him for a few seconds more before inching the door open wider. She stepped aside to allow him entrance.

Luca waited for her to lock the door, noticing that she left the chain off. She didn't trust him and he didn't blame her.

He followed her through the house. She had done well for herself, though he knew Ross Dillard would try to take the credit for the lavishness surrounding them. He was not someone Luca would have chosen for her. Luca always thought Ross had too many faces, but then he was sure there were a few people who would say the same about him. If they asked, Luca could sum up his life in two lines. "He wasn't a saint, but he was a family man" or "He wasn't a saint because he was a family man."

Luca watched Brenda's hips sway in the burgundy lounge jumper with its wide, flowing legs and long sleeves with the shoulders bared. He wondered what man first came up with the thought to design a top that covered a woman's midriff and cleavage but left the shoulders exposed. They obviously knew women's bodies as well as what men found fascinating about the curves of a woman. Luca tore his eyes away from her form and took in more of the house. He listened out for another presence but had it on good authority that Ross' flight wouldn't get in for another hour.

Brenda led him into the kitchen and off to the side where there was a kitchen table nestled in a nook. He would have chuckled if he didn't think she had purposely led him to the kitchen where all the knives were.

Brenda sat down closest to the stove, leaving Luca with the chair next to the window if he wanted to look straight at her. She didn't offer him any refreshments. She just stared at him and waited for him to tell her why he was there.

"You're looking good, Bre... Grace."

Brenda's eyes narrowed ever so slightly but she didn't respond. She was still an extraordinarily beautiful woman. He had glanced at a new photo or two of her over the years, but it was more out of necessity than want. He had to keep an eye on her because the one time he hadn't she had nearly gained more of his family than he could spare.

Brenda's skin was still flawless without wrinkles or blemishes. Her lips wore the same shade as her outfit, which enhanced the contrast between her complexion and eyes. She could have been fifteen years younger easily, but her eyes told on her. Luca could read almost every tale in them, and most of them leaned toward the dark end of the spectrum.

Luca shook himself, getting his thoughts back in line. He had to leave here with a definitive answer from her, and he would do what he could to draw one from her that would be beneficial to everyone.

"Brian told me your visit with Melanie didn't go well." Luca didn't get a reply or reaction from her, so he continued speaking. "I wanted it to go well for her sake. She has been the only one in your corner besides me." He watched the left side of her mouth twitch then smooth back out. *Well, it was something.*

Luca chose another angle since rousing her anger hadn't worked to loosen her tongue. "You're playing with fire, Grace."

"All of my life." Her words were said with indifference as though she were tired... like him.

"Angelo's nephews are cunning and zealous. They aren't known for their temperance or impulse control. They don't hold the old guard in as high esteem as we would wish. They are much like their uncle that way." Luca said the last on an exhale, leaning back in his chair and crossing his legs.

"So you're here to threaten me?" Brenda asked, sounding more resolved by the moment.

Almost four decades had passed since he'd last been face-to-face with her, but one conversation brought them right back to where they left off. Grace didn't play games with him then and she didn't do so now. She didn't deny knowing Angelo's nephews, and chances were she wouldn't deny working with them behind Angelo's back.

"No, I came to warn you." He tamped down on the memory of her eyes lighting up then, just as they were now, and forced himself to take a deeper look at the woman in front of him. There was spirit and life behind the blaze when she was young, but now it was fueled by an unquenchable anger and it made him... sad.

"Would it help if I apologized for all the pain I caused you?" He sensed she wanted to laugh at him but held back so he worked harder to convince her. He uncrossed his legs and leaned forward in his chair, pinning her with his gaze. "I'm sorry for being too weak to deny my feelings for you and not keeping my word to you." He meant it from the bottom of his heart and let her see and hear it with each word.

Finally, like a flower held dormant in winter's grasp that felt the first rays of spring's sun, she began to open up to him. There was no smile or loosening of the tension around her shoulders, just the almost imperceptible softening of her features.

"That's something, but it would help even more if you made the choice to avenge me now."

His gut began to roil, and his throat threatened to constrict around his larynx. "You know that's impossible."

Brenda shrugged. "So you say." There was no bitterness in her tone, just a matter-of-factness that left him cold. He could make men tremble with one hard look, but he couldn't convince this woman to save her own life. He spoke as if she hadn't said a word.

"Besides, I don't believe you would be able to forgive me or let go of your hatred that easily after forty years. It's in your blood now," he bluffed.

"Also true," she countered.

He decided to throw pretense out the window. "Then what? What will it take to get you off this road of destruction?"

"Why does this mean so much to you? It's not like I'm really family. Melanie... is not yours." He saw her swallow before the last words and almost wished that the girl was his, but that would have been catastrophic. No. Things were the way they were supposed to be, and it could all turn out all right if Brenda would just let go and grasp hold of what she had instead of what she'd lost.

"Melanie is the mother of my great-grandson and great-granddaughter. She's family."

Her eyes flashed something he'd never seen in them and thus couldn't recognize. Then the light dimmed and she looked down, hiding them from him. "How does your wife feel about that?"

Luca's heart pressed against his breastbone. Helena was off-limits, but if he could give Grace this one thing, maybe she would be appeased. "She took care of Brian and B.J. when they were young. She loves them, and she will love Melanie and Paige as well."

Brenda nodded twice and took a shuddering breath. Her bottom lip trembled before she bit it hard enough to leach it of color. Brenda inhaled deep and slow and exhaled the same before looking up at him with moist eyes. She threw him a watery smile before standing up from her seat.

Luca didn't want to assume that he'd reached her. He needed her to be clear about her intentions.

"What are you going to do, Grace?"

She looked him in the eyes without blinking. "Like you said, Luca. It's in my blood. I'm going to see this thing to the end."

He didn't move to stand. He had time. "It may just be your end."

"So be it."

"You could have a good life."

"My husband's going to be home soon, and I don't think he will take too kindly to *you* being here."

"Did you tell him about us?" Luca asked, curious, seeing one more angle he could use.

"It might have come up."

He watched her carefully before speaking. "Does he know that you're using his credentials to smuggle drugs into the country?"

Her eyes met his then skittered away and he had his answer.

His heart tripped over itself for a moment. "Oh, Bren, what are you doing?

She leaned in close. "What you didn't."

"If you mean ruining your family, that's all on you." He stood up, just stopping himself from throwing up his hands in frustration. "This isn't revenge, it's suicide."

"I am getting what's due me," Brenda said, seeming to feel none of his emotion. It was like talking to a wall.

"And what is due you? You nearly brought their company to their knees and you're still living to tell about it. No one does that. You got your vengeance."

"My vengeance is done when his body is in the ground. He took my future from me. I was going to the top. I had everything to live for. I had a future that would have shown my family that they were wrong to give up on me, to abandon me, but I had to go and fall for you. You, who took me to the stars and instead of keeping your word and letting me go, you led the wolves to me. And if that wasn't enough, when all I had left was hope for revenge, you sent me to no-man's-land. I want the life I'm owed. Nothing else will do now."

He let go of the pent-up feeling with one long exhale. He looked at her intensely one more time, tracking the light from the low-hanging lamp over the kitchen table. His Brenda was gone. In her place stood a woman he no longer recognized. He nodded and headed for the door, feeling an emptiness he knew wouldn't go away anytime soon. He'd lost.

His hand was on the doorknob before she spoke again.

"I'm going to trust you one last time to keep your word regarding Melanie and Paige. If you don't, their blood will be on your hands. Mine might be too tainted for God to care, but those two believe in Him with such fervor, it is hard not to believe He's real when you're around them. You won't be dealing with my wrath this time if you fail to do what you promised. You will have to deal with His."

Luca stared back at Brenda for a few seconds before nodding and crossing over the threshold to the outside. He had the feeling that she had gotten everything she intended from their meeting, and he'd come away with more and less at the same time.

Luca dipped his head against the wind and walked briskly to the car waiting for him, never looking up or to the left or right of him. He was overwhelmed by his thoughts, emotions, and... failure. He'd failed to right what he had wronged. Yet even as he emotionally flogged himself he saw the fragile chance of redemption she'd handed him. He'd do for Melanie and Paige what he'd done for his Brian and B.J. He would protect them, take them in as he'd said, and call them family. He just hoped they would accept his olive branch.

Chapter 32

Paige walked through the terminal in Madison not looking forward to the long flight home to Los Angeles, but almost giddy at the thought of going somewhere warm. It didn't matter how many layers she wore in negative five-degree weather. The cold seemed to seep into her bones. She hadn't been warm since Montana nearly a month ago. That would teach her to join the northern circuit in the winter. "How cold could it be?" Carmen had said. "I hear they have new designs in thermal underthings," she'd whispered conspiratorially. If Carmen scheduled anything north of Utah before March next year, Paige was dragging her with her. That would end any future arguments quickly.

Paige found her gate and made herself comfortable in a corner seat near the window so she could watch the planes take off and guess where they were headed by their direction.

She missed her family. She missed Melanie who texted her every morning alongside Vivian and Gladys' quick video chats. They had fallen back into their morning routine soon after the New Year, and it made the homesickness a little less intense. She took out her phone and scrolled through some of the latest quotes Melanie had taken to sending her at random times throughout the day. Some were extremely insightful like the one she'd sent earlier in the week which was a small modification of Henry Miller's quote. "Don't always look for miracles. *You* are the miracle." She'd printed it out and kept it in her wallet next to her bills and had read it every time she gave some money or received change. It reminded her that she was indeed a miracle on many levels, and she would embrace the thought every chance she got.

Paige focused back on a plane, watching it gain speed then tip its nose up in the air before lifting off. It spoke to her somehow. Maybe she was being nostalgic but seeing the movement from the outside gave her an almost opposite perspective from being inside. The thrill of the speed when she was inside was lost as she watched from the terminal, but the experience of watching the plane take flight was no less splendid when she thought of what it took to gain and keep flight. She had once thought her relationship with God was like taking off. She thought that if she could just get off the ground she could float and glide without much effort, but it seemed that once she got into the air she had to fight to constantly stay in the air. She admitted there were many times over the last year that she had stalled out, only to be bailed out by God.

Paige praised Him, thinking she couldn't get any higher one minute and yelled at Him for the unfairness of her life the next, and He never let her go or gave up on her. He had chastised her, sure, and warned her of the path she was heading for, but often enough he would set up buffers in the way of people to talk her back or give her just enough insight to help her see the path she was on from another angle and change her direction. He kept her close, and she felt so blessed by that fact, it didn't bother her that she couldn't say or do things other Christians thought were permissible.

She had been set aside for not just one purpose, but for many with chance after chance to prove herself when she sang words like "I surrender all." Paige finally got that understanding as she stood in front of a crowd of women and was led to share... not the testimony that went along with the fictional book she was promoting about her cousin's life, but about her darkest moments after Brandon passed. She hadn't discussed her marriage to Brandon in public before that night. It was something sacred and not easily explained, so she usually gave those who were privy to her personal life a general overview of her and

Brandon's far too short marriage. She suffered the pitying looks and quickly changed the subject.

That night in Billings, Minnesota was different though. The presence of the Lord was so heavily felt, even before she began she knew something special was going to happen. She just didn't know it would have to do with her.

Paige was in the middle of her talk about the importance of seeking God's perspective when the Holy Spirit impressed upon her the moment her perspective changed regarding Brandon's passing and what she thought God had taken away from her.

Paige shared some of her darkest thoughts with the audience. She shared the shift that happened when she spoke to her spiritual mother and received her first letter from Brandon. Part of her hated to share that piece with the public, but as with everything else in her life, she had to surrender it to keep from turning it into an idol.

She knew it was the Holy Spirit because the shame she'd felt months before was gone and there was just a knowing. Saying Brandon's name still squeezed her heart to near pain, but she welcomed that.

Paige finished her talk, greeted readers, signed books, and accepted some words of encouragement and gratitude for being so transparent, but still felt a restlessness in her spirit that made her uneasy.

She'd gone to bed and slept fitfully then got up and prayed before beginning her day, which looked much like the one before if their schedules were anything to go by. She did a little sightseeing with one of the other authors before the evening panel and couldn't resist stepping into a bookstore.

They hadn't taken two steps when she heard a gasp from someone to her right. Paige looked over to see a woman, maybe a year or two older than herself covering her mouth with both hands. Paige looked around her, including at her friend to see who the woman was looking at. The woman slowly walked toward her as if she were trying to contain herself or present herself as nonthreatening, which if Paige were honest, didn't really work.

"I'm sorry that I gasped," the woman said by way of greeting. "I was just startled to see you. You don't know me," the woman quickly added, seeming to read Paige's mind. "I saw you last night at the Women's Overcoming conference. Your testimony changed my girlfriend's life last night. I spent the evening comforting and praying with her so she would receive her full deliverance from what you started."

The woman paused to breathe and Paige did too, allowing it to relax her some. The woman wasn't overzealous or threatening in any way, she was just excited. Paige understood that.

"Praise God, I'm glad she had you to guide her through that. How is she doing now?"

The woman smiled broadly. "She's asleep, so I thought I would come out and do a little sightseeing, but it is cold as dickens out there, so I came to my second-favorite spot." She lifted her hands to gesture to the bookstore.

"I definitely understand. What's your name?"

"Reesie. Reesie Thompson. I'm from Helena, just up north. My friend and I won tickets to this conference at church a couple of months ago and made it a road trip."

The name caught Paige's attention causing her to look at the woman more carefully. "Well, congratulations." Paige felt a nudge from her companion.

"I'm going to go over to the speculative fiction section. I'll see you in a moment."

"Okay," Paige said, feeling a moment of indecision, but her companion waved her off.

"I'm sorry. I'm sure you came out here to get away from all the pulling on you, and here I am taking up your free time," the woman said, looking embarrassed.

"It's called 'free' for a reason. I can spend it any way I choose." Paige replied.

The woman's eyes danced for a moment reminding her of Vivian's. "I don't know how you will take this next part, but know that if you choose to go, I won't try and stop you or feel any type of way about it. I have tickets for tonight so I will be there regardless."

Paige tried to mask her feelings of apprehension but obviously didn't do a good job.

"I'm messing this all up. Okay, I will just come out and say it," the woman said as she stepped back from Paige, which was odd since she just said she wanted to share something with her.

"The reason why I gasped when you walked in was because I was led to tell you something last night but I didn't know how I would be able to get enough time with you to deliver it. When my friend reacted the way she did to your message I thought I had heard wrong and was actually relieved to take care of her instead of approach you." Reesie glanced at her sheepishly and Paige understood her dilemma. There had been times when Paige had been prompted to tell people something the Lord wanted them to hear. She hadn't always been obedient and had suffered in different types of ways for it.

It was a delicate thing. She wouldn't deny the woman her blessing for being obedient, but she would also receive the message with God's covering and the Holy Spirit's guidance. If it wasn't a confirmation of what God had already spoken to her, she would ask God to confirm it if it was in fact from Him.

"Okay."

"Okay?" Reesie repeated, looking even more nervous than before.

"Yes, I am a child of God. Why wouldn't I want to hear what He has to say?"

"Yes," Reesie said, seeming to relax. "Here it goes...You are generous with your love and your forgiveness to all except the one who needs it the most. Just as no one can love Me as you can, no one can help deliver this gift to her as you can."

The impact of the woman's words nearly brought Paige to her knees. She didn't waste her time asking the woman how she knew what Paige had been struggling with. It had been a constant push and pull over the last few months. Paige asking God for guidance, but being too fearful to actually listen long enough for His answer.

Oh God. I don't know if I can do it?

"You would not trade a moment of surrender for her eternity?"

Paige wiped at her tears before staring the woman in the face. "Never lag, never doubt. Just be obedient. Thank you very much for delivering that message." Paige hugged Reesie.

"When you come tonight, please see me before you leave. I want to give you and your girlfriend signed copies of my books."

"I didn't give you that message to get anything," Reesie said, sounding uncomfortable.

"I know. I'm just saying thank you for being obedient. Please do this for me," Paige said with determination. It worked because Reesie's current smile outshined her last one, and she gave her a huge hug.

"May I pray with you?" Paige asked, moving farther from the door so she wasn't in the way. It dawned on her that it was the same thing Reesie had been trying to get her to do without saying anything.

"Absolutely," Reesie said, backing up a little more so they were slightly obscured by a row of books.

Paige took the woman's hands and bowed her head. "Dear Aba Father, thank you for your guiding hand and your perfect ways. You seek us out constantly and we call ourselves blessed to be your children. You adopted us into your family, making us heirs to your kingdom with your only begotten son, Jesus Christ, and we thank you.

"Lord, I praise and thank You for my sister, Reesie. I lift her up to You right now and ask that you continue to bless her greatly. You have gifted her by using her to share Your word in a very special way, and I ask that you give her a holy boldness to render Your word to those you have chosen it for. Let her continue to be timely and humble in her telling. Let the reverence for you stay in her heart even as the confidence that you give her in delivering Your message shines through.

"I lift up her friend to You ask and that You continue what you started last night that she may be whole in body, mind, and spirit even as You heal me. Give these two women traveling mercy, and greet them each morning with a new song on their lips.

"We will continue to give you all the praise and the glory because it is yours alone. In Jesus', name, amen."

378

"Amen," Reesie repeated. Her eyes were wet but just as bright as her smile. She hugged Paige to her again, and Paige returned it in strength, feeling the restlessness ease.

"Thank you so much. I will see you tonight. Have fun in here, and please tell your colleague I apologize for infringing upon your time." She didn't give Paige a chance to respond, just waved and made a beeline for the cashier. Paige waved back, bemused, and went to find her friend and colleague as she replayed God's message over and over in her head.

The women came up to Paige after the evening's events were done, and Paige surprised them with not only her books but a book from each of the panel authors that she'd gotten signed. As she hoped, the women were overjoyed, and they talked until it was time to leave the room.

Afterward, Paige dragged herself to her room, exhausted, and more than satisfied with the week's events.

The call for passengers at her gate to begin boarding rang over the PA system, pulling her back to the present.

Paige checked her watch and figured she could get off a few texts before she boarded, including one to Mason. They'd talked earlier that day as they had almost every other day or twice a week since Christmas. He asked her to send him a message letting him know when she was about to board. Though her mind often wanted to analyze their relationship she never indulged in it, preferring to just enjoy his attention while she had it. One day he would meet a woman he could see himself with for the rest of his life, and their talks would take a back burner to his life.

Paige dug her phone out of her purse and noticed that she'd missed two calls between the security entrance and the gate. She checked her voicemail and smiled when she heard Brian's voice.

"Hey, Baby Girl." He'd begun to call her that sometime over the last month and Paige didn't mind. He'd embraced her fully from the moment she'd met him, and she couldn't begrudge him the endearment even though she was still taking her time warming to him.

There had been a speed bump in their communication. Well, she'd avoided his calls for a few days, or a week, when Melanie told her, he and B.J. had lied about the home they'd led Marc and Melanie to when they first reunited. Melanie understood their need for privacy and secrecy, but Paige was insulted on her mother's behalf and wasn't so quick to forgive him.

After a week of voicemails that never escalated in aggression beyond Brian's request for her to give him a call so he could explain, she conceded and called him, listening to him with an open mind. By the end of the call, the rough patches had been smoothed, and Paige was more than willing to resume their communications.

"When you have a moment, maybe today or tomorrow, give me a call. Something important has come up, and I think you are going to want to be a part of it. I will be available on my phone for the rest of the evening. I pray all is going well in Minneapolis. Talk to you soon."

Paige wondered if he was talking about Grace. She'd asked him to keep her apprised of anything he found out about her while she was touring. Paige had considered interrupting her part of the tour and prayed about it, but the urgency wasn't there. She knew before she spoke to Grace in person or on the phone she would have to fully work out her anger and guilt surrounding Grace and her own children. Every time Paige thought she had gained some ground a thought would come to mind that would put her teeth on edge. Logically, she knew the forgiveness was for her, but she also had a feeling that it was something she needed to do in order to help Grace and that was where she struggled.

It was hard to explain how she was able to forgive her cousin, who betrayed her trust and violated her but couldn't forgive her mother.

Paige saved the message and apologized silently as she dialed for being one of those people who held a phone call in a small space.

"Hello?"

"Hi, Paige. I'm glad you could get back to me so soon," Brian greeted.

"I'm about to board a flight back to Los Angeles, so it would have been hours before I could get back to you."

"Understood. I'll make it quick. Luca finally spoke to Angelo Mauro," Brian said.

Paige counted the weeks since she'd found out what Grace was up to with Angelo's nephews at Christmastime.

"I think he was trying to give Grace a chance to change her mind or at least her ways, but she hasn't. He had to do it now because he wouldn't have been able to explain why he waited until a recent shipment made it across the border, putting Angelo's business in jeopardy.

Paige understood Luca's dilemma. For all his faults he had given Grace a lot of leniency.

"Angelo Mauro wants to meet both you and Melanie."

"I thought it was just going to be Melanie... in a public place... with a whole lot of security?" Paige stopped her forward motion, momentarily stunned by his news. She was glad she wasn't yet in front of anyone.

"Yes, but in light of what Luca revealed to Angelo, he's wary, to say the least." Brian's tone was apologetic.

"He should be," Paige said before she could stop herself.

"Yes, but we've all done things we wish we could outlive," he responded, the words ringing true in her heart.

"Yeah," Paige said, feeling chastised even though she had the feeling Brian was speaking about himself.

"Paige, I just got you and Melanie back in my life. I wouldn't do anything to jeopardize that." Brian's voice was quiet yet firm over the line, and she didn't doubt his words or feelings.

So, you will give it some consideration?"

"Yes. Do you know where and when yet?"

"Melanie and I discussed that earlier today. We thought with your next circuit stop being in Chicago in three weeks, we could arrange something in two weeks. Melanie said Gladys will be on spring break, so she will come but stay with Mason and Vivian."

"Geesh, it sounds like you two have already organized everything," Paige said, not quite sure how she felt about that.

"We wanted to make it as convenient for you as possible if you decided to come."

His last few words went a long way to relax her. She still had a choice. "Thank you. I appreciate you taking that into consideration."

"I do more than take you into consideration. I know it's hard to believe because you just recently learned about me and your brother, but I thought about you every single day of my life, and when I learned my prayers could go further than my thoughts, I started doing that as well."

His words warmed her, making her wish once again that she had learned about him sooner, but she had him and her brother in her life now.

"Now that Angelo knows about Grace's part in his nephew's deception, what will he do?"

"Angelo said he wouldn't make any moves regarding Grace until after he met you and Mel." Paige's relief was immense. She had more time. "Okay, good. All right. If it will help, I will come."

She glanced up to see that she was only a couple of passengers away from the gate attendant and fished her ticket out of the front pocket of her carry-on.

"Very good," Brian said.

"Look, I have to go. I'll call you tomorrow, okay?" Paige said as she handed her ticket over to be scanned.

"Okay, yes. Talk to you soon. Have a safe flight," Brian responded, speaking quickly.

"Thank you. Bye, Brian."

"Bye, Paige," Brian returned before disconnecting the call.

Paige heaved a sigh before heading through the gateway. She had an overwhelming urge to speak to Mason. They'd talked about Grace a few times, and he was always able to give her another angle to consider regarding Grace's actions in her life. He had also made her laugh before they hung up. It seemed the more intense the conversation, the harder he would work to get a laugh out of her. Paige dialed before she could reconsider. Right now, she really just wanted to hear his voice.

And that is exactly what she got after four rings—his voicemail. Paige listened to his greeting while she searched for her assigned seat.

When the beep came she made a last-minute decision to leave a message.

"Hey, I'm sorry I missed you. I'm about to head back to Los Angeles, but you will probably be asleep before I get home. I got a call from Brian a few minutes ago. It looks like I will be arriving in Chicago a week early. Please give Vivian a kiss for me and throw in a hug for yourself. I'll call you tomorrow." Paige ended the call and arranged her belongings and sat down feeling deflated and more than a little concerned about the meeting she agreed to.

She resisted the urge to go through her purse and reorganize her makeup bag, manicure case, pill bag, electronic charger case with its cords and outlet chargers, her change purse, and USB holder, for want of something to do with her hands and mind. People she was in close quarters with usually frowned at all the moving around. It unsettled them even as it soothed her, but the spike in her anxiety wouldn't be ignored. Paige made fists and took slow breaths until she remembered the game app Gladys downloaded on her phone and showed her how to work before she left. It was a group of puzzles where objects had to be packed in virtual bags and boxes just so or they wouldn't fit, there were also ones with hidden objects, and jigsaws made from some of the pictures they'd taken at Christmas and her favorite picture of cherry blossom trees in full bloom.

She worked the puzzles, allowing the repetitive motion to soothe her and was feeling a modicum of her control return just as they were taking off. She was going to add to whatever allowance Melanie was giving Gladys when she got home.

***

Paige looked around her once she, Melanie, and Gladys walked in the door. She was impressed and pleased to see that there was little evidence of their packing even though Melanie kept her updated on how many boxes they sent to Atlanta or placed in the storage unit she and Brandon rented when they first moved in together. The apartment had a minimalistic feel to it, but Melanie and Gladys had rearranged the furniture to fill in the gaps left by smaller pieces and knickknacks.

Paige had decided to move with Melanie, Marc, and Gladys after her tour. She'd prayed about it for weeks and spoke to Lady Menagerie and Pastor Lawrence before sharing her decision with Mel who whooped and jumped around like a child. It wasn't until then that Paige realized how much Melanie wanted to stay in Atlanta but was willing to make a life on the West Coast just to be near Paige. She was happy to do something to give back to her mom.

Marc was back at work in Atlanta and was happy to receive the packages as they arrived. Paige had agreed to stay with Mel, Marc, and Gladys for at least one year as she relearned her way around the city and possibly made a friend or two.

The only person not excited about her moving was Mason. It had nothing to do with him or Vivian visiting her because Atlanta was a shorter flight. He was concerned about her well-being and just how much she was giving up in moving with her family. What Paige pointed out to him more than once was the fact that she was moving *with* family, but figured he wouldn't be convinced until he saw her in Atlanta, smiling.

"You guys have done such a great job. I feel bad that you are doing all this packing, and I haven't been here to help," Paige said on her way to her room. Melanie had moved her things into the twins' room for the time that Paige was home. She didn't mind. She'd missed her bed. Paige noticed that even less had been disturbed in her room and was more grateful than she could express.

Melanie and Gladys walked in behind her. Gladys lay across her bed, and Melanie leaned against the doorjamb and shrugged. "It's the only thing that has kept me from going mad. It has been fun and a bit of a challenge to pick and choose things that could be packed and shipped until we are ready to go in a few months. The next time you come back it will look desolate," Melanie said both in warning and with pride.

Paige walked back over from her closet and gave Melanie a long hug. "Thank you."

"You're welcome," Mel replied, rubbing her back softly.

"How're you doing? Miss Marc much?" Paige said, moving to sit on the bed next to Gladys.

Melanie hugged herself and nodded. "I can't tell you how happy I am that he will be coming up to Chicago to meet us. I don't think I've spent this much time away from him in all the time we've been married. The only other time I've been away from him more than a week was when you were in the hospital after you donated your kidney to Vivian."

Paige's heart went out to Melanie. She was happy she would be able to get some time with Marc. Paige glanced at the clock. "What do you say about having a pajama-unpacking party?"

Gladys perked up. "Can we have ice cream and popcorn?"

"Sure," Paige answered after sneaking a look at Melanie.

"Can we watch a movie too?" Gladys asked.

"It wouldn't be much of a party without one."

"Can I pick?"

Paige was about to say yes but caught the small shake of Melanie's head.

"Uh, I think it depends on what you're thinking of," Paige said, trying to be as diplomatic as possible.

"*Everything is Everything.*"

Melanie groaned.

"What? It's a great movie." Gladys said.

"Yes, I agreed the first and second time," Melanie returned.

"Is there anything you've been wanting to binge-watch?" Paige had nothing early to wake up for, so she didn't mind staying up as long as she possibly could.

Gladys bounced up and down on the bed. "Oooh, that would be great. I've been considering at least a half dozen. We can all decide." Paige knew this meant Gladys would decide after she shot down all their suggestions and objections. Paige smiled indulgently at her daughter and kissed her forehead.

"Deal."

Gladys scrambled off the bed to make the popcorn, and Paige reached for her suitcase.

"Brian told me you said 'yes' to meeting with Angelo Mauro," Melanie said, taking Gladys' place on the bed.

385

Paige glanced at her then heaved her suitcase on the bed. "Yep."

"Why? You don't owe anyone anything," Melanie said.

"No, I don't, least of all Angelo Mauro, but if it will smooth things over for Grace, it's a small concession. Besides, I will get to spend more time in Chicago on someone else's dime," Paige ended flippantly to keep the discussion light.

"Paige," Melanie said, placing a hand on hers to stay her movements. Paige looked up reluctantly.

"If this becomes too much... if you change your mind..." Melanie faltered. Paige didn't even try to lessen the scowl she was directing at Melanie. She had been done being coddled after Mel's first month in Los Angeles.

Melanie raised her hands in surrender then let out a breath. "Thank you. That's what I meant to say."

"You're welcome," Paige returned before turning back to her suitcase and pulling out an armful of toiletries. She knew how broken up Melanie had been about having to sever ties with Grace. It did nothing to sever her love for her mother though. It didn't help Paige's struggle to forgive Grace when she continued to cause Melanie undue stress and pain, but both women were well and above the age to take responsibility for their actions.

Paige focused her attention on the items in her arms and concentrated on doing what God had been leading her to do.

Chapter 33

"Are you sure you'll be ready to get back on another plane when your conference is over here? That ride was rough," Melanie said as they walked what seemed like the mile-long corridor to the baggage claim.

Paige shrugged. "I guess it depends on how well it goes here. The fact that I'm going to get some off time before and after won't hurt."

"No, I guess not, but you can *keep* the whole traveling thing for three to six months out of the year. If I didn't know before, I know now that I am a homebody."

Paige smiled over at Melanie knowingly as Gladys picked up her pace overtaking them. "I know one great thing about traveling," Paige said.

"Really? What's that?" Melanie asked, preoccupied with digging something out of her purse.

Paige saw who was waiting for them on the other side of the security exit leading to baggage claim. They were probably who Gladys was half running, half-speed walking toward at the moment.

"Waiting loved ones," Paige said.

Melanie looked up at her then down the hall. Paige watched her face split into a wide grin and didn't even try to keep up when Melanie began speed walking to Marc at the end of the hall.

Paige smiled as Gladys ran and jumped into Marc's arms for a huge hug. He squeezed her tight before letting her down so she could then run over and hug her sister, and it wasn't a moment too soon with Melanie taking a small leap of her own into Marc's arms.

Nice catch, Paige thought to herself.

The kiss that Melanie laid on Marc after she was sure she was secure was not something Paige needed to see, though.

Paige looked over to see Mason watching her. Her heart did a little fluttering dance and she chalked it up to the excitement of the moment. She smiled and waved when she was still two dozen or so feet away. He smiled back, and she found herself moving faster to greet him. At the last second, she decided to play a joke on him and pretended to run at him, bags and all. She saw his eyes go wide and his stance change, but when she got to him she pulled up short.

"Hi," she said, slightly winded when she was in front of him then started laughing.

"Hi," he greeted back, straightening.

"I was just playing. I wasn't going to jump."

"To bad. I would have caught you," Mason said.

Paige laughed to conceal the all-over body shiver that thought gave her. "Good to know."

"Hug?" Mason asked as he opened his arms.

"Much safer," Paige said as she walked into his arms.

Mason gave her a long squeeze that warmed her from her shoulders to her toes. She noticed that her head came to just under his shoulder. He was always such a good hugger she was hard-pressed to let go when he loosened his hold.

Paige looked up at him. "You are such a wonderful hugger."

"It takes two, so right back at cha," he replied with a grin.

"If you don't mind, I'd like to give Brat a hug," Marc said, standing next to Mason.

"Just don't kiss my cheek. I see where your mouth has been," Paige razzed as she stepped into Marc's arms.

Marc hugged her then turned and blew razzberries into her cheek making her squeal and try to remove herself from his arms. "I'm sorry, I'm sorry." She half apologized and half pleaded to get him to stop.

"It's just love," Marc said, laughing as she wiped her cheek with her palm. Paige deep breathed as she tried hard not to think of Marc kissing Mel just before spitting all over her cheek. She pushed Marc away and pulled Vivian into her arms letting the scent and feel of her child soothe her. After a few seconds, she exhaled and let Vivian go.

"How're you doing?"

"Great, now that you're here. My teacher loooooves your new book, and I wanted to know if you would sign a copy for her."

"Okaaaay," Paige said, trying not to be offended.

"Got you!" Vivian said, laughing.

Paige conceded. "Yeah, you did."

"Sorry," Vivian said, shrugging sheepishly. "I missed you though."

"I missed you too, and we have even more time together this trip."

"Yeah, Dad hasn't stopped talking about it," Vivian said, peeking around Paige to her dad.

"Thanks a lot, kiddo," Mason said.

"What? You said you were looking forward to seeing Paige face-to-face 'cause..." Mason moved around Paige and Vivian almost faster than Paige could track. He covered Vivian's mouth from behind and spoke over her mumblings.

"Anybody hungry?"

"Me!" Gladys yelled, raising her hand.

Melanie wrapped an arm around Paige. "Come on, let's get our bags so we can go eat. I refused to pay twelve dollars on the plane for a turkey sandwich."

Paige let herself be pulled away, finally understanding what Melanie had been trying to veil from her. Mason liked her.

When they got a few more steps away she glanced back to see if he was still watching her. He was. *Huh.*

Melanie told Paige where to sit at the table. It happened to be across and one person down from Mason. Paige didn't resist. She thought it was funny and worked hard to keep the smile off her face. When Melanie got into protector mode there was no going against her.

A passing thought wiped the smile away though. Was Melanie being so protective because she didn't like Mason? No, they got along well. Maybe she didn't think he was good enough for Paige. Maybe the Mason before…"

"Hey, the gang's all here." Brian's voice pulled Paige from her thoughts, and she was happily distracted.

Paige suffered more kisses to her cheeks, trying not to think about how many more people just indirectly kissed Melanie. She was going to have to wash it off. Maybe she should excuse herself and go to the ladies' room. She had some facial cleanser in her makeup bag…

"So, 'Big Time,' what have you been up to?" B.J. asked, sitting to her right.

"'Big Time'?" Paige turned to him, confused.

"You've been hopping all over the country, sharing, and signing books, speaking on women's views, sharing your testimony, praying over people." He caught her attention with the last part of his sentence.

"How do you know all that?" Paige asked, watching him closely.

B.J. blinked. "I guessed."

"Try again," Paige said.

B.J.'s shoulders slumped a little. "I hacked into a camera feed."

"You can do that?" Paige asked, too surprised to think.

"It was digital," B.J. said, looking at her with a wary expression.

"Wow, why?" Paige asked.

B.J. stared at her for a moment. "You aren't angry?"

"Impressed but certainly not angry. I didn't know you could do that. Why, again, did you do that?" Paige asked.

"I wanted to see you." He shrugged. "I was curious. You are anointed to do what you do. I felt proud to know you." He threw her a sheepish look. "I even bought your book."

"Why did you do that? I would have given you one if I thought you were interested," Paige said, feeling extremely flattered.

"I wanted to buy it, but would you sign it?" he asked.

"Of course. You don't even need to ask. You're my brother." Paige said the last without thinking.

B.J.'s smile lit up the restaurant. He grabbed her and kissed her cheek. She smiled back and then got up from the table. "I'm going to go to the ladies' room to wash... my hands," Paige said before heading to the back of the restaurant with her purse.

An hour later the mostly sated family sat around the table thinking about the next day's meeting between Angelo Mauro, Brian, B.J., Melanie, Marc, and Paige. Marc had gone over the security issues and directions twice, though they were easy enough to get the first time. Paige didn't say anything because she knew how nervous the thought of Melanie meeting the elder Mauro made him. She sat back and listened to everyone's opinions, along with Brian's input about the layout of the restaurant they would be in the next day and B.J.'s offer to set up a camera in or audio recorder near enough to record what was said in case there were any threats.

Paige groaned to herself. B.J. had just unknowingly ratcheted up Marc's wariness. Marc's eyes practically glowed with intensity, and the conversation lengthened at least another half hour.

Paige passed Melanie a look who was sitting across from her.

"He's just being thorough," Melanie whispered.

Paige nodded. Melanie would never know how hard it was for Paige to keep from rolling her eyes.

Paige glanced at Mason to see how he was holding up. He was leaning back in his chair staring up at the ceiling. Paige glanced up to see what he was looking at but not noticing anything, looked back at him to find him watching her. He crossed his eyes and stuck out his tongue, which caught her off guard. She bit down on the laugh then returned the face. Mason came back with another face, and she answered with the pig face she'd learned as a child.

It took Paige a moment for her to realize that the table had gone quiet. She swallowed before looking at Melanie in front of her and was relieved to see her fighting to keep the smile off her face. Paige looked up at Marc and her humor left at his thunderous look. She looked down at her hands.

She heard Marc exhale. "Paige, I'm not talking just to hear myself speak. This is for your safety as much as it is for Melanie. Can you tell me the last thing you heard before you began playing funny faces with Mason?"

Paige looked back up at Marc. "Melanie will enter and sit between you and Brian, and I will stay between Brian and B.J. at all times. All food and drink will only be consumed if it comes from one waiter because the food will be watched from the time it is prepped to when it is delivered at the table. If I need to use the facilities B.J. will accompany me. If Grace shows up, I am not to say anything to her, just get up and walk out between Brian and B.J." She took a breath and opened her mouth to continue, but Marc held up a hand to stop her.

"Okay." He looked around the table. "It sounds like you all have this down. What time are we meeting in the lobby tomorrow?" Marc asked, speaking to no one in particular.

"One o'clock sharp," Melanie said loud and clear.

Paige wanted to whisper "teacher's pet" but figured she was already in enough trouble.

Paige got up when everyone started pulling away from the table. Marc came around and gave her a hug. "Sorry about that. This whole thing is making a little crazy."

His apology made Paige feel bad about her behavior.

"No, I'm sorry. I know this is hard on you. You know a great deal more about this man than we do, so I understand your concern. Just know that I will follow your instructions tomorrow to a 'T.' The last thing I want to do is put anyone in jeopardy," Paige said, leaning back to look him in the eye.

"How about this." He tapped her nose. "I will continue to plan... and pray, and you pray more."

"I can do that, Chief," Paige said, giving him a mock salute.

"It's good to see you laugh and display that crazy humor of yours," Marc said, looking down at her with love shining in his eyes.

"Wait until it comes back full force." She raised her eyebrows at him.

Marc just smiled at her. "Bring it on."

"Remember you said that," Paige said, letting him go.

"Are you going to make me regret it?" he said, placing a hand on his chest.

"Only a little bit," Paige said, showing him her forefinger and thumb that were barely an inch apart.

Brian came around to her other side draping his arm around her shoulder. "I can see you were a handful when you were young."

Paige glanced up even farther at Brian before looking back at Marc. "He thinks I stopped when I was young. You're going to have to school him, Marc."

"I don't call her 'Brat' because I'm feeling nostalgic," Marc said to Brian.

"Do I get to call you 'Brat' too?" Brian asked.

"No. One endearment per person, and you have already chosen yours," Paige said, feeling feisty.

"So you're okay with 'Baby Girl'?" Brian asked, smiling down at her.

"It's not bad, but you can only say it with a smile."

"Done," he said. "Now let's get out of here so you can get to your room. Tomorrow's going to be a big day."

Paige sighed at his statement. Tomorrow. What she wouldn't give for it to be the day after. That would be fun. She couldn't wait to see B.J.'s face when she gave him his birthday present. No one had said anything, so Paige figured they were all preoccupied with the lunch meeting and forgot about her and B.J's birthdays, which was fine with her. She never liked all the fanfare, and she didn't know how she would feel with not being able to share it with Brandon.

Chapter 34

Melanie stepped out of the sleek Town Car holding Marc's hand. She hadn't slept a wink and her eyes felt gritty. She applied more eye makeup to cover up that fact and sunglasses over that which she would have to take off in a few seconds. As they stepped aside to wait for Brian, Paige, and B.J., Marc placed his hand on her lower back and leaned into her.

"How are you doing?"

"Somewhere between nervous and terrified," Melanie said, barely opening her mouth so no one looking at them could guess her feelings.

"I won't leave your side at any time," Marc whispered before pressing a kiss behind her ear."

"Okay," Melanie replied.

When B.J. was smoothly behind Paige they moved forward. Melanie noticed one of Paige's hands inside the fold of her sleeve and knew she was running her fingers over the texturized, beaded bracelet she wore in high-stress situations. She sent a small prayer up to God and redirected her thoughts to her husband.

Melanie allowed Marc to step in front of her and distracted herself by watching him move in the slate-gray suit with a hint of metallic thread woven through it that she'd bought him for his last birthday. It had cost a mint, but it was worth it. The color showed off his broad back and slim hips. It was lightweight, so he could wear it during the spring and summer. His long legs ate up the sidewalk, and she shifted her attention to the restaurant doors in front of them.

When Marc stepped inside the front door he was stopped. He was asked to widen his stance and raise his arms by the biggest man Melanie had ever seen in person. Her blood pressure spiked, and she could feel her ears grow hot. He was at least a foot taller than Marc and half a foot taller than Brian, with massive shoulders and arms that strained the suit he was wearing. He patted Marc down, and Melanie waited for her turn, wondering if she would be able to get her feet to move when the time came.

When Marc stepped aside, a woman came forward, dressed much the same as the man, but her features were less intimidating. Melanie let go of the breath she'd been holding and stepped forward. Melanie relaxed a little when the woman stepped in front of her with a wand. The fact that the woman looked as if she could bench-press her, gave Melanie little concern because her eyes were kind. She didn't smile, but she did look Melanie in the eye before she started waving the wand in front of her.

"Please hold your arms out."

Melanie followed her instructions and within a few seconds was done and told to stand next to Marc.

"Still good?" Marc whispered.

"Good enough," Melanie said, watching for Paige who was safely ensconced between her father and brother. She felt Marc's hand guide her farther into the restaurant and took a moment to look around. The place Brian had chosen was opulent with ivory tablecloths, plush carpeting, and sconces on the walls with dim lighting, giving the restaurant an intimate atmosphere. Melanie noticed the only thing that was missing were diners. Well, except for the people sitting at the table in the center of the room.

Once Brian was done, she peeked around him to see how Paige was doing. She caught her eye and gave her a nervous thumbs-up, and Melanie relaxed even more.

Once B.J. stepped away from Mauro's security, they all were ushered to a table in the middle of the restaurant. It didn't hit Melanie until then the type of money these men had at their disposal. She wondered if Brian and B.J. were among them then quashed the thought. It was none of her business.

The men at the table rose as they approached. Melanie's eyes went to the older gentleman in the middle, and she recognized him right away from the photos Marc showed her the night before. He hadn't wanted her to be thrown off by anything. Now, as she had last night, she got the feeling there was something slightly familiar about him, but she couldn't put her finger on it.

Greetings started with Marc who seemed to purposely obstruct her from Mr. Mauro's view, but she figured Marc had his reasons. From what she could tell, Angelo Mauro was accompanied by his personal lawyer, Tomas, with a last name she would have to hear again to pronounce, and a good friend of the family, Giovanni Bianchi. The name rang a bell, but Melanie's thoughts fled when Marc stepped aside to reveal her.

Angelo's reaction was impossible to miss. Melanie wondered, as she looked at Angelo Mauro, how Marc had known seeing her in person would throw him off guard. Angelo had a swarthy complexion, but it went almost gray when Melanie stepped forward with an outstretched hand to greet him.

His friend Giovanni asked him if he wanted to sit down, but he shook his head to the negative and held out trembling fingers to shake her hand. It was as if he'd seen a ghost. His dark-green eyes contrasting drastically with the pallor of his skin but they didn't leave her face. Melanie knew she resembled Grace. The eyes made it hard not to, but whereas her mother's face was round, Melanie's face was oval and on the lean side. Her hair was thick, but the curl was looser than Grace's.

It wasn't until Brian stepped forward to introduce himself that Angelo stopped staring and then he brightened with interest.

"The chameleon," Angelo whispered at him before Brian stepped aside and Paige faced him head-on.

Angelo's gaze shot back to Melanie before returning to Paige. "Do all the women in your family have those golden eyes?"

"I'm the last, I'm afraid," Paige said before introducing herself to all three men. B.J. introduced himself, shook everyone's hands, and they all sat down.

"It looks like our ancestors are visiting us today," Angelo said, looking first at Melanie then Brian and Paige.

Melanie thought it was an odd phrase but it didn't take but another second before Angelo explained. "Melanie is the spitting image of my grandmother Liolli," Angelo addressed the table but looked at Melanie. It was disconcerting but not uncomfortable since his gaze was more curious than anything else.

"She didn't have your exquisite eyes or coloring, but you share her jawline and nose," Angelo went on, "The men in my family are on the shorter side. As we age, our wide chests get wider along with our middles, but the women are gorgeous, and you two are no exception," he said graciously.

Normally, Melanie would blush at such praise, but a part of her didn't want him to be pleased by her. She wanted it to be a struggle for him to look upon her knowing how she was conceived. Much like his initial reaction. She also knew that none of this would be resolved that way.

"I only wish we weren't here under such strained conditions."

Ha. Did the wealthy learn lines like that in school? *Strained conditions. He didn't know what a strained condition looked like.*

"Would you tell me about yourself while I try to put some of these ghosts to rest?" Angelo asked before taking a sip of his water.

"What would you like to know?" Melanie asked, not giving anything away. Her voice was firm and direct.

"Where do you live?" Angelo asked.

"I live in Atlanta with my husband," Melanie answered, wondering if she should try to be a little more courteous.

They all looked up when the sommelier arrived to take their drink orders. Angelo and his companions ordered wine. The rest of the table ordered tea and soda.

"And Paige, here is your daughter?" Angelo asked.

Melanie looked at Brian before answering. At his nod, Melanie turned back to Angelo. "Both Paige and B.J., uh, Brian Jr., are my children."

Angelo's startled eyes focused on Brian then B.J. "And you are Luca's grandson," Angelo said, and Melanie could see where his mind was going. There was a proverbial future powerhouse sitting at the table in front of him.

When Angelo recovered from his shock he looked back at Melanie. "Forgive me. I don't mean to be indelicate, but how old are your children?"

"They will be twenty-eight tomorrow," Melanie said without hesitation. "I was..." She gestured to Brian. "We were very young. It's a story I would rather not get into at a lunch or dinner table," Melanie said, and she wouldn't budge on that. Let him look it up.

"Excuse me," Brian broke into the conversation. "You said the word 'chameleon' when you greeted me. What did you mean by that?"

Angelo looked at him as if trying to read him then waited as their drinks were delivered.

"Would you like the waiter to come out and take your order at this time?" The sommelier asked.

"Give us a few minutes," Angelo said with a small wave. The man bowed and moved away quickly.

"Your grandfather told me that you work for him as Marco Sanza." Angelo shifted slightly forward in his chair. "There were many whispers about you and who you were to Luca. I hear even your father didn't know who you were. You were called the enigmatic Marco or 'chameleon.'"

"In my line of business, as you know more than anyone else, it is important to know who you work with. There was more than one family who did a background check on you, trying to figure out who you were. It was a source of some discomfort among us. I'm glad Luca could trust you. He is a good man." Angelo looked down, straightening his utensils before looking back up at Brian.

"Maybe one day you could tell me why you chose to remain invisible for so long."

Brian nodded, and Angelo's gaze returned to Melanie.

"I'm sure Brian shared some of my story with you, and your husband dug up everything he could to prepare you for this visit with me, but do you have questions of your own?"

Melanie didn't look to Marc for permission because she was going off-script. She just couldn't continue to trade niceties with this rapist in a suit that would have cost her more than one month's salary. Both Marc and Brian shared some of his recent exploits and the foundation he'd started to help raise awareness about the opioid crisis. Boy, had Grace been going for the jugular with her scheme.

Though Melanie could tell that the man before her wasn't the same man in character who assaulted her mother, her mother's words and description of the incident still had Melanie looking through a haze of red. The way he answered her next questions would shape their relationship going forward, if there was going to be one.

"I'm not supposed to ask you who ordered you to assault my mother out of respect for you and Luca. I'm also not supposed to ask you if you would have gone so far as to kill my mother because your lawyer there wouldn't want you to answer, but I am going to ask you another question now that we have met." Angelo didn't say anything. He simply nodded his head, his forest-green eyes going darker still.

"I know this meeting is so we could feel each other out and see if we can at least, trust one another." Melanie paused and Angelo nodded again.

"Have you considered the possibility that this formal acquaintance might grow into something more?"

"I have given it considerable thought, yes."

"Well, if you or I decide to take this acquaintance further than this meeting, I am going to need an apology. We can make sure it's out in the middle of nowhere. An open field, if you want, but if reconciliation is something you may want in the future, it will have to start there."

Melanie felt Marc's hand rest on her thigh but refused to look his way. She had to say this while she had the nerve and before she learned something that would make objectivity a challenge.

399

"Also, as you may have guessed, I am not one to hide behind formalities." She gave Angelo a rueful smile. "What you see is what you get. If we get to a place in this relationship where you want me at any time to acknowledge you as my biological father, then you will have to do the same in public. I will not *knowingly* be a dirty secret."

"What would that entail?" Tomas, Angelo's lawyer, asked.

Melanie thought about the question. She hated the thought of asking Angelo Mauro for anything but if she could leave this meeting with a commitment from him or his family not to seek retribution against Grace for her recent actions, Melanie would breathe easier. She figured if Mauro didn't deny her existence or parentage in the public eye, it may also keep him from causing Grace harm.

"It would start with, Angelo not denying the existence of children in the future if he is asked." She turned back to the man in question.

"And is there an underlying reason for this?" Tomas asked.

"Yes. It won't exonerate my mother, but it will help to explain to the other families why she did what she did almost forty years ago."

"You want to put the weight of your mother's decisions on Angelo?"

"No, I just want him to share some of it," Melanie replied. "Grace has been shouldering it all for the last three decades and more."

"Are you looking for some kind of public statement of his guilt, because I can tell you right now, that it won't happen."

Angelo laid a hand on Tomas' arm, and the man took a deep breath. "My apologies. I let my emotions get the better of me. I'm sorry for my tone."

At first, Melanie thought his apology was almost overly gracious, but when she felt more than saw Marc and Brian, out of the corner of her eye, relax a little, she understood the reason for his quick capitulation. *Her men.*

"I don't need you to make a public announcement. The statement your lack of denial will make regarding me is more than enough. It may bring up some uncomfortable questions, but I will leave you to answer those as long as you do not disparage my mother or defame her character."

"I just want to get this straight," Giovanni jumped in this time. "You came here today for your mother?"

Melanie knew her eyes flashed with anger but didn't try to hide it. "No, I came here for myself because at the end of all of this, I'm the one who will have to live with the decisions I make today," Melanie stated resolutely. She wasn't sure, but she thought she saw a look of admiration in Giovanni's eyes. *Who was he?*

"I was prepared for your mother to show up, but I am glad we are able to handle this in a more civilized manner. Your love and loyalty for your mother are commendable." Angelo said with no condescension Melanie could tell. Marc's hand tightened on her thigh, and Melanie laid her hand over his to soothe him.

Angelo continued, "I know the last thing you need from me is a compliment. I can only imagine the magnitude of the hatred you felt for me upon receiving the news you did from your mother. You've handled yourself with a great deal more decorum and graciousness than I would have at your age."

"That being said, I promised Luca that no harm would come to Grace by my hand or anyone in my family. I plan on keeping that promise."

Melanie tried not to show how relieved she was, but she knew she failed when Marc's hand released its hold and began rubbing in circles around the area.

"What about your nephews?" Marc asked, drawing both her and Angelo's attention.

"They are being...disciplined. It will be some time before they could be considered a threat if they choose to do Grace harm." Angelo delivered the cryptic sentence as if he'd just handed over family secrets. Melanie looked at Marc to see if he understood Angelo's answer any better than she had. The crease between his brows told her everything.

"I would very much like to get to know you and the rest of your family. I have no right to ask this of you, but I would like you to be under the protection of my family name as well," Angelo continued, and Melanie turned back to find him watching her.

401

"I'm married. I'm not changing my name," Melanie said before she could catch herself.

Angelo smiled for the first time since the meeting started. Melanie saw more of the man and less of the monster she'd painted him as, but she steeled herself against softer feelings toward him.

"No, that is not what I am asking nor would I wish it with your husband's protective presence," Mauro said sliding a look at Marc before continuing. "I am merely requesting that in addition to the Sable family protection you receive, you would welcome protection from the Mauros as well."

Melanie had no idea what that entailed. She barely understood how Luca kept her and her mother from being hidden at the bottom of a body of water all these years. *Was that a stereotype?*

"You've just met me. You barely know me," Melanie said, uncomfortable with agreeing with something she knew very little about.

"I must confess that I am not as ignorant of you as I first portrayed," Angelo said, looking a little uncomfortable.

What? Melanie thought.

"What?" she voiced.

"I have known about you since your early teens. I just assumed you were Major Morganson's…"

"Colonel," both Melanie and Paige corrected.

Angelo seemed to remember Paige at that moment and stared at her before speaking again.

"My apologies, Colonel Morganson." He gave Paige a slight bow and turned back to Melanie.

"After Grace left Chicago, but before she turned state's evidence, I was given the task of watching her. It was from afar and only to make sure she stayed away from Chicago."

"Why?"

"I'm sorry, I can't say, but after Grace was released from witness protection, I was curious about her reappearance. I thought Paige was her daughter the birth certificate had your mother's and father's name on it." He blinked at her, but Melanie made no move to explain.

"Anyway, I would look you up from time to time from afar. I could never find a good picture of you though." He looked at Marc. "I'm guessing that was your doing?"

Melanie followed Angelo's gaze to Marc catching confusion cross his face.

"That was me," Brian said, raising his hand.

"Then me," B.J. said.

Angelo looked between the men with something akin to pride. "I see you have more resources than I first believed."

Melanie was going to have a talk with Brian and B.J. after this meeting, but surreptitiously reached over and squeezed Brian's forearm in gratitude.

"As I was saying, the reason I was surprised when you stood in front of me today was that I was never able to obtain a close and clean picture of you. Your presence today, however, has only confirmed the character I was able to witness over the years. It always was and continues to be completely in your hands as to whether you want to have anything to do with me from this day forward." Angelo finished.

Melanie watched Angelo. She couldn't read any guile in his eyes, but she knew very little. She tamped down on the fire roiling in her gut. Could she forgive this man who had helped place her mother on the path of vengeance? She didn't know.

"I don't know," she answered honestly.

Angelo regarded her for a few seconds. "You have a very good heart. I honestly thought you would straight-out reject my offer."

Well, that was something. At least he knew where he was supposed to stand.

"At the risk of sounding like I'm trying to buy your forgiveness, I want to let you know that there has been a trust established in your name. It is more in name of back child support."

"Shouldn't that go to my mother?" Melanie asked.

Angelo gave her an apologetic smile. "My legal counsel advised me against that, but there is no law stating that you can't share those funds with her. There will be another account established for you as my daughter. It will be reserved in an escrow of sorts until you decide whether you wish to expound on what has begun here. As an extension of my family line, there will be one established for Paige and B.J. as well." Angelo looked over to her daughter.

"Um, Paige, I couldn't help notice that your husband wasn't here today. You did state your title as Mrs., did you not?"

"I am widowed... six"—she cleared her throat—"six months now," Paige responded.

Angelo crossed himself as well as Tomas and Giovanni. "My condolences, sweet child. Any children?"

"I have twin girls from a different father. They will be fourteen in June," Paige said, her voice gaining volume.

Angelo frowned, his mind obviously going through the calculations. Melanie could tell he considered asking but changed his mind. Paige offered the information Melanie wasn't sure he even wanted to know after she gave him a few more seconds to think about the possibilities.

"It wasn't by choice nor was it with my consent, but I adore my children and wouldn't trade them for anything.

"But you... you were a bambina... a baby," Angelo blustered, indignant on her behalf.

Paige shrugged, used to the reaction. "Does it really matter what age? Is rape better at any age?"

Her question hit the table like a pile of bricks. Melanie looked at Paige, wondering if she'd led the conversation to that very point, but Paige's eyes were only sad.

Melanie looked back at Angelo who slumped back in his chair looking as if he'd aged twenty years in the last few seconds.

"No," he answered.

"No," Paige repeated.

And Melanie saw the understanding of his actions hit Angelo head-on. God bless her daughter.

Melanie looked down so no one saw her preen over her daughter's wisdom, but her desire to gloat was cut off by Paige's next words.

"But it ends with me. My girls will not carry the sin of my grandmother," Paige said.

Melanie's whole being went still. She kept her head down, rocked by Paige's words.

"What do you mean?" Angelo asked solemnly, bracing himself as if expecting another blow.

"Grace chose anger and hate instead of forgiveness, and it ate her up from the inside out. My... Melanie is my heart. I love her deeply, and in some ways I am just as protective of her as she is of me. I would do anything to keep her from hurting. I defer to her decision. If she chooses to have nothing to do with you, that includes me, but for whatever offense we are speaking of today, I forgive you. I hold no ill will toward you because I choose not to. It ends with me. My grandparents' sins will not be visited upon my children." Paige finished with the same quiet firmness she began with.

A handkerchief appeared in Melanie's lap, and she used it to dab at her eyes as Marc's arm came around her shoulders.

"She's a mighty little thing, isn't she?" Marc's words startled a giggle out of her, helping her gain her composure.

"Yes," she answered, drying her eyes and taking a deep breath before looking up again.

"I'm thinking lunch wasn't the best idea," Angelo said, looking tired. Melanie's heart went out to him. She knew Paige was right, but Melanie wasn't going to force something she wasn't ready for.

"Do you have a card or a phone number I can call when I make up my mind?" Melanie asked Angelo, seeing some of the lines smooth out on his face. He reached into his suit pocket and pulled out a gold card case. He removed a card and wrote something on the back.

"This is my personal number. You may use it at any time."

Melanie accepted the card looking down at his smooth script before looking back up at him. "Okay."

He gave her a sad smile. "It was an extreme pleasure to meet you, Grace Melanie Miller and you, Paige Tatum. You as well, gentlemen," Angelo said before getting to his feet.

"If you wish, lunch is on me. The food here is excellent."

"Thank you," Marc said, standing and shaking hands with each of the men. "I think we may head out as well. Brian and B.J. followed suit in standing, but Melanie and Paige remained seated though they shook everyone's hands.

When Angelo and his companions left, Marc held his hand for Melanie. She took it, and he hauled her up and into his arms for a hug so tight it was just shy of painful. She welcomed his strength, taking from it what she needed for the moment.

"You did good, love. You did good," Marc said, and she wanted to cry all over again to release some of the emotion sitting on her chest, but resisted the urge.

She pulled out of his arms and turned to face her daughter. Paige was in the midst of being ribbed by her brother. "You are a force to be reckoned with, little sis."

"Little sis? I'm only like two hours younger than you," Paige said, frowning.

"Yeah, you are also little in stature but not in spirit. You are the real deal. You carry that everywhere you go."

"That what?" she asked, baffled.

"That... fire, that... conviction," he said, seeming not quite satisfied with his descriptions.

"Don't you?" Paige asked him matter-of-factly.

"Not as much as I wish," he returned.

"Then work on it," Paige said with a shrug as if it were that easy.

B.J. looked at Brian and shrugged like Paige, and Melanie couldn't help her smile.

Melanie stepped toward Paige, taking her face in her hands. "Listen to me carefully, and don't interrupt until I'm done." Paige's lips quirked into a smile at the irony of her statement.

"I am sorry I didn't have the wherewithal to decree what you just did, but I am so proud of you, Baby Girl, for taking that on and going after the root of this tree we have been bearing the fruit of. You inspire me to be better, to do better. God blessed me with someone precious in you." Melanie kissed Paige's forehead and draped an arm around her shoulder.

"I don't know about you, but I'm up for a big juicy burger with chili fries. Let's go get the girls and Mason."

"Your wish is our command," Brian said, gathering everyone and moving them toward the door of the restaurant. Once they were outside, Melanie noticed everyone taking deep breaths.

Melanie looked up at the sky and whispered a small prayer. "God, please help me forgive Angelo, not just for him, but for myself and my children. I think he could benefit from a real family, and we could heal some of our pasts."

"You ready?" Marc asked her, holding the car door open for her.

"Yes I am," Melanie answered before gifting him with a smile and a kiss before climbing in.

Chapter 35

Mason ran his hand over the letter in his pocket again, wondering if he'd missed his moment to give Paige the birthday letter from Brandon. He was happy it was the first and only one Brandon had asked him to give to her. He didn't know how Brandon would know that they would be spending this day together.

His whole relationship with Mason was rather uncanny. Mason had now communicated more with Brandon after his death than he had while Brandon was alive. Some people might find it morbid, but Mason was grateful for each note Brandon had written him in his notebook. There would come a day when he turned a page in the notebook, and there would be no new writing, and he would be on his own in his relationship with God, but he was sure he would still talk to Brandon. How odd would it be if Paige one day turned his way and truly saw him as a man instead of the father of her daughter and a good friend. Would he still talk to Brandon? Probably not about Paige, but definitely about everything else.

"So, what's in your pocket?" B.J. asked, scooting on a chair closer to him in the bowling alley where B.J and Paige were starting their birthday celebration before dinner.

As he thought about his answer, Mason watched Melanie take her turn at sending the bowling ball down the lane toward a set of pins, coming one pin short of a strike. He glanced up at the projected scorecard. Melanie was in the lead again.

"What pocket?" he asked, still looking up at the scorecard as he calculated what his team, consisting of Gladys, B.J, and Marc, would have to score to get back in front. B.J. patted his jacket in the place where Brandon's letter lay, scorching a hole in his suit.

Mason shied away and consciously kept himself from touching his jacket again.

"I have to warn you. If that's a ring. It's way too soon. She isn't ready."

Mason turned to B.J. confused. "What?"

"I was just saying. I think you are a really good guy and all, and I can tell Paige has a special fondness for you, but I don't think she's ready for a commitment."

Mason couldn't believe what B.J. was saying. Why would he think Mason would propose this close to the death of her husband? She was still grieving. Almost every other conversation they had, she mentioned Brandon in one way or another. Mason understood the need to keep Brandon present for a little while longer.

Mason wished he had someone to talk to who knew Rachel when she passed so he could keep her close a little longer. Vivian was open to talking about her and he tried a time or two but he always felt so bad about failing her by not finding a cure for Rachel... not that there was one to be had. It didn't matter, he still ended up bawling like a baby when he left Vivian's room.

"Man, I'm not proposing," he hissed. "I'm carrying a birthday letter from her husband."

B.J. gave him a peculiar look. "Were you two good friends?"

"Not until the end," Mason said, making sure they couldn't be overheard.

"And how long have you been in love with Paige?" B.J. asked, sobering.

"Sometimes I think it was from the moment I ran into her in the hospital when she came to talk to me about donating a kidney for Vivian," Mason answered, slipping back to that moment before coming back to the present with a thud when B.J pushed him.

"Stay with me, man," B.J. said. "What happened?"

409

Mason looked around, feeling uncomfortable with speaking about his feelings around Paige's family members who could walk up at any time. He watched Gladys walk up to her lane, squat down, and push her ball hard. It rolled down the middle of the aisle, taking at least twice as long as Melanie's to reach the pins, but as it had the time before, rolled right through the middle of the set knocking each pin down.

Mason shot up out of his chair in exultation to cheer and congratulate Gladys. "That's what I'm talking about! Give me ten!" He held up both hands, and she slapped them hard enough for them to burn.

"I'm coming back," B.J. said, pointing at him before passing them to retrieve his ball and take his turn.

And that is how it went for two hours of bowling. B.J. would grill him on his relationship with Paige, commiserating with him one moment and encouraging him the next in between plays. By the time they were all ready to go to dinner, Mason's team was ahead by fifty points mostly due to Gladys' stellar skills, and he was tired of reminiscing.

"How long would you wait for her if you knew she would eventually come around?" B.J. asked him while they were washing their hands in the men's restroom before going to their table. Mason, no longer distracted by all the things going on as they bowled, looked at B.J. in the mirror.

"Are you asking me these questions because you want to know about my relationship with Paige or because you are in need of advice for yourself?"

B.J. became focused on washing his hands... again, and Mason knew he'd hit the nail on the head.

"My answer is, 'There is no amount of time I wouldn't wait for her.' Now tell me what her name is."

"Simone," B.J. said before moving to dry his hands. "I've known her since high school. I knew from the moment I met her that she was the one, but my situation with my dad wasn't favorable to anything as serious as marriage. It's kind of hard to build something when you limited on what you can share. I'm hoping that now that I'm free to

410

share everything about myself she won't leave me for not being one hundred percent truthful."

"There's only one way to tell."

B.J.'s face fell. "Yes, I know. Tell her, but there is more to it."

Mason waited for him to elaborate, but B.J. clammed up.

"Come on. Everyone is probably waiting for us to join them, and I've worked up an appetite since lunch. I think the best time to give Paige the letter is when you are alone with her after dinner. I'll buy you some time with the girls. Paige will probably have questions as to why you are handing her the letter anyway." B.J. balled up his towel and threw it in the basket before exiting.

Mason followed him, wondering just how fast B.J.'s mind worked if his mouth was that quick and who this Simone was.

***

Dinner was a festive affair. Mason had chosen a family-oriented American cuisine restaurant with great views of the pier, and he could tell Paige enjoyed it immensely. After dinner, their waiter rolled out a three-tier, white-and-blue birthday cake with "Happy Birthday B.J. and Paige" on it, compliments of Brian. There were sparklers on top, and Vivian and Gladys were so taken with them Mason made a note to get sparklers for their birthday cake as well.

The sparklers were extinguished and one candle was added for each of them. "To your first year celebrating your birthdays together. May this be the start of a tradition that lasts a lifetime," Brian announced, and everyone cheered and sang "Happy Birthday" before the birthday twins blew out their candles.

The waiter cut the cake, and Mason was pleasantly surprised to learn that each tier was a separate flavor. He chose the chocolate fudge just like Paige and sat back to watch as presents were passed out to the two.

Mason got Paige a rejuvenation spa package from him and Vivian with reservations for the next day in the hotel she, Melanie, and Marc were staying in. Paige opened the envelope unable to keep the grin off her face. When she read the gift certificate her eyes widened then grew dreamy. "How did you know? This is exactly what I need."

He shrugged, feeling self-conscious. "Vivian and I noticed how much you were traveling and knew that those long, uncomfortable plane rides were probably taking their toll."

"You two are spot on." Paige kissed Vivian, who was sitting on her left, on the cheek then stood up to lean over the table. Mason met her halfway, and she kissed his cheek as well.

Her eyes sparkled when she leaned back. "Thank you."

Mason just nodded because his heart was halfway up his throat, probably in an effort to reach her.

Brian reached over and handed Paige another envelope. "Happy birthday slash housewarming," Brian said as he sat back down to watch her open the envelope.

Mason watched her face, curious to see if her reaction would give away the present.

Paige read the piece of paper and started laughing. "Really?" She looked from Brian to Marc and Mel who nodded then back at Brian and laughed again. "This is too much."

Oh Lord, please don't tell me he bought her a house. Mason prayed.

"Brian got me one of those sheds you can turn into a studio. Since Marc and Melanie have all that room in the backyard, he bought me a ready-made writing studio."

"That's fantastic!" Mason said with a little too much enthusiasm, and Marc looked at him strangely, but Melanie grinned knowingly. He brought his cheering down a level.

Paige pulled a box out of her purse, handing it to B.J. "What did you do, Paige?" B.J. asked even as he unwrapped the box. Mason watched as Paige looked on nervously. She seemed to flourish around her family.

"No way!" B.J. exclaimed, taking a plastic-encased comic book from the box. "This is the first issue. Do you know how hard this is to find? How did you ever get it?" B.J. said, not taking his eyes off the comic book.

412

Paige shrugged. "I know someone who knows someone." She smiled brightly.

"I like the people you know," B.J. said, putting the book back in the box and passing it to his dad who read the cover and gave a low whistle.

"I think you just made his decade, Paige. I think you're good for at least five more birthdays and Christmases."

Paige preened and blew on her nails before rubbing them against her top until Melanie threw a napkin at her head obscuring one eye. Instead of immediately taking it off, Paige tilted her head so she could still see everyone. Mason chuckled at this silly side of Paige, and Vivian and Gladys laughed riotously.

"Hey, it's still early yet. Dad, I'm going to take Vivian and Gladys to the arcade near uptown." He looked toward Marc, Melanie, Paige, and Mason for permission. They all nodded, knowing B.J. would protect the girls with his life if need be.

"I'm going to turn in. It's been an intense couple of days," Melanie said and Marc yawned.

"You going to be all right?" Melanie asked Paige. Paige looked at Mason.

"I'll make sure she gets back safe and sound," Mason said.

"Oh yeah, go on old-timers," Paige said, getting a warning look from Melanie.

"Hey, B.J., drop me off on the way, would you?" Brian asked B.J., and just like that Mason was going to be alone with Paige.

Everyone hugged and kissed each other goodnight and headed their separate ways.

Mason walked Paige out of the restaurant and into the cool evening. "Does it ever stay warm at night?"

"Yes, in the summertime."

"Mmmm," Paige said, seeming to give it consideration.

"Would you like me to take you right back, or would you like to take a walk?"

413

"A walk sounds nice after all of that food and cake. I feel like a roly-poly," Paige said, taking a breath and looking up at the sky. Mason started walking to the east toward the more crowded section of town.

"Funny, you don't look like a roly-poly. You look like a beautiful and very mature twenty-eight-year-old," Mason said, allowing himself one compliment about her looks.

"Thank you," she said, flashing him a smile but it faded away too soon. "Sometimes I feel much older."

"I get that. You've been through a lot in the last couple of years," he said, measuring his steps to hers.

"Is that all? Sometimes I think I will look back at my cousin's funeral and see that ten years passed by," Paige said, going quiet for a moment.

"I spoke to Dominy today. He called me for my birthday along with Ava, Makayla, Marjorie, Victoria, Richard, Lady Menagerie, and so on." Paige laughed. "I didn't even think I knew that many people.

"Dominy and I talked for almost an hour. It seems we had some catching up to do. He and Robin moved to Montana and are expecting another baby. I wish he would have returned any of my calls. I could have visited them when I was in town."

"He took Brandon's death extremely hard as well, and he doesn't have the same foundation in God as you do."

"Yes, I know it wasn't personal, but I miss him. He promised to keep in touch and send me baby pictures. I bet Nicky is huge now."

Mason didn't respond, thinking she just needed to get that off her chest.

"Thank you again for that spa package. I'm going to really enjoy myself. I haven't pampered myself in a long time."

"I figured as much what with you taking care of Gladys, holding Thanksgiving and Christmas at your home…" he said.

"It goes by quickly on one scale and doesn't seem to move on the other," Paige said, sounding nostalgic, and Mason knew she was thinking of Brandon.

"One day they will balance back out."

"Yes, one day," she mused.

414

With the mood she was in he figured there was no better time. He reached into his inner jacket pocket and pulled out the envelope. "One more present for you," he said as he handed it to her.

She gave him a quizzical look before looking down at the envelope and stopping short. He watched her read Brandon's writing a couple of times before looking up at him.

"You had this?" Paige asked.

"Yes."

"How long?" He could tell she was trying to put something together but didn't know what.

"A couple of months. Ava gave it to me and told me it was for your birthday."

"How did she know we would be together for my birthday." Paige's voice had gone whisper-thin.

"Brandon was the one who told her to give it to me for you."

"Really? She said that?"

Mason nodded in affirmation.

Paige looked down at the letter.

"If you want to, there are some benches on the next street. You could read it there."

She shook her head without looking up. "No, that's okay. I'll wait until I get back to the hotel." Paige held on to the letter for another block before putting it in her purse.

Once it was out of sight, Paige came back to the present. She asked him to give her a mini-tour, and he guided her toward Millennium Park. He showed her the Crown Fountain, and she posed against one of the lighted towers. He led them toward the pavilion and back around to the car since he wanted to be home before B.J. took the girls back to his place.

Mason parked and walked Paige to her hotel room where he intended to say goodnight, but when she looked up at him anxiously with her big golden eyes and asked if he would stay just long enough for her to read the letter, he could do nothing but concede.

He stepped inside and sat on the couch and called B.J. to get up an update. He told him it would be at least another half an hour before the

415

girls were ready to go, and they were about twenty minutes from his house. He thanked B.J. and hung up. He waited in silence for a few minutes before getting restless and turning on the television. It was a few minutes more before he heard crying coming from the bedroom. He turned off the TV and listened to her sob: his heart hurting.

Mason got up and slowly walked through the living area to the door of the bedroom almost afraid of what he would find. When he peeked around the doorway, he saw Paige on the bed curled in a ball and felt compelled to comfort her.

Wordlessly, he slipped his shoes off and crawled up on the bed behind her and curled himself around her. Her body shook with her sobs, and he held on tight just to keep her from splintering apart. It was another ten minutes before she calmed though it felt like ten years as he could do nothing but hold her.

"Thank you," Paige said when she'd gained enough composure to speak. "I'm sorry. I don't know why it hit me so hard. It's not like I haven't said goodbye to him before, but it felt so real this time. Like he was letting me go so I could let him go, and that is so like him. So unselfish. It used to make me so angry sometimes... just like it did now.

He felt her take a deep breath and realized he was still holding her tightly. He loosened his hold and moved back to give her some room.

"Do you have to go?" she whispered.

"No, not just yet," he said and scooted back more to make room for her as she turned around.

"I know this sounds off, given that I am lying here in my own tears, but thank you for being obedient and giving me that letter and thank you for a wonderful birthday."

He chuckled and pulled her into him again tucking her head under his chin and stroking her hair. He took in her scent and hitched breathing and both ranted at and thanked God for this opportunity. She was asleep within five minutes, but he held her for five more before he removed himself from around her and the bed.

Mason walked around to the other side of the bed and pulled the covers over her. He stood there watching her for a moment before giving in and laying a kiss on the crown of her head. Mason turned off the lights and retreated from the room feeling for the first time angry at Brandon for putting Paige through this with his letters. If there were any more letters, Ava would have to deliver them herself.

Chapter 36

Paige flopped down on the couch in her room, her muscles feeling like jelly. She couldn't remember the last time she felt so relaxed. Her thoughts were clear, and as many times as Brandon's words from his letter came back to her throughout the day, they didn't devastate her as they had the night before. It was as though she'd purged the heaviest part with her tears, and the masseuse did the rest.

Melanie walked out of the bathroom and sank onto the couch next to her. Melanie had surprised Paige by joining her at the spa. It was even better than if she'd gone by herself with her nonstop thoughts.

"Why can't I feel like this all the time?" Melanie murmured.

"Because then we would flow into the drain in the bathroom."

"But what a way to go."

Paige could think of better ways to go but to each his own.

"Are you sure you'll be okay with Marc, Gladys, and me leaving tomorrow?"

"Yes, Brian and B.J. will be in town until I start back on the circuit next week. Besides, Mason and Vivian are here, and they promised to show me the town when I can move again."

Melanie let go of a half-hearted giggle. "I'm glad to see you feeling better. You were quiet this morning."

"After everyone left last night Mason took me for a walk through Millennium Park and handed me a letter from Brandon."

"What? How did he get it?"

"Ava. It seems Brandon has been orchestrating from the great beyond," Paige said with only a little ire.

"I take it the letter wasn't as good as the one you received for Christmas," Melanie said, sounding winded.

Paige tried to shake her head but gave up. "Nope."

Melanie let out a groan.

"Exactly. Mason walked me to the door, and I asked him to stay until I read the letter. I sensed this one wouldn't be as lighthearted as the last one and I was right. I went into the bedroom to read it, and it made me so angry and sad, but there was no one to take it out on, so I ended up on the bed in the fetal position, crying my eyes out. Somewhere in the depths of my pain I felt someone come up behind me and put their arms around me. You know for a moment I thought it was Brandon, but I caught the scent of Mason's aftershave and in a way that was better. It's hard to explain." Paige finally got up the strength to look over at Melanie.

"He held me like he thought I might shatter into a million pieces and let me cry out my frustration. I turned around to talk to him about how I was feeling, and he tucked me in next to him and held me until I fell asleep." Paige paused for a moment, wondering if she should share her next thought, but there was no one but God closer to her than Melanie.

"I had a dream about Mason in the early morning on the day after my wedding," Paige said quietly.

"You're kidding me," Melanie said, sounding aghast.

"No, I am not," Paige replied with her head resting once again on the back of the couch and her eyes closed. She didn't need to see Melanie's face; she heard everything she needed to in Melanie's voice.

"What did you do?"

Paige scoffed. "Turned over and tried to forget it."

"Good girl."

"I didn't though. I thought about that dream, wondering if I was supposed to have chosen Mason or if I harbored undealt with feelings for him."

"It was that kind of dream?"

"No, but I felt cherished... safe... on fire as if I'd been struck by lightning." She went quiet for a moment, thinking of the dream. "Finally, I chalked it up to the enemy trying to cause problems or the extra-rich chocolate mousse I'd had the night before." Paige giggled.

"Why did you share that with me?" Melanie asked.

Paige thought about her answer for a few seconds. "It was one of the reasons I was so jacked up when Brandon died. Albeit, it was a very small piece of the puzzle, but it presented itself with all the other doubts about whether I should have married Brandon."

"I'm glad you resolved that issue. I would hate to think of you giving up that testimony."

Paige smiled to herself. "Me too."

"It sounds like Mason gave you what you needed though. Last night," Melanie said nonchalantly, but Paige wasn't fooled.

"Yes, he's very good at that in general." Paige paused for a beat. "How long has Mason liked me?"

"What? I... I guess you're going to have to ask him?" Melanie stuttered.

"When B.J. started asking me questions about Mason in the car on Christmas night, did you discourage him from continuing because you knew then?" Paige countered.

Melanie let out a sound somewhere between a groan and a growl then struggle to sit up. "Yes. Okay?"

Paige laughed. "What's the matter?"

"I didn't want the thought of how Mason feels for you to get in the way of your friendship with him. You two get along so well, and I don't want the fact that he has feelings for you to cause any awkwardness."

Paige thought of Melanie's reasoning and understood why she would come to the conclusion she did, but what Melanie hadn't considered was Paige's feelings for Mason.

"Do you think he will act any differently if he finds out I know?"

"Well, I won't tell him, but I'm talking about how *you* will act toward him," Melanie said.

Paige shrugged. "Why should it change?"

Melanie directed all her focus on Paige. "Are you saying you welcome his feelings?"

"I'm not saying that I'm ready to do anything about them, but the thought of Mason having feelings for me isn't revolting."

"What?" Quick as a blink, Melanie turned from mother to girlfriend.

"You like him? You like him." Melanie gasped.

Paige felt her ears turning pink as she shook her head while she tried to organize her thoughts.

She finally shrugged because she didn't know what else to do. Paige looked around the room trying to find a place for her focus to land. "I don't know if I can confess it. It feels like if I say something it becomes real and that both thrills and scares the mess out of me."

Melanie leaned into her line of sight, forcing Paige to look at her. "No one is rushing you. If Mason has liked you for as long as I think he has, he is going to be the last one to expect anything from you."

"What if I'm never ready? I mean, what if my feelings don't grow past a great friendship, fondness, and underlying awareness. What if he gets tired of waiting?"

"Only two of those questions are ones you can do something about. The other is completely up to him?"

Melanie placed her hands on Paige's shoulders and turned her so they were face-to-face. "This is what I was trying to save you from, though you would have to work your way through these questions at some point. You are still grieving and still dealing with a lot of emotions. The fact that you've noticed Mason is a good sign, but take care of yourself. Find your footing again. Ask yourself if you are even interested in another relationship and this time with your child involved."

Paige put up her hands, feeling overwhelmed. "Okay, I'm not ready. I'm not ready."

"No, but when you are, it will be a wonderful thing," Melanie said, taking Paige in her arms.

"You think so?" Paige laid her head on Melanie's chest.

"Absolutely."

"Do you think Brandon would be upset with me choosing Mason?" Paige asked quietly.

"Why? You chose him the first time."

Paige laughed more out of surprise at Melanie's perspective than humor. "I did do that, didn't I?"

"Yes, Baby Girl, and you made a very good choice."

"I did, didn't I," Paige said, envisioning Brandon smiling down at her.

"Yes," Melanie said, punctuating her answer with a squeeze.

***

Happy Birthday, baby,

We both know I wish I could be there to celebrate it with you, so I won't even go there. Happy 28th birthday! I hope you did something spectacular. I'm afraid I'm going to have to make this one a short one. I don't have as much energy as I did before. I sometimes wonder if I should have written you more letters or if this will get my message across.

I love you through space and time.

Live, Paige, with every fiber of your being. Shine so brightly I can see you from heaven. Not for me, but for you and those who are fortunate to share your life. It is a gift.

Continue to change lives. You've changed mine for the better.

Now it's time to give someone else a chance to bask in your light.

Until we meet again.

You have all my love except what I take with me.

Brandon

Paige folded up the letter from her birthday and placed it with the other letters she'd received from Brandon while he was courting her, while they were married, and after. She'd found a gorgeous ornate box while window shopping in Richmond one afternoon and knew right

422

away it would be a good home for the letters. Paige ran her fingers lovingly over the pieces of paper before closing the box and holding it to her heart for a few moments.

It was hard to believe that eight months had gone by since Brandon passed. She'd made it eight months when she first thought she wouldn't get through eight hours. Her heart squeezed at the thought of ever being back in that place. It was definitely a good argument against time travel and possibly falling in love again. Paige placed the box in her suitcase then began packing her other belongings around it.

She came across one of the journals Vivian had given her almost a year before, and her mind went straight to Mason again.

Paige had broken her promise to herself. She'd responded poorly toward Mason since confirming with Melanie that his feelings for her went beyond friendship. At first, she told herself that she didn't want to lead him on but realized he hadn't asked for anything before she found out. Then she told herself that it was inappropriate for her, a new widow, to have any thoughts of Mason outside of friendship, let alone the thoughts she'd begun to have right after her birthday.

She'd relegated their talks back to Saturday afternoons and then only spoke with him for a few minutes using business or tiredness as an excuse. He'd sounded disappointed and that hurt her, but it was better than breaking his heart if she got it wrong.

Paige had just come off a three-day fast, praying, and holding up one question to God. She took every dream, wish, or thought of what she now desired and set them at God's feet. She asked Him if it was part of His perfect plan that she, Mason, and Vivian become a traditional family with her and Mason becoming man and wife.

She made peace with her thoughts and her heart, opening herself up to whichever answer He gave her. For the last two days she prayed, feeling a peace grow in her heart, giving her the courage to look at her relationship with Brandon from the beginning to the end with as much objectivity as possible. Paige went over all the places she'd surrendered to Brandon that weren't his burdens to carry. One was her barely managed anxiety that she unfairly placed in his lap, looking for his love for her to cover and soothe her disorder when she and God had already worked out a perfect form of management.

Paige knew she had grown in so many ways since dedicating her life to God, but the constant need to feel safe drove her to make decisions she knew deep down were unfair to others.

That morning Paige had awakened with the answer on her heart and cried like a baby in both relief and praise for the God she served who would take such painstaking care of her from her innermost desires to the emotions that would trip her up.

It was hard not to constantly go over what God had put into place regarding her family from the time before she was born. Paige thought her praise for Him inadequate when she came into the knowledge that both of her children were alive. Now she was overwhelmed by the magnitude of it all. There was no place in her life she could think back to where God wasn't shifting, moving, or staying the hand of the enemy for her sake. It was hard to contain. It flowed through her, making her want to share it with everyone she encountered, in some form or fashion.

Paige wanted to call Mason, but the conversation she needed to have with him couldn't be conducted in the half-hour it would take to get to the airport. Neither was it a conversation she wanted to have over the phone. She owed it to herself to look him in the face when she asked him if he'd asked God if she was his wife. The thought brought a smile to her lip, but that same smile dimmed a little as she considered the things she had to do before she could see him again.

Paige looked again at her suitcase and shook her head. It was no coincidence that she would finally come to these realizations right before she went to DC. Tension rolled through Paige at the thought of what would be coming at the end of this trip because she couldn't leave DC without visiting her mother. She prayed she didn't get in front of God on this; that she didn't allow the fear and shame she'd associated with Grace for so long to prevent her from doing whatever it was God wanted done.

Angelo Mauro had kept his word and didn't touch Grace, and it went a long way toward shortening the rift between him and Melanie who had called him only a couple of weeks before.

Melanie said it wasn't long, and there was no commitment for more. She just had a conversation with him, asking how his health was and how work was going. She told Paige that she asked him how the weather was in Chicago, and the man had just started laughing, but Melanie said it sounded like he didn't laugh much, so she didn't comment. Melanie refused Angelo's invitation to his home for a family get-together for the Fourth of July but told him she would call him again and she had earlier that week.

From what Paige could discern, it had gone much the same way, and Melanie believed Angelo was just fine with the gradual building of their relationship. It looked like Melanie was on her way to truly forgiving Angelo Mauro. It made Paige wonder how Melanie could forgive her father who brought her into the world under such violent circumstances, but Paige couldn't seem to let go of the desire to hear her mother acknowledge just one of the offenses she'd made against Paige, even after everything she'd said in the restaurant.

Paige shook herself out of the thought. Grace had suffered all her life from the hands of men and herself for decisions she'd made decades ago. Who was Paige to make sure she got her drop of blood in restitution for what Grace had done to her while blinded by pain?

I'm a child of God, that's who, and I matter, Paige thought to herself.

"You are also a child of mine and I will hold her accountable if you will only surrender it to me."

Paige tried to find comfort in His words but struggled in her mind to let go of the debt she knew God should have. She wanted to negotiate with Him regarding the surrender of the debt and request that He not turn around and pardon Grace. Paige wanted Grace to have to work out at least some of her debt, but it was pointless. Besides, what measure of punishment, above and beyond what Grace had already gone through, was enough?

Paige stomped her foot, giving in to the last piece of resistance in her body and gave up her mother's debt to her Heavenly Father.

"It's yours," she said to the ceiling, and in a symbol of her words, she took a deep breath, closed her suitcase, gathered the rest of her belongings, and left the room.

Chapter 37

"Hello?" Paige said into the phone, letting her sleepy voice tell whoever was calling that it was way too early.

"Paige."

Her sister's tear-filled voice was like a dousing of cold water, waking her instantly. "Melanie, what's wrong?"

Paige tried to make sense of the words through Melanie's sobbing. All she could understand was shot and Ross? He was a nice guy, but was Melanie crying hysterically because Ross was shot?

"Ross was shot?" Paige asked.

"No…" Melanie's words were too garbled for Paige to understand.

"Melanie, is Marc there? Can you put him on the phone?"

The phone hit something as it was being passed, and Paige took her ear away from her phone for a moment.

"Paige?"

"Yes."

"Sorry, I'm on the other line trying to arrange a flight to DC. Paige, the word is that Ross shot Grace."

Paige's hearing narrowed as if someone muted the sound of the world. *Oh no. Oh God, please, no. I never talked to her. I never got to…*

Marc's voice pulled Paige out of the tunnel. "It doesn't look good. Can you get to Georgetown General?

427

Oh, thank God, she was still alive. Paige didn't even stop to think—"yes, I can get there." She would take a cab. He would know how to get her there.

"Paige, Grace was admitted into the trauma center a half an hour ago. Be careful, Paige. It's all over the news. A neighbor heard the shot and came out to investigate. He saw Grace laying in her doorway and saw Ross driving away in his car. Law enforcement is looking for him now," Marc said, then the phone sounded like he was holding his hand over the mic. When he came back on she heard a weird echo, like he was in the restroom. "I'm trying everything I can think of, but it doesn't look like we will make it in time."

Paige closed her eyes at the thought that Melanie wouldn't get to say goodbye to Grace. "Have you called Brian, B.J., Luca, or Richard?"

"Um," Marc started, and Paige interrupted him.

"This is what family's for. Emergency or not, you need to be able to call one another if you need help. Call them, then take their help and get on a plane with Melanie to DC. I'm getting dressed now, and I will head straight to the hospital."

"Yes, ma'am," Marc quipped.

"Tell Melanie I will call her back when I get an update on Grace," Paige said, looking around for her pants and shoes.

"Okay."

"I love you, Marc. Tell Melanie I love her too, and we will get through this."

"I love you too and we will. We've been through worse," Marc replied.

"Yes, later," Paige responded before hanging up. She called a cab from the courtesy hotel book and got dressed.

Fifteen minutes later, the cab pulled up in front of the hospital. Paige paid for the ride and practically ran from the car to the main hospital information desk. She gave them Grace's name, date of birth, and that she was in the trauma center or trauma (ICU). The nurse looked up something on her computer and directed Paige to the next level down. She told her to check-in at the nurses' station, and someone on the trauma team would come out to speak to her.

428

Paige followed the woman's directions. When she arrived at the next station and told the nurse who she was there to see, Paige was asked to fill out some paperwork while she waited and was directed to a family waiting area. She answered the questions that she could and left the rest blank. She just couldn't concentrate on all the information she needed and how to get it at the moment. Paige looked around the room and took a few deep breaths before praying for guidance.

When she opened her eyes, she saw a family huddled together in the corner of the room. The mother had her arms around a boy of about ten and a girl somewhere around eight. They were both crying softly, and Paige's heart went out to them. She began to pray for them and expanded her prayer to include the other people in the waiting room, as well as who they were there for.

Paige was in the process of praying for the nurses at the desk when her phone rang. She got up and stepped into an alcove when she saw who it was.

"Paige?"

"Hi."

"I just got a call from Richard. Are you okay?" Mason's voice came through the phone. His concern was clear in his tone.

"Yes, I'm at the hospital waiting to hear something from one of the doctors," Paige said, looking around to make sure she could see the waiting room doorway.

"Do you know what happened?" Mason asked.

"Not really. Marc said a neighbor heard a shot and found Grace at her front door. He thought he saw Ross driving away. I haven't had a chance to find out much more," Paige said, biting her nail then forcing herself to put her hand down.

"Paige?"

"Yes?"

"Are you okay? Do you need anything?"

You

"Um, no, I don't think so."

"Do you want me to hang on the line with you?" Mason asked.

Paige checked her phone. She had a full charge, and her purse had an independent charger in it.

"Yeah, that would be great."

"So how did the conference go?"

"What?" Paige asked, caught off guard by the question.

"Your conference," Mason repeated.

"Oh, yes. It went better than expected," Paige said, shifting from foot to foot. "We shifted the discussion a little to cover some of the current topics in the DC area such as some of the police violence. People participated, and though the discussion got a little heated at times, there was a lot of interaction, which made the night go quickly."

"You sound tired." The concern was back in Mason's voice.

"Yeah, Melanie pulled me out of a dead sleep."

"Not sleepy, weary," Mason clarified.

"Ah, yes, that too. It's been a long tour. Thank goodness it's almost over. I just want to go home and sleep for a week."

"Are you all finished packing? When do you have to be out of your apartment?" Mason asked.

"My lease isn't up until October, so I have plenty of time," Paige said, her attention becoming divided when a doctor walked in and looked around.

"Grace Dillard's family member..."

"Mason, I gotta go. The doctor is here."

"Okay, call me anytime if you need anything."

"I will," she said as she took the phone away from her face and approached the doctor.

"I'm Grace Dillard's daughter," Paige said, raising her hand.

The doctor's face didn't show a bit of relief at seeing her. *That wasn't good.*

"I'm Dr. Crane. Your mother sustained a gunshot wound at close range. The timeline isn't certain, but we believe it was an hour and a half ago. It looks like the bullet ricocheted off a rib, puncturing her liver." He glanced over her shoulder briefly before returning his gaze to her eyes. Paige resisted the urge to turn around and continued to give him her undivided attention.

"A lacerated liver can go from treatable to fatal depending on how severe the blood loss and our ability to contain it." He paused a couple of seconds before continuing and she wondered if Grace was already gone.

"I'm afraid your mother's liver suffered significant damage. Though we were able to slow the bleeding, we are unable to stop it. She is as comfortable as we can make her right now." He stopped even though his voice went up as if he would say more. She stared at him while she tried to make sense of his words.

This was it. There was no more time. Paige's throat closed for a moment, and she thought she wouldn't be able to get the words out.

"Can... is... may I see her?"

"Yes. I'll take you back," he said before turning around.

She caught up to him quickly. "Did you work on her?"

He gave her a wary glance. "Yes. Myself and a few others."

Paige nodded. "Thank you for your efforts."

Dr. Crane looked at her and swallowed hard. "You're welcome. It's my job."

"Then thank you for not calling in sick." Paige wasn't sure why she'd said what she did. She chalked it up to nerves.

Dr. Crane went quiet, and Paige took that moment to update Melanie before she stepped into no-phone land. She quickly tapped out a text to her sister trying to give her as much information in as few words as possible:

Mom is in Trauma ICU
The doctor said they are unable to stop the bleeding.
She has little time. I will tell her you love her whether she is awake or not.

Paige followed him quietly for a moment then remembered why her mother was there. "Did she say something about who shot her?" Dr. Crane met her eyes briefly before looking away. "A DC private detective came by and got a statement from her when she was lucid enough after surgery. They're looking for her husband. Is he...?" He faltered.

"He's not my father. I barely know him. I've only met him once," Paige said, then fell silent again as the doctor led her through the emergency room then the Intensive Care Unit. She went over the information again in her head. Ross, the one who said he wanted the family to get along, shot Grace. Paige wondered if it was over what Grace had been into with the Mauro nephews.

Paige forced herself to concentrate on the moment. She would deal with everything else later. Right now, she was just trying to get her emotions under control. *Why her?* Why would she be the one to be the closest geographically to Grace at a time like this? Melanie should be the one. Grace should get peace in her last... what—minutes, hours?

Paige checked her emotions, and surprise of all surprises, she felt cheated... cheated of the time she hadn't wanted to take in the first place.

Paige wanted Dr. Crane to speed up then she wanted him to slow down. It could take a half-hour to get to the room if they walked very slowly, couldn't it? Time. It was time that was working with and against her. At this moment it was also time that was working against her mother and would be for eternity if Paige did not get herself together.

Dr. Crane opened one last door into a room with beds set against the wall, separated by curtains, then led her to Grace's cubicle.

"She should come around any moment," Dr. Crane said as he stood aside and allowed Paige to step to the side of Grace's bedside.

This woman looked nothing like the overbearing and intimidating woman Paige grew up with. She looked fragile and pale and holding on by a thread. Paige hated this. Eight months and she was right back to another family member's deathbed.

Had she missed something the last time that she was supposed to get right this time? Paige took in the tubes running to and from the different machines to different parts of Grace's body.

When she saw the doctor move out of the corner of her eye, Paige turned to him, giving him a watery smile. He nodded and left. She would have to remember to pray for him.

Paige moved forward and rested her hand on her mother's cold hand. It too had a thin tube running from it to an IV bag set to the side. Paige glanced back up at Grace's face to find her watching her. Grace's eyes were sharp, which was disconcerting with everything they were probably pumping her with.

"Hi." *It's me. The one you never wanted.*

Grace didn't respond. She just stared at Paige, and Paige wondered if her first assessment of Grace's eyes was wrong. She tried again.

"Sorry, it's just me. I was the closest," Paige said apologetically. "The rest of the family is on their way." Paige blabbered on, wanting to apologize again, feeling wholly inadequate. "I was at a conference. It ends Thursday. I was coming to see you on Friday to talk. To make amends," she finished with a shrug.

"Perfect," Grace rasped, and Paige came a little closer to figure out what she meant. Was she mocking her or being serious? Grace's mouth lifted in something between a smile and grimace and Paige realized Grace had meant her presence was perfect.

"I'm sorry," Grace said.

Paige stared at her for a moment, stunned by the two words she never thought she'd hear come out of the woman's mouth, let alone directed at her. Two words, and in one second, twenty-eight years of pain drifted to the background.

Paige's lips tipped up into a soft smile as she looked at her mother. "I need you to do something for me because I really want to see you again."

Grace frowned in confusion.

"I need to tell you about the night I was going to give up and take my life in high school," Paige said, pulling the sole chair in the space up to Grace's bed.

Grace looked at her with sad eyes.

"Don't worry, it has a very happy ending," Paige said, catching Grace's look.

433

"I had a friend in high school who kept inviting me to Bible study. It was ironic since I thought I was the last person a church girl would want to be seen with. I was low. I think at my lowest. I was slowly siphoning off Dad's new wife's valium and had enough to do some real damage, but I decided to take my friend up on her offer and promised myself if I didn't get the answers I needed, I would go home afterward and take them all." Paige took a breath.

"Still bad," Grace said, grimacing.

"Don't worry. It's about to change." Paige wasn't sure if Grace's grimace was from pain or her story, but she decided to do some condensing.

"I wasn't in the church for more than two minutes when a small-framed mother of the faith approached me and asked me if she could hug me. I didn't want to offend her, so I went with it. After a few moments, I began to get uncomfortable, but she kept hugging me then she told me something I will never forget," Paige said, emphasizing her words by rubbing Grace's hand.

"She said, "Baby, God's been waiting for you. He says He is going to prove to you you are worth it." I asked her what she meant by 'worth it' and she said, "Worth His Son dying on the cross.""

"I won't deny that I was confused, but her next words hit me like a ton of bricks. She said, "His Son died on the cross, baby, so that you don't have to." Then she told me what God had revealed to her about me, including what I was thinking of doing later that night."

Paige gazed into Grace's eyes. "I'm not going lay your life out before you, but I do want to offer you an invitation."

"To Bible study?" Grace whispered, and Paige saw the small flare of life in her golden eyes.

Paige smiled at her joke but sobered quickly. "To accept Jesus in your heart so you may receive eternal life with God instead of eternal pain and suffering away from Him."

Grace's eyes had become misty and she swallowed. "I deserve pain."

Paige's heart dropped at her words because she could see Grace believed them. "Don't you think you've suffered enough?"

434

Grace went still but Paige kept rubbing.

"None of us *deserve* eternal life. You can't work for it. It's a gift, and yes, Grace, you are worth it, but He won't force you. God isn't like that. You have to accept willingly."

"I'm not good. I've hurt you," Grace said, her eyes growing sad and unfocused. She grimaced again, and this time Paige knew it was due to pain.

Paige leaned in close. "You're right. You have hurt me, but I truly do not believe that God would have been urging me to forgive you and come to see you since the beginning of this year if He didn't want me to be right here, right now, trying to convince you that you are worth saving." Paige leaned back, her vision going blurry with tears. "You can have peace."

"Peace," Grace whispered. "I don't remember what that feels like." Her eyes became unfocused again.

"Let me show you," Paige said, not taking her eyes off her mom's face, though she was tempted to try and read the machines. If God wanted this done, He would give them time.

"What do I do?" Grace asked and exhaled, and Paige had to swallow down a sob of joy.

"You just repeat after me."

"Dear Lord," Paige began.

"Dear Lord," Grace repeated, closing her eyes.

"I accept your Son, Jesus Christ."

"I accept your Son, Jesus Christ."

"In my heart," Paige said, giving her hand a little squeeze

Grace's breathing became labored. "In my heart."

"I believe He died for my sins."

"I believe..." Grace said, then took a couple of breaths, "He died for my sins."

Paige watched as a tear escaped from the side of Grace's eye and ran into her hairline and nearly lost it. She swallowed down the emotion and continued with a firm voice. "And rose from the dead."

435

Paige gave Grace some time to collect her strength. She watched her intensely, waiting. When Grace finally breathed in deep, Paige took a breath with her and mouthed the words while Grace said them.

"And rose... from the dead."

"Jesus is my Lord and Savior," Paige said slowly and softly, watching her mother fade.

"Jesus... is"—Paige saw more than heard the breath Grace took— "my Lord... and Savior," Grace said, then smiled ever so slightly.

Paige had heard of people's faces transforming right before death, but she'd never seen it for herself until that moment. The lines etched by anger and pain on Grace's face faded, and the smile became serene.

Grace took another breath, and another, then let go of one last exhale.

"Amen," Paige whispered, unable to keep the tears at bay any longer. "I'll see you again, Grace. I'll see you again. Then she laid her forehead on her mother's hand and sobbed in earnest at what God had done for her mother, for His child.

It was a few minutes before she felt a hand on her shoulder. "Miss?"

Paige sat up, drying her eyes with her sleeve and taking another look at her mother's body before turning to the person wanting her attention. It was one of the nurses she'd seen moving back and forth earlier.

"I'm sorry, but we need to unhook her and get her body ready..." She gave Paige a gentle and apologetic smile. Paige nodded then turned back to Grace's body as she slowly let go of the hand she held.

"She went peacefully. You can see it all over her," the nurse said as Paige got to her feet.

The tears started again, and Paige struggled to speak. "Yes." She looked over at the woman giving her a watery smile.

"Yes, she did."

"Was she your mom?" the nurse asked as she moved Paige to get to the machines.

"Yes," Paige said, meaning it from the bottom of her heart. "She was my mom."

"She was blessed to have you," the nurse said by way of conversation, but it reverberated through Paige.

"Thank you," Paige said, stepping back, not quite sure what she was supposed to do now. She looked around the large room again and felt selfish. Her mother got to go home, but would these people?

"There is a counselor available to walk you through the rest of this process. Since your mom was a gunshot victim and died due to overwhelming trauma and blood loss from a lacerated liver and perforated bowel, her body is now part of an investigation and will be taken to the county examiner's office. Your mother's personal effects will go along with the body to assist in the autopsy. I'm sorry. It's protocol in these situations."

Paige nodded at the woman, taking in the information, but her eyes kept straying to the other beds in the room.

"The rooms you would normally be taken to for family members in your situation are still being occupied. I deeply apologize for the delay. It has been a very long night. If you would just step to the side of the nurses' station over there"—she pointed to a space to the side of the counter seemingly out of the way—"the counselor should be here soon to take you back," the nurse continued before she pulled the sheet over Grace's head. Paige closed her eyes briefly, trying to keep herself rooted in the present.

She walked over to the place the nurse directed then began to pray for each person in each and every bed for physical healing or eternal healing with God. She prayed for every nurse, orderly, and doctor she saw and when she'd covered everyone, she took out her phone and called Marc but there were no bars.

"Miss?"

Paige looked over to see a small woman looking up at her.

"I'm Dr. Rashi. Are you family to Mrs. Dillard?"

"Yes," Paige answered.

"I am so sorry for your loss."

"Um, thank you," Paige said automatically.

I'm here to take you to a family meeting room. Will there be anyone else joining us?"

That was fast, Paige thought. "Yes, but I'm not sure how long it will be…" Paige let the sentence fade since she didn't know how many hours it would take for Marc and Melanie to arrive.

"We received a call from a Luca Sable. Is he any relation to you?"

Paige blinked at the woman, confusion clouding her thoughts. "Um, he's my, my great-grandfather."

Dr. Rashi nodded. "Will you come with me. We've made some arrangements for you and your family."

She led Paige back through the door of the trauma center and down the hall to a room with a huge window overlooking the grounds behind the hospital. It looked like an extended stay hotel room with a table in the corner, a wide-screen television on the wall, and a number of couches and recliner chairs. "There is a small refrigerator next to the sink over there." The woman pointed to the divider Paige was standing next to. She peeked around it, spotting the items in a small alcove.

"Would you like to go over the next steps now, or would you like to wait for the rest of the family?" Dr. Rashi asked.

"I'll wait," Paige said, feeling relieved not to have to go through the process alone.

"Very good. We will direct your family here when they arrive, but otherwise, you will not be disturbed. There are blankets and pillows in the cabinet to your right."

Paige looked around the room again, not sure of what she wanted to do first then looked back at Dr. Rashi. "Thank you very much."

Dr. Rashi gave her a short bow and left the room.

Paige's phone gave a short vibration in her pocket alerting her to a message. If she got a message that meant she had a signal. She took out her phone and tried dialing Marc again.

"Paige." Marc's voice sounded wary as if he'd been waiting for her call and hoping it wouldn't come.

"Yes." Paige swallowed trying to put off from saying the words a second more, knowing how it would affect Melanie. She exhaled slowly. "Grace is gone."

"What did she say? Has she seen Grace?" Paige heard her sister's voice in the background and winced.

"Okay," Marc replied to Paige. Then she heard him cover the phone as he turned to give Melanie the news.

The moan and whimper Paige heard in the background tore through her, but it still didn't prepare her for the deep, penetrating silence and wail that came out of Melanie the next second. Paige reached out, catching hold of the back of a chair to keep herself standing. She shook from the effort and barely heard Marc when he spoke again.

"Luca's sending his jet. We are on the way to the airport right now. We should be there in a couple of hours. Brian and B.J. are already on the way."

Marc exhaled. "They have an APB out on Ross Dillard, so I think you should stay at the hospital until we arrive."

Paige could hear Melanie crying in the background.

"Take care of Melanie. I'll be all right."

"Okay, talk to you soon," Marc said before hanging up.

"Okay," Paige responded because she didn't know what else to say.

She stood there in the middle of the room trying hard not to hear Melanie's cries in her head over and over again.

Page looked for something to keep her mind occupied until the rest of the family arrived. Paige took her phone back out and called the organizer of the author circuit to let her know that she probably wouldn't be able to participate in the last two days of the conference in DC due to a death in her family. Then she called Carmen, her agent, to let her know what was going on and that there was a chance that she might have to miss the Christian Writer's Symposium in New York if her mother's autopsy took longer than expected.

Paige walked around the room touching various objects and seeing how the different appliances worked. She perused the small shelf of books and looked out the window at the trees blowing in the wind. The day was just dawning, and she felt like she'd lived a decade. She sat down in the recliner closest to the window and continued to stare out the window, letting the shifting leaves and the quietness of the early morning soothe her.

Paige didn't know she was asleep until she heard her name and felt something brush her cheek.

"Paige."

She opened her eyes, feeling a little disoriented then turned to see Brian crouched next to her. How long had she been sleeping?

"Hi, Baby Girl," he greeted.

"Hi," Paige whispered in return.

His eyes were sad, and it brought back the circumstances of the day. Tears rushed to her eyes but she held them back. Brian's eyes softened, and he leaned in giving her a hug. Paige rested her head on his shoulder for a moment and let his strength seep into her.

When Brian released her and leaned back, Paige noticed a pair of legs on either side of him.

Paige looked up, seeing B.J. first to Brian's right and Mason to his left. *Mason. Mason was there?* She was stunned into inaction for a moment and just stared at him. He gave her a ghost of a smile, his expression telling her he wasn't sure if she would welcome him, and she regretted all the time she'd wasted.

"Hey, Paige."

Page forced her gaze from his face and looked over to her brother.

"Hey, B.J." Page moved to stand up, and Brian gave her a hand. She got to her feet, feeling stiff and more tired than she'd felt in a long time.

Paige moved, greeted her brother with a hug then turned back to Mason. She meant the hug to be quick and perfunctory, but his arms felt so good, and she remembered the night he'd held and comforted her until she fell asleep.

She felt Mason's head come closer just before he whispered in her ear. "It's okay. I've got you now."

The dam that she reinforced to keep the tears at bay broke, and she held fast to him as she cried. She didn't have to go through this alone.

"Thank you," she said when the worst of the tears abated. "I hoped you'd come. You are always there when I need you."

"And I always will be," he whispered, hugging her to him a little tighter before letting her go.

Paige bowed her head, a little embarrassed by her loss of control, but Mason bent down and wiped the tears from her cheeks with his thumbs.

"What time is it?" Paige asked.

"It's a little after seven," Mason answered.

That meant nothing to Paige. She didn't know how long she had been sleeping.

"Marc and Melanie should arrive in fifteen minutes," Brian added.

Okay, so she hadn't slept all that long. Paige looked around at the three men staring back at her with varying degrees of concern on their faces. "I'm okay, really I am. I am just really happy to see you all."

She watched their shoulders relax and walked over to the area set up like a living room with a couch and chairs placed relatively close. Paige sat at one end of the couch and Brian and B.J. followed suit.

Mason went to the sink and counter that held an individual-cup coffeemaker and a small microwave. "Would you like some coffee?"

The thought made her smile. "Yes, please."

He smiled back, and though he looked a little tired, his hazel-green eyes sparkled. When he turned to the coffee machine, Paige looked over at B.J. who was also smiling.

"What's up?" she asked, wondering what was so amusing.

"Nothing. I just missed you," he said, his eyes looking just like Gladys' when she told half-truths.

"You mean you didn't see me last night?" she said, referring to his penchant toward hacking.

He glanced at his dad quickly before turning back to her with wide eyes.

"I was at work last night. I'm sure I don't know what you're talking about," B.J. said.

"She's talking about you hacking into her conference's digital feed," Brian said, crossing one leg over the other. "I saw it over your shoulder when I came in the other night. You owe them ticket money."

"Yes, Dad." B.J. sounded contrite, but Paige saw his lips twitching.

"Granddad said you got to see Grace before she passed," Brian said, turning to Paige.

"Yes," Paige answered.

"Was she lucid? Did she say anything?" Brian asked, uncrossing his legs and leaning forward.

Paige wasn't sure what to say. Did she share the conversation they'd had? She hadn't thought of asking Grace about Ross. She was focused on saving Grace's soul.

"I, um, we talked, but it wasn't about her injury, sorry," Paige said, feeling awkward.

Brian looked at her with confusion written on his face. "Then what did you talk about?"

"Her soul. She accepted Christ before she died," Paige said, looking at them then Mason when he turned to look at her with something akin to astonishment.

Brian's face cleared and he shook his head, smiling at her.

"Told you, Dad. God's anointing on her is powerful." B.J. grinned proudly.

Paige blushed under their praise. If they only knew what it took for God to get her there. Maybe she would tell them sometime... or not.

"When Melanie and Marc arrive, we will talk to the counselor about where they are taking Grace's body. Melanie will want to see her," Brian said, and Paige nodded.

Mason brought her the cup of coffee and sat down beside her on the couch. She took a sip and hummed. "Thank you."

"You're welcome."

She saw Brian looked at Mason then the coffee machine before looking over at B.J. who burst out laughing. Paige smiled to herself and took another sip.

"Would you like some coffee, Dad?" B.J. asked.

"Why sure, son. Thank you for asking," Brian responded before looking at Mason who looked between everyone and flushed beet red.

She patted Mason's hand to soothe him. "I appreciate the special attention. I needed a little bit of that."

Mason relaxed, but she saw he was trying to control his smile. She looked at Brian, wanting to warn him to behave, but he just rolled his eyes.

A few seconds later, they all turned to the door when it opened, and the moment Melanie walked in the door, Paige handed her cup to Mason and met her sister with a hug, feeling like the day could finally move forward.

Chapter 38

Melanie took the proffered handkerchief from her husband. She would have to buy him a dozen or so to replace a few of the ones he'd loaned her. They now had makeup stains she was pretty sure wouldn't come out. She dabbed at her eyes, hoping her waterproof mascara did its job.

Melanie looked up at the casket set at the front of her church wishing it was closed. The embalmers couldn't capture the air of serenity and peace Melanie had seen on Grace's face when they were led in to see her at the hospital. If she hadn't witnessed it herself Melanie would have had a hard time believing Grace had received the peace she'd rejected all her life.

When Paige told her that Grace accepted the Lord, Jesus Christ as her savior, Melanie felt such profound gratitude for God and her daughter that she hugged Paige and began jumping up and down with her in the extremely comfortable and expensive-looking room the family met in at the hospital.

Melanie stage whispered what she wanted to shout. God was awesome. His works were perfect and there was no one greater. She gave Him the highest form of praise with her lips, but it didn't feel like enough. She could praise God every moment of every day and it still wouldn't be enough to convey her gratitude for answering her prayers with a "yes" and "amen." Melanie would see her mother again. Her mother was happy and at peace. She was finally healed, inside and out, and God had used her daughter to lead her to Him.

Every so often throughout the days leading to the funeral, Melanie couldn't help but break out in a shout, unable to contain the joy in her heart. Paige had kept her word. She'd ended the curse that had started generations before. It stopped with Paige because she let go of her right to seek retribution and forgave Grace. The thought caused the tears to come again, and Melanie laid her head on her husband's shoulder.

It seemed that no one needed to seek retribution in their immediate family even if they had wanted to. Ross Dillard had been stopped at Reagan International Airport trying to leave the country under an assumed identity and fake passport. The DC Police Department spotted his vehicle through a traffic camera but lost him when he changed vehicles in the middle of the morning.

Ross may have gotten away if he hadn't purchased a ticket under the name Grace had given the detective when he came to question her in the hospital. When asked about any alias he might have, Grace mentioned a passport she'd found in one of his bags months before but didn't ask him about it. She explained that Ross was a contractor for Homeland Security and could have had it as evidence of some sort. That piece of information panned out when Ross Dillard presented the fake passport and was taken into custody immediately for the murder of his wife who he later said had cost him his job, career, and reputation when she'd used his credentials to schedule a shipment of black-market opiates into the United States.

When Angelo flew in to offer his condolences and assistance in making arrangements for the sale of Grace's estate and funeral costs he also, very quietly, asked her if she were fine with Ross living out his life in prison. It took only two seconds for Melanie to understand what he was asking. She responded in no uncertain terms that Ross needed to serve whatever sentence he was given and that she wanted Angelo Mauro to promise never to offer her such a proposition. She also made him promise to come to church with them the next time he came to visit. He agreed to both as she'd known he would.

Melanie felt Marc turn and kiss the top of her head, and she let go of a quiet sigh and listened to the choir's rendition of "I'm Going Up

Yonder." It definitely reminded her of her mother, which made her cry happy tears all over again.

"You'll make yourself sick, baby," Marc said, referring to her tears. She would probably wake up with a doozy of a headache after all her sobbing today, but it couldn't be helped. "They're mostly happy tears."

"Okay, baby," Marc said, but she was sure he didn't believe her.

Melanie raised her head to check on the rest of the occupants in their pew. She looked around Marc to see Paige sitting up straight, eyes wet, staring at the casket. She was about to ask Marc to check on her when Mason turned to Paige. She watched as he whispered something in her ear and Paige closed her eyes on a long blink and let the tears cascade down her cheeks. Mason placed a tissue in one of Paige's hands and took the other in his as he pressed a kiss to the side of her head.

Paige smiled softly before dabbing at her eyes. *When had that happened?* Sure, Mason had been more attentive since they'd all met at the hospital, but this was something more.

Melanie looked beyond Mason at Vivian and Gladys who watched Paige and Mason and whispered back and forth between each other. She locked gazes with Brian who winked at her then looked at B.J. who seemed lost in his own world as he stared out the window to his right.

She wondered, not for the first time, where he went when he spaced out that way. Wherever it was it didn't seem like a happy place for her usually lighthearted son. She would have to find some time alone with him soon.

Melanie glanced behind her at Victoria and Richard, thankful they were not only able to make it but agreed to come. There was no love lost between them and Grace, but Victoria said they were there to support the living, and that was more than good enough for her.

Melanie's attention was pulled back to the front when the music stopped, and her immediate family shifted so that Paige could reach the side aisle. Melanie had strongly debated with Paige about saying anything during the funeral. Melanie told Paige she could say she was too emotional to speak on behalf of the family, but Paige said she wanted to do it, so Melanie conceded. It was as close to a eulogy that

Grace was going to get, and who better to do it than the person who was there at the end of her life.

Melanie looked up to see Paige watching her. She nodded her head, and Paige gave her a brief smile before she began.

"Good afternoon, everyone. I'm Elder Paige Morganson Tatum. Known to some as Baby Girl, others as Brat and then still some more as Lil' Sis, but first and foremost I am a child of God, and I can say that so is my entire immediate family." Paige's eyes moved back and forth along the pew and beyond. She smiled at a few people behind Melanie, her eyes lighting up and hovering on one section before returning to her notes.

"I am speaking on behalf of my family today because I wanted to tell you about the life of Grace Morganson Dillard, a woman who bred chaos, confusion, and dissidence among most of this family." Paige raised a hand to halt the people's murmurs in the church. "Bear with me because there is a happy ending." The attendees quieted down, and Paige continued.

Paige read her message to Melanie the night before and Melanie had promptly called her pastor to warn him and let him know that the intent wasn't to disparage or defame Grace's character, not that it was easy. He let her know that he'd seen quite a bit in his time and wouldn't interfere unless it got out of hand. Melanie assured him that it would not.

"Grace came from money and was well cared for as a child, but she was extremely independent and wanted to show her family that she could make it on her own and ended up on her own once out of college. She moved to Chicago and began to make a name for herself. She was recognized by some powerful people with powerful connections and ended up making some extremely poor decisions that followed her throughout her life.

"She was victimized but instead of being forgiving and finding a way to heal, she chose to become a victim of her own hatred and obsession with revenge."

"Did you know she was going to say this?" Marc whispered.

"Yes."

"Does it get deeper?"

"Not much."

"Good 'cause my mom is here," Marc said, looking over his shoulder.

Melanie followed his gaze and smiled at her mother-in-law who was a long-standing member of the church. She thought it only fitting to warn Mrs. Miller earlier that morning about Paige's "message", since she served in a couple of the auxiliaries and was held in high esteem. Mrs. Miller told her she'd witnessed a great deal in the church over the years, but wasn't too concerned since Melanie had only ever spoken of Paige's advocation and reverence for God as inspirational. After giving her approval Mrs. Miller had rushed Melanie off of the phone so she could finish getting ready.

"I know. I warned her already."

"Really?"

"Really."

Melanie saw Paige scan the small crowd, her face growing intense. "Grace followed that road for four decades. Can you imagine being angry, bitter, and bent on revenge for forty years?" Paige relaxed her features, her eyes softening and growing sad, and Melanie wondered if she'd seen where *she* may have ended up.

"It's hard to receive love that way. It's hard to receive forgiveness too… but God…" Paige said, and whispered agreements went up in the pews. Melanie heard Vivian and Gladys repeat Paige's last two words as well.

"I had the extreme honor of leading Grace to Christ seconds before she stepped into eternity. I wouldn't have had the opportunity if I hadn't forgiven her first." Melanie watched as Paige stared down at her paper for a moment then out into the sanctuary half full of people.

"I didn't share Grace's life with you to encourage you to do whatever you'd like in life, then quick, find someone to lead you to Christ before you take your last breath. I shared it so you would be that person who leads those who might be on their way to hell, to Christ. Whatever the reason, life is too short, and eternity is too long not to ask for forgiveness right now and forgive those who have hurt you.

448

"I shiver sometimes, thinking about the forty years worth of moments where Grace could have left this earth and stepped into an eternity filled with her emotional meter stuck between anger and fear with no peace, no love, and no hope for parole. But I praise God for the one minute she said yes to the peace, yes to the love, and yes to accepting Christ in her heart. Because it was the one that counted.

"God bless you," Paige said before stepping away from the stand.

Melanie stood up with the rest of the family and clapped in gratitude and pride. It was echoed behind them, but Melanie only had eyes for her girl who had chosen love over anger and hate.

***

As they stood in the receiving line to greet and receive condolences from the attendees before the dinner, Melanie saw Paige bounce in place before kissing and hugging Dominy and Robin who was pregnant with a baby in tow. How long had she been gone with Marc? Paige's eyes lit up with excitement, and they exchanged another round of hugs before Dominy and Robin continued up the line to her and Marc.

"I'm so glad you could make it, Dominy." She gave him a hug. "You too, Robin. Thank you so much. It really means a lot to Paige. She misses you."

Dominy gave her a sheepish grin. "Yeah, I could tell. I told her we would be around more. We actually came with the Tatum family."

That surprised Melanie, although she didn't know why. It made perfect sense that Brandon's family would keep Dominy and Robin from getting too far.

"When are you due? Melanie asked Robin.

"October," Robin said, rubbing her stomach.

"Wow, three months. Congratulations.

"We're holding up the line. I told Paige that we would be back to see her soon now that we lived closer to one another."

"I look forward to it too," Melanie said, shaking his hand.

A few people behind the Hartemans were Ava and Elias Tatum Sr.

Melanie reached out and hugged Ava before turning to Brandon's father.

"I'm sorry for your loss," Pastor Tatum said as he took her hands in his.

"And I am sorry for yours as well."

"Yes, well, they are both in a better place," he said, letting her hands go.

"Very true."

"Paige seems to be doing well," Elias, Sr. said.

"It's been a very rough year, as you well know, but I believe her father and brother coming back into her life have helped. Now that she has moved to Atlanta, would you consider coming to see us from time to time for holiday meals, and we will do the same?"

"That would be lovely," Ava said. "We've missed Paige."

"And I know that she's missed you, so we will do it soon."

"Absolutely," Ava said before moving away.

***

Dinner came and went in a blur, and it was all Melanie could do to keep her eyes open as she sat with Marc, Gladys, Vivian, Brian, Paige, Mason, B.J., Victoria, and Richard around the living room. It was such a wonderful feeling to be around family. It was also good to be done with all the ceremonies and events surrounding Grace's death and estate.

Melanie and Paige planned to fly to Washington DC the next week to go see if Grace kept any heirlooms or sentimental items from their childhoods. Paige would then go to New York for the Christian Writer's Symposium to finish her author circuit.

At the thought of Paige, Melanie popped up from the couch. She picked up her half-full cup of coffee and Marc's who opened his mouth but closed it at her look. "Paige, will you assist me in the kitchen? I want to get myself and Marc more coffee. Anyone else?" She glanced around to make her ruse look more legit. "No? Okay." She gave Paige one of her "Mother says" looks and walked to the kitchen.

Melanie placed the cups and saucers on the counter near the coffee machine and turned when she heard Paige walk in. Her confused expression cleared when she saw Melanie's stance and expression. Paige moved in closer, obviously not wanting anyone to overhear them.

"So, what's going on between you and Mason?" Melanie asked without preamble, thinking Paige should give her credit for waiting this long.

Paige gave her a little shrug. "Nothing. He's been here to support me and the family."

"I've seen Mason supporting you and the family. This is much more than Mason supporting you and the family," Melanie shot back.

"I don't know, Mel. We haven't talked yet, but I think I will be open soon to whatever happens," Paige said.

"Really?" Melanie asked, feeling a weight slide off her shoulders.

"Yes, I mean, I'm not ready to profess my love for him in a releasing-of-the-doves ceremony or anything like that, but he's a beautiful man with a beautiful heart, and he is exactly what I need when I need it, and I want to be that for him as well."

"You could do that just being his friend."

Paige gave her a look. "Uh, no."

Melanie squealed then put her hand over her mouth. "So you're saying there are other feelings there?"

"Yes, but that's all I'm going to say before I talk to him," Paige said firmly.

Melanie did a little hopping dance before coming over to Paige and hugging her tight. "I know... I know this doesn't make everything instantly better, but I am so happy for you. I think he's a great guy, so you have my blessing."

"I couldn't tell," Paige said once they parted.

"Don't sass me, child," Melanie said before breaking out into another smile.

"Are you thinking of moving to Chicago?" Melanie asked, her mind racing.

"Mom," Paige whined.

Melanie stopped, her mind and body going still. "You called me 'Mom,'" Melanie said, placing her hand on her mouth.

"I've called you 'Mom' before," Paige said, but doubt crept into her features.

"Not to my face, and after last year I thought it might never happen," Melanie said.

"I might have considered you my sister, but you've always been more of a mother to me than anyone else." Paige shrugged. "I guess I don't feel as though I'm betraying Grace by saying it, even though she was really only my mother in name."

"We haven't had a chance to talk one-on-one about your time with Grace. How do you really feel?" Melanie asked.

Paige took a deep breath. "I feel honored." Paige swallowed, and her eyes grew bright. "I feel liberated. I don't have to keep track of the reasons why I'm hurt so I can charge her with them when I see her. God gave me that... or well... took that away before I saw her... before she apologized."

"She apologized? I don't remember you saying that."

"I guess I forgot it because though it touched me, it wasn't what I was focused on at the end."

Melanie nodded in understanding. "Yeah." She reached for Paige one more time, hugging her tight.

"I'm so proud of you. You make the pain worth it," Melanie said.

Paige shook for a moment in her arms. "Why'd you have to go there. I've been doing so good," Paige said, pulling back and wiping her eyes in disgust.

"I love you, Paige," Melanie said, sobering.

Paige gave her a small smile. "I love you too, Mom."

Melanie draped an arm around her shoulder and began to lead her back to the living room. "What about the coffee for you and Marc?" Paige asked, trying to slow their forward movement.

"He doesn't need any more coffee, and I sure don't after this day. I want to be able to sleep when my head hits the pillow," Melanie responded before guiding Paige out of the kitchen, feeling satisfied.

Chapter 39

Paige smiled and signed her book while trying to stay engaged in conversation with the woman in front of her. It was becoming a daunting task at this hour, but she gave it her all because this was one of the reasons she wrote. She wanted to provoke thought and possibly introduce her readers to a few different perspectives on real-life issues. This was a culmination of that work.

It was the last hour of the last night of the Christian Writer's Symposium and Paige was spent. She was happy that she was able to join back up with the panel after missing the last two nights of her conference. Everyone had welcomed her back with hugs and warm greetings. She even received a few flowers and cards from them at the mortuary. The authors, schedulers, and agents of the event were all so sweet, she wanted to immediately accept the invitation to do it again the next year, but she stopped herself at the last second and thought about her future and all the places she could be in a year.

Paige handed the woman her book with a smile and readied herself for another book and another conversation, but all thoughts left when Mason stepped forward with one of her books in his hands. Paige couldn't help the blush that came to her cheeks or the smile that came to her lips.

"I heard that Paige Morganson Tatum was at this symposium and I knew I had to come," he said, handing her the book to sign. She glanced around him, seeing only five people left in the line.

"I'm your biggest fan," Mason said, his eyes light with humor.

"Melanie may beg to differ," Paige said as she began to sign the book. "What are you really doing here?"

"I wanted to see you."

"Really?"

"Really."

She glanced around him again. "Okay, it looks like I'm almost done. Would you like to get dinner?" She finished signing with a flourish and handed him the book.

"I think that's my line, but yes, I would love to. I'll just look around for a bit and come back," Mason said, grinning at her.

"Okay," Paige said, aware that she was smiling hard, but she couldn't help it.

The tiredness from moments before drained away, and she went back to signing, answering questions, and asking a few of her own. Twenty minutes later, she was kissing and hugging Carmen and the fellow authors goodbye. She turned away from the last author and came face-to-face with Mason. She gave him a smile, feeling shy all of a sudden. Mason held out his hand, never taking his gaze from hers. Paige felt like he was asking for more than just her hand, but either way, the answer was yes. She slid her palm against his and held on.

He pulled her next to him. "Where to?"

Paige had no clue. She opened her mouth and closed it again.

"I can think of someplace," he said, looking at her with a secret smile.

Paige followed Mason noticing that he hadn't let go of her hand. She loved that.

She quietly walked beside him for a block before having the urge to speak; she was so happy to see him.

"How's Vivian?"

"She's good. She is staying with her girlfriend for a couple of days. She convinced me to come actually."

"Oh." Paige didn't know how she felt about him having to be convinced to come see her.

"I wanted to wait until you were back home for a week. You know, when you were rested. Vivian thought it would be great to surprise you." He jumped in front of her, giving her jazz hands. "Surprise."

Paige burst out laughing then feigned surprise. "Don't do that." She placed a hand over her heart.

He chuckled and retook her hand before they continued walking.

It took a couple more minutes of walking before she realized where they were going. "We're going to that little all-night café, aren't we?"

"You remembered," he said.

"Yes," she said, looking up at him, and he grinned at her and led her around the corner.

Once they were inside and seated with coats off and warm drinks in their hands, Mason began to look uncomfortable, and Paige's attention focused on him even more.

"I came to New York for a specific reason," he began looking down into his cup of hot chocolate. "When you came into my life and nearly knocked me down in the hospital waiting room..."

Paige thought to interrupt him, but caught his teasing look and giggled instead. "I was shaken by you. I thought the surgery might do you more harm than Vivian good and I thought what a travesty that would be because you were exquisite."

Okay, he was coming straight out of the box with his feelings.

She couldn't halt the smile or the blush and stopped trying.

"I was divided between wanting to save my daughter and keep you from irreparable bodily harm. I was glad it didn't come down to me making the decision. I would have been a wreck," he said, giving her an apologetic smile.

"I ended up wrecked for other reasons though. Once when I found out that Vivian was your biological daughter and when it became clear that you'd chosen Brandon." Mason smiled ruefully. "That was a bad month."

Paige's heart dropped. This was where Mason told her why he couldn't be with her. Paige swallowed and tried to smile back.

"I did things that I wasn't proud of in the name of coping with a situation I couldn't handle. I got drunk to forget how much it hurt to finally want to live but denied what brought me back to life. When I finally pulled my head out of the sand and stopped feeling sorry for myself, I realized that you had done me a favor," Mason said, glancing up at her quickly, before his gaze to his cup.

"I didn't know why you drew me to you even as you sent me away, why I kept wanting to be in your space, even knowing I couldn't be everything you needed me to be. You did me such a great service when you told me that you couldn't see yourself with someone who you couldn't discuss the love of your life with. I didn't want to get it then, but it kept coming back to me with different relationships and circumstances, and I couldn't deny what I was fighting, what I had been avoiding, and you set all of that in motion when you didn't compromise your beliefs or settle for less than what God had for you.

"I wasn't ready to be what you needed at that time and you were right not to settle."

Paige knew she should be flattered, but his words were hollowing her out. He was telling her she was right to have rejected him, not to choose him, and a part of her agreed, but couldn't he see that he wasn't that same man?

"Okay," Paige said, just to try and be agreeable. There must have been some of what she was feeling in her voice because Mason looked up at her and searched her eyes. Paige swallowed to keep the lump growing in her throat from choking her.

"So..." Paige cleared her throat. "So, you want to just remain friends," she voiced to clarify what he'd been saying.

Mason frowned at her as if she'd pulled her statement from thin air. "No," he said adamantly then closed his eyes and breathed. "I mean yes, that too." He put his elbow on the table and rested his forehead in his right hand. "I thought I was doing such a good job of explaining this."

Mason took a deep breath. "What I'm trying to say, Paige, is I want to be your friend and hopefully someday your lover, but I know more now than I knew then what that entails."

Paige was so relieved she couldn't pull the tears back quick enough. She picked up her napkin and dabbed her eyes quickly.

Mason went still. "Do you not want that?"

Paige looked up at him. "Just the opposite."

Mason didn't react right away as she expected him to. Instead, he thought over her response. "I need to ask you something, but I don't mean to offend you. I just need to be sure we're on the same page."

Paige sat up straighter in her chair. "Sure, go ahead."

"You're not just saying these things because I was there for you, as you say, exactly when you needed me. You really feel something outside of friendship for me? Understand that it is all right either way. I will be your friend no matter what."

Paige wasn't offended. They were reasonable questions given her pendulum act between her birthday and Grace's death two months later. "I have to confess that I realized you had feelings for me during the week I was in Chicago for my birthday."

"You didn't know before that?" Mason asked her, sounding incredulous.

"I might have suspected but I wasn't ready to see it before then. As it was, when I did realize your feelings went deeper than friendship, I still wasn't ready to handle it. I retreated a little, as you might have noticed, but it was because I needed to concentrate on my own feelings and then prayed about who you were to be in my life," she said.

"What do you mean by what I am to be in your life?"

Paige felt a little uncomfortable and even embarrassed to admit that she'd asked God if Mason was to be her husband, and she hesitated while she tried to think of a way to explain it without sounding presumptuous.

"Did you ask God if I was your husband?" Mason asked in a teasing tone.

Paige didn't know how to deny that without lying, and she busied herself by taking a sip of her hot apple cider.

"You did," Mason said, sounding both astonished and pleased.

"I wanted to make sure I didn't lead you on or hurt you if it could be avoided," Paige said.

"Did you get the answer you wanted?" he asked in a quieter voice.

Paige nodded without looking up.

"Good," Mason said, sounding pleased and not at all uncomfortable, causing Paige to look up. She was about to open her mouth to ask him a question when their server came up to the table and took their orders.

When she left, Paige asked the question she'd been holding. "Did you ask God if I was your wife?"

"Yes, but I didn't need to ask God to know that you were the only woman for me. I even tried with someone else. She was a perfect Tabitha but a shadow of you," Mason said, looking at her with an intensity she wasn't used to seeing from him.

There were so many parts of that statement that hit both the right spots in her heart and wrong places in her emotions, but addressing any of them would take them off the subject.

"Then why did you ask Him?"

"I figured you'd want to know."

"Do you truly believe He has a say?"

"Absolutely. It's just that I was a little more concerned with getting someone else's blessing at the time I asked."

"Who."

"Your husband."

Paige gasped at his answer. Not because she didn't believe Mason would do such a thing, but because she believed he did, and it shook her to the core.

Did she want to know the answer to her next question? Could she live with it, with knowing they discussed her?

"Do you want to know what he said?" Mason asked when she kept quiet.

"I don't know," Paige said honestly.

Mason nodded. "Understandable, but it wasn't what you think. He told me he wanted you to be happy."

"Oh," Paige said, letting go of the breath she'd been holding. Another thought occurred to her.

"Did Brandon write you a letter?"

Mason began to look uncomfortable. "Um, yes he did."

"No need to look uncomfortable if he wrote you a letter. It's not like I didn't get a couple of my own," Paige said, feeling gracious.

458

"He didn't write me a letter, necessarily," Mason said.

"Oh, was it two, like me?" Paige asked.

"It was more like a notebook full," Mason said, and Paige blinked, trying to wrap her mind around what he was saying. "A notebook? How big was this notebook?"

"It's about the size of a journal," Mason answered.

"He wrote you a journal full of letters?" Paige asked for clarification. She didn't know how she felt about that. Well, jealousy was one emotion that came to mind quicker than the others. Mason had gotten a journal full of letters from Brandon and Paige had gotten two? *Two measly letters? Not even two whole ones. One was like a half. She'd received one and a half letters.*

"What was in these letters? Did you discuss me?" Paige asked, feeling sick by the prospect.

"No, you might have been mentioned in passing once or twice, but no more than that. It was mostly Scripture study and questions that would lead me to a conversation with God."

Paige couldn't express her relief at his words. She felt wrung out from the yo-yoing her emotions had just done. Maybe it would be best if they just kept this conversation about the two of them.

"I need to tell you something, and I don't know how you will take it, but I have to tell you so my fear of how you will respond won't compromise anything we build," Mason said as he leaned forward and rubbed his hands together.

She couldn't fault his logic. It was refreshing to hear, but she needed a moment to catch her breath and get her bearings. Paige lifted a hand to stop him. "I'm feeling a little overwhelmed by all of this. Could you give me a few minutes?"

Mason looked like he wanted to argue but nodded. He glanced up over her shoulder, and Paige followed his gaze and was happy to see the server coming their way. *Good, they could eat.*

She didn't remember it being this complicated with Brandon. Paige winced at her thoughts. That was completely unfair. Mason was his own person and comparing him to Brandon wasn't only wrong, it would bring an end to any relationship they were able to build.

459

Paige dug into her food as if she were starving, and Mason didn't do too bad himself with his plate. Once her initial hunger was quenched, she felt a little less fragile and looked up at Mason who looked troubled.

"I'm sorry," she said, setting her fork down.

"For what?" Mason asked.

"I want to be open with you regarding everything. I have wanted to have this talk for a long time and because of that, I am feeling a level of anxiety I am not comfortable with. My emotions have hit the ceiling and the floor with this conversation, and I just needed them to stay somewhere in the middle for a few minutes. I'm not trying to avoid any topics, I'm just trying to be able to filter the emotions as best as I can. I hope I'm not making a mess of this."

Mason shook his head. I understand what you're saying, and I should apologize. Vivian told me when she came to stay with you for her birthday last year, that you were acting differently. Brandon told her that sometimes you get emotionally overloaded and have trouble letting go of feelings. She said it makes you anxious and you have activities to put that energy into. He even showed her your medication just in case he was out of the house and you needed to take something to help."

Paige hadn't been ready to discuss her challenges with her obsessive-compulsive disorder with him, but in a way, she guessed she'd brought it up herself.

"Okay, yes, I have struggled with obsessive-compulsive disorder since around the time I was raped. It took a while for the doctors to diagnose it, but I have learned what my triggers are and when I am beginning to feel overwhelmed. My quiet time with God is a huge help because of the meditation and the security I feel in going over my thoughts and cares with Him. There were a lot of red flags I ignored around the time I got married, which resulted in some concerning episodes, but I won't do that anymore—not on purpose," Paige said, knowing what she said was true.

Mason's lips slowly tipped up in a smile. "I'm going to hold you to letting me know if you are feeling overwhelmed, like earlier. I can't adjust if I don't know what to look for."

"You don't need to adjust..." Paige began, but the look she got from Mason stopped her.

"There will be things I need you to adjust to or call me on and I will do the same for you. I don't know how to do this in any other way. It's all or just friendship," Mason said firmly.

"You sound like your mind's made up," Paige said. "What if I'm not ready yet?"

Mason shrugged. "I wanted to have this conversation, so you knew how I felt, not to bulldoze you into anything. I'm fine with waiting as long as it takes. I've already waited forever." Mason finished, looking at her solemnly.

"Why forever?" Paige asked, curious about his word usage.

"When you married Brandon, my wait was as good as forever. This...This is a walk in the park."

If Paige wasn't sitting down, she was sure her knees would have buckled. She didn't know if she'd heard anything so profoundly beautiful in her life.

"When I'm ready, will you still court me? I mean we are doing things kind of backward. We have a child together and all..." Paige faltered, but she wanted to know if she would have to give up the notion of being romanced.

Mason's head tilted to the side as if he were trying to make sense of her question before he answered. "For the rest of your life."

She couldn't have thought of a more perfect answer, so she just nodded in agreement.

"Are you ready to hear what I had to tell you before dinner came?" Mason asked with patience in his eyes and voice.

"Yes," Paige said, giving him her undivided attention.

"During the Thanksgiving holiday, Ava came to me and asked me if I thought you were ready to receive Brandon's first letter. She said he asked that you not receive the letter until you were in a place in your grieving where it would do more good than harm. He didn't want you

461

to make a shrine out of the letters. He just wanted you to accept them as something he did to stay connected with you a little longer." Mason watched her for a moment and when she nodded, he continued. She already had an idea of where he was going with this since she didn't get the letter until Christmas. He had been right to keep the letter from her. She hadn't been ready for it in November.

"I told Ava you weren't ready. It was the hardest thing I've ever done, but it just didn't feel right here." He touched his stomach under his solar plexus and she smiled to herself, knowing who guided him." She reached out and touched his hand on the table to ease his conscience.

"The timing was perfect. Thank you for being obedient to the Holy Spirit," Paige said, squeezing his hand.

Mason blinked once, then twice more quickly. He swallowed convulsively then looked down seemingly overcome with emotion. His shoulders shook before he was able to gain some composure. He removed his hand that had fisted under hers.

"Sorry," he said, not looking up at her. He took another huge breath and exhaled slowly. It all happened so quickly, Paige hadn't been able to react. She wondered if she should get up and come over to comfort him. She made to do so and Mason held up a hand to stop her.

"I'm okay. It was just... it's been laying heavy on me. I was relieved that you didn't blame me, but it's a little overwhelming to realize that the Holy Spirit guided me so clearly." He finally looked up, and she saw that his eyes were bright and wet and absolutely beautiful.

Paige rose from her seat, leaning forward to wipe a stray tear from under his right eye. She smiled gently at him and palmed his cheek. He leaned into her hand and her heart swelled, but the moment he brought his hand up to cup hers heat ran up her arm and spanned the rest of her body, suffusing her in a warmth that made her scalp and toes tingle. She slowly removed her hand afraid she'd fall over before she sat down. *Lightning.*

Paige smiled to herself.

"You okay?" Mason asked.

"Yes, perfect."

Chapter 40

One year later

Whose idea was this again? Oh yes, his.

He really needed to get his ideas vetted more carefully in the future. Mason sat down in the church next to Paige. He wiped his palm on his slacks before taking her hand across the divider as he had done every other time they sat anywhere over the last few months. He felt a flash of heat, but this time it had nothing to do with touching Paige. He still wondered at that reaction sometimes, but always thought it best not to over-analyze it. It was more romantic that way.

At times Mason couldn't believe he could openly and freely rub Paige's arm, hold her hand, hug her, or kiss her temple or forehead. He'd been denied it for so long. At least he no longer jumped when she initiated the affection. He remembered the first time she took his arm when they were walking through Chicago on one of her many visits. He was showing her a building she'd asked about when they had gone back to Millennium Park the day before. He was pointing out the unique architectural points when she moved closer and put her arm in his. Startled by the foreign feeling, he jumped slightly and pulled back. When he saw the hurt in Paige's eyes, he rushed to explain what he was feeling.

He also told her that the only way to overcome it was to have her touch him more often. She's given him one of her sassy responses. Something like "I'll think about it" or "I'll see if I can do that."

He hadn't realized she was so sassy. He knew she was intelligent and extremely quick-witted, but this playful side she only showed to him was a gift. She was a gift.

In the months after her mother's funeral, Paige had laughed more than he'd ever seen. It wasn't all outright guffaws or giggles, but her eyes laughed or showed a quiet mirth that always made him curious about what she was thinking.

He loved being with her. He couldn't get enough of touching her. Yes, first it was to reinforce that they were a couple, but it soon became more from the fact that she lived in Atlanta with her family and he lived in Chicago. He wanted her to be with him 24/7 but knew that she wasn't ready for that. Paige had just gotten her family back and he wanted her to spend time with them, plus get reacquainted with Marc's family before Mason swooped her up and relocated her to Chicago with him.

Vivian taught him how to work the video apps on his phone and tablet so he could see Paige at least once a day when they were apart. It was hard to keep his mind on anything but Paige and Vivian in those early months of his relationship with Paige.

If he had a dinner meeting, he would look on the menu for things Paige might like in case he wanted to take her there. He could imagine them cooking dinner together, and since there was only one hour's difference in their time zones, he would turn on the video connection on his tablet and cook dinner while they talked. It was almost like having her in the kitchen. Almost.

Paige would come up to Chicago by herself or with Melanie every couple of weeks. Melanie's relationship with Angelo Mauro had been growing, so Mason wasn't surprised when Paige asked if they could all have dinner together. He had no reservations about meeting Angelo Mauro after everything Paige shared with him about the man over the months they'd been seeing each other.

It was funny that Mason left the restaurant feeling a modicum of fear that he hadn't before meeting the man. Mason had never doubted that his relationship with Paige would lead to marriage and he stated at much when Mr. Mauro asked him about his intentions. The man had the nerve to narrow his eyes at Mason and ask him if he was taking advantage of his granddaughter's state of mind and grief to gain her love and affection. Feeling Paige stiffen next to him, Mason reached out and rubbed her back. He told Mauro that Paige had the strongest will and mind he knew and if she didn't want to be with him, no distress or death in her life would cause her to do something she didn't want to, including having Mr. Mauro in her life.

Mason would admit that his hand shook a little when he went back over his words in his head and realized he had just thrown Angelo Mauro a challenge, but the man had made Paige uncomfortable and he couldn't stand for that. Mr. Mauro stared at him for a couple of seconds before shifting his gaze to Paige. "You have a good man there. I think he would do anything it took to protect you."

Paige replied without hesitation. "Yes, he is. He would even protect me against you if he had to. He wouldn't like it because he doesn't want to see me unhappy, but he would do it all the same."

Mr. Mauro watched Paige a couple of seconds before smiling at her with a bit of admiration and nodded his head.

He then turned back to Mason. "I apologize if I came off as rude or overbearing. That was not my intention."

Mason accepted his apology on Paige's behalf and breathed a sigh of relief on his own. The man was intense.

It took a couple of days after meeting Paige in New York for him to understand the reason for her question regarding whether he would court her. He had studied the Word as it pertained to winning a woman's heart. From what he could tell from some biblical stories and commentaries he'd read, as well as watching how Marc treated Melanie, winning a woman's heart was done daily, not just until she said: "I do." He guessed Paige had wondered, with the fact that they had both asked and received a 'yes' from God, if he would still woo her. She didn't know it, but she had set forth a challenge to him to not only woo her but make every day a special day for her.

He was glad that Brandon hadn't shared anything personal about Paige in his journal. Mason was having fun discovering her likes, dislikes, quirks, pet peeves and habits. She was the neatest and most organized when she was close to a deadline. The cleaning and straightening helped to both relieve stress and keep her To-Do list clear. When he was on deadline, he was so focused, he considered it a plus if he had clean clothes when he was done.

Vivian had started doing her own laundry when she was twelve. She watched a mom and her daughter do it on some informational video and followed along.

Vivian was over the moon regarding him and Paige. She'd told him that she was happy he'd become the type of man Paige should marry. He had nothing to say to her compliment since he agreed. The finalization of adoption had become official in August last year, and they had all celebrated with a get together in Atlanta with Marc's family. Brian and B.J. had flown in from Chicago and Victoria and Richard from Oklahoma. It was like a two-day family reunion with a trip to a theme park that Saturday and a dedication service that Sunday at Melanie's church.

It was the second time the family as a whole was there in two months and the pastor was more than pleased, having led the altar call after Paige's 'message from the family' during the funeral and witnessing a surge in youth and young adult participation. Paige hadn't sat on the pew long. With her letter of recommendation from Pastor Lawrence and Lady Menagerie, Paige had joined the Young Women's Ministry and visited a couple of the rest homes in the area Marc's mother visited on occasion.

Mason couldn't be more proud, but knew it would take a toll on her when she left. He had gone in to talk with his pastor about Paige and what she'd done in both Los Angeles and Atlanta and asked if he would talk with her once she moved to Chicago. It was important to him that he do what he could to make her transition as smooth as possible. There were some big differences in the protocol since the churches she attended in Los Angeles and Atlanta were a different denomination than his. But one thing remained the same. They shared the same faith.

Paige seemed to enjoy herself when she attended church with him and Vivian, and she loved the Children's Ministry. She told him she thought it was more advanced than others she'd seen and credited Vivian's earlier bible knowledge to it.

Not until recently had he been feeling Paige out to see if she was ready to take the next step with him. He hadn't asked her point-blank, but he'd hinted at it and asked her questions about how she thought her move to Chicago would impact her career and family. Both of her answers were to his liking, so he started making plans for today.

It had been a few months from their talk in New York before she told him she was ready to take their relationship beyond friendship. Even with that go ahead, he let the Holy Spirit guide him and found the shift to be effortless.

This, not so much.

As Mason sat there between his daughter and Paige, growing more nervous by the second, he was beginning to have second thoughts about getting up in front of this congregation. He beat them back ruthlessly, replaying some of the memories he'd already made with Paige...

"Daddy, it's time." Vivian's voice pulled him out of his reverie, and he blinked at her a couple of times before he looked up at Pastor Lawrence who then gestured for them to come forward. Vivian got up, and he followed her lead before turning to pull a surprised Paige to her feet. She still had no clue. *This was going to be great!* Mason walked up to the pulpit, holding both Paige's and Vivian's hands.

He shook hands with Pastor Lawrence and exchanged hugs with Lady Menagerie, who had joined them. He stepped in front of the microphone at Pastor Lawrence's beckoning.

"Good morning," Mason said, and waited for the membership to respond. "I'm here today with Elder Paige Morganson Tatum and our daughter Vivian to ask you a very important question. A few years ago, I met Paige when she offered to be a living donor for Vivian. We were both surprised to learn that Vivian was Paige's biological daughter, switched at birth. As some of you know, the operation didn't go as smoothly as we have liked, and Elder Paige ended up staying in Chicago to rehabilitate for so time. During that time, we got to know each other and my feelings for her developed into something more." He glanced at Paige. Her eyes were huge and confused, so he smiled reassuringly and turned back to the members.

"She didn't share my feelings. There was another person vying for affections by the name of Elder Brandon Tatum. Though I didn't want to admit it at the time, he was the better man for her. He was a man of God who was mighty in spiritual and emotional strength. His obedience to God was and is one of the reasons why I am here today. Brandon befriended me and we talked almost daily during the last couple of months of his life, unbeknownst to Paige.

"He knew how I felt about Paige before they were married and that I had been unsuccessful in purging myself of those feelings, though I kept my distance and even tried unsuccessfully to move on with someone else. Brandon didn't sugarcoat his feelings about me or my lifestyle at the time. He told me I would have to make some changes for myself and for my daughter way before I could even consider thinking of doing some changes for Paige. He was one of the most selfless people I knew, and he was my best friend when he passed." Mason paused as he swallowed back the emotion.

"I don't have time to share all of our talks with you, but one thing he impressed upon me was the fact that he thought I was a good man, but good would only take me so far. He knew, regardless of how soon it would happen, he was going to heaven to be with God the Father for eternity, but if I didn't get my act together, I might be headed in another direction." Mason lifted his eyebrows at some of the members he locked gazes with, and there were a few snickers.

"It's a long story about how I allowed what others did to me to hinder my relationship, as it was, with God. Either way, I was headed towards a life of pain and an afterlife of more pain. So, we talked and talked and talked and on the day of Brandon's funeral I accepted Christ back into my heart."

Mason was startled to hear clapping begin from one area and looked over to see Ava and Makayla Tatum sitting next to Melanie and Marc. Mason couldn't stop the burning at the back of his eyes no matter how hard he tried to tamp down the emotion the realization of their attendance gave him. He spared them a small smile before returning to his task.

"A year ago and several life-altering situations after Brandon passed, I approached Paige with my feelings and asked if I could court her. Though she asked for some time, she eventually accepted. I brought her and my daughter here today because I wanted to ask you, her first church family, for your blessing in asking her another question." He waited a couple of seconds, listening to the overbearing silence in the room. Pastor Lawrence stepped beside him and spoke into the microphone. "You have my blessing." The church members followed suit, and Mason breathed a sigh of relief. Pastor Lawrence patted him on the shoulder, chuckling as he made his way back to his wife.

Mason turned to Paige who now looked like a deer caught in headlights. He pulled the ring box out of his pocket and got down on one knee.

"Paige Rosen Morganson Tatum, you blessed me with one of the most precious people in my life when you had Vivian, and then again when you saved her. I should be satisfied, but I am a greedy man." He got a giggle from Vivian after that line, but he never took his eyes off Paige, who had begun to cry.

"I want it all. The relationship with God, a healthy daughter, my best friend and the only woman I can imagine spending the rest of my life with. Will you bless me even more by becoming my wife?"

Paige raised her hands to her mouth and murmured something. Lady Menagerie stepped over and pulled Paige's hand from her face.

"The people outside of your head would like to hear your answer too."

469

"Yes." Paige nearly shouted, and Mason exhaled with relief and the members cheered as he slipped the classic platinum diamond princess cut, solitaire on her ring finger. He stood up and took her face in his hands before smiling down at her and lowering his head so he could touch his lips to hers, sealing the engagement with a kiss. It was over too quickly for his taste, but the sun wouldn't set before he finished it.

Paige was pulled away from him by Lady Menagerie who hugged her and whispered in her ear before pushing her to Pastor Lawrence.

Meanwhile, Mason hugged and kissed Vivian, who whispered a loud, "Good job!" in his ear. He laughed, warming at her compliment.

He hugged Pastor Lawrence and Lady Menagerie before they walked down from the pulpit, and was surprised when Pastor Lawrence announced that there was going to be a light repast in celebration of their engagement. Mason was touched that he would be so eagerly received.

After that, the service sped by. Mostly because the hardest part for him was over. He was engaged to Paige. She'd said yes.

***

"Thank you for the most amazing day," Paige said, leaning against the door to her and Vivian's hotel suite. Mason hadn't yet gotten used to the luxury her grandfather's wealth provided, but she had only just started accepting what Angelo called a small allowance.

Mason knew that Angelo Mauro had no other children and wanted to spoil both Melanie and Paige rotten, but they were both very independent women who hadn't found a need for the opulence he tried to press upon them. They would though, from time to time use his money to gift others. Hence the set of suites Paige had upgraded them to when they arrived at the hotel yesterday.

"You are welcome," he replied, slowly moving closer to her. He saw Paige notice his movements and try to hide a smile. They were alone. The first time the whole day. Vivian wanted to go up to the rooftop pool, and Melanie and Marc agreed to take her. Paige had made

470

excuses, saying that she wanted to catch a nap before the light supper they'd all planned to have in the hotel restaurant later.

"So, what are you going to do while I'm taking my nap?" Paige asked, her golden eyes turning bronze in the light of the room as she looked at him.

"Remembering this," he said, staring into her eyes a moment longer before dropping his gaze to her lips. She opened her mouth to say something. It was probably going to be sassy. It could wait.

He closed the distance between them swiftly but met her mouth gently. He pressed his lips to hers once, twice, then sealed her mouth with his, becoming consumed by the feeling of her mouth moving under his.

His lips, cheek, and jaw tingled where she'd just placed her hand and he moved closer, wanting to wrap himself around her, take in her essence and warmth and just be. Oh, how he loved this woman. There was nothing in him that didn't want to be close to her, to protect her and see her happy.

Mason broke the kiss, needing to catch his breath, but he didn't release Paige from his embrace, and she didn't seem in a rush to let go of him either. He rested his forehead on hers, content to hold her and share breaths with her. He opened his eyes and caught a glimpse of a tear.

Mason pulled back to get a better look at Paige's face. Her eyes were wet which sent his heartbeat into overdrive for the half-second it took for him to glance from her eyes to her mouth which was smiling wide.

"Lightning," she murmured, and he couldn't help the chuckle that rumbled up from his chest.

She'd told him after their first kiss a few months ago that kissing him was like uncorking lightning from a bottle. He lit her up inside. He took that as a very good sign.

He grinned at her, trying to come up with something romantic but she beat him to it. Her hand that had been resting on his shoulder, moved to his chest as her smile turned soft.

471

"I love you, Mason Jenson. Very much."

His heartbeat picked up again at her words. He wouldn't have been able to stop the overflow of emotion coming from his eyes if he'd wanted to. This – this right here was where he'd been heading all his life. He'd finally obtained this sense of fulfillment that had eluded him for so long. He closed his eyes and took it in.

"I love you too, Paige, more than I ever thought I could, but still less than you deserve. So, I'll be working on that."

Paige grinned at him, and he saw the mischievous glint in her eyes just before she spoke. "I'm not gonna complain."

"That sass," he said, grinning back just before he kissed her again.

Epilogue

Six months later

"B.J., get a move on. I am not going to be late. Not today. I will leave you if I have to," Brian said from the other room.

"Hold your horses, old man. I'm coming. Besides, we have a whole hour before we have to be at the church and it's only a twenty-minute drive," B.J. said loud enough to be heard throughout the two-bedroom suite.

B.J. sent out another text as he slipped on his sneakers and double-checked the list on his phone against what he saw through the plastic window of his garment bag. He saw his tuxedo, socks, shoes, tie, handkerchiefs, cummerbund and cufflink box. His wallet was in his left pocket and the ring was in his right.

"Los Angeles traffic is unpredictable, even on a Saturday. Don't underestimate it," Brian said, coming to stand at the door of B.J.'s bedroom.

"What are you doing?" Brian asked, looking at the phone in B.J.'s hand. His nervous gaze grew concerned when B.J. didn't answer right away.

B.J. cleared his phone and slipped it in his back pocket. "Simone hasn't called. I'm not sure if she made her flight."

"Son. Please hear me carefully. I know you are concerned about Simone but you did everything but put her on the plane an escort her here. If she doesn't want to come, you can't make her. She is as much of an adult as you. She didn't want to travel with us, and you can't reach her now. What does that say to you?" His father implored.

As much as B.J. wanted to get angry, he couldn't fault his dad for his point of view. It wasn't like his and Simone's relationship was easy going. It hadn't been easy going for a while and this was just one more disappointment. He didn't know how to reach her heart now as he had when they had first gotten together. She also was a different person than the Simone he first fell in love with. He'd asked God to relieve him of his feelings for her, but here he was, in deeper than ever. Love was definitely not doing him any favors.

B.J. looked at his father and put his thoughts as far back in his mind as possible. "It tells me, love is hard. It seems none of us come by it easily. We have to struggle and fight for our happy endings." B.J. saw the nervous excitement in his father's eyes dim at his comment and regretted the words even though he'd been referring to Paige. His dad nodded, then dismissed the conversation altogether.

"So, you ready?" Brian asked him.

"Yep," B.J. answered as he picked up his garment bag.

"Well then, let's go and get your sister married."

Neither said another word until they were in the car.

"Is Gran already at the church?" B.J. asked, referring to Victoria.

"Yes. She's like a child in a candy store."

What did you and Richard talk about late into the night?

"Richard had some meetings. He's going back to Uganda at the end of the month. I'm thinking of going with him?"

B.J. looked over, astonished. "Really? I didn't know you had any interest in philanthropic work?"

Brian shrugged as he looked through his side-view mirror and changed lanes. "Luca has been getting on me about getting a hobby. I thought I would see what Richard was involved with. If I wasn't interested, the least I could do was contribute."

"Do you think he'll take it?"

"Richard is a smart businessman. He's done his time and has nothing to prove. I think he will."

B.J. nodded and stared out of the window. His mind started wandering and he turned back to his dad. "So, you have your speech ready?" he asked with a teasing grin.

"Don't play. I've been going over it all morning."

"As I said before, you could just use your phone. No one will be offended."

"I will not toast my daughter and son-in-law's new life by reading off of a gadget. I got this," his dad said, poking at his head.

"What time is Nonno arriving?"

"He should arrive in an hour. He wanted his appearance to be a surprise to the family, so he didn't infringe upon Angelo who is the Don at this affair. They spoke a week ago."

"Who would have ever thought there would be such a merge," B.J. said.

"Yes, well, he was right to keep us hidden for as long as he did. Can you imagine the amount of security we'd have to have for you if Don Matani was still alive? He forbade houses to align. Too much power."

B.J. thought about the legacy he carried and shivered slightly at the obligations that came with it. He'd been approached by Angelo Mauro six months before to see if they could meet. B.J. told him he would be more than happy to meet with him... along with Luca. Luca wasn't happy that Angelo had reached out to him before conferring with Luca, but he agreed with the meeting, which was still due to happen.

"Speaking of speeches. Do you have yours?" Brian asked.

"Yep. Right here as well," He said, pointing to his temple.

"How do you think Melanie will handle Paige moving to Chicago?"

B.J. shrugged. "I think she's happy that Paige is happy and marrying a good man. If she misses Paige too much, she can always just buy a jet with all the money Angelo is dumping on her."

"Want to say guilty cash?"

"Guilty cassssssh," B.J. said before he laughed. "He better be careful. If he hangs around Melanie and Paige long enough, he might mess around and get saved."

"One can only hope," Brian replied.

"Do you have something against Angelo?" B.J. asked, feeling an underlying tension in his father.

"Assaulting and raping Melanie's mother wasn't enough?"

"If she can forgive him, why can't you?"

"Probably because I knew him when…" Brian answered.

"He's not the same man," B.J. said, before thinking.

Brian glanced at him. "You sound like you are getting a little personal."

"Why? I can't have an opinion? You knew *me* when. Am I a monster?" B.J. asked, then shut his mouth.

The car was quiet for a few minutes. "I'm sorry, B.J. It's just hard to separate his person from all the heartache he indirectly caused Melanie."

B.J. understood his father's frustration. He'd always held a special place in his heart for Melanie. "I understand, Dad. But if things hadn't happened the way they did, Paige and I wouldn't be here."

Brian looked over at him ruefully. "You're right, son. You're a gem I would not give back."

B.J. just hoped his dad would feel the same way if he decided to take Angelo up on the offer he believed he was going to make him when they finally all got together.

***

"You are so beautiful, I'm not sure Mason will remember his vows," Victoria said as she took in her beautiful granddaughter in a cream gown of charmeuse satin and tulle that looked like it was made with silk and clouds. It had a simple sweetheart bodice but the skirt had layers and layers of tulle with colorful butterflies embroidered on one of the layers of the skirt so it looked like they were flying around her legs as she walked. It was exquisite.

"It's a good thing Pastor Lawrence will remind us of what to say right before we have to say it," Paige whispered to Melanie who was bending over her as she pinned one last rhinestone clip in her hair.

"I heard that, Smarty-pants," Victoria said.

"Mason says she's got a sassy mouth," Melanie said as she stepped back from Paige and they both just stared at her for a moment.

"I don't want to hear about anything Mason says about Paige's mouth," Victoria said. "I can't believe his good fortune. First my daughter then my granddaughter. Which, when said that way... sounds kinda odd."

Melanie and Paige both frowned and nodded, their eyes thoughtful.

Melanie tapped Victoria on the arm with the back of her hand just hard enough to startle her. "Keep your mind out of the gutter. Mason was talking about Paige's playful and spirited side. She doesn't show it to everyone so consider yourself fortunate."

"I do," Victoria said, looking at Paige. "I definitely do."

"I have a small gift for you. I'm glad you didn't wear those sleeves all the way to your fingertips. It will allow this to stand out." Victoria handed Paige a jewelry box.

"You've already given me so much with the first-class trip to Auckland, New Zealand."

"It was the least I could do. You will be spending half of your honeymoon trying to get to your destination. You should do it in luxury," Victoria said as she watched Paige open the box and gasp.

"Oh my goodness. This is gorgeous. It's so unique, and it matches perfectly," Paige whispered, referring to the platinum bracelet with five matte butterflies elevated from the thin band at the top. They shook slightly giving the effect that they were hovering over her wrist.

"I've never seen anything like it," Paige said, running her hands over the butterflies and closing her eyes in bliss. Then opening them with a startled look in the mirror at Victoria.

"They're textured. They are all slightly different in height and smoothness," Paige said, looking from Melanie to Victoria.

Melanie raised her hands. "I didn't say anything."

"Richard bought that for me. That man was always so observant. I used to get these bad anxiety attacks whenever I needed to go talk to the bank about the farm. One of his clients was a psychologist that told him about a friend that made sensory jewelry. It was so new, very few people did it.

"Anyway." Victoria waved her hand, feeling a bit anxious herself. "I saw your prescription bottles when you came for that long visit. I didn't want to say anything, at the time because we didn't part on the best of terms and I didn't want you getting angrier at the time. But I figured with it being your wedding day you would be very happy and willing to forgive me for being a nosy nanny."

"Literally," Melanie said, and Paige burst out laughing.

"It's perfect. Thank you so much," Paige said, getting up and turning to her to give her an air kiss and hug.

The door opened and Vivian and Gladys walked in looking like identical snow princesses in their silver gowns that almost matched their eyes. They had butterflies embroidered on their dresses as well, but the thinnest layer of silk organza covering their satin dresses.

At fifteen, their features had matured. Their faces were no longer rounded with big cheeks. Their now oval faces held high cheekbones, full lips, strong jawlines and dark eyelashes that only emphasized their big silver eyes. In a word, they were gorgeous. It also didn't help that they'd gotten their grandfather's height. At five feet eight inches, they were already three inches taller than their mother and heading towards their uncle's height, though Victoria was sure they would taper down soon.

Mason told Victoria he was thinking of buying a shotgun when they'd all gotten together for Vivian and Glady's fifteenth birthdays.

"Mommy you are so beautiful. Daddy will be speechless," Vivian said.

"Told you," Victoria said.

Paige screwed up her face. "No more talking about my soon-to-be-husband being mute."

"You are gorgeous, Mati."

"Thank you, Babies. You two might be in trouble after this, though. When your dads see you, they will want to lock you up until you are at least twenty-five."

Vivian and Gladys struck a pose and gave Paige a pouty lip look.

"That will not help your cause," Victoria said.

"We were peeking over the balcony. The church is packed. Even Don Mauro is here," Gladys said, making Victoria wince. Not one, but two Dons in the family. She just hoped they kept trouble from their doorstep. Well, at least Antonio wasn't coming. He was still licking his wounds from when Luca announced the year before that Brian would be taking the helm when he retired.

"So, we came down to see if you are ready. Dad is wearing a hole in the carpet and Pastor Lawrence is looking at him like he wants to say something, but Lady Menagerie keeps shushing him," Vivian said.

Paige took a deep breath and looked at all of them before addressing Victoria. "Well then, we better go. Have you seen Brian?"

"He's as nervous as a virgin..." She glanced at the girls. "He's as nervous as a cat with a long tail at a rocking chair convention."

"What?" Vivian asked her.

"Never mind. He is very nervous. He's treating it like it might be the most important job of his life," Victoria said.

Melanie was shaking her head, trying hard to keep her mouth straight.

Paige frowned at Victoria, but she turned and flounced to the door. "Stop dawdling and come marry my son-in-law so you can make me some more of those precious great-grandbabies."

"Ahhhh, Gran. I didn't need to hear that," Vivian cried, covering her ears.

"And *I* certainly didn't need to hear that. I get enough of that mushy stuff with Mom and Dad," Gladys said.

"You owe me five dollars. I told you she would mention great-grandchildren before I got down the aisle." Paige said.

"Fine, fine," Melanie murmured, picking up Paige's bouquet and handing it to her before picking of her own and walking towards the door. "You just couldn't keep your mouth shut for ten more minutes," Melanie said as she passed Victoria.

"It is not really what I'm known for, Sweetie," Victoria said as she held the door.

When Paige crossed the threshold, she looked at Victoria. "I love you, Gran."

"I love you too, Love," Victoria returned.

***

"Well, I guess this is it," Brian said somberly to Paige as they stood behind the closed door to the church.

"I'm not being executed. I'm getting married," Paige replied, looking at her handsome father in his long-tail tux.

"I feel like I just met you and now you're going off to get married," Brian said.

"Once again. I am getting married, not joining the circus," Paige said, smiling up at him.

"Do you know how beautiful you are?" Brian asked, his eyes growing moist.

"Don't you do it. I forbade you to cry. If I drop one tear before I get to Mason, Gran will kill you and if she doesn't, then Mel will."

Brian sniffed, but he blinked quickly. The next time he looked at her, his eyes were relatively dry.

Paige shook her head. She felt like everyone's mother today. What was going on?

"I could not be more proud of you if I had a hand in molding you for the last thirty years," Brian said as the doors began to open.

"I love you too, Dad," Paige said, feeling sentimental.

Brian's bottom lip began to tremble.

"Don't." She pointed at him. He bit his lip and took a deep breath.

She refused to continue to look at him and watched as the doors continued to open. She felt Brian shift next to her and she slid her arm through his and felt him place his hand on hers.

Paige looked down the aisle, following the pews full of people to the pulpit and then to Mason who was already watching her.

"Ready?" Brian whispered.

"Absolutely," Paige replied, and they stepped forward.

The walk up the aisle took forever and no time at all, but she never lost eye contact with Mason. Her father led her up the steps to where Mason stood under a wedding arch. His eyes wide and a little glassy.

She smiled at Brian then looked back at Mason who continued to stare at her, now in wonder.

"Dearly beloved…" Pastor Lawrence began.

"You're so beautiful," Mason said, seeming unable to help himself. "And you're mine."

"Not yet, which is why we are gathered here today Mr. Jenson," Pastor Lawrence said.

There were some giggles and chuckles amongst the wedding party, but one look from Pastor Lawrence silenced them.

"Are you going to be trouble, young man?" Pastor Lawrence asked in a quieter tone.

"No, sir... Pastor sir," Mason said, startling a laugh out of Paige.

Pastor Lawrence looked at her and she sobered and dropped her eyes.

Pastor Lawrence heaved a sigh and began again. "Dearly beloved, we are gathered here today in the sight of God to join this man, and this woman in holy matrimony..."

Paige followed along, smiling now and again at Mason until it was time for her father to let her go.

"Who gives this woman in holy matrimony to this man?" Pastor Lawrence asked.

"I, her father, along with her mother and stepfather do," Brian said proudly.

Paige just barely held back the giggle.

Brian released her hand and turned her to him so he could lift her veil. He kissed her cheek and whispered. "I love you, Baby Girl," before placing her hand in Mason's.

Pastor Lawrence led them through the recitation of their vows. Once they were done, Paige breathed a sigh of relief that the small hitch in the beginning of the ceremony didn't continue through the service.

"The wedding ring is an unbroken symbol of the everlasting love and commitment between man and wife. May we have the rings?" Pastor Lawrence requested.

Melanie handed Paige Mason's ring and they waited for B.J. who did the classic pat-down dance of his front pockets... twice before touching on the ring box in a back pocket and handing it to a very relieved looking Mason. Paige had so many questions, but she told herself she would let them go until later.

"With this ring, I thee wed," Mason said. With shaky fingers, Mason slipped the beautiful three stone wedding band next to her engagement ring then smiled up at her like a toddler who just guessed that the ball went into the round hole.

"With this ring, I thee wed," Paige repeated, trying to hold back her laughter as she slipped his ring on his ring finger.

"What God has joined together, let no man put asunder. With the power vested in me by God and the state of California, I now pronounce you man and wife. You may kiss the bride," Pastor Lawrence said and stepped back.

Mason pulled her to him and gave her a quick hug. "Not a word, sassy mouth." He whispered before looking at her. "Your sassy mouth," Paige said quickly.

"I love you, wife," Mason said on an exhale, his eyes growing soft.

"I love you too, husband," Paige replied and met Mason's lips in an electrifying kiss.

~The End~

Dear Reader,

Thank you so much for joining me on this path through the lives of these families as they realized what they had even as they were searching for more.

I can't tell you how much this series spoke to my heart and all of the times God had me write something only for me to read it back and go "Hey. That's me." This has been a very personal journey for me and it has been a source of healing in many ways. I hope I have not been alone.

I pray that even now, words, phrases, and messages that God placed in these pages for you, speak to your heart, feed your soul and heal every place in your being that needs to be made whole.

If you have read through this series for the entertainment but a word or scene has touched your heart and you wish to know God and receive His gift of salvation, please read these words with your heart and out of your mouth.

Dear Heavenly Father,

I come to you as I am. I confess that You are the one and only living God who sacrificed Your Son, Jesus Christ for my sins. I also confess that Jesus died on the cross, but He rose on the third day with all power in his hands.

I accept Jesus Christ as my Lord and Savior, into my heart and I thank you for your mercy and grace. In Jesus' name. Amen

Welcome to the family!

I do suggest that you find a church to attend that speaks to your heart. Allow the Hoy Spirit to guide you with His peace.

Thank you for reading and I hope you share your thoughts with me on this series or my others.

Please send your questions or thoughts to me at tawcarlisle@gmail.com.

You can also visit my website at www.tawcarlisle.com and follow me at www.twitter.com/traciwcarlisle and www.facebook.com/traciwoodencarlisle

Until next time,
Keep reading and expand your dreams
Traci Wooden-Carlisle

My Books

Promises of Zion series

My Beauty For Your Ashes
My Oil of Joy For Your Mourning
My Garment of Praise for Your Spirit of Heaviness
Stolen Promises
Promises Fulfilled

Chances Series

Chances Are…
Taking Chances

Chandler County Series

Missing Destiny
Missing Us
Missing the Gift
Missing Under the Mistletoe

A Symphony From Heaven
The Prayer Warrior
God is Waiting for You in a Quiet Place of Praise

If you enjoyed this book, please join Christian Indie Author Readers Group on Facebook. You will find Christian Books in Multiple Genres with opportunities to find other Christian Authors and learn about new releases, sales, and free books. Here is the link: https://www.facebook.com/groups/291215317668431/

About the Author

Traci Wooden-Carlisle lives in San Diego with her husband. She designs jewelry, writes as much as she can and freelances as a graphic artist. She loves her coffee in the morning and fuzzy slippers at night. She loves to read anything romantic – the more inspirational the better. For fun, she dances and makes swag for herself and other authors.

Made in United States
North Haven, CT
26 March 2024

50532821R00271